THE
ELEVENTH
V1CT1M

THE
ELEVENTH
V1CT1M

NANCY GRACE

HYPERION

NEW YORK

Library of Congress Cataloging-in-Publication Data

Grace, Nancy.
  The eleventh victim / Nancy Grace.
    p. cm.
  ISBN 978-1-4013-0345-7
  1. Women lawyers—Fiction.   2. Women psychotherapists—
Fiction.   3. Grief—Fiction.   I. Title.
  PS3607.R3266E44 2009
  813'.6—dc22
      2008052944

Hyperion books are available for special promotions and premiums.
For details contact the HarperCollins Special Markets Department
in the New York office at 212-207-7528, fax 212-207-7222, or email
spsales@harpercollins.com.

Book design by Karen Minster

First Edition

10 9 8 7 6 5 4 3 2 1

THIS LABEL APPLIES TO TEXT STOCK

We try to produce the most beautiful books possible, and we are also
extremely concerned about the impact of our manufacturing process
on the forests of the world and the environment as a whole.
Accordingly, we've made sure that all of the paper we use has been
certified as coming from forests that are managed to insure the
protection of the people and wildlife dependent upon them.

To Prince Dragonfly and Princess Lyric

aka My Parents

Mac and Elizabeth Grace

THE ELEVENTH V1CT1M

A LITTLE SOMETHING. WHAT WAS IT? SOMETHING . . . SOME DETAIL WAS wrong.

He couldn't just leave the body lying there like that. There was something missing. It was biting at him. He'd tried to go, walking back to his car in the dark twice now, but the nagging in his brain wouldn't let him leave until she was absolutely perfect.

He looked at her lying there in the moonlight. Her dead body was absolutely stunning. Before, when she had been alive, sitting in the passenger seat of his car, talking and talking about her life and herself and her journey from Anniston, Alabama, to Atlanta to break into acting, he thought his head would blow up like a bomb. She just wouldn't shut up.

What did she think it was . . . a date? She was a hooker. He spotted her climbing the steep steps out of the MARTA subway station downtown. She got straight into his car with a big smile when he offered her a ride.

Once inside, driving, he kept looking away from the road, stealing glances at her neck. Something about it drew him. Maybe the shape, the curve—or maybe it was the soft hollow spot at the bottom. It was the only thing about her he could stomach.

He lowered the automatic windows so her conversation would fly out into the night and he wouldn't have to hear it. Her teeth and lips revolted him. The shiny pink lip gloss she was wearing had thickened in spots across her lips and some had smeared onto her front teeth. Looking over at her as she talked, Cruise thought it was the most disgusting thing he had ever seen.

Back to the task at hand. What was it? It was maddening . . . he couldn't bring himself to leave until everything was just right . . . perfect, in fact.

Every detail mattered. Like a delicate soufflé or performing his specialty, decorating with boiling-hot spun sugar, perfection was achieved only by acute attention to detail.

There, in the dark of the clearing, it hit him. Turning, he walked to his car and reached through the open window into the glove compartment and got it. The baker's twine. It was his favorite brand—it was actually the only twine he would ever consider using—just shipped in from France.

He had posed her on her back. The four bright-red puncture marks torn into her mid-back didn't bother him at all. In fact, the dark red against the white skin created a vivid contrast that was somehow pleasing to him. Walking back to her body, which he had spread carefully on a bed of soft grass to more suitably frame her pale limbs in a night lit only by the moon, he paused again.

He needed the perfect spot. He couldn't rush this or he wouldn't sleep all night. The wrist? Like a bracelet? No. She was wearing a tacky, gold-tone watch. That would ruin the whole thing for him. And he couldn't bring himself to actually touch the timepiece she wore there on her right wrist. It looked cheap; he was sure the gold-tone finish was turning dark at the edges of the band.

The neck? No. It was much too close to the lip gloss. The gloss had a faint, fruity odor, foul as gasoline fumes to Cruise, and that alone made him want to retch. It would totally destroy the twine's effect.

Sometime during their "date," fresh, damp dirt and a little grass had smeared horizontally across her mouth and worked its way up into her nose. He left it there. That was a beautiful and poetic touch of nature, but the lip gloss . . . disgusting.

As he stood there at the foot of her body, staring into her face, her own eyes stared away from him and straight up into the sky, her lips still slightly parted just as they had been in life . . . just as they had been at the zenith, that incredibly beautiful and intimate moment when she exhaled her last breath into the night. And as he relived that moment, it came to him in an epiphany.

He decided . . . the left ring finger. Perfect.

He squatted down and gently picked up her left hand. The wrist was still limp.

He tied a single, perfect bow around her ring finger just before rigor set in . . . before the body went stiff and cold and hard. He placed the hand back gently across her stomach.

Backing away a few feet to take in the whole picture, finally, he could relax. Every detail was exquisite. Finally, he could get some sleep.

The bow was perfectly symmetrical, and there, in the moonlight, it was just gorgeous. Almost like a wedding band.

Atlanta, Georgia

THE PIERCING ERUPTION OF A TELEPHONE STARTLED SPECIAL Prosecutor Hailey Dean, still at her desk late on a Friday night preparing for a Monday-morning trial.

It was probably Fincher, her longtime investigator and sometime bodyguard. Together, they worked felony investigations from inner-city housing projects to this latest, which involved one of North Atlanta's elite country clubs.

"District Attorney's Office, Hailey Dean speaking," she said absently into the receiver.

The silence that greeted Hailey on the other end of the telephone line caught her attention.

"Hello?"

Still nothing.

Realizing what was likely coming next, Hailey quickly reached for a notepad.

"Hello?" she repeated and waited for the recorded announcement that the call was from the prison. After she accepted the call, which she always did, an inmate would come on the line to offer information in exchange for a full dismissal of his own charges or, at the least, a lighter sentence or a transfer to a better facility.

As if a dismissal would ever happen.

No way would Hailey go to hell to get witnesses to put a devil in jail . . . she said so up front to each and every snitch.

Still, she'd talk, listening carefully, turning their tips into evidence in court—if she believed them. Then it would become necessary, like it or not, to cut some kind of deal.

She had never broken a deal, and so far, her snitches in turn had displayed a certain degree of decency. Not one had ever backed down on the stand, even when things got tense in the courtroom or behind jailhouse bars, where her informants lived day to day with the very defendants against whom they were testifying.

In fact, Hailey often trusted her rats more than her fellow attorneys, whom she routinely fed with a long-handled spoon, keeping them safely at arm's length.

"Hello," she repeated into the phone, wondering if the call got dropped by the prison switchboard. It wouldn't be the first time.

Silence.

Just as she reached to hang up, she heard a faint, "Miss Hailey?"

An older, Southern woman was on the other end of the line, she realized—a woman who still functioned under the rules left over from the fifties that demanded a respectful "Miss."

"Yes, hello?"

Still nothing.

"Can I help you, ma'am?" she asked, trying not to sound impatient, but she had a lot of work to do before she got out of here. "The DA's office is closed right now . . ."

"Excuse me for calling so late. This is Mrs. Leola Williams."

Williams . . . Leola Williams . . .

Hailey's mind whirred like a computer trying to place the name.

"LaSondra was my first baby girl."

Ah. Connection.

Leola Williams as in LaSondra Williams.

Otherwise known as Victim Eleven.

Hailey instinctively started taking notes on the pad, neatly writing "V Eleven" across the top of the page and underlining it. Eleven women across Atlanta, all in their twenties, had been raped, sodomized, and strangled. As the coup de grâce, each woman was stabbed with a deadly, signature four-prong weapon, piercing the lower back, moving upward through the lungs.

LaSondra Williams was the final woman they knew of to die at the hands of a ruthless serial killer who evaded the Atlanta Homicide Division for well over a year, striking with no real pattern, but always the same MO. It had taken a long time for cops to even connect victims One through Seven, mainly because the victims were prostitutes.

Most of the city's residents dismissed the murders as the price streetwalkers paid to make a living. Even as the body count rose, there was little pressure on police to stop the killing and solve the murders.

The corpses of young women slowly piled up, necks mangled and torsos ripped, left in open fields behind strip bars, cocktail lounges, crack holes, and flop houses.

From the get-go, Hailey believed the murder scenes were staged. Once she started comparing notes from each murder, she realized that a "calling card" was left on each victim.

The autopsy reports referred to it simply as "string" found on or around the body—no detail, and no description whatsoever. No wonder nobody connected the dots.

Various rotating doctors had performed the eleven autopsies and, as a result, there was no big picture, no overview, no single go-to doctor at the Medical Examiner's Office with all the answers. When Hailey ran down one of the doctors who performed two of the postmortems, she had to press hard to actually view the effects, that is, every single item found "on or about the body."

But there it was. In separate plastic bags marked with an ME's Office case number, thin but sturdy string. She insisted on seeing the chief medical examiner, known across the jurisdiction as "Jack the Ripper." After a closed-door meeting, he ordered all the effects in each case assembled for Hailey's inspection. Her theory was laid out before her eyes.

Eleven of them were arranged on a sterile metal table there in the morgue.

A bow of twine was always there, sometimes on an ankle, sometimes tied around a pinkie or toe. Victim Five was nearly excluded from the series of murder victims when no twine was found on the body. It was only during the routine dissection of the head that the twine was found, shoved up the left nasal cavity.

The twine was forced so deeply into the ear of Victim Seven that blood had trickled down the side of the woman's neck, indicating the bow had been painfully inserted during life while blood still flowed freely.

Hailey had the twine traced and analyzed by the FBI. It was high-end imported baker's twine. Sisson Imports, made in France, sold in tightly wound balls, three hundred inches of pure white linen kitchen twine—preferred by chefs because it neither burned nor frayed during the cooking process.

Each body was found cold, with an unmistakable wound to the delicate flesh of the lower back—four thin, perfectly symmetrical puncture wounds, like a quartet of exactly paralleled, venomous snake bites.

Callous headlines referred to each of the victims not by her name, but by her profession.

She was a hooker, so who really cared?

I cared. I still care.

It was all running through her head rapidly, like a home movie on fast forward. Hailey lit a fire under the Atlanta Police Department to at least attempt to make the women aware they were being stalked, but that was a daunting task. How do you effectively reach an underworld made up of streetwalkers, escorts, junkies chasing johns for a hit of crack, and strippers turning the occasional trick?

Finally, as a last resort and at Hailey's urging, the city's night court took action. Officials began reading a form warning to every woman processed through the city jail when she was booked in and fingerprinted for soliciting prostitution. The same warning, in writing, was then placed in the hand of every hooker at every guilty plea, court date, and trial. The Xeroxed warnings were subsequently found littering the courthouse steps, the ladies' bathrooms, sidewalks, and the bus and trains stations at the courthouse stop. But Hailey insisted that they continue handing them out. Begrudgingly, they were.

"Miss Hailey, I can't hardly bear you all calling her what you called her in the paper. LaSondra, she went to Mt. Zion Baptist real regular. She just got her a new job keeping the books for a man up in Tucker. She didn't walk no streets, Miss Hailey." The pain in Leola's voice cracked through the receiver, and Hailey's chest hurt hearing it.

"I know, Mrs. Williams, I know she was good." She tried her best to keep an impersonal, professional tone. She steeled herself.

It was easy to forget that these women, these prostitutes, were once somebody's little girls.

But Hailey knew better than to let emotion get in the way of a case, or let sympathy cloud her decisions on a trial matter.

Sentimentality in a courtroom angered judges. Anything but a cool head resulted in adverse rulings from the bench, botched cross-exams, bad trial tactics, and not-guilty verdicts.

Tonight, with a high-profile case looming on Monday's trial calendar, she couldn't afford to get emotionally attached to a voice on the other end of the phone line.

"You've got to make them stop saying those things about her, Miss Hailey. You don't know what it's been like for me, waking up every morning and remembering she ain't comin' home again."

Hailey swallowed hard. "No," she lied softly, "I don't know."

"Promise me you'll make them tell the truth about her. That she didn't walk no streets. Promise?"

Hailey didn't make promises she wasn't sure she could keep.

Instead, she said, "I'll get to work on it right now." Never mind that "now" was 10:30 p.m. on a Friday night, long past time to go home.

"Thank you, Miss Hailey." The woman's voice shook with gratitude as she gave Hailey her phone number. "You call me back, then, when you know more."

"I will."

"I'll be up all night."

"Oh, no need to do that, Mrs. Leola."

"Miss Hailey," the woman said flatly, "I ain't slept through the night since I found out about my baby girl."

"I . . . I'm sorry" was all Hailey could think of to say.

That, and *I know. I know how you feel . . .*

But she didn't—couldn't—say that. Even after all these years, she never verbally acknowledged that she still suffered the same grief, the same sleepless nights, the same nearly disabling pain.

Hanging up the telephone, Hailey spun around in her desk chair, toying with the silver Tiffany pen hanging from a black silken cord around her neck.

She had never been attached to many of her possessions, but the pen was a gift from Katrine Dumont, whose fiancé, Phil Eastwood, had been murdered.

It had been one of Hailey's very first cases. The newly engaged couple—both just twenty-two, with their whole lives ahead of them—stepped out onto the patio of their apartment to sip wine and watch the sun set over Atlanta. They toasted each other and their future and were about to call their families to tell them about their upcoming wedding—but they never got the chance.

Two brand-new parolees with heavy rap sheets ambushed them from behind a thick hedge surrounding the patio. Phil tried to fight back and was immediately gunned down at point-blank range. His fiancée was dragged into the apartment and repeatedly raped and beaten.

To complicate matters, Katrine had been so emotionally devastated, so weak and fragile, no way could she take the stand and survive cross-exam. Without an eyewitness to the shooting, Hailey knew a guilty verdict would be nearly impossible.

At the outset, Hailey rejected a lenient plea deal that both the defense and the trial judge, Albert Grimes, tried to push on her. A pushover on the bench, the trial judge had a reputation of always siding with defendants no matter how petty or brutal the crime, and for displaying his Harvard degree in the foyer of his chambers for all to see. After Hailey kicked back the deal Grimes had cooked up with the defense, the judge was in a foul mood at actually having to preside over a case throughout the weeks to come.

It had been especially tough for Hailey personally, dredging up all the old memories of Will's murder. But after a three-week presentation of evidence, the jury convicted. Hailey was exhausted and drained at the end.

Katrine came to see her not long after, still a fragile wisp.

"I'm sorry I couldn't be there to testify at trial," Katrine said, handing her a sky-blue velvet box.

Inside was the pen, etched with the words, FOR HAILEY, SEEKING JUSTICE, KATRINE DUMONT-EASTWOOD.

They hadn't been married, but Katrine, Hailey learned, had officially taken his name after his death.

"I know it sounds crazy, but in my heart, I'm his wife."

No. It didn't sound crazy at all.

For the next ten years, Hailey wore the pen hanging on a black silk cord around her neck during every jury trial and often in between.

Now, she gazed out the window at bright lights shooting upward at Turner Stadium, slicing the dark sky. The night air hummed with cars flying past on interstate I-75.

Just for the moment, she allowed herself to consider the eleven women, long silenced, dead in their graves.

Hailey had studied the eight-by-ten crime scene photos, hundreds of them, at length, from every possible angle in the weeks leading up to trial, poring over each one to determine any possible probative significance she could use to State's advantage in court.

But tonight they haunted her, not as potential evidence at trial, but as photos of the suffering of real people. Now the media was circling the case like vultures, threatening to pick clean the bones of the women by exploiting them again, this time in sensational news accounts.

The headlights blurred, flying by outside her window. She thought of LaSondra Williams, strangled, her slender neck marred by three long, angry scratch marks and her torso ripped open. If the papers had their way, her name . . . and lifestyle . . . would make city headlines, maybe further if the Associated Press picked up on the trial from the death-penalty angle.

It's the least you can do, she told herself, leaving her office and heading to the record room to start running rap sheets.

By midnight, Hailey's eyes were red and irritated from squinting at the computer screen.

Fingerprints don't lie, and they told Hailey that Leola Williams's first baby girl, just twenty-four, was a crack hooker.

LaSondra worked motels near the strip clubs on Stewart Avenue skirting Atlanta's Hartsfield-Jackson International Airport, the seediest piece of highway with the highest crime rate in the entire state. LaSondra was just part of the scenery outside strip bars, motels that rented rooms by the hour, and crack houses doing their business.

And LaSondra hadn't *just* been arrested. She'd been arrested over a dozen times for soliciting sex for the purpose of prostitution, pleading guilty or no contest under oath every single time.

In addition, her record was dotted with at least a dozen other charges for pandering, minor possession of cocaine, and one conviction for spitting on an officer at the time of arrest. They were all actually petty crimes, none warranting hard time . . . maybe an occasional overnight in the city jail, maybe a fine.

Hailey could see how LaSondra's family had never known the truth.

And what a series of mug shots. The girl was beautiful, thin, with gorgeous dark hair floating in waves down one side and pinned back on the other. But Hailey spotted telltale facial bruises on one mug shot and a gaunt, hollow-eyed searching stare in others. La Sondra was thin, all right. Cocaine thin.

As Hailey stared at the photos in the bright, overhead lights of the records room, the girl in the picture stared right back.

She closed her eyes to block out the image, and another face, a beautiful face with chiseled features and deep blue eyes, appeared before her. Another murder victim.

Will.

It happened late on a beautiful, vivid, spring afternoon, three weeks before their wedding. Countless minor details were still etched in Hailey's memory, mundane things that unfolded in the minutes before her life was destroyed.

She remembered hurrying down the marble steps in the university's Psychology Department and out into the sunlight. She was elated, having just finished the last essay of her final exam for her Masters in Psychology. She'd actually finished a year early.

Practically skipping home from campus, she burst through the door, tossing her books and her favorite coral-colored raincoat onto the scratchy plaid sofa.

Her last thought before she turned toward the answering machine, with its blinking red light, was that she'd been wrong about the raincoat. That morning, she'd had the feeling she might need it, heedless of the forecast, but it hadn't rained after all. It was sunny.

The message was from Will's sister.

"Hailey—please call me. As soon as you can."

That was all there was to the message. Just nine strained words, and a click.

Hailey's hands shook as she reached for the receiver, fluttering over the dial like moths batting around a porch light in the dark. Instinctively, she knew.

Will was dead.

For months, it didn't register. Will was murdered. Murdered in a senseless act of what the police called "random violence"—a mugging. Hailey's beloved fiancé had taken five shots, four to the head, one to the back, over his wallet containing thirty-five dollars, credit cards, driver's license, and a picture of her. The credit cards were thrown to the ground beside his body.

Her world skidded to a halt.

Nothing mattered anymore; the days, weeks, months that followed melted and blurred, one into the other. Hailey wouldn't eat, couldn't sleep, went days without speaking. Then days turned into weeks.

The clocks in her parents' home were removed when the ticking drove her crazy, and the house stood completely quiet. It was as if time stopped along with the clocks. Her wedding dress hung in the closet and no one dared suggest she put it away. She wouldn't pack away his clothes, his letters. Even her notebook of wedding plans sat unmoved at her bedside with the blue pen on top, as if there were more to write.

The fresh-faced girl with the world waiting for her was dead. She died alongside the man she loved on a sunny spring afternoon.

Eight months later, the first, thick package in plain wrapping arrived, jammed into the mailbox at the end of the driveway.

It was from the first law school that wrote her back, answering her query with an application. That single envelope started a trickle that swiftly became a torrent, triggering long nights typing essays, researching scholarships, ordering transcripts, lining up references.

Her original plans—to teach college psychology or counsel patients in a quiet carpeted office—were out of the question, no longer even a remote option. The anger, the rage, but most of all the pain, were simply too big to fit into an antiseptic lecture hall or a muted psychologist's office.

One year to the day after Will's murder and with little fanfare, Hailey loaded her belongings—including her wedding dress, delicately folded into a big white box—into her car and left her family standing in the driveway, waving good-bye until they were just a tiny snatch of color in the rearview mirror.

Hailey opened her eyes and saw LaSondra still staring back at her.

Stuffing the photos into the back of the trial folder, she went padding in stocking feet out of the overhead fluorescent glare and into the lamplight of her own office.

There she dialed by heart the number for Christian Brown, managing editor of the *Atlanta Telegraph*, on his private office phone at his faux–Italian rococo behemoth on West Paces Ferry. His wife had dreamed it up. No children, just lifestyle.

No way would Brown budge on headlines for the sake of one bereaved mother's feelings in South Atlanta, but there was more than one way to skin a cat.

"Christian, Hailey Dean. Problem." Brown knew her well, so they dispensed with polite hellos.

"What's up?" He sounded sleepy.

"Listen, I'm doing you a favor."

"How's that?"

She reached down deep . . . and lied. She lied for all she was worth and in great detail delivered the news of a lawsuit hatched by a few personal-injury lawyers just that afternoon after arraignments.

"Christian, I hate to call you at home this late and on a weekend, too. But I knew you'd want to know immediately . . . they're going up against the paper for twenty mill on libel, the hooker headlines on the murder case."

She made it up as she went along. She broke every cardinal rule of testimony on the stand, her story getting more and more elaborate.

"They're already sweet-talking the victims' families one by one, meeting in their homes and showing up with all the paperwork ready to be signed."

Receiver wedged between shoulder and ear, she pictured the usual clientless hacks roaming the courthouse halls, nursing Styrofoam cups of coffee, belts riding low to make room for girth.

If it were true, the suit against the *Telegraph* could easily pass the time while they waited for judges to hand out appointed cases to them. An appointed case was a fast three hundred bucks in exchange for a swift, easy, and unprepared guilty plea from inmates. Judges loved clearing their calendars and defense attorneys loved the three hundred dollars.

"But my God, they *were* hookers!" Christian exploded, as if that would get him out of a lawsuit.

"Yeah, if you can prove it," she followed up, "but imagine a jury when they see eight-by-tens of eleven murdered women, then listen to their families break down in tears on the stand one after the other, including *their mothers*, Christian. Can you imagine? Plaintiffs will have a field day, even though they normally can't try their way out of a paper bag. It's over, Christian, and it hasn't even started."

She knew Brown's head was spinning as he realized he'd shot his own foot for one day's circulation boost. Hookers in headlines always sold copy. He hadn't bargained on a lawsuit.

"Vultures, all of them, Christian," she went on. "Vultures. You should have heard them. A couple million in a settlement against you makes the good life possible for them. Watch out."

"I'll see what I can do," he told Hailey.

Without the least bit of guilt over the huge lie she'd just told, Hailey placed the phone back in the cradle, then immediately picked it up again.

Rap sheets in hand, she dialed the number Leola Williams had given her.

With a pang of hurt for the loss of Leola's first baby girl and no mention of LaSondra's extensive rap sheet, Hailey promised into the phone that Leola's daughter would not be mistreated by the press. Easier said than done, but she had to try.

"Thank you, Miss Hailey. You see that justice comes to the man who did this. You make sure he pays."

Atlanta, Georgia

F OR OVER TWO MONTHS, HAILEY CRUISED THE STRIP IN AN UNDER-
cover county car with Fincher behind the wheel.

The Odd Couple—that's what they were called around the County
Courthouse. Fincher was a dark-skinned black Marine, six foot three,
heavily muscled, and always packing heat hip and ankle. Hailey
stood five foot one, slight, blonde, and always unarmed. Secretly, she
still recoiled at the sight of handguns, ever since Will's murder years
before. Even when guns came in as evidence in murder or assault trials, she held them lightly, as if they burned her fingertips.

After driving the streets for a while, they'd get out and go on
foot from one "gentlemen's club" to the next.

Fincher, badging their way in at the door, flashing his gold detective's shield, always starting by asking for the manager.

They carried with them several huge albums of mug shots: every
rapist, sex offender, Peeping Tom, obscene phone caller, and pervert
booked in the city during the last four years, literally hundreds of
suspects in the serial murder investigation. They were, at best, remote possibilities—but they were all Hailey and Fincher had to
go on.

Most of the hookers who danced the strip bars wouldn't ordinarily bother to look through the photos. But since the managers
didn't want any problems with the District Attorney's Office, they
made the girls go through the book in a break room, one by one.

That night, Hailey and Fincher interviewed nearly forty dancers, all of whom looked bored, thumbing through the album without a glint of recognition.

Then they met Cassie.

"I'll look at your pictures under one condition," she'd said
shrewdly, looking from Hailey to Fincher.

"What's that?"

"I want dinner. You buy."

"Deal."

The three of them went across the street to an all-night Denny's, where Fincher and Hailey got coffee and Cassie got the works, building her own Grand Slam platter for five ninety-nine.

From across the table, Hailey watched her switch off bites of bacon and a side order of onion rings as she thumbed through the album.

After about twenty pages, she stopped and sank back in the booth.

"Oh, sweet Jesus, help me." Her eyes widened and her face went pale under heavy stage makeup. She shoved her plate away, holding her right hand palm-flat to the base of her neck and reaching for her cigarettes with her left.

Hailey instinctively flicked on the recorder inside her purse. "What is it, Cassie?"

"It's him." Cassie lit a cigarette with a trembling hand, took a few puffs, then ground it into what was left of the Grand Slam. "He put his hands around my neck. He was supposed to give me a hundred dollars for a half-and-half—that's what we call it, Hailey, when—you know."

"I know," she said quickly. She'd tried enough street crime to know what a half-and-half was and didn't need a tutorial in a booth at Denny's.

"Then, out of the blue, during the last half, he put his hands around my neck and choked me so hard I puked up right there on the blanket."

"What blanket?"

"He put out a blue blanket in the park, down at the turnaround past the club. He got it out of his car trunk. We were supposed to just be there a little while and he promised a hundred dollars. I saw him in the club a few times when I was dancing, he seemed okay and the tips were always pretty good. So...I went with him." Cassie lit up and took a long, shaky drag on a new cigarette.

"So why did he stop?"

"Well when I puked, he lost it, everything stopped. He got all embarrassed, said he didn't mean to hurt me. But he did hurt me, I was trying to get at his hands and he wouldn't . . . until I threw up."

"Then what happened?"

"He gave me the hundred dollars in tens and he dropped me back off at the club. I never saw him again. I didn't think about it too much at the time. But you know, later that night when I got home and I was getting ready for bed, I felt inside like I had been touched by something pure evil. I know it sounds crazy, but after all the men I've been through, I never felt like that before."

Fincher looked hard at the woman across the booth. "Why didn't you report him? If this is the right guy, you know how many women he killed? Women just like you? *Eleven* that we *know* of. And I bet there are bodies out there we never found."

Fincher was breathing hard and irritated. It was late and they were dead tired, but they both felt an unspoken surge that they had stumbled onto something.

"Well what was *I* supposed to tell the cops . . . that I was turning a half-and-half out behind the club and the guy got crazy on me? That sounds like a confession to me. That kind of talk will get you ninety hours in the city jail for solicitation. Plus, the man gave me the hundred. Hell, *no*, I didn't tell the police."

Cassie ground her cigarette into her plate beside the first butt and started collecting her things to leave. She was pissed. She hadn't come here for a sermon. She grabbed her purse.

Hailey couldn't let her go, couldn't screw this up. Too much was riding on it. She had to smooth it over.

Because out there, somewhere, tonight maybe, he was roaming. Waiting. Looking. Every extra day Hailey spent working the case meant one more night he was free to stalk the city of Atlanta. For all she knew, he was there, outside, this very moment.

"Fincher, go to the car and call back to the precinct. Get this guy's rap sheet."

He stalked out sulking, knowing full well he was banished from the booth for reprimanding a woman who could end up being the State's star witness.

"Cassie, please . . ." Hailey reached out and gently touched the hooker's bony, tattooed arm. "Don't go."

"I don't need this shit."

"Listen, I'm sorry about that. We just don't want to see another woman, or you, killed. Fincher feels the police didn't work the case because the dead girls were hookers. Or dancers—like you, Cassie. Please. You could be saving a life. I need you. Don't you have a little sister? Or a little girl? Would you want this to happen to her?"

Hailey pulled out a crime scene photo of one of the victims and handed it to Cassie.

Cassie paused, looking at the photo. Then, she put her purse back down beside her in the booth, got out a cigarette, and lit it up.

Thank God, a second chance.

"When did it happen, Cassie? Did you ever see him again? Just tell me what you remember."

"It was July, last year." She exhaled. "It was sticky hot the minute I stepped out of the back of the club and came down the steps."

"July. Good. When in July?"

Cassie thought hard about it, as Hailey calculated . . . July of last year would have been nearly two years ago . . . when Homicide figured he'd first started the killings. Cassie must have been one of his first victims, but he had gotten put off by the vomit and quit. But by the time he geared up for his next victim, he was past backing out. The next girl wasn't so lucky.

"You know what?" Cassie said at last. "It was probably, like, the week after the Fourth. I remember because I had made a little outfit for a special show at the club for the holiday and I wore it the next week, too. It had red, white, and blue sequins and a matching sequined choker. I wore the leotard part of the outfit again the next week but without the red tux jacket. It was that night, the night I went with him in the car. He tore the neck of it in the park."

"Tore the neck out?" Hailey alerted to the significance.

"Yeah. Just the neck was torn."

"What else? Just tell me what you remember . . . every detail. It'll come back to you."

Cassie shrugged. "It was late, like four a.m. I stepped out of the back of the club. He was waiting for me in his car, looking up at the door when I came out."

"What kind of car?"

"I don't know . . . it was big, but I don't remember what kind. I thought we'd go to a hotel room or even in the car because it was so big, but he wanted it outdoors. I figured it'd be quick and at that time of night in the cul-de-sac, nobody would be around for sure, so I took him there."

"Did you ever see him again?"

Cassie shook her head. "He never came back after that night, and up 'til then, he had been pretty regular, same seat every night for about a month. Good tips, too. Then—poof! Gone. Never came back. I told some of the other girls about it. They remembered him, but they said it, too—you know, that he never came back in the club."

She stopped talking and got quiet, looking down at the ashtray.

"What else can you remember?" Hailey coaxed.

"Yeah . . . thinking back . . . you know, I wouldn't have thrown up, but I had just had my dinner break. He smelled funny, like a kitchen smell, like real strong garlic. But it wasn't his breath. It was just *him*. It like . . . came out of his *pores* or something."

Hailey's thoughts raced as they sent Cassie on her way and pulled out of the Denny's parking lot. All they needed was a break . . . one break. One hint, one clue, one sign.

They finally had something . . . same MO, outside in a secluded area located off the strip, prostitute-victim, half-and-half, manual strangulation during the trick . . . a fascination with the victim's neck . . . it was all too similar *not* to be connected.

The sheer impact of how close this woman had come to losing her life, *if* this was the right guy, slammed into Hailey like a tsunami.

"Fincher . . . stop the car."

"What's wrong?"

He was out there.

"Nothing. Just . . ." She turned, looking out the back window, and watched Cassie until she was out of sight, back in the club, safe.

Safe for tonight, at least.

IIIIIIIIIIIIIIIIIIIIIIIIIIIIIIIIIIIIIIIIIIIIIIIIIIIIIIIIIIIIII **3** IIIIIIIIIIIIIIIII

Atlanta, Georgia

"LOOK, I KNOW IT SOUNDS CRAZY," SHEILA GRAHAM TOLD HAILEY as they sat facing each other across her living room coffee table, "but I just can't get involved in this again."

"It doesn't sound crazy at all, Sheila. I've heard it a million times. Nobody wants to get involved. But what I'm telling you is that he could get out. If I get evidence suppressed or the jury just doesn't like the victims, for whatever reason, Clint Burrell Cruise could walk, he could get out. Then who do you think he'd want to come back to? You, that's who."

"I can't do it."

"Please, Sheila . . . we need you. Believe me, I know how difficult it will be for you to come face-to-face with Cruise again, after what he did to you. He almost killed you, I know that."

Cruise—the woman's former live-in boyfriend—had harassed her with a series of late-night, sexually obscene phone calls. Then, when she'd continued to rebuff him, he broke into her apartment, crept into her bedroom, and tried to rape her. When she'd fought back, the sex attack turned into attempted murder. He tried to strangle her there in her own bed.

If it hadn't been for her sister, sleeping over in the guest bedroom that night and calling 911, Sheila would be dead. As it was, the sister left town and couldn't be found after Cruise threatened to come after her.

Even in the darkened bedroom, Sheila could still make a positive ID, and a voice ID as well. Prints lifted off the back window matched Cruise's. The case was rock solid.

It was that arrest and book-in photo that landed Cruise's photo in the mug-shot album, where Cassie recognized him from the strip club. From Cassie's identification, a warrant for Cruise's blood evidence, which meant DNA at trial, was suddenly possible.

The prosecutor at the time dropped the ball and didn't push when Sheila refused to testify against her ex-boyfriend at trial. But even though the case had to be dropped for lack of prosecution, the mug shot was still there, still there in Hailey's fat book of photos.

"What makes you think she'll do it now? For somebody else? When she wouldn't even do it for herself?" Hailey asked herself, sitting immobile on the sofa, not willing to give up just yet but knowing inside it was probably futile to try and convince her.

But without Sheila, the evidence would just be the dry testimony of scientists from the crime lab on the stand, and maybe Cassie, too, if she didn't OD or disappear before trial.

"It's not just what he did that day that's so painful for me to face," Sheila said slowly. "It's what he was like before that. I thought he loved me, Hailey. He had me fooled. I thought he was perfect. Sweet, charming, he could dance, he brought home a paycheck . . . everything."

"Classic psychopath," Hailey thought.

Sheila was her only hope. Here was her chance.

"Sheila, this isn't just about what he did to you. It's about the eleven women he murdered after you broke up with him. But really,

Sheila, it's about your little girl. Until he's behind bars, she's not safe. Didn't you say she was the only thing you cared about? That's what you told me on the phone. What about her? It's not just about you, Sheila. You're a mother now. It's not all about you anymore."

Coming down on her was a risk. It could make her furious and land Hailey back out on the sidewalk where she came from, empty-handed.

It started with one tear, and quickly Hailey was searching for Kleenex. Sheila broke down. The woman really had been through so much and here was Hailey, badgering her.

From the moment Hailey first laid eyes on Sheila, she had the nagging sensation that she knew her, that they must have met somewhere in the past. But Sheila said no, and she didn't have a record. She was a nurse at Northside Hospital pediatric NICU without a single blemish on her record, not even a speeding ticket.

But there on the sofa, watching her movements, listening to her speech patterns as she talked, the way she dabbed at her eyes with the Kleenex . . . there was something familiar . . .

Hailey came up dry. She couldn't place her. The woman must be telling the truth. She had never been in the courthouse as a defendant, suspect, or witness. Nevertheless, Hailey instinctively continued to look her up and down, staring intently whenever she looked away.

There was something about her . . .

"Want some coffee? It'll only take a minute to brew."

"I'd love some, thank you, Sheila."

Hailey stood up, too, and followed Sheila into the kitchen. Her baby girl was there, playing on the kitchen floor. Hailey sat down at the kitchen table and started playing with her.

"What do you take in it? Milk?"

Hailey looked up to answer and, glancing over to Sheila's profile, there at the kitchen sink, it hit like a ton of bricks.

Hailey realized where she had seen Sheila before. In autopsy photos. Ten of them, anyway.

All Cruise's victims—with the exception of LaSondra, the very last—looked just like Sheila, front and side. All had the same slight, ghostly pale features, with hair cascading down over one shoulder. Sheila had dark brown eyes, they had dark brown eyes. Even their height and weight . . . Sheila was five foot one, ninety-five pounds. Cruise's victims were all between four foot nine and five foot two, not one weighing in over one hundred and five.

How had Hailey overlooked that?

She couldn't take her eyes off the girl. It was as if the victims had come to life again, through her.

Here was motive, handed to her on a silver platter. The State didn't have to prove it, but juries without exception expected to hear a motive, especially in a murder case.

Over and over, with each woman he attacked and strangled, he relived Sheila's rejection, acting out the same rage over and over. With each murder, he got her back.

"Please, Sheila," Hailey begged. "Please say you'll testify. I know you can do it. For their sakes."

She laid out the eleven folders on the kitchen table, setting them carefully one by one and opening their covers to reveal eleven photographs of eleven dead women.

Sheila stared at them for a long time.

"And to protect her." Without turning away from Sheila, Hailey gestured toward the baby girl sitting on the kitchen floor.

Sheila looked over at the baby, then back up at Hailey. Her eyes filled with tears.

"All right," she said at last. "I'll do it. I'll testify."

Walking back out to her car, Hailey glanced back to see Sheila standing at the window, baby on hip, looking out after her.

"Maybe now I can pull this thing off . . . maybe . . ."

Atlanta, Georgia

I N HER OFFICE AFTER HOURS, HAILEY POURED OVER A MOUNTAIN OF evidence against Clint Burrell Cruise in the murders of eleven women.

Evidence that was now under attack and in jeopardy of being suppressed by a defense team led by Matt Leonard.

Leonard knew every trick in the book and was pulling out all the stops on this one. First, he papered her with motions, knowing she was trying the case solo. She wrote and argued every response herself. He knew that.

Already, he had taken the use of DNA evidence up to the Georgia Supreme Court, arguing that between junk science, possible police corruption, and contamination both at the scene and at the crime lab, it was not reliable enough to use in cases so serious as to warrant the death penalty, cases like this one. Leonard argued that, unlike a sentence of years behind bars, once the death penalty was imposed, there was no possible "reversal," as far as his client was concerned.

Luckily, she had insisted on a warrant for backup DNA testing at the crime lab, so the Court felt secure that not one but two DNA tests pointed to Cruise as the strangler in ten out of eleven cases. With the startling similarities in MO in all eleven murders, she was determined to prove the last victim, Victim Eleven, Leola's daughter LaSondra, was Cruise's as well.

The circus Leonard created was designed to throw her off her game and distract her from trying the case.

The next morning, a mortal blow was delivered to the State. The judge ruled the strangling incident with Sheila would not come into evidence at trial in his courtroom. He bought into the defense theory that to introduce evidence of another bad act—not the ones on trial—was more prejudicial than probative ... that it wasn't evidence proving the murders and just served to taint Cruise's reputation before the jury.

But Sheila alone showed motive. The judge couldn't care less. Sickened by the decision, Hailey stood alone in the courtroom as it emptied.

She held her left fist to her mouth, the right twisting the silver pen. What to do ... what to do? The jury would never hear motive and if they didn't accept the DNA or disbelieved any of the cops, Cruise would walk. Look what had happened in O. J. Simpson's double murder trial ... one bad cop and it was all over.

The case was sacked, with Leonard winning round one of pre-trial motions.

Hailey heard the rush of air when the courtroom door behind her was pushed open and she turned.

It was Leonard.

He stopped short when their gazes locked, but he continued to eye her from across the State's counsel table.

"Ready to bite the bullet and drop the case?"

She laughed. "When hell freezes over, Leonard. Not a day before."

"If I get the blood warrant thrown out on legal grounds, it's over. But I can make it easy on you. I won't tell the press, and you dead-docket the case. Nobody'll know. You can tell everybody there just wasn't enough proof."

"Well, you've finally lost your mind, Leonard. I've seen it coming, though, no surprise here. Too much pressure?"

"Face it, Hailey, you can't win them all, as much as I know that disappoints you." His tone was cruel and sarcastic, belying the half-smile playing on his lips.

Hailey looked at him, really looked at him, for the first time after having handled countless guilty pleas and various other negotiations and motions with him over the years.

To her he was just another defense attorney, one out of hundreds she dealt with in the course of handling the State's business.

She had never really noticed the thin curve of his upper lip, the twist at the corner of his mouth, the cold glint in his gray eyes, his bulky frame. His face was pale but his skin was blotchy, as if he'd had severe acne as a teenager.

Leonard had been an Atlanta cop for several years but never rose above street cop status, and he still stayed in close contact with his old cronies. Many of them had risen in the ranks. He still had the body of a cop, with a barrel chest and thin at the waist. He was a fitness buff, spending hours watching himself work out in front of mirrors at the gym. He even had to have his suits specially tailored wide at the shoulder and then taken in for an almost freakishly thin waist and bottom. Word was that he left the police force with an Internal Affairs file as thick as your fist, filled with police brutality complaints. Gossip or lore, Hailey never knew the truth of it.

He'd gone through five wives that Hailey knew of. She saw the most recent one at the annual Lawyer's Club Christmas party: a bleached platinum blonde, tiny, in her early twenties, incredibly frail and thin. She couldn't have weighed more than ninety pounds and was dressed like a runway model. She never said a word, though, looking ill at ease and nervous. Her frosty red lipstick kept glomming at the corners of her mouth, giving her an unnatural clown frown. Hailey later heard they, too, had divorced.

Standing there, facing Leonard's steely gaze and imposing figure, Hailey had no problem believing that the brutality rumor was true.

"Take the dead-docket, Hailey. It won't spoil your record. That's what it's all about for you, right? Undefeated?"

"This isn't about my record, Leonard. It's about what went down on the strip. It's about your client and what he did. You may win one round in court, Leonard, but it's not over . . . *yet*. I've just gotten started with you."

"What do you want, Dean? To rot in a job as a local prosecutor? Nothing but dopers, thugs, killers?"

"Like yours is any different? Except, oh yeah, you *defend* the dopers and the thugs and the killers. You put them back on the street." She shot it right back at him.

"Some life you've got going here, Hailey. No family, no kids, just a worn-out, bitter prosecutor. How's that working for you?"

His hulking frame was hovering closer, his hands clinched, the knuckles white as they gripped the other side of the State's counsel table. Instead of playing his game, Hailey turned her back on him and started packing her files to leave.

"Don't do it, Hailey, you're being stupid," he hissed, low in the silence of the courtroom. "Here's the deal. You can go on to a judgeship. I can make it happen for you. That's what you want in the end, don't you? To be a judge? Don't go down the tubes over some dead hookers. Your career is everything to you, right? It's all you've got left . . . why blow it now? Play this case right, don't make enemies."

She snapped, turning around to look him square in the face.

"Leonard, I think you should go get into your car and drive out to the jail to see your client and tell him he's getting the chair. You know, the electric chair. 'Old Sparky,' I believe they call it, Leonard. Ever heard of that? 'Old Sparky'?" She gestured her head toward the parking deck.

"You little bitch . . . you just won't play ball with the rest of us, will you? You think you're all about justice. You think you're above us all, don't you? You're nothing but a prima donna and I'm bringing you down."

Leonard advanced around the corner of the table. Too close. Too menacing. She saw his trademark nervous tic erupt across the corner of his lip and eye, his fingers working that ridiculous family crest ring encrusted with rubies. It was monstrous. Pompous ass.

She'd never do it in front of a judge or jury, but now, without anyone watching, she smiled openly at Leonard's nervous twisting. With all that twitching and sniffing, he unwittingly turned off jurors and witnesses by the drove.

"Now *here's* the deal, Leonard. If Cruise walks free out of this courthouse, he'll do it over my dead cold body. Unlike everything and everybody else, this is one thing you and your politician brother won't be able to buy. You know why? Because you don't have a single thing I want, including a judgeship. And I don't need friends like you, Leonard. You and your client are both freaks. Now get out of the courtroom."

"When this is over, Dean, I'll have the nameplate off your office door, and your law license, too." He let it out low, flinty eyes boring a hole through hers.

"I'll keep that in mind." She turned, picked up her briefcase, and left.

It took all her willpower not to turn at the courtroom door and look back at him. As she walked alone down the courthouse's wide hallway, she could feel his presence right on her heels, like he was going to pounce on her from behind.

IIIIIIIIIIIIIIIIIIIIIIIIIIIIIIIIIIIIIIIIIIIIIIIIIIIIIIIII **5** IIIIIIIIIIIIIIIIII

Atlanta, Georgia

"THIS, MEMBERS OF THE JURY, IS THE WEAPON DEFENDANT CLINT Burrell Cruise used to murder eleven innocent women. This, and his own brute strength as he circled his fingers around their throats." Hailey held up the poultry-lifter in her left hand, arm outstretched, slowly walking the length of the jury rail in a courtroom packed with relatives, court watchers, and media. Witnesses lined the halls outside the courtroom, waiting to be called in one by one.

The jurors stared at the weapon, some with their mouths open. This was the weapon that had stumped Atlanta PD for so long. Several of the jurors actually recoiled backward in their seats as she walked slowly before them, intentionally holding the lifter just beneath their chins.

Blood from the last victim, LaSondra Williams, was still on the prongs that left an unmistakable, signature death wound ripping open the lower back of each victim.

Hailey's mind flashed back to the exact wording in the autopsy.

Angle: 45 degrees, upwards, back to front, just below the lung cavity.

Even with Cassie's lead, it had taken a while to piece together the puzzle and make an arrest.

Between baker's twine, the murder weapon itself, and what Cassie said about the smell of garlic oozing from the pores of her attacker, it all slowly fit together. The killer was a chef.

The murder weapon had taken a while to figure out. Months of studying the mortal wounds, their angles of entry and exit, their lengths and their widths, and searching for microscopic fibers or particles left behind inside or around the puncture marks had ended with nothing. Nothing. It was only after Hailey's comparison of the baker's twine and Cassie's observation that a murder weapon was finally identified . . . in a specialty gourmet kitchen boutique.

The killer used a poultry-lifter to deliver each of the four-pronged stab wounds. A solid stainless-steel Norpro poultry-lifter had prongs sharp and sturdy enough to handle even the biggest birds. The long, seven-inch stainless-steel prongs were easily identifiable once they knew where to look, the individual tines widely spaced to allow a chef to balance the bird.

He'd always ended by staging the scene, postmortem, with the signature bow, tied with baker's twine around the victims' bruised neck, wrist, ankle, toe . . . almost always varying the anatomical location, like a little surprise.

Cruise wrapped each victim like a present to the Homicide Unit. Then later, after the papers announced that Hailey was named head of the investigation, it became a mocking gesture to her alone.

When the murder weapon was finally found in Cruise's home, pursuant to a search warrant, it was in a Ziploc double-zip bag, wrapped in a stark white bath towel and stuffed inside a gym bag. The bag was concealed far behind a row of perfectly lined shoes in Cruise's bedroom closet. The rubber grip should have revealed latent fingerprints, but multiple grooved markings on the handle made prints impossible.

Still, nothing could stop the DNA trail in the identical series of murders, which were so similar any court in the nation would affirm their introduction into evidence.

The trial itself was a DNA nightmare: Ten of the eleven murders pointed to Clint Burrell Cruise. But the final victim had been found without a trace of the killer's DNA on her body.

LaSondra Williams.

And she alone had the odd marking on her neck—a small cluster of shallow cuts, fresh fingernail scratches. Hailey assumed LaSondra's nails were inspected and yielded nothing. It had to be from Cruise's nails, but by the time he was arrested months later, the DNA was obviously gone.

Hailey didn't know what it meant—probably nothing—but she knew Leonard would use it against her at trial. As usual, she over-analyzed. Neither the lead defense counsel nor his fleet of sycophants had caught it in the autopsy report. She guessed Leonard wasn't as sharp as he was cracked up to be.

LaSondra's mother, Leola, was at the trial every day, sporting one beautiful, tailored suit after the next, eyes fixed either with gratitude on Hailey, or with hatred on the man who had snuffed out her daughter's life, leaving a wake of pain behind him he seemed unable to comprehend, sitting in court every day, nonplussed . . . as if he were above it all.

Hailey tried the case solo as usual—no other lawyers to back her up as second chair. Just Fincher sitting with her at the counsel table for the State. The table was strewn with stacks of notes, evidence books, and brown paper bags containing clothes, shoes, earrings, and hose that once belonged to the dead women, each bag sealed and marked separately.

The photos of the crime scenes and close-ups of the victims' faces in death were burned into Hailey's brain. One in particular disturbed her. It was a photo of dirt and grass pushed up into La-Sondra's nose and mouth from being shoved facedown into the ground during the attack. In it, the angry, red elongated scratches on LaSondra's neck were clearly visible.

But the photos—and even the media frenzy surrounding the case—were the least of Hailey's worries.

Matt Leonard was at the helm of a fleet of high-priced attorneys and their hangers-on: paralegals, investigators, and unpaid clerks plotting to count the trial as "experience" when they padded their résumés at the end of law school—all of them banded together, determined to beat a murder rap on behalf of the most prolific serial killer ever to stalk the city of Atlanta.

Especially Leonard, who was unaccustomed to losing in court to anyone.

Hailey could feel the venom in his gaze right now as she went on with her closing argument.

She could see him out of the corner of her eye throughout the trial, though she never let the jury catch her looking over at the defense table.

She finished in a hushed tone in a rapt courtroom, barely speaking above a whisper, leaning over the rail, addressing the jurors directly. This was not for the press, not for the judge, not for the packed courtroom. It was for their ears alone. The court reporter strained to take it down.

"These women had families. Mothers and fathers, husbands, children, sisters and brothers. Families who waited for them to come home. They never did. They never did, because they crossed paths with Clint Burrell Cruise. It's in your hands now. Do not turn away from the evidence. Your voice is the only one they have. Please, please, convict this man and return a verdict that speaks the truth. Show him the same mercy he showed his victims. None. He is *guilty*." After a brief moment of complete silence, she turned from the jury and took her seat at the State's counsel table.

Now, with Hailey's closing arguments ended, it was finally out of her hands. She had done all she possibly could during months of long nights and weekends working. Now she could only pray justice would prevail.

"Miss Hailey?" Leola Williams came up behind her as she gathered files into her briefcase. "I want to thank you."

"No, Miss Leola. I only hope the jury does the right thing and you find some peace." Hailey hugged her tightly, knowing that even a death sentence for Cruise wouldn't bring back Leola's girl.

They broke apart and went to the courthouse cafeteria for iced teas, going over and over the witnesses, the evidence, everything that had happened during the trial. And then, back up the elevator and to the courtroom.

Hours passed as they all sat on the courtroom's hardwood pews, waiting. Once, when she caught Leonard staring at her again, he turned sharply away from her, pretending to study the far wall of the courtroom in deep thought.

Out of the jury's sight, Hailey turned slightly to study Cruise as he sat at the counsel table. He was angled away from her, but she immediately noticed Cruise hungrily biting the nails on his right hand, almost like an animal. During the investigation, she retraced his movements through credit card statements and knew he must miss the weekly manicures he had gotten on the outside. Something about his gesture struck her as odd, but she was wrenched from her train of thought when the courtroom bailiff placed his hand on her shoulder. He nodded to her, giving her a heads up, silently communicating the jury was done. Almost immediately, a buzzer inside the jury deliberation room buzzed loudly in the courtroom. They had a verdict.

Guilty . . . on all eleven counts. Hailey published the verdict, standing alone in the center of the courtroom looking directly at Cruise. It hardly seemed real, reading out loud in a clear voice. It rang out in the courtroom as she spoke.

"I didn't do it!" Cruise bellowed out when the last count was read. All hell broke loose in the courtroom. Cruise, in a rage, lunged at Hailey across the defense table. Books thumped to the ground, papers flew up in the air, the jury and spectators leaped to their feet.

In a matter of seconds, eight sheriffs strategically positioned about the courtroom when major verdicts came down attacked Cruise, dragging him away from Hailey. But it was just long enough for Hailey to feel what his victims had felt—Cruise's cold hands closing around her neck.

In that moment, Hailey knew she was finished.

Years of trials and the endless parade of victims silently looking out at her from crime scene photos and autopsy tables at the morgue had taken their toll. But it wasn't Cruise's lunge at her that did it. It was the photo, the photo of the dirt and grass, smeared up and across LaSondra's face.

This was Hailey Dean's final war with a powerful and cunning Atlanta defense bar, a last stand.

She was ready now, ready to turn her back on the justice system and leave the practice of criminal law—and Atlanta itself—behind.

With Cruise off the street, Hailey Dean resigned from the District Attorney's Office.

And on that night, the papers wrote, the city's pimps, thieves, and killers . . . and their defense lawyers . . . danced in the streets with the Devil.

Reidsville
State Penitentiary,
Georgia

THE SMELL COULDN'T BE DISINFECTED AWAY.

No ammonia, no cleanser, no air purifier yet known to man could erase the funk left behind by thousands of killers, rapists, and child molesters. In fact, the industrial-strength cleansers mopped into the floor and scrubbed into the sideboards only added their own unique ingredient to the mix. It was a stench to remind visitors, long after they'd left the cluster of concrete buildings, just how sweet their own freedom smelled.

Clint Burrell Cruise sat in his cell on a metal bunk bolted to the floor. Imagining. Remembering.

He had been the premier star, the up-and-comer in the small, ultra-prestigious world of nouvelle cuisine called "infusion art." He'd even convinced himself he had actually coined the phrase.

Cruise was even approached by the Food Channel to launch his own televised daily hour of infusion art. He was all set to be up there alongside the others, Rachael Ray, Paula Deen, the Iron Chefs, and maybe one day, Martha Stewart herself. Many times he'd imagined lingering over the made-for-TV kitchen counter, casually straddling a bar stool, sharing techniques with Stewart.

It could happen.

As much as he adored Martha Stewart, he hated Emeril Lagasse with that frickin' "Bam!" every time he did something. God he hated that man. He, Cruise, should have Lagasse's fame.

Screw him and his worn out "Bam!" routine.

The last time some ass had turned on Lagasse in the rec room, Cruise picked up a metal folding chair and threw it at the TV. He got thirty days in solitary for that, but if Lagasse said "Bam" just one more time Cruise swore he'd kill him dead with his own two hands.

The Food Channel . . . just when it was all coming together . . . it all came crashing down. Because of her. Hailey Dean. That bitch hunted him down like a bloodhound.

After his arrest, she came to the jail. He could smell her halfway down the cellblock. She smelled like cold wind, like the night air in Atlanta after it rained. Even that memory plagued Cruise now, made him twist at night in a sweat on the two inches of flat cotton over rusted springs they called a cot.

When she'd come to the jail that day, she had him pulled out of his cell with a warrant and dragged to the sick bay. He knew what she wanted and he fought like hell until two guards forced him into a seat and cuffed him to the chair. There, she watched the nurse jab him with a needle to draw blood from his arm. He stared right back at her, neither one ever once breaking their gaze, even when the needle bit into his skin.

Not one muscle moved in her face, even though behind her, talking into her ear the whole time she watched, there had stood a huge black man wearing a heavy coat and a black fedora. She seemed to listen to him, but never once responded, never looking away from Cruise's face. When the blood was drawn and siphoned into separate vials, she stepped around the glass wall and into sick bay. Even as she spoke to the jail nurse, she still kept a razor lock on Cruise.

"Mark it, please. Name and cell," he heard her say. "And would you hand it directly to my investigator? I can't touch it myself, can't break the chain of custody. I'd hate to be a State's witness in a murder case I'm prosecuting myself. And ma'am, let me give you this subpoena in case the drawing of the blood is called into question by the defense."

The nurse marked the two glass vials and handed them over to the investigator.

"Fincher, seal it." Hailey stood completely still, never laying a finger on the vials, vials that literally held Clint Cruise's future within their thin walls. Fincher placed them into a brown manila envelope, and sealed it.

Hailey Dean handed the nurse a court order of appearance, then backed toward the door. Still staring him in the face, she fired one last remark, like a hollow-point bullet. "DNA evidence is a miracle. Isn't that right, Fincher?"

"Sure is, it's a miracle."

They both looked at him with no change of expression, then turned on their heels and walked out.

Later, at trial, Cruise learned Hailey Dean was so concerned about the admissibility of DNA evidence at trial, she was shoring up her evidence before the jury was even struck. She knew full well that defense attorneys far and wide labeled DNA "junk science" when it suited their defense.

With Fincher by her side, Hailey had drawn up an additional warrant for the trial judge presiding over Cruise's murder trial and presented it to him in chambers. She'd sworn in Fincher using the judge's desktop Bible, and asked him a series of quick, carefully constructed questions they'd rehearsed in the elevator on the way up to the judge's chambers.

The questions were all regarding the Atlanta serial murders, and their answers would support the judge in signing the warrant to look for additional evidence to prove the State's case. The "search" amounted to having a second, backup series of Cruise's blood drawn for comparison to sperm found in and on the bodies of several of the victims.

Several, but not all of them.

There was one victim, the last one, whose body offered up no trace of DNA matter to compare: no blood, no sperm, no hair.

LaSondra Williams.

The eleventh victim haunted Cruise every night.

Couldn't they see she wasn't his type anyway? Why hadn't Leonard argued that to the jury?

LaSondra Williams looked nothing like the others, all of them slight and pale-skinned, with hair parted over to the right and falling in waves down to their shoulders. LaSondra had been tall and gangly, much taller than Cruise himself.

With no DNA, Matt Leonard, if he had taken his head out of his ass for one minute, could have argued the State was wrong about Williams's murder and, therefore, could likely be wrong about the other ten hookers. Then he could have argued the rest was planted by police. . . . It only takes one juror to hang a jury.

Most nights now, in the quiet of maximum security in the inner-most cells of Reidsville, Cruise woke up sweating, back in the courtroom with Hailey Dean staring him down. Hailey Dean passing just inches from him as she questioned each witness on the stand. Hailey Dean so close he could feel the whisper of air melting around her as she passed, always wearing black, hair always pulled back tightly from her face.

Her voice was sharp as a whip on cross-exams, yet cajoling and hushed on direct with her own witnesses. During her closing argument to the jury, she spoke so softly, leaning in with her fingers resting on the jury rail, that Cruise had to strain to hear her words. His mouth went dry, his palms sweaty as hell as he'd watched the jury leaning forward toward her, and he caught himself doing the same.

Then, without warning, she turned on him and lashed out loudly, causing the jury to look directly at him while she practically shouted out the evidence.

His stomach burned with the memory.

And the stench of this place was giving him another pounding headache. Like the kind he used to get each time he'd go hunting for the next woman, the next victim. The tension building, he'd watch his own hands at work in the highest-tech kitchens in Atlanta. Then, later that same night, almost as if in a dream, off Stewart Avenue, hidden in the shadows of motels lining the strip, he'd have the hooker facedown in front of him, his hands choking, out of control, pulsing as if they belonged to someone much stronger, someone superhuman.

Only after, when he walked away and headed for his car, could he ever breathe again.

His body needed the kill, needed the feel of skin under his fingertips, digging, digging into flesh, to feel alive.

And who were the "victims" anyway? They were all hookers. He was doing the city a favor.

In court, the photos of the women's necks showed mangled flesh, as if the killer had torn the skin with his fingers in the frenzy of the strangling. Once, as Hailey Dean looked down at crime scene photos she was holding in her hand, he thought she was going to crack.

A flush of victory loomed for Cruise when her voice broke in the middle of questioning a lead homicide detective. She'd been looking at a shot of the knees of one of the hookers, scratched and bruised from the dirt where she'd knelt.

It was LaSondra Williams.

This whole mess was his lawyer's fault. That stupid ass. He had never finished working Cruise's alibi for the night LaSondra Williams was strangled. Cruise knew Leonard didn't believe him. But he'd stood there lying that the private investigator couldn't locate the leads Cruise gave him.

Here in Reidsville, he had plenty of time to relive the trial, all the errors his lawyer had made, and all the other indignities Hailey Dean subjected him to.

He followed her career from behind bars. He had gone to the law library and Xeroxed every document he could find on her. He had every news clipping, every blurb, every shred of information on Dean. It was too obvious to just thrust it under his cot, so instead, at night, he'd meticulously tear apart the thin layers of cotton that made up his mattress and press each article between the strips. He had to be careful.

He read all about her cases, every appeal of every case she ever tried, even the hard-luck story that came out about the murder of her fiancé. The thought of her and the memory of his attorney screwing him over consumed him.

The day the verdict was handed down, she was pale. Her hair was pulled back and he couldn't take his eyes off her neck.

He remembered watching her neck as the verdict was read.

Guilty. All eleven counts.

The courtroom turned into a reddish, hazy blur when the last count was read, the last verdict of guilty, for the murder of LaSondra Williams.

His body took over, his hands felt the electricity surging through them, shooting through his wrists down to his fingertips and he leaped.

Lunging across the table, strewing law books and notes and paper cups . . . he made it. He made it all the way to where she stood, unprotected in the center of the massive courtroom. Her investigator was several rows back in the courtroom sitting with the State's witnesses. He had stupidly let his guard down and left her alone. In that one moment, Cruise made it across the courtroom to Hailey Dean.

He reached out and barely fingered her neck, when a pain burned through his skull as the sheriffs clubbed him from behind.

Idiots. They couldn't understand the artist's mind, a mind like his. They thought he was enraged over the verdict. But all he wanted was to touch her neck. His hands were pumped with energy, and they ached to circle her neck, just below her chin.

Dean stood silent when they dragged him off her, eyes still locked on him, as if he had never touched her.

Tonight, in the dark of his cell, his hands felt hot with electricity, that old feeling that took hold of him. He was superhuman again.

He thought of her. She wasn't so smart. A smile spread across his face.

He was the only one that knew just how stupid Hailey Dean really was. Because he, Clint Burrell Cruise, hadn't strangled LaSondra Williams.

Imagine Dean's expression when she finds out the truth. Stupid bitch. So stupid, she didn't have a clue.

If his own incompetent lawyer had proven him innocent on the eleventh murder count, doubt would have been cast on all the other murders and the jury would have let him go . . . let him walk out of the courtroom and onto the elevator. Down to the lobby and out into the street, mingling with all the others on the sidewalk until he disappeared into the evening.

The cell row was deafeningly quiet. Cruise's hands were so electric tonight he thought he'd come out of his skin.

Hailey Dean.

It was like she was here, in his cell with him. He still remembered her smell. In the dark, he could still smell her, like the outdoors.

|||||||||||||||||||||||||||||||||||||||||||||||||||||||| **7** ||||||||||||||||

New York City
TWO YEARS LATER

WAVES OF HEAT SHIMMERED OFF THE GRASS IN THE CLEARING where she sat cross-legged in the red Georgia dirt. The sun baked the pine trees and their sap boiled over, spilling onto the trunks, making the air even heavier with the scent. Digging with a spoon from the kitchen, the girl's skin felt as if it had been baking, too.

Suddenly, her tiny fingers tensed around the spoon handle.

Someone was coming. Something was wrong.

She sensed it before she heard faint footsteps.

Peering between slender trunks, she made out the form of her own mother.

But momentary relief gave way to apprehension . . . her mother was moving slowly, stealthily toward her, creeping across a smooth floor of strewn pine needles and cones.

Her mother approached with neither word nor recognition, raising a sharpened hoe over her head that the child had only seen used for planting daylilies or digging in the fields on Saturdays.

She dropped the spoon to the ground. Palms up on her knees, she saw the hoe raised up evenly, then pulling back, her mother's face like a stone. And in one smooth, violent, powerful plunge, the woman thrust the blade forward.

At the very last moment, the child squeezed her eyes shut.

She never cried out, opening her eyes to see her mother sink without a word to her knees.

There, just inches beside them along with the little dirt pies, lay a Southern timber rattler, its head neatly chopped from its body, still coiled in fat and convulsing circles.

The girl sat still as her mother rose up from the red earth, scooped her to her feet, and without a word between them, carried her across the field and into the house.

Once inside the darkened kitchen, everything was safe again. The world was right. . . .

Then Hailey was spinning, spinning . . . comforting arms on a sunny afternoon were gone and suddenly, it was dark.

The pain in her chest made her think for a moment she was having a heart attack. Her heart beat violently, her blood pumping hard, her fingertips throbbing, her ears ringing.

Somewhere in the night, a car slammed on squealing brakes and then, gunning its motor, took off down Fifty-fourth toward the East River.

Hailey Dean sat up abruptly, clutching her chest.

In the dim light, her bedroom began to materialize, pieces of furniture reassembling themselves in the darkness. Tonight, in the dark of her Manhattan apartment, it was all real.

Clutching the sheets of her bed, she remembered how her mother had saved her life that day. Her life was saved, but she hadn't been

able to save Will's, not all the lives that had touched her own since—
all the victims whose cases she went on to prosecute.

Two years ago, she kept a promise to Leola Williams and sent
her daughter's killer to Death Row.

And then, she left. In a new city, she started a new life.

The old dark days were thousands of miles and years away.

Years of courtroom battles and an endless parade of victims
looking out at her from crime-scene photos and autopsy tables at
the morgue had taken their toll.

It was January in New York City, yet sweat bathed her forehead.
The hair against the back of her neck was soaked and perspiration
beaded across her chest. Her nightgown was twisted around her
waist and tangled with the sheets.

As always, she ordered herself to be free of it all . . . if only her
mind would let her.

It never did. Will was dead and he had been for years.

Hailey lay awake until the sun came up and the alarm went off.

She showered, then returned to the bedroom. She did her best to
ignore the cardboard box on the top shelf as she pulled a couple of
outfits on hangers from her closet.

Inside, her wedding gown and veil lay carefully folded between
layers of crinkly tissue paper.

The dress was champagne silk, off the shoulder, simple; not too
much of a train, but a train nevertheless. The veil was brocade. The
two, gown and veil, should have swished gently down an aisle
sprinkled with flower petals and lit by candlelight, should have
been admired by hushed onlookers. They should have been memo-
rialized in wedding photos displayed to the delight of children and
grandchildren to come.

Hailey hadn't sealed the box. But in all the years since Will's
murder, in all the years since she had finally folded her wedding
gown carefully away, she never once opened the lid.

The box was always close at hand. She carried it like a treasure to
law school. It was her only traveling companion when she headed
to Atlanta after graduating.

She purposely chose a post in the inner city. The gritty downtown topped the charts for violent crime, thanks to the well-traveled drug courier route from Colombia to Miami to Atlanta, for distribution throughout the States. High-volume violent crime was just what Hailey wanted, despite her family's wishes. Dodging the traffic speeding north up the freeway, their protests that the work would be too dangerous rang in her head just under the music thumping on the car stereo.

Wherever she moved, the white cardboard box went with her.

There was more, of course. Furniture, books, posters, plants, clothes, kitchen appliances, dishes . . . all crowded into a single U-Haul attached by a trailer hitch to the back of a Saab she bought used and drove for years. Only the box rode silently along with her. Sometimes she even buckled a seat belt across it.

The white box had taken on its own identity over the years, a reminder of another life in another time, another girl who would have grown into a very different woman.

She brushed past dozens of suits in all colors, and fresh, crisp blouses mixed in with the silks. Reaching up to a wooden peg in the closet, she took down her jeans and a denim shirt and sweater. Bending down, she picked up her cowboy boots and began to dress. For all those years, she had to wear dresses, suits, hose, and heels. No more.

Back in the bedroom, she opened her jewelry chest and grabbed her favorite earrings. She touched her hand to the back of her neck. It felt bare and she thought, briefly, of the silver pen she used to wear every day. In one of life's grand coincidences, she had lost it in court on the final day of her final trial.

Back in the kitchen, Hailey filled the copper teakettle and set it over the flame on the stovetop before heading over to her computer to see what landed in her e-mail overnight. It whirred into action, first alerting her of today's weather in New York and Georgia, followed by breaking news.

Spam . . . spam . . . more spam . . . bills . . .

And Fincher!

A smile crossed her face.

Every time a few days passed without hearing from him in Iraq, worry set in. For years, she gave Fincher hell about cashing a monthly paycheck for being in the Military Reserves in exchange for "playing soldier" on base every six weeks. Now those checks could cost him his life. She couldn't even bear to think of it. He had been at her side for every jury trial, every guilty plea, every investigation—the highs and the lows. Somewhere deep inside, she believed she would somehow know, immediately sense it, if something happened to him.

The e-mail was just a few lines but enough to let her know he was still alive. She typed a quick note back about innocuous doings, the weather, news stateside, and the usual back-home local political shenanigans. There was always something, and even now she still had an ear in the courthouse. She closed with just her initials, never saying good-bye.

She meant to leave now, to spring up, toss on her coat, and head to work. Instead she clicked out of the screen and sat staring off into the patch of sky out her window.

The teakettle on Hailey's stove whistled loudly, sending Atlanta, the courtroom, and the parade of victims back where they belonged. The past.

This was the here and now, and she was already late. Hailey hustled back to her morning routine with an eye on the clock. She had a full day of appointments ahead.

She'd lingered too long and had no time today to walk the first part of her commute, as she ordinarily did. She somehow beat out the others for a yellow cab to carry her through heavy East Side traffic the forty blocks downtown.

In the heart of Greenwich Village, the cabbie pulled up in front of the brick townhouse that was home to three small psychology practices upstairs and dental offices on the first two floors. Not a happy group of patients all around, Hailey often thought.

Chilled wind whipped around her legs as she leaned in to pay the cabbie, then darted up the steps to the red front door.

Someone had obviously arrived before her and adjusted the heat. The warm interior and the amber-colored wallpaper in the entrance hall was comforting against the cold New York winds and the gray day outside.

Reaching the third floor, Hailey saw that her *New York Post* was missing from the foot of her door. She slowed as she approached—feeling suddenly that old instinct that something was off.

Why was her office door unlocked? The paper was gone and the door stood open a fraction of an inch.

The sound below had disappeared and the old brick three-story had gone unusually quiet. Hailey placed her gloved hand on the door handle and pushed it open into the darkened foyer of her office. Stepping silently across the threshold, she heard the sound of running water in the kitchenette.

Had an intruder left it running?

Or was he still here, lurking in the shadows, watching her?

She crept through the office, glancing around to make sure it hadn't been ransacked. Warily, she looked inside a closet, behind the couch, in the bathroom.

Only the kitchenette was left.

Hailey slipped silently toward the doorway, wondering what she would do if someone was there.

Holding her breath, Hailey poked her head around the corner—

And smiled. There was Dana, the attractive bottle-redhead who had the psych practice across the hall. Hailey had loaned her a spare key over a year ago when Dana's restroom plumbing went on the fritz.

Hailey felt sorry for Dana—and relieved, as that would have been her own office and was actually still listed in her name. Dana had mistakenly thought it was larger, and for the same price, had rented it just before Hailey formalized in a written-lease contract the handshake deal she'd already struck with the landlord. The landlord had never updated the files, and Hailey was still listed as tenant in the front office suite.

Hailey had initially been miffed, but in the end, when the two offices turned out to be the same size, Hailey was glad she'd lost out on the other office after all. From her desk, Hailey's view overlooked a courtyard, and one longer, narrow window in the corner of the office revealed a sliver of the street out front. Much better than staring at the building across the street, windows dark and empty, vacant for renovations.

Dana bit into a bagel soaked with butter and read Hailey's *Post* while she waited for the coffeepot to fill beneath the tap. She was clutching Hailey's favorite coffee mug, now branded with shiny pinkish-purplish lipstick, and looked up when Hailey came through the kitchen door.

Hailey long ago renamed Dana's trademark shade "pinkle." Pinkle was everywhere, on mugs, Kleenex, water glasses, soda cans, cigarette butts. She once even found pinkle on the mouth of a jug of orange juice in her office refrigerator.

Dana held up the *Post*. "This is yours. You don't mind that I grabbed it, do you?"

"Other than a near heart attack thinking I had a break-in, you know you're welcome to anything I have." Hailey gave Dana a quick hug.

For all Dana's neediness and insecurity, Hailey had really grown fond of her. She saw her not so much as needy and whiny, but as someone who goes through life lonely and deeply disappointed in love.

Watching Dana pour water into the waiting coffeemaker, Hailey realized that she herself was alone, too, but not lonely . . . not so much disappointed as circumspect. She didn't want to put herself out there again, go out on a limb, risk having her world explode. She couldn't afford the damage it could cause. It had taken years to pull herself back together. It just wasn't worth the risk now. End of story. But which was worse? Disappointed and bitter like Dana, or emotionally shut down?

"Hey, Hailey, what are you doing later? Why don't we go out to happy hour after work?"

"Not tonight. I had a really long week."

"But it's Friday! You can sleep in tomorrow morning."

Dana's man-hunt had been in overdrive ever since Evan, her latest boyfriend, had broken it off, claiming she "talked too much." Dana had since been set up on three dates. All three had been miserable. Although apparently Dana had met a new guy that she was keeping on the QT. They saw each other infrequently and on short notice. He was a lawyer and Dana perceived that as promising. Hailey hoped he was as single as he claimed.

Meanwhile, she was accustomed to fending off Dana's attempts to join forces to hunt down well-to-do single men in New York City.

"Come on, Hail, it'll be fun."

"I really can't. I've got a full day and I didn't sleep at all."

"Who does when they're alone? Let's just go have a glass of wine. Just one."

"That sounds so nice but I really can't. I mean it. Hey, coffee's ready . . . at least enough for a full cup." She gestured at the still-percolating pot, which came with a brew-interrupt mechanism.

"Oh, you can pour the first cup. I'll wait," Dana said graciously.

"No, really . . ." Hailey grabbed the pot and filled Dana's mug.

As Dana closed the door behind her, leaving a smear of butter on the inside handle, Hailey remembered her paper.

Dana took it with her.

Hailey wanted to read it, but she didn't have time to open the door and start the whole process with Dana again. Her first patient would be here any minute. She pulled Karen Elliot's file, then returned to the kitchenette to watch coffee trickle into the pot.

Dana, bagels, pinkle, coffee . . . it all melted into a world a million miles away.

Hailey stared at tiny particles of dust that floated across a shaft of morning light coming at a slant through the den's window. Not at all the same type of golden warming light as afternoon sun, but welcome anyway. It suddenly reminded her of the golden gleam that spilled from the antique fixture hanging in her parents' Georgia kitchen.

Hailey's mind was drifting, rare in itself. She was not prone to daydreaming.

The three of them . . . sitting there at the kitchen table under the warm glow of the kitchen lamp. She could hear her parents' voices, desperate to stop her from taking a job prosecuting a series of murders in court that would only dredge up obvious memories of Will's violent death.

"The money they're offering you is nothing for a lawyer with your grades," her father said, shaking his head. "We just want you to have everything we never did. We want you to be happy, not just scraping by your whole life, sweetheart."

"How can you just throw away a hard-earned degree?" her mother wanted to know, well aware of the big-money offers Hailey had received from high-profile Atlanta law firms.

"Money isn't everything," Hailey responded.

How could her parents argue with that? Those were their own words, words uttered frequently. In fact, they had preached against materialism for as long as she could remember. They had always had a happiness that money couldn't buy; it didn't have a price tag.

But this wasn't really about the money for them. Hailey already knew that.

"But you'll be going after killers, drug dealers, child molesters." Her father looked pained. Hailey wanted to tell her father that it was too late—that nothing else could hurt her now.

"I'll be fine. It's what I want. I want to do something good."

Victims and witnesses from the most disturbing and heinous violent crimes, child molestation victims too young to know their ABCs, rape victims silent and unspeaking, hate-crime victims who endured inexplicable violence, communities full of outrage over drug turf battles on their playgrounds . . . they all spoke through her.

With each guilty verdict, Hailey's aching heart would ease, but just for a moment.

Then it was on to the next victim, the next case.

For ten years, from the pits of the courthouse, she spoke. With a single purpose, she grew into the most notorious prosecuting attorney in the entire southeastern United States. Her plea negotiations were brutal. Nothing but maximum time behind bars for violent crime could satisfy her.

Guilty verdicts wrung out of one jury after the next weren't enough . . . she was always searching for the next case, racking up thousands of guilty pleas and over a hundred jury trials and a 100 percent win record.

It was unheard of: Hailey Dean had never . . . *never* . . . lost a single case.

The downstairs buzzer rang, signaling the arrival of one of her clients.

As she hurriedly buzzed the door open, she glanced at the blue sky beyond the window, where limbs of the courtyard gingko tugged back and forth in the wind.

Karen walked in and closed the door purposefully behind her, trying to keep her back to Hailey, who immediately spotted her reddened eyes and nose.

Obviously James, her live-in, was at it again.

Karen flung herself deep into the sofa, chestnut-brown hair falling in soft waves around her face and spilling over the collar of a bright-pink wool coat.

"It's the usual. It never ends, Hailey, no matter what I do. I'm so beat down."

Karen's live-in was wearing her down to a nub, but the story wasn't new. Not drugs, not gambling or booze. There were no angry beatings in their apartment at night. There was no "other woman."

No. "Other *woman*" was not entirely accurate. There wasn't just one. There were hundreds, as a matter of fact, each one more beautiful than the last, and all of them were hot for James.

Online "pen pals," porn sites, phone sex, and strippers had dogged their relationship since it started. The harder he tried to hide it from Karen, not "actually cheating" he said, the harder she tried to listen in on phone messages, pick through his pockets at night, and read e-mails sent to and from his super-secret screen name.

Hailey sat, feet curled under her on her red sofa, drinking tea as Karen switched topics from James's impotency and online relationships with other women to her human resources job and her struggle to advance against her male counterparts.

The hour flew by.

"So, same time next Friday?" she asked as Karen headed for the door.

"Definitely yes. Thank you, Hailey. For everything. Bye." Karen slipped into her coat, picked up her shoulder bag and briefcase, then reached out and hugged Hailey good-bye, as always. She still had a red nose from crying, but at least now it was topping a big smile. Karen closed the door and her steps echoed down the hall.

Hailey knew most therapists disapproved of doctor-patient hugs, but it seemed so natural she never tried to resist. Instead, she hugged back just as tightly.

Hailey made a few quick notes in her file, then checked her schedule. Karen's session had run late, but there was still no sign of her next patient, Melissa Everett—not unusual, as Melissa often barreled in late and breathless.

She always had an excuse, but Hailey suspected the real reason Melissa ran late was that she didn't look forward to tackling the raw pain dredged up by some of her memories. An adult victim of child molestation that had been inflicted years before, Melissa still could find no real peace.

CPA Nathan Mazzelli, whom Hailey suspected was on the take, had a late-afternoon slot. He probably needed more than a shrink. All things considered, a criminal defense attorney could soon move to the top of Mazz's shopping list. Mazz was obsessed with a recurring dream character, an evil carnival monkey who doubled as a secret henchman for the IRS who was looking for him. Whenever Mazz thought he'd lost them, the monkey would literally jump on his back, screeching at the top of its primate lungs to alert the government predators to his location.

The patient who followed was one of the sweetest and the loneliest . . . Hayden Krasinski, an incredibly talented graphic designer just over twenty years old and already worn out with the world.

Somebody sat rudely on their car horn outside. Hailey instinctively looked out the sliver of window that faced the street.

She couldn't help but smile as she watched Karen, with the perfect form of an Olympic sprinter, aggressively pursuing a cab back to work. In her full-length neon pink coat and loaded down with a staggering briefcase and jumbo-size shoulder purse, Karen displayed serious agility and beat a guy in his early twenties to the pass, nabbing the taxi herself.

"You go, Karen," Hailey whispered aloud, followed quickly by, "James, you big idiot."

||||||||||||||||||||||||||||||||||||||||||||||||||||||||||||||||| **8** |||||||||||||||||||

Atlanta, Georgia

BALANCING AN ARMLOAD OF RESEARCH, LAW CLERK JIM TALLEY knocked on the door of Judge Clarence E. Carter's chambers.

"Come in."

The Judge—"C.C." to his political cohorts—eyed the stack of documents suspiciously. "Son, what is that you've got with you? I hope it's the Sports section from the *Telegraph*."

Jim exercised immense self-control in not rolling his eyes and reminded himself that a thousand third-years would give their eye teeth to get a spot with the State Supremes.

Jim might have graduated first in his class at Mercer University, one of the oldest law school in the state, but he had received the coveted appellate-court clerkship purely through connections.

Upon learning his class ranking, the judge quickly informed him that grades didn't matter. "It's not what you know, son. It's who you know and how you use it. Remember that, son, and you'll go far."

The judge had dispensed that advice a hundred times, and Jim wholeheartedly believed it.

After all, his father was on the boards of two major corporations that contributed heavily to the judge's campaign . . . a campaign that was never fully waged because of C.C.'s surprise appointment to the bench, rendering voters unnecessary. Jim happened to know that for reasons mysterious and unspoken, the judge held on to all the campaign money to create his "war chest," as he called it.

"Sorry to say it's not the sports page, Judge," he told C.C. "It's the research for that opinion pending on the docket."

The judge looked momentarily blank.

"You know," Jim prodded, "the one we talked about? The death penalty appeal."

Ah. The light dawned in C.C's eyes.

"Son, I'm going to let you handle that on your own. It's time you took on more responsibility and I think you're ready for it. I've taught you what I know on the subject. Make me proud, boy."

Maybe Jim should have been thrilled with the idea of changing the course of legal history by writing the judge's opinions totally unsupervised. But the truth was, he didn't want to be responsible for a political hot potato.

Still, if Jim did as he was told, he figured the clerkship with Judge C. could set him up for an associate position over at Lange and Parker, the South's premier law firm, the crown jewel of the Georgia Bar.

His *Mercer Law Review* cronies would be livid.

"So, Judge, we affirm, right?"

With shifting support for the death penalty, Jim thought he should at least get Carter's okay before taking the judge's usual hang-'em-high position and affirming the death sentence. He'd worry about finding a legal basis later.

"Son, which slimy SOB is it this time? These days you got to be a real bastard to get the chair."

"It's the chef. You know, the Atlanta chef that posed all those hookers after he strangled them."

"Shit, son. He must've been one mean son of a bitch to get a death sentence out of a bunch of intellectual left-wing snoots and all the rest. . . . Well, you know who sits on Atlanta juries. They wouldn't even give Wayne Williams the chair. He strangled how many boys . . . twelve, before they caught him?"

"No sir. Twenty-one."

"Twenty-one what?" It had clearly been a rhetorical question because C.C. had no idea what Jim was referring to.

"Wayne Williams allegedly murdered twenty-one little boys and teens before they got him, based on fiber evidence. But Williams still says he didn't do it . . . that he was set up."

"Set up? Son, you scare me when you talk like that. Allegedly. Allegedly, my ass. A jury convicted him."

"So, Judge, we affirm?"

"Did you say he says he was set up? Set up by who? God? Sit in jail long enough, and they all think somebody set 'em up."

"The chef, Judge, you want to affirm the DP on the chef, right?"

"Hell, yes, affirm it, by God," Judge Carter bellowed, slapping his beefy hand on the desk so hard the obligatory framed family photos rattled. "You want me to lose my spot on the bench? The voters would burn down the Court if we let that one go. He'll never see nothing but the inside of the bus on the way from Reidsville Prison to Old Sparky at Jackson."

"Sir, just to be clear—it's a constitutional challenge to the use of DNA without obtaining an additional warrant on each separate murder charge. They also claim overzealous prosecution against the State. It was Hailey Dean again."

"Son, you're botherin' me, now. You know I have to affirm . . . both the guilty verdict *and* the death penalty sentence. It ain't the liberals keeping me on the bench, son. Remember that."

"But the DNA—"

"I'm fine by DNA and there is no such thing as overzealous prosecution. Unless it's against me. That's a joke, son. Lighten up."

Jim nodded woodenly, but managed to laugh at just the right volume and with just the right amount of heartiness.

"Yes, sir. It's affirmed. He's headed to Old Sparky."

"That's right, son. It's between him and the Lord now. And son," the judge added, dipping his right hand back into his top drawer, "could you bring me that Sports section? I wanna find out how the Dogs look for the weekend."

"Will do, sir." Jim closed the door behind him and exhaled. C.C. wouldn't know the law if it jumped up on the bench and bit him right in the neck.

He headed down the quiet hall outside the judge's chambers to his own office.

Well, that was done . . . the appeal was over. The death sentence was affirmed.

The prosecution at trial could rest easy.

"WHAT THE HELL DO YOU WANT?" CRUISE SPIT THE WORDS
through the wall of glass that separated him from
Leonard.

The attorney's lips curved into a thin smile. "Not happy to see
me? What's wrong, Clint? I thought you'd be happy. Come on,
show some enthusiasm . . . it's not like you're flooded with visitors."

If it weren't for a wall of thick plate glass that separated them,
Cruise would have made a lunge for him. As it was, all he could do
was sit here, chained in shackles, waiting for his useless lawyer to
say whatever he had to say and make Cruise read or sign whatever
he had to read or sign.

Useless. That was what Cruise thought of Matt Leonard and his
weak, pathetic performance at trial. Damn him, the way Hailey Dean
walked all over him. Cruise knew the deal. Leonard wanted the celebrity of being the big-time death penalty hero, but he just couldn't deliver. Cruise had read up on him, found out his firm was rolling in
federal and state grant money for the so-called Death Penalty Project.

Cruise didn't know exactly how much money, but he did know
both Leonard and even his paralegal drove Mercedes. Thanks to
Google and the penitentiary law library Internet, he also knew
Leonard lived in a huge three-story on Habersham near the governor's mansion. Leonard's crapper was probably bigger than Cruise's
whole cell.

Damn Hailey Dean, too.

The day of the verdict, he went for her in court and made it all
the way to where she stood, alone in the middle of the courtroom.
Because of her, he was clubbed in the head from behind. Then, they
nearly tore his arms off pulling him from the courtroom. He turned
back for one last look, and saw a juror had actually made it around

the jury rail and was hugging Hailey Dean, right there at the podium. Over the juror's shoulder though, Dean was staring straight at him, watching when they hooked the leg irons on him.

The moment the sheriffs got him alone in holding just outside the courtroom, they cursed him out and punched him over and over, right in the stomach. The walls were soundproofed, though, and Cruise knew no one in the courtroom heard a damn thing.

"This is for Hailey, you sick little perv," one of them said, landing a punch that knocked out one of Cruise's teeth. The beating went on.

At the end, Hailey's investigator, Fincher Henson, sauntered back into the holding pen. The other sheriffs got real quiet when he strolled through the door, like the damned President walked in.

Cruise remembered it like it was yesterday.

"Uncuff him," Henson said.

The cell went quiet and nobody moved. Not one sheriff so much as shifted his weight. Who the hell did he think he was . . . God?

Cruise would be damned to hell if he'd have given him the courtesy of looking up.

"Uncuff the son of a bitch," Henson turned and barked at the nearest sheriff, who stepped up to Cruise, jangling the cuff keys attached to his belt.

The cuffs were unlocked and removed.

"Stand up, asshole," Fincher growled low in his throat.

Cruise had stayed doubled over against the wall. No way would he stand on command.

"I said, stand up!"

Cruise paused for one moment before hurling a thick wad of spit on Henson's shiny black shoes.

"I don't give a damn if you spit on me, you little asshole. But you will *never* touch Hailey Dean again. And *this* is to make sure you don't forget. Remember, Cruise, if you ever *do* see the light of day, which you won't, I'll be waiting for you." Fincher lifted him up with one muscled arm. From the other, Cruise took a single blow to the face that had knocked him out cold.

He'd come to lying on the holding cell floor. He was soaking wet all over, covered in piss. Those assholes, each one of them, had taken turns pissing on him after Henson cold-cocked him. Henson was gone, the sheriffs were gone, and except for Cruise, the holding cells were empty.

Even now, Cruise remembered the putrid smell, drying on his skin.

One day, he'd get to her. Somehow, some way.

And he knew damn well she thought about him, just like he did her here in Reidsville. He read about her in *Atlanta Magazine* when he was in sick bay last year. About her starting over in Manhattan. And he'd bet there wasn't one night that passed that she didn't think of him, Clint Burrell Cruise, and the moment he had her neck in his hands.

He'd never forget his last glimpse of her.

Nor would he ever forget his last glimpse of Matt Leonard in court that day.

As they were clamping the irons on Cruise's ankles, Leonard was sitting there looking all put out, like *he* was the one headed for the electric chair. Then, before they could even get Cruise out the door, Leonard started clearing up his papers and packing his trial files to leave, as if he were just wiping crumbs off his hands after a picnic.

Next case, next fat fee. That was all he meant to Leonard, that asshole. He was just another statistic Leonard could use to get all his federal money.

"Guess what, Matt?" he crooned through the plate-glass wall.

"What?" Leonard looked leery.

"I'm writing all the newspapers about my case. The same ones that stood in line to cover my death sentence . . . the same ones there on the edge of their seats in the death chamber when I'm strapped in the chair and they give me the juice."

He casually tossed off even that last part. Never would Cruise let Leonard see him the least bit affected by the idea of Old Sparky.

No one would ever see that, see him cringe whenever he thought about the Waiting Room. Inmates were forced to stay there in the weeks before they were electrocuted. The jail said it was for security and ease of transporting the inmate.

BS. It was to make the prisoner sit, sleep, eat, and breathe just feet away from the electric chair. To force the inmate to *really* think about what was coming.

Twisted assholes.

Cruise heard the Waiting Room was a little bigger than his regular cell on the Row.

There was one big difference: the view.

The view from the bunk in the Waiting Room made inmates refuse to eat, lose their appetites, lie on their sides on their bunk, turned away from the barred door. Visible through the bars of the Waiting Room doors was a twenty-four-hour-a-day, round-the-clock view of a wall covered with the wires, boxes, and levers that would ultimately activate the juice to run through your body and kill you.

Cruise's stomach churned just thinking of it.

Pushing aside thoughts of Old Sparky and the sickening view from the Waiting Room, he focused instead on the matter at hand.

"You know what, Matt? I bet the papers will listen to what I have to say."

Cruise watched Matt's eyes narrow.

Protected by the wall of glass and the knowledge that he had nothing to lose, Cruise went on, leaning in closer to the glass toward Leonard. "They'll listen, all right, especially if I'm willing to admit to ten of the murders."

"Believe me, you don't want to do that."

"Oh, but I do."

"You don't." Leonard's face was paler than usual and his voice was so soft Cruise almost had to lean forward to hear it.

"Any letter you write to the *Telegraph* outlining the evidence," Leonard added in a hushed tone, "will ruin your chances of reversal."

That was bullshit, of course. Cruise knew there would never be a reversal. Leonard was blowing smoke up his ass, again.

"You know what I think, Matt?" Cruise's voice wasn't anywhere near a whisper. "I think you don't want the public to know the truth about what a sorry-ass attorney you really are."

Matt merely shrugged. But when he reached up to straighten his tie, Cruise noticed a tremor in his hand. Noticed, too, he was still twisting the same ruby ring that had his blue-blood family crest on it.

"So," Cruise concluded, "I just thought you should know first . . . about me writing the papers, giving all the details to the murders. All except the last one. And if the jury was wrong about one, who's to say they weren't wrong about the others? I'm even thinking of adding a claim of incompetent counsel to my federal appeal. How will that look in the paper, Matt?"

"You son of a bitch, you can't . . ."

"There's a lot of things I can't do these days, Leonard. But this isn't one of them."

And right there, even though he knew it wouldn't touch him through the glass, Cruise spat right at Leonard. A big glob.

With a curse, Leonard got up and walked away without a glance backward.

O UTSIDE C.C.'S SQUEAKY-CLEAN WINDOW ON THE TOP FLOOR OF the Judicial Building, the Atlanta skyline sparkled in the morning sun.

C.C. gave it only a cursory glance, winced at the sunlight, and turned back to watch his new assistant close the door behind her. He contemplated her backside, the real reason he hired her if the truth be known. Now that she was done buzzing around his desk and with her rear end completely out of his view, C.C. eased a silver flask from his desk, uncapped it, and took a long pull of pure Kentucky bourbon, followed by a second.

No mixer for him; he liked it sweet and strong, just like his daddy did. C.C. was just one step away from the governor's office and he could feel it down in his bones, unless that warm tingle was just the bourbon, now down to nearly half a flask.

Yes, today he'd take that final step.

He pressed the intercom button on his phone. "Amanda?"

The response was nearly instantaneous. "Yes, Judge?"—silky on the other end.

"Get Eugene's office on the phone and confirm the tee-off time, will you?"

"Yes, Judge."

C.C. leaned back in his chair, spinning it back toward the plate-glass window.

From here, it seemed, he could see all of Atlanta.

Including the governor's mansion.

The twenty-four-thousand-square-foot redbrick Greek Revival palace sat on eighteen acres of lawn just a few miles northwest. But C.C.'s eyes never strayed from the prize. It was his legacy.

C.C. made his living in politics just like his daddy and his grand-daddy had. Their empire was built on backbreaking slave labor in the southernmost part of the state of Georgia, Dooley County. Dooley historically kept one of the lowest income levels pro rata in the entire region, just a hair above poverty level.

But somehow the Carters, headed by Talmadge Carter, who bought the land in 1817, managed to make money hand over fist. It didn't take long to position his son, T. Carter Jr., in the mayor's office of the county seat, Vienna, Georgia.

T. Carter's grandson, Talmadge Carter III, made it to state senator. That came in awfully handy when interstate I-16 was in the works. With T. Carter's minor adjustments to the plans submitted by the Georgia Department of Roads and Highways, the interstate—and all its motels, gas stations, 7-Elevens, and roadside fruit stands for the Yankees who didn't know better than to pay five dollars for a nickel sack of Georgia peaches—had cut a swath directly through the old home place.

To hell with the home place. They were multimillionaires at last, the stars were aligned, and the political power C.C. was meant for was on the cusp.

With "family money" as a springboard, T. Carter's great-grand-son C.C. made one political deal after the next until he got the sweetest appointment of all: a spot on the Georgia Supreme Court. He had jumped from one political appointment to another like a frog jumping rock to rock on the Flint's muddy brown water.

Now, silk stocking attorneys across the state—even the elite Lange and Parker, a blue-blood law firm that stabled four former U.S. senators and every past mayor of the city of Atlanta—would have to kiss his redneck ass, and he knew it.

But he felt instinctively that a judicial position did not wield sufficient political clout. He wanted more. Needed more. His legacy *was* more.

It was time to make a move and make his dear, departed daddy proud.

He spun impatiently in his chair and reached for the intercom again, but there was a knock on the door instead.

He hurriedly stashed the flask in his top desk drawer and called out, "Come in."

Amanda appeared in the doorway. "I just spoke to Mr. Eugene's assistant, Judge."

"And?"

He smiled at her, the perfect campaign smile, courtesy of braces as a teenager and thousands of dollars of caps over the years. Never mind that too much Kentucky bourbon had yellowed the caps and gifted him with a bulbous nose, red-veined around the nostrils.

Amanda smiled sweetly. "The tee-off time is set for noon, like you asked."

No, he didn't like doing business on another man's turf one tiny bit. But after weeks of trying every trick in the book to engineer a meeting with Floyd Moye Eugene—and finding that he, a Georgia Supreme Court Justice, couldn't get even a simple phone conference with the man, much less arrange a meeting—the invitation to play a round of golf came as a surprise. It all fell into place so much more easily than C.C. had ever anticipated. Eugene was playing right into his hands.

The support of one man was about to swing the balance for C.C. and make his political dreams come true. Floyd Moye Eugene happened to be the chairman of the Georgia State Democratic Party.

A man after C.C.'s own heart, Eugene played the party ranks all the way from grass roots in Columbus to the Democratic National Convention. Eugene had been the power behind every man to grace the governor's mansion on West Paces Ferry since it had been re-built in 1968, and the next election would be no different.

C.C. had done his research—or at least commissioned his willing law clerk, Jim Talley, to do it for him.

Eugene had attended UGA just like C.C. Just like him, Eugene was a huge UGA football booster and drank Kentucky bourbon.

Also like C.C., nobody knew exactly what Eugene did to make a living.

Pulling the flask from his drawer once again, C.C. imagined they were twins.

C.C. had dispatched his staff operatives to do whatever it took to ferret out Eugene's weaknesses. But in the end, extensive snooping, including various political snitches in the know and the services of not one but two private investigators, uncovered not a single vice C.C. could use to his own advantage. Nothing. No drugs, no love child, no porn habit, no secret male lover he could slip a few Gs to. Nada.

"*Too bad...*" C.C. thought. "*A mistress. I could have at least worked with that ... a mistress.*" There was always hope.

Meanwhile, Eugene worked out of offices in the Capitol, across the street from C.C. in the chambers of the Georgia Supreme Court. If he had a mistress here in Atlanta, she was well-hidden.

Eugene's single vice seemed to be an insatiable thirst for power. He had been relentless and merciless in his quest for control over his family, the Georgia House, Senate, even the governor himself. C.C. was an amateur when it came to power play, just a distant planet rotating around Eugene.

How Floyd Moye Eugene had attained his power may have been a mystery, but it was now a force to be reckoned with, not bested.

C.C. was about to enter the game with high hopes and an eye on the prize.

Again, he spun his chair to view the city sprawled below—and not far away at all out there, the governor's mansion, glittering in the morning sun.

St. Simons Island,
Georgia

HOW LONG DID IT TAKE A PERSON TO BUY GROCERIES? VIRGINIA Gunn was starting to wonder that as she sat crouched down behind the wheel of her Jeep in the Kroger parking lot.

She herself had spent just twenty minutes inside the store—in and out well over an hour ago with a week's worth of organic produce, soy milk, and the all natural bread she used to make sandwiches every day for lunch.

It was as she rolled her own full cart through the parking lot looking for her Jeep that she spotted it.

A Volkswagen Beetle, circa 1977, badly beaten up but sporting a brand-new shiny Greenpeace bumper sticker.

Ah. Perfect. Hardcore reconnaissance and quick deductions were in order.

First she loaded her groceries into the back of her Jeep, then drove through the parking lot to the row behind the Beetle. From there, she could keep watch—and she had been, for over an hour.

Damn, it was hot, even with all the windows rolled down. So hot that she was almost tempted to run the engine, just for a few minutes, with the air-conditioning on.

Almost. But Virginia had been an eco-fighter long before Al Gore invented the Internet or starred in *An Inconvenient Truth*. In fact, she had some news for Al Gore. He could take his private jet and shove it straight . . . *Damn it was hot in here!*

She smelled under her arms. *Not terrible . . . yet.*

Come on, it's not like you're having heat stroke. How can you even consider burning fossil fuel and emitting all that exhaust when you're just sitting here in a parking lot?

She wiped a trickle of sweat from her forehead and reached for the cup in the cupholder. She had filled it with cold tap water before leaving home early this morning, and left it in the car. Now it was hot enough to steep a tea bag in, thanks to the sun glaring off the windshield.

How she longed to get back to her house, with water views and sea breezes billowing the white sheers.

Virginia Gunn had spent her entire life on St. Simons Island, with its magical strip of coast on either side and in between, acres of live oaks decorated by nature with low-hanging, sea-green Spanish moss.

For hundreds of years, Georgia natives debated which was more beautiful, the ocean coast or the marshland, a hybrid formed of half-land, half-ocean, creating a unique habitat.

The Spanish American War's Battle of the Bloody Marsh had been waged on the southernmost tip of the Island, not far from Virginia's childhood home. General Oglethorpe had galloped directly into the Spanish line and attacked. Her father told ghost stories about soldiers willing to die rather than give up the Island jewel, ghosts that still haunted the Bloody Marsh, where, as a child, Virginia and her friends dug up old Spanish bullets.

Southerners also fought and died for this strip of beach at the most bitterly contested battles during the War Between the States. And Daddy personally recalled the era, during World War II, when German U-boats trolled the coastal waters. Back then, the locals, armed with shotguns, sabers, and kitchen knives, prepared to take on the hulking tubs of iron all on their own.

Now, the unsuspecting Island faced a new threat. And like her Island ancestors, Virginia was prepared to do whatever it took to save it.

So here she sat in the unbearably hot car, thirsty, hopefully checking out every customer emerging from the store and heading this way.

So far, no contenders.

The middle-aged woman in head-to-toe Lilly Pulitzer couldn't belong to the Beetle.

The elderly man in shorts and black dress socks couldn't either . . . nor the pair of high-school boys wearing madras and loafers without socks.

Virginia took a closer look at two women in their mid-to-late thirties, both with identically cropped early–Chris Evert hairstyles, both with gold wire-rimmed glasses and both with baggy hiking shorts. From where Virginia sat, the only physical difference between the two was that one wore Birkenstocks over white socks and the other topped her white socks with hemp-woven clogs. Pay dirt.

Sure enough, they started loading a cart full of groceries into the Beetle.

Virginia gratefully exited the steaming Jeep, sneaking between rows of parked cars for a few moments, then approached casually by foot. They had their heads together and were laughing, arms grazing as they put bags into the car, and Virginia deduced an intimacy indicating that they were probably more than roommates.

"Hello, there."

They both looked up and offered surprised return greetings.

"Gorgeous day, isn't it? Do you live here on the Island?"

Woven Clogs looked a little wary, but Birkenstocks answered, "Yes it is, and yes we do!"

"So do I. Have for years. Not a stone's throw from the water. You know, sometimes, before the Island got so crowded, I used to see whales breaching in the sea right from my deck!"

Woven Clogs lost the wary expression in a hurry. "You did? That must have been amazing!"

"Oh, it was. It was," she said, with just the right note of bittersweet wistfulness. "They're such beautiful creatures, don't you think?"

"Absolutely," Birkenstocks assured her.

Woven Clogs asked, "Did you see that two-hour PBS special a few months ago?"

"Which special was that?"

"The one about an Indian tribe hunting whales once a year in the Pacific, as part of ancient Indian ritual."

"No, I hate that I missed it . . ."

"It was the most horrific thing Renee and I have ever witnessed." Birkenstocks tossed the last bag into the car and slammed the door hard, clearly incensed just thinking about it. "Those poor whales, savagely slaughtered, and for what?"

"For what?" Renee echoed, shaking her short haircut, eyes solemn behind her wire-rims.

"That's the kind of thing that really makes a person want to stand up and take action," Virginia said carefully. "You know . . . do some good to offset the bad."

"Oh, we did, didn't we, Dottie?" Renee asked, nodding at her partner.

"What did you do?" Leaning back on the battered VW, Virginia instinctively knew—right here in the Kroger parking lot—that she had struck gold.

"We had an epiphany, right there on our living room sofa that night after the special. We just looked at each other, and we didn't even have to say a word. We knew what we had to do."

"We took two full weeks of vacation time to drive north to Alaska in the VW and stage a protest."

"All the way to Alaska? I'm stunned . . ."

They were perfect.

Casually, she asked Renee and Dottie, "I don't suppose you're free tonight? You and maybe some of your Greenpeace friends?"

New York City

WHEN THE DOWNSTAIRS DOOR BUZZED, HAILEY GLADLY SET aside the bills she'd been paying and opened the door to meet Melissa. Standing in the doorway, she could hear footsteps flying up the stairs, could feel Melissa's stress vibrating toward her, even before she burst into view down the hall.

Her straight, dark hair, almost down to her waist, was wind-blown back from a face that had a delicate, almost childlike beauty. When the light hit her just right or she flashed a rare smile, it was especially evident. But Melissa's nose was crooked, having been broken a few too many times—and her brown eyes were perpetually troubled and rimmed with the dark circles of chronic insomnia. "Sorry I'm late, Hailey—track trouble on the number four train."

"It's okay. Come on in. Want some coffee?"

"Definitely."

Hailey didn't bother to ask her how she took it. She already knew. Black.

Just like her outfit: black skirt, black boots, black leather jacket. Hailey wondered whether it was a fashion statement or a reflection of Melissa's state of mind. Maybe both. It only accentuated her pale, drawn features.

"So how are you?" she asked when she and Melissa were settled in her office—Melissa with her coffee, which Hailey noticed she clutched in both hands, as if trying to warm them. She looked so frail sitting there, like she could barely hold the mug. Hailey hoped the coffee wouldn't slosh over the rim and burn her.

"I'm a little better," Melissa said. "I saw Tammy this week."

Tammy was her half-sister, with whom she had recently reconnected.

"That's really good. Did you talk?"

"You mean . . . about . . . anything?"

Hailey nodded. "Anything" would be Melissa's stepfather—Tammy's father—who had beaten and sexually abused her from the time he came into her mother's life when Melissa was eight until she ran away at sixteen. She'd have left sooner, but she was worried about Tammy becoming the next victim.

As far as she knew, Tammy hadn't.

"We just talked about this movie we both want to see, and her haircut—she got her hair cut. It looks good. She told me I should cut my hair too, but . . ." Melissa shook her head.

"You like your hair long."

"Right."

The better to hide behind, Hailey knew. Melissa's hair frequently fell over her eyes and across her cheeks, begging a hand to brush it back, but she never did.

They'd come a long way in the two years Hailey had been treating her, but they had a long way to go. There were still sessions when Melissa would sit, silently rocking in her seat, hugging herself, lost in memories forced to the edges of her mind, examined only at great emotional cost.

"Last week, we talked about the day you and your sister went to the church carnival," Hailey told Melissa gently. "Do you remember? You said that your sister made you go on the Ferris wheel because she was too young to ride alone, and you were afraid, but then when you were spinning around high in the sky, with all those lights dazzling below you, you felt strong. Remember?"

No smile, but Melissa nodded. "I remember."

"And it felt good to come up with that memory. Remember how happy you were?"

Another nod, slower to come than the last. A key part of their recent sessions involved Melissa integrating happy childhood memories along with the disturbing ones.

"Did you share the Ferris wheel memory with Tammy when you saw her?"

"I did, but she doesn't remember it. She doesn't remember a lot of things."

Her sister, Hailey knew, had once accused Melissa of making it all up—the beatings, the sex abuse.

It was Tammy's way of protecting her father, or maybe protecting herself.

But she wasn't Hailey's patient. Melissa was. And for all the progress they'd made, Hailey knew they had a long way to go.

"Can you think of another happy memory?" Hailey asked. Melissa immediately shook her head, a curtain of hair covering her face.

"Maybe something else about the carnival," Hailey suggested. "Did you eat anything there? Cotton candy, maybe? Snow cones? I love carnival food."

So had Will.

"Snow cones." Melissa nodded slowly, a hint of recognition in faraway eyes. "We ate snow cones. I had purple, Tammy had red."

Instinctively leaning forward to help her patient once again delve into the past, Hailey had to acknowledge Melissa wasn't the only one haunted by memories.

An hour later, Nathan Mazzelli replaced Melissa in the chair opposite Hailey. Mazzelli likely needed a defense lawyer more than a shrink. Hailey kept her expression carefully neutral as he described his latest intricate, sinister nightmare.

As always, it was about an IRS agent.

"So there I was"—Mazz twisted a sweat-sopped Hermès bandanna in his lap—"trying to fly away from him—"

"Fly?" Hailey interjected.

"Yeah, in the dream, I was a housefly."

Interesting. A fly. She made a note on her pad as he went on. "But I saw him coming after me. Big guy, and he was wearing an incredibly plain navy suit. You know—not even pinstriped—and a white dress shirt, a white plastic ID card on his lapel."

Typical. In Mazz's dreams, IRS agents were always dressed in stark contrast to Mazz's three-thousand-dollar Armani suits and

Hermès ties. Sometimes the agents even sported plastic shirt-pocket protectors neatly stuffed with multiple black-ink plastic pens.

"Oh," Mazz added, "and he had on a synthetic tie. Maybe poly-rayon. I don't know."

Judging by his expression as he delivered this piece of information, a synthetic tie was a crime worse than . . .

Well, worse, as far as he was concerned, than anything Hailey suspected Nathan himself had done. He'd never actually confided anything illegal.

In Mazz's dreams, the agents always chased him relentlessly through confusing mazes. On foot, he ran for his life through hair-pin twists and turns, secret passages and trapdoors he never knew existed in the bowels of his own building, and resurfacing in buildings of clients.

"And did they find you behind the cabinets this time?" Hailey asked him as he wound down the narrative.

"Nope."

Not yet.

The unspoken phrase hung in the air.

Hailey snuck a glance at the tiny clock surreptitiously placed on a shelf behind his head and realized they were out of time.

"Looks like we'll have to pick it up next week, Nathan," she said, as though it were just too bad the session was over.

"Okay, okay . . . by then, I'm sure I'll have had a couple of new dreams."

Maybe another couple of dreams . . . but Hailey was willing to bet they wouldn't be new ones.

Hayden Krasinski was next.

For all the months the brilliantly talented, tousled blonde graphic artist had been seeing Hailey, sessions invariably went in fits and starts, depending on her mood. She was either way high or low.

Today, she was down. Way down.

They sat in silence for the first five minutes.

Then Hayden said bleakly, "I just don't know."

The statement, which hadn't even been preceded by a question from Hailey, was punctuated by a heavy sigh.

"Hayden, why don't you tell me about something positive that happened to you since we met last week." Hailey tried a gentle, upbeat approach.

"I can't think of anything" was the prompt reply. "Not a single thing."

"Try."

Hayden sighed again and fell silent, running her right forefinger up and down the scars on her left forearm.

Depressed, and not just over the accidental drowning deaths of her mother and kid brother two years ago, she repeatedly self-mutilated, methodically slicing horizontal grooves down her arms and along the insides of her thighs.

"Have you written anything this week?" Hailey wasn't giving up.

"A poem."

"Do you want to share it?"

Hayden shook her head. "No. You said to think of something positive. That wasn't a positive poem."

"It's a positive thing that you wrote it. You told me your writing is cathartic."

Hayden nodded, staring at her scars.

Hailey paused before deciding to plunge ahead with an idea that had struck her the other day in the elevator of her building, where she'd run into one of her neighbors, an editor at a small publishing house.

"You know, I've been thinking about your poetry, Hayden, and the pieces you've shown me are really good."

Hayden looked up sharply.

"Really, really good. And you know I'm not just saying that," she added, reading Hayden's mind.

A hint of a smile lit Hayden's pretty brown eyes, though she said nothing.

"Maybe you could publish them."

"Who would want to publish them?"

"I have a friend—she's an editor. She's done quite a few poetry collections featuring poems from new talent, and I'm sure she'd be willing to take a look."

"What if she hates them?"

"What if she doesn't?"

Hayden considered that. "I don't know," she said heavily again, but at least this time it was relevant.

"Think about it. Okay?"

"Okay."

Hailey smiled. "Okay."

At least they were making progress.

She knew the dichotomy of Hayden would haunt her long after the workday ended. It always did.

She jogged nearly every evening after work, alone along the East River, just as the New York skyline began to twinkle with lights against the darkening sky. The river was deep and gray and beautiful. Tugs and speedboats and huge container ships passed by under bridges that were lit up against the skyline. On days Hayden had been in, Hailey would look out over the dark waters and dwell on the patient with sharp scars marking her arms and beautiful poetry and drawings tucked into her backpack.

Something Hayden had told her once, early in their work together, remained stubbornly stuck in Hailey's brain.

"I'm going to die young, like my mother," Hayden had said, with a cryptic shrug. "Only a lot younger than she was."

Hailey first assumed she was suicidal, but over time, had ruled that possibility out . . . almost.

"It's just a feeling I've always had," Hayden told her recently. "You know—that I'm not going to be here for very long. I just don't belong here, I don't fit in."

The feeling could very well be a symptom of her depression, but it waved a red flag. Hailey worried deeply about her between sessions and always met Hayden at her office door with relief that she had shown up again and all in one piece, dressed as always in

T-shirts and worn, baggy jeans covered in ink and marker draw-ings, knees showing through.

She hoped and prayed Hayden was wrong because she had a whole lot of life ahead of her. When Hayden smiled or laughed, which was rare, she lit up the room.

They were making progress.

||||||||||||||||||||||||||||||||||||||||||||||||||||||||||| **13** |||||||||||||||||||

Atlanta, Georgia

AS C.C. RECLAIMED HIS SEAT ON THE BENCH AFTER AN EXTENDED visit to the men's room and tried to look serious-minded, he couldn't help but feel the heat from Florence Teasley. Giving her a glance sideways, he saw her give him the evil eye.

Old bat.

She was nothing but a do-gooder who had terrorized him ever since she'd made it to the bench.

However he voted, Teasley automatically took the opposite opinion and seemed to relish actually writing the opposing opinion herself, attacking him at every turn.

Damn reformer.

At case conferences, she baited him in front of the other justices, lording her own Harvard-degreed intellectualism over his self-titled "down-home Dooley County common sense."

But why did *he* need to know the law? That was what law clerks were for.

C.C.'s main worry wasn't Teasley's insinuations he was not a deep legal thinker. Instead, he was deeply concerned Teasley knew he occasionally took a "nip" during oral arguments. As an arch death penalty opponent, she never missed a chance to suggest the electric chair was appropriate only for drunk drivers, and she always looked straight at him when she said it. And she always seemed to be able to smell bourbon on him, openly sniffing when he was near.

She could probably do with a drink or two herself. Old-maid-spinster-liberal, but the only thing C.C. had ever seen her drink since she took the bench three years ago was hot water with lemon on the side. She'd sip it like it was a fine wine and damn if she didn't eat the damn lemon peel behind it, every single time.

He watched her go through her high-tea protocol every Thursday during the Justices' weekly case review. It nearly made him jump out of his skin but he couldn't drag his eyes away when she peeled the lemon off the rind with her teeth.

Vegan lunatic.

At last, after grueling hours of sitting on a huge leather easy chair positioned directly next to Florence Teasley and trying his best to chime in with questions occasionally, oral arguments came to a merciful end. Maybe he should just take a cue from U.S. Supreme Court judge Clarence Thomas and just keep his piehole shut. Better to remain silent and let others just suspect he was in over his head than actually speak and confirm their suspicions.

He was pretty sure Lincoln said that.

C.C. shed his black rayon-polyester robe as fast as he could unzip it and hopped the private elevator down to LP, Lower Parking.

Augusta National . . . here comes the judge!

Then . . . the governor's mansion.

He wondered if what was left of the Allman Brothers would play at his inauguration party. Without Duane, would it even be worth it? Poor bastards.

C.C. slipped the keys into the ignition of his midnight-blue Cadillac and cranked the music and the AC both on high.

This was his favorite Allman Brothers CD, and even though he didn't know all the lyrics it didn't stop him from singing along all the way to Augusta. There, he tooled around for fifteen minutes looking for the route to the famed Augusta National Golf Course.

At last, he was driving his Caddy down Magnolia Lane. When visitors first entered the sanctity of the world-renowned course, they took a winding route lined by deep-green Southern magnolias. Breathtaking. But C.C. wasn't here to soak up nature.

He was here to bag Floyd Moye Eugene.

C.C. entered a set of tremendous gates, humming along on "Ramblin' Man" with Duane Allman. It was virtually impossible to get on the course here, much less obtain a membership, even through bribery. C.C. had tried.

At the guardhouse protecting the entrance, he was met by a uniformed employee who sized him up with a brisk, "Morning, sir. Name, please."

"Nearly afternoon, son," C.C. observed, not taking kindly to being treated like an outsider.

"Your name, sir?"

The guard didn't take the bait. He had seen it all . . . everybody and their great-grandmother trying to get into Augusta.

"Judge Clarence E. Carter. I'm a guest of a longtime member, Floyd Moye Eugene."

"Carter . . . Carter . . ."

You'd think he'd recognize C.C.'s name or at least the personalized plate on his car, "GAJUDGE1."

Between the name and the plate, he'd never been ticketed after being pulled over on traffic infractions—which happened regularly. Especially around his favorite strip club, the Pink Fuzzy. Didn't cops have anything better to do than try to trick unsuspecting drunk drivers into an arrest? But at least the Georgia State Patrol usually managed to put two and two together and let him go with a wave and a respectful "You have a good evening now, sir."

But no, not the deputy dogs here at Augusta. Here, they were treating a State Supreme Court Justice just like anybody else, keeping him waiting expectantly while they took their time checking his name against a list of expected guests.

Never mind, they'd beg him to play a few rounds here when he was *Governor* Clarence Carter.

Once he made it past the gestapo Checkpoint Charlie, he continued his trip through perfectly manicured grounds.

Time to reset his sights and wipe the sweat off his neck. With the backing of the head of the State Democratic Party, the single most powerful body in the region, the rest of the state would fall in line. Challengers would back off or be kicked to the curb without the party's support.

In exchange for Eugene's support all the way to the mansion, C.C. was prepared to offer anything Eugene wanted. Thanks to a fruitless investigation of all things remotely connected to Eugene, C.C. had no idea what exactly that might be. But whatever it was, he'd get it.

He knew he had to be subtle at first, lead him up to it. He couldn't hit the man over the head with an offer.

Floyd Moye Eugene was the kingmaker, and C.C. would be king.

After parking his car, he was met by a pale, stooped, older man, slightly balding and wearing a crisp white uniform bearing the Augusta crest.

"Nice to meet you. I'm George, and I'll be ushering you to the clubhouse."

"Oh, I'm sure I can make it on over myself," C.C. said quickly, not wanting to stand out as a mere visitor.

"I'll escort you," the attendant said again, kindly, but leaving no wiggle room for C.C. to roam free.

But as they made their way, C.C. realized that without George at his side, he wouldn't know where the hell to go and would *really* stick out as one of those who made it in riding somebody else's coattails.

Good thing he was perfectly decked out in the most expensive golf clothing available in the resort wear department of Saks Fifth Avenue at Phipps Plaza.

"Beautiful day, isn't it, sir?" the man asked.

"Perfect for eighteen holes."

"So I take it you play a lot . . . Ever been here before, sir?"

"Oh yes . . . yes . . . many times," C.C. lied, embarrassed that a man of his standing in the Georgia legal community had never before been invited to Augusta National—much less invited to join.

The man chatted him up as they headed toward the clubhouse. Damn, this place was swank.

Once inside the clubhouse, the guide discreetly disappeared.

When C.C.'s eyes adjusted to the dark room, he scanned the whole place and could finally make out Eugene, still wearing darkened aviator sunglasses and sitting alone at a table in one of the far corners of the paneled bar.

Damn, was C.C. that late? Eugene was nearly through with his drink.

As he strode toward him, C.C. silently cursed the guard for the delay at the front gate. He'd see their minimum wage asses hauled into their supervisor's office and fired.

He put on his game face and stuck out his right hand.

"Floyd Moye, how are you? Have I kept you waiting?" C.C. couldn't possibly smile any wider, giving Eugene a clear view all the way back to the fillings in his wisdom teeth.

When Eugene stood to take C.C.'s hand, his grasp was firm and cool on C.C.'s overheated palm. "No, Judge," he said, "I'm just early. Bad habit of mine."

That was a lie, of course. C.C. was late. But in the South, a social faux pas such as arriving late for a tee time would never, ever be pointed out under any circumstances. That would be rude and considered an open act of hostility.

"Judge, would you care for a drink before we hit the fairways?"

"Sure, Floyd, not a bad way to start eighteen."

Eugene had read his mind. The judge had cottonmouth in the worst way.

Or did Eugene simply know for a fact that C.C. never minded a cocktail? If that was the case, what else did Eugene know about him?

He got his answer a moment later.

"Maker's Mark, two rocks, am I right?"

Damn, Eugene was sharp.

"Yes siree, Floyd Moye, I'm impressed."

"I assure you, Judge, it's mutual."

C.C. wondered what he meant by that. Could he be impressed with some of C.C.'s legal opinions?

Or maybe Eugene admired C.C. after reading about him in the papers, one profile after the next. C.C. had even been on television a few times, addressing the State Bar Association on legal ethics. Or maybe he supported C.C.'s stalwart pro-law-and-order stance.

"Lewis, two Maker's on the rocks, sir," Eugene said to the elderly waiter in a white jacket standing unobtrusively a few feet away.

"Yes, sir."

"Judge, how was your drive down?" Eugene turned his focus toward C.C., taking him in from head to toe. Something about Eugene put him on edge.

"About three hours," he said, "but it's worth it, Floyd."

"Played the greens here at Augusta much?"

"Oh yes. Quite a bit. Beautiful course."

"Really?" Eugene's eyes locked on him like radar.

The judge felt his face flush.

"Damn! Why did I lie? Save the lies for something important."

He'd told himself this a million times . . . it was always the details that bite you in the neck . . . *always.*

Could Eugene know? Shit, of course he knew. He was a member here.

Anybody who was anybody played here all the time and knew the place like the back of his hand. C.C. had mostly just seen it from his own den, on TV, a gaping hole in his social pedigree. And that was usually on a Sunday afternoon after a couple of bourbons.

He had to take the obvious route and lie, again.

"Of course, not recently, you know," he quickly amended, trying to wade out of the muck. "The workload on the bench is very demanding. *Very* demanding."

Eugene nodded thoughtfully. "I'm sure it is."

Had he gotten out of that one? No way to tell. He was relieved when the waiter returned with warmed cashews and Eugene turned his attention away from C.C. for a moment to chat with him.

C.C. raised his glass to his lips and fought the urge to drain it in one mighty gulp as Eugene, thank God in Heaven, paused before turning his attention across the table again.

"How's your wife?" he asked C.C. "Betty, isn't it?"

Of course it was. The man was good.

"Betty's just fine, Floyd." He considered returning the question, but he was pretty sure he knew how Eugene's wife was—and that bringing her up might very well sour the conversation.

"How does Betty find life down in Dooley County after time in the big city?"

It was all he could do not to snort at the thought of Betty in Atlanta. She hated it.

"She likes to stay close to home," he told Eugene.

Home with her family. Even in light of his current position, they loathed him. He could feel it. The pained greetings, formal airs, exchanged glances whenever C.C. talked. He hated the way Betty's bunch didn't drink, smoke, or curse, and sat all pinched up on the front row of the First Baptist Church every damn Sunday. He hated the way they guarded the old grandmother's china at Sunday lunch, like C.C. might just take a big bite out of one of the salad plates.

He guessed they were still mad he got a little drunk at the wedding, but what the hell was wrong with that? C.C. never understood it. His daddy and his daddy's daddy owned Dooley County. Now Betty was the wife of one of the most powerful men in the state.

"Does she come up to Atlanta much?"

"Not too much, Floyd. She pretty much stays put when court's in session. She gets lost every time she gets anywhere near I-285."

"Does she? I don't blame her."

"Oh, yes." C.C. nodded vigorously. A gift from Heaven . . . they had something else in common to talk about. They both hated traffic.

"Ever since they built that damn perimeter around the city, I swear tourism's been on the decrease. Once they're on it, nobody can figure out how to get off the damn thing and get into downtown."

C.C. knew he was rambling but he couldn't seem to stop himself.

"Yep, I wish Betty'd get the hang of it and visit more. Atlanta can be a lonely city, Floyd Moye, a lonely city indeed," he added. C.C. put on a sad, thoughtful face. Wistful, in fact.

Actually, he hadn't thought of Betty in days.

She adored C.C., of course, but whenever Mrs. Clarence E. Carter considered the prospect of a four-and-a-half-hour drive to spend a weekend in Atlanta with her husband, she seemed to develop a sudden and immediate migraine that caused her to take to her bed, sometimes for the entire weekend. Betty was better off down on the farm where she was happy. He was entirely certain that navigating the sprawling behemoth called Interstate 285 was the sole barrier that kept her in Dooley County.

Thank God for Atlanta traffic.

A few more minutes of small talk, a couple of swallows of Maker's Mark, and the two finally made it out of the clubhouse.

It was none too soon for C.C., who could only hope he'd do better with his hands occupied. No more uncomfortable one-on-one conversation. It was nerve-racking, especially when he couldn't figure out how to do away with the yak and get to the governorship.

"Why not be honest for once? That's right . . . honest and up front. Just put it out there. Wait . . . Don't just put it out there . . . Let things breathe . . . No need to do anything radical . . . Play it cool,"

C.C. told himself as they headed out to the tee. He could chat all night if he had to.

"Plan on taking a cart, Floyd?" C.C. asked hopefully, blinking in the hot Georgia sun.

"Well, Judge, we use the caddies here. No carts anywhere on the grounds . . . kind of a tradition."

Busted again, dammit! Fricking details!

Why didn't he notice there wasn't a single cart parked anywhere near the area, just a group of older men standing near the clubhouse? On TV when Tiger won the Masters, there wasn't any damn cart!

"Right! That's right! I remember that!"

C.C. and Eugene set out walking, two caddies following discreetly behind.

For a while, it was just about golf—and it was all C.C. could do to stay on his game. He tried, but Eugene was better. A lot better.

Was it any surprise?

C.C. couldn't focus. As the two approached the fourth hole, Eugene asked, "Ready for the Crab Apple, Judge?"

"I beg your pardon?"

Was it some kind of drink? C.C. hoped so.

"Crab Apple . . . It's the name of the fourth hole. Each hole is named after a tree or bush here."

"Yes . . . very unique, very unique. I've always thought that."

Damn him to hell. Was Eugene torturing him on purpose?

Then, out of the blue, Eugene said casually, "You know, Judge, I admire your work on the bench. Have for years."

Suddenly, he no longer hated Eugene. He was now elated.

Maybe he should seize the moment and plow ahead with his offer.

But before he could speak, Eugene went on. "But I can't help but think a man of your caliber, from such a fine family with politics in the blood, fine education at the University, who's been doing his duty to the State of Georgia on the bench for all these years now . . ."

Uh-oh. Where was this going? It couldn't be good. C.C. felt sick.

"You could be doing something even greater, Judge. Such a waste of talent."

What? What did he just say? A waste of talent? Did he say that?

"Well, Floyd, I'm flattered but . . ."

No one had ever called him talented before. Not even the newspaper profiles, the TV interviews, not even that sorry bunch of suck-up law clerks had ever accused C.C. of being talented.

Even his girls, the strippers he picked up at the Pink Fuzzy on weekends, normally full of compliments, had never suggested such a thing as talent.

His head was swimming. Where would it lead?

He needed a drink, but this was not the kind of place where you brought along your thermos, and he knew better than to pull out a flask in front of Eugene.

"Have you ever thought of a run for governor?"

C.C. didn't miss a beat. "Well, Floyd, you're not the first who has proposed just that."

Giddy with his success, he could hardly keep walking without jumping up in the air.

He hadn't even had to push it, no bargaining back and forth.

Obviously Eugene wasn't the operator he was cracked up to be.

Whatever, it was clearly meant to be.

Eugene was on his side.

God was on his side.

The way things were going, he might not have to offer Eugene a bribe after all.

Walking eighteen holes was no easy feat for a Supreme Court Justice who, at most, walked from his car to an enclosed underground elevator, just nearly fifteen feet, twice a day. And even that was air-conditioned. Nobody wanted the judges breaking a sweat.

Thank God they weren't lugging their own clubs.

Speaking of clubs, C.C. had asked the pro at his country club to outfit him with the most expensive clubs the store carried. He dropped a load of money on Pings in hopes Floyd Moye would notice. If he had noticed, he hadn't mentioned it . . . yet. C.C. made a point to swing with great flourish and flash the Ping markings whenever he could.

Somehow, though, C.C. managed to keep up with Floyd Moye, the two walking side by side, casually crushing beneath cleated soles the prized Bermuda grass that was somebody's life's work.

C.C. noticed little of his surroundings. Not the grass, the heat, the botanical beauty around them, not even his shrieking calf muscles. He just kept walking, listening, enthralled as Eugene laid it all out for him, describing the inner workings of the State party machinery and how it would all play out. C.C. was mesmerized.

The rest was all details as far as C.C. was concerned. He'd been to the mountaintop and he could see the Promised Land.

With each approaching tee, Eugene spun a gubernatorial web around C.C. He touched on power bases here, weaknesses of possible opponents there, and solutions as to how the party could work it all to their advantage.

"We want a winner. Come next January," Eugene said, just before teeing off at the eighteenth hole, "Governor Carter will run the State Capitol. What do you think about that?"

C.C.'s hand was burning not to whip out his flask and have a congratulatory shot of bourbon. It seemed wrong not to.

"I . . . I'm ecstatic," he finally managed to say.

After the eighteenth hole, the two headed back to the clubhouse.

"Let's have a drink and celebrate, Judge. What'll you have? Another Maker's Mark?"

"You know it, and the drinks are on me."

It was the least he could do. All that walking and talking, Eugene laying it all out for him, and the man had never once asked a thing in return.

"Don't be silly, you're my guest. Lewis!" He waved at the waiter.

A real class act, Floyd Moye Eugene. Peculiar, but classy.

"My associate here will have another Maker's, two rocks," Eugene told Lewis, and C.C. glowed.

"I'll have ice water with lime, Lewis."

"I thought we were celebrating," C.C. protested, dismayed at Eugene's teetotaling.

"We are. You go ahead and enjoy your drink, and I'll enjoy my ice water."

C.C., who didn't have to be asked twice, knocked back another drink, and then one more, as Eugene drank water and added up a majority of Georgia counties they could count on.

"I have to say, you've got me feeling mighty optimistic, Floyd," C.C. said as they walked to his car.

"Good, good. You should."

The valet already had the Caddy waiting, with the AC and radio on high for him. It had been tuned to an Allman Brothers CD, as C.C. recalled, upon his arrival. Not anymore.

Now Motown was on the radio. Diana Ross belting out "I'm Comin' Up."

It was a sign. The stars were aligned.

He got behind the wheel and reached for the electric adjuster to move the seat back. It'd be one hell of a joy ride back.

Eugene stood between the car door and the seat, still talking.

"Thanks again, Floyd Moye, for golf, the drinks, the fine conversation, and—"

"One last thing, Judge."

C.C. looked up, and Floyd Eugene's expression gave him pause. A tiny bit of the effusive warmth seemed to have dribbled away.

"Anything, Floyd Moye."

"Before we begin working the campaign seriously, there's one matter I need cleared up. It ought to be routine for a man of your standing."

"Sure, Floyd."

Routine . . . Eugene probably wanted a spot in the new regime. Completely understandable.

"What can I do for you?"

"I have a friend, a very dear friend indeed, who has a concern about the legality of a conviction of a young man, a talented man by the name of Cruise."

"Oh . . . ?"

"We both think, my friend and I, that there is a very strong possibility this young man was wrongly convicted. We certainly wouldn't want that type of thing clouding your candidacy."

"Oh, no, Floyd, absolutely not," C.C. was quick to agree. "Not at this, let me say, critical juncture."

"Exactly. The poor soul is facing death row on something to do with some hookers in Atlanta a couple years back. It's a real mess. Anyone could have committed the crime—God only knows who those women had been with. You know they'll do anything for a hit of crack."

"Don't I know it," C.C. murmured, briefly glancing away from Floyd and toward his steering wheel, then caught himself. "Not that I know anything about hookers *personally* . . . but my *work* . . . You know, I've read about it. . . ."

"No, no, of course you wouldn't. Anyway, Judge, it's just terrible . . . and just a *hell* of a mess for an innocent young man to be trapped like that. Don't you think so?"

"I surely do."

"A reversal should do the trick."

C.C. sat there like a lump, not getting it.

Did he say reversal?

Eugene went on. "Justice can be so blind. Thank God there are men like you, C.C., to rise up and do the right thing."

Mistaking his lack of grasp on the situation for squeamishness, Floyd Moye forged ahead. "It was all a damn setup . . . Some angry as hell gal behind it all . . . One of those *liberated* female prosecutors had it in for him. . . . You know what I mean, Judge."

C.C. wasn't sure that he did. He was trying to take it all in, but he just couldn't. What the hell was Eugene talking about? Who had talent and was wrongfully convicted? Who got liberated?

"It was all a setup from the start," Eugene went on. "She was probably just trying to advance her own career. . . . You know the type . . . right, Judge?"

"Oh, yeah . . . I know the type all right. . . . But I don't get it. Where do I fit in?" C.C. asked at last, not wanting to appear stupid, but finally breaking down. He knew that whatever Eugene was talking about, the most C.C. had done was read about it over a cup of coffee.

"As I said, he goes free, and chances are, he's innocent. He could go on and cure cancer, for all we know."

"He's a doctor?"

"A chef. He's a chef, Judge." Eugene was starting to look impatient. "That's not the point. The point is, he needs to go live his life. Do some good in the world. He's an innocent man."

C.C. tried to digest it all . . . A chef that might have the cure for cancer?

Eugene leaned in, his arm resting on the top of the open door.

"After all, they *were* just hookers. Nobody'll *miss* them. Now, isn't that right, Judge? They were hookers, every last one of them, and the city's better off without a used-up fleet of hookers. Am I right about *that*, Judge?"

Eugene was so close to C.C.'s face he could feel the heat of his body and smell the lime on his breath.

C.C. was still in the dark and couldn't figure out quite what to say or exactly what it was that Floyd wanted him to do.

"Well, the city *is* a mess . . . That part *is* true, Floyd."

Floyd continued on, his voice lowered. "I mean, if you look at it realistically, why waste the State's money keeping him up on death row for ten . . . more like twenty years of appeals? It's the taxpayers' money. We've got to keep their best interests in mind, too. Especially come re-election time . . . right, Judge?"

All at once, it dawned on him.

C.C. went pale. It was all coming up . . . up his throat. He could taste Kentucky bourbon and the Monte Cristo sandwich he'd had back on the ninth hole at the back of his throat.

He couldn't puke right here. Not in front of Floyd Moye Eugene. Not at Augusta National.

Cruise was sitting in jail after the jury convicted; the case was up on appeal at that very moment. A reversal would set him free . . . let him walk right out of his prison cell and onto the streets with decent, normal people . . . including C.C.

C.C. swallowed it down.

"I'll take a look at the case, Floyd."

"Well, Judge, let me know as soon as you can see fit to. We'll need that taken care of before we can move forward on the campaign."

The dirty work clearly behind him, Floyd quickly shifted gears again. He straightened and all but brushed his hands against each other. "So, I believe Dooley would be just the place to announce. It *is* your home jurisdiction, your *symbolic* headquarters at the outset, correct?"

"Correct." C.C. got it out, still fighting back the Monte Cristo.

"Of course, then we'll have to move you to Fulton County. Although Macon *is* technically the geographic center of the state, and we do need to appeal to more than just Fulton and metro Atlanta this time, but it's just easier to work out of Atlanta. You know what I mean. We'll get started as soon as you can take care of that legal problem. Right?"

"Right."

"Good, good, good. It's been a pleasure, Judge, or should I say Governor?" With that, Floyd Moye's face melted into a smile.

"Oh, no. It'll always be C.C. for you, Floyd Moye."

Before C.C.'s Cadillac could turn the bend much less disappear out of view, Floyd Moye let out a single snort—a silent laugh through his nose, not taking the effort required to make a sound— half in amusement, half in disgust.

Eugene flipped out his cell phone. Waiting for the connection, he walked coolly away from the valet, well out of earshot. Cell phones and pagers were banned at Augusta and this was one call that didn't need a witness.

Glancing around, he spoke. "The rabbit's in the hole. How's the view on the beach?"

"Temp is warm and sunny. Slight breeze on the island. Sand white as sugar and not a soul on the beach. Just two island sea turtles."

"Not for much longer," Eugene responded.

In a few hours, the fate of an island would begin to change. Pristine and protected, St. Simons Island was the jewel in the crown of the Georgia coast. Not since 1862, when Confederates ripped apart the Island's lighthouse to thwart Yankee troops, had the Island been faced with such upheaval, nor come closer to another invasion, this time with tourists.

"Okay," Eugene said into the phone, "he got his. Now I want a call after they meet tonight. I can't wait another twenty-four hours. Things are heating up. We knew at the beginning timing was the key."

"It's a done deal. Count on it."

Eugene nodded and clicked off.

||||||||||||||||||||||||||||||||||||||||||||||||||||||||||||| **14** |||||||||||||||||||

St. Simons Island,
Georgia

THREE BLOCKS BEHIND GLYNN COUNTY MIDDLE SCHOOL, A QUARter mile from the beachfront pier on St. Simons Island, Virginia Gunn took the last sip of her Amaretto and crushed one cigarette into a green ashtray shaped like a seahorse after lighting her next off its smoldering butt-end. It was always the best sip, having been down at the bottom of the ice the longest.

But she had to be sharp tonight.

"I'm coming, little babies, wait for Mommy!" she called to her dogs, barking out on the deck. "I know you're hungry, but these aren't for you! You don't want chips! Remember what they did to you last time? All that poopy all over the house? You don't like Ranch-Flavored Doritos, so stop asking!"

She laid out chips and dip on the bar between her kitchen and den, filled another ice bucket, and lit candles scattered artfully around the house.

The dogs kept barking, but for once, she made them wait. Everything had to be just right.

This evening, she had a feeling, was going to be another one of those turning points in her life.

Tonight might be right up there with when she resigned as chief county commissioner of the Island after a vote of no confidence by the Commission eight years ago.

The other commissioners sold her out over the construction of a secluded but still highly offensive goofy-golf course near the United Methodist Center. Naturally, she opposed goofy-golf in all its forms, not only because it would encroach upon nearby marshland, but how could Virginia Gunn, in her right mind and with a straight face, represent to the taxpayers that goofy-golf was anything but tacky?

Virginia had to pour herself another Amaretto on the rocks, getting all worked up again just thinking about it.

She'd simply had no choice but to draw a line in the sand when it came to the Island's beaches and marshland. Next thing she knew, there'd be Seashell Shacks, mini-marts, beach towel emporiums, and roadside stands peddling brushed-velvet portraits of Elvis and the Last Supper.

Well, of course, the measure had passed anyway. But fate intervened. Before the concrete could be poured and covered with Astroturf, the goofy-golf investors had gone broke and the thing never happened.

By then, though, Virginia had written a scathing letter to the editor of the *St. Simons Herald* in which she blasted the other Commission members, exposing them for what they were . . . crass materialists.

At which point, the vote of no confidence went down. She'd stormed out of the middle-school auditorium after claiming that the St. Simons establishment was hell-bent on developing every square inch of the Island.

For eight years now, Virginia had laid low, operating just under the radar of the County Commission.

Only one close call . . . but so what if they suspected *she* was responsible for hacking down the first and only parking meter at the Pier? It happened in the middle of the night, when the St. Simons police were always on "shift change" at the Donut Hole. A squad car happened along just as she was finishing up, and she dove into a thick hedge of dwarf palmettos just in time. Those suckers' leaves were like *swords*!

Then there was her greatest coup of all: blackmailing the new Commission chairman, Toby McKissick, just before the last vote on constructing a major bridge connecting the Island to the mainland.

From that moment on, Gunn knew she had found her calling. She was a guerrilla. A counter-terrorist fighting the Commission and all other forces seeking to destroy the Island's natural beauty.

Hence, the chips and dip now laid out neatly on Virginia's bar.

A new assault on the scarce Island Sea Turtle was in motion.

Euphemistically referred to as "beach replenishing," it consisted of pumping sand from the ocean bottom onto the Island's beaches, to build them up for tourists. Doing so would all but destroy the turtles' mating grounds. Moreover, there was no guarantee where the sand would come from, and a likely location was just off an industrial point near the mainland. The sludge there was replete with toxic buildup, thanks to dumping from a paper mill. To have that dumped on the Island under the disguise of "replenishing" would be a crime. But now it was in the works.

Something must be done.

Something on par with—or perhaps, even greater than—what she had done to McKissick.

She'd tell her new friends all about it later tonight, Virginia decided, and clenched another cigarette in her smiling lips as she went to let the dogs in.

||||||||||||||||||||||||||||||||||||||||||||||||||||||||||||| **15** |||||||||||||||||||||

Back Roads
One Hundred Miles
Southeast of Atlanta,
Georgia

THE SPEEDOMETER READ NINETY-EIGHT, THE *BEST OF THE ALLMAN Brothers* CD was turned up, and C.C.'s flask was empty.

He'd already pulled off the interstate to search his trunk for reinforcements, but it was dry. Damn! He needed to think!

How the hell was he going to explain to the Court that he was reversing his decision on the serial murders?

He'd already given the law clerk his orders—the opinion had been written in rough draft and circulated to the other judges weeks ago. He was writing the Court's opinion, leading the majority of five against the other four weak sisters who always dissented, on principle, to the death penalty. If those pansy-asses had had the chance to fry Jim Jones in his own damn Kool-Aid, down in Guyana, they'd still vote against it.

After twenty-eight more miles of nothing but asphalt, C.C. pulled off the highway to a Bar-b-que stop. Beside it was a thin neon sign, thank God, for a liquor store. It even had a drive-through window tacked onto the side, he saw, and steered toward it. *God bless America.*

"Bottle of Maker's to go, partner. Would you throw in a plastic cup for me?"

Yes, sir, his partner in the drive-through window sure would.

God bless America, C.C. thought again as he paid up through the window and scratched off.

He took a big swallow of the bourbon. Damn, that was good.

Now all he needed was some boiled peanuts. That should be easy enough to find. Roadside stands selling boiled peanuts and fresh-picked fruits and vegetables were everywhere along the back roads off the Georgia interstate, mostly to lure the Yankees headed to Florida.

C.C. cut away from the interstate to begin a search-and-recover mission for boiled peanuts.

And it couldn't be *just* boiled peanuts, it had to be fresh-boiled *green* peanuts. They had more of a kick, anybody'd know that.

After churning up nearly twenty more miles of narrow two-lane back road, C.C.'s dreams came true just outside the Georgia–South Carolina border. Three bucks, and now . . . he could think.

Washing down a handful of peanuts with a gulp of bourbon, he told himself it wasn't as if he *cared* about some idiot convicted and sentenced by a jury; somebody who was getting what he deserved . . . the chair.

And he sure as hell couldn't care less about the idiot's mother crying into a TV microphone or a bunch of tofu-eating liberals holding votive candles outside the penitentiary the night Old Sparky lit him up.

The reality was . . . he had his own reputation to maintain. How the hell could he vote no on a penalty case?

With another swallow of Maker's Mark, genius struck.

Just recently, C.C.'s little suck-up law clerk had come in sniveling about a moratorium on the death penalty somewhere up north.

Claimed it was based on a series of so-called "faulty" convictions where innocent men landed on the Illinois death row.

C.C. knew in his right mind that it was all bullshit, of course, probably just political maneuvering trying to throw focus off someone's own sorry career.

But . . .

What if, based on that, C.C. claimed his vote change wasn't anti–death penalty . . . it was pro-justice by God!

Yeah, and he'd say he wanted the "real killer" punished! Like in O.J. Well maybe not O.J. He'd make his law clerk think of another example.

The more he drank the more it made sense.

He could actually do this thing. The bourbon was settling in and the tingle was fine. Back on the interstate, he set the cruise control to eighty-nine. No need to speed in excess and get caught. Plus, he was protected by his "GAJUDGE1" plate. No state trooper who wanted to keep his job would pull him over.

Taking his right hand off the steering wheel, he uncorked the Maker's, just to top it off. The plastic cup was now filled to the very rim but amazingly, he didn't lose a drop. The peanut shells were piling up on the floorboard of the passenger's side.

Flicking a soggy peanut shell off his car-installed cell phone, landing it on the passenger's leather-upholstered door, he hit the speed dial to Jim Talley.

After four rings, it transferred into the law clerk's voice mail.

"Talley. It's the Judge, here. I'm working on a weekend, son. Long hours are just part of the job description. Nobody said the bench was easy, son. Remember that."

He flicked away another soggy shell. This one landed on his shoe and stuck. C.C. paid no attention.

"I've been doing a lot of soul searching, boy. I think our colleagues on the Bench are right about this one. The constitutionality of it all is disturbing me, Jim, disturbing me greatly. I'm very torn, Jim."

Yeah, he could do this. It was perfect. He *did* care about the Constitution . . . deeply.

"That Atlanta death penalty case? I've changed my mind, boy. No man is too great and should never be too proud to change his mind for the right. That includes even me, son . . . and I now firmly believe that boy was wrongly sent to the death chamber. If we're wrong . . . he'll do it again. You've seen enough of these cases, son, he'll go right back to his old habits and *then* the State can string him up good. No sense to rush a case. Let it *mature* . . . like a fine wine."

He rambled on in a hazy, bourbon-laced attempt to justify the about-face. "I mean, son, we've got to administer the law in a realistic manner, a manner in which the *people* of the state of Georgia are protected. We can't waste the State's money keeping him up on death row for twenty years of appeals. It's the taxpayers' money. We've got to keep their best interests in mind, too. Don't forget the little people, Jim. And above all else, son, we've got to be fair. Justice is blind, son, don't forget that. Justice is blind."

He pressed the "End" button and cranked up "Lord I Was Born a Rambling Man." The keyboards were pure inspiration. One more hour and he'd hit Atlanta.

It was Saturday night, he was the governor-to-be, and he was feeling fine.

It was definitely a Pink Fuzzy night. Nothing like a good strip club to calm him down.

Duane Allman was in a serious groove.

God, C.C. loved Duane Allman.

Why did Duane have to die?

Duane held a screeching high note on his Gibson.

Nirvana.

New York City

"I'M SO GLAD YOU CHANGED YOUR MIND, HAILEY," DANA SAID OVER the rim of her wineglass—her third in less than an hour. It was stained with pinkle. "Should I have one more?"

Dana cased the bar area again, pausing at each potential future husband. "But who's counting?" she'd asked with a shrug as she ordered another glass of her favorite wine. "It's not as if I've got to drive."

Maybe not, the subway was a block from the Bleecker Street bar where they sat, and it could have Dana back to her place in minutes. There were plenty of cabs, too, at this time of night. But Hailey never enjoyed witnessing Dana after too many drinks.

"I really can't stay much longer," Hailey told her—again.

"Yeah, yeah, I know . . . you've got to get home." Dana shook her head. "I don't know why you won't come out dancing with me. I told you, I know the doorman at—"

"The last thing I want tonight is to be packed like a sardine in a club."

"Hailey, just answer me one thing. When was the last time you had any fun?"

"I have fun all the time!"

"No, you don't."

"Not if 'fun' means clubbing around the city with a bunch of twenty-year-olds!"

"Plenty of people our age go to clubs."

"Maybe. But not people who have to get up and go to work first thing in the morning, and Dana, seriously, that's both of us."

"I can get by on very little sleep."

So could Hailey. She did it every night. But she wasn't going to get into it with Dana, who knew only that she lost her fiancé years ago, was an attorney in Atlanta once upon a time, and didn't like talking about either of those things.

Lucky for her, Dana was always much more interested in her own future than Hailey's past. But truthfully, who could blame her?

"Do you think I should get my hair cut tomorrow?"

"You mean, short?"

"Are you kidding? Never *short* short. Just a trim, but maybe with layers. Men like women with long hair. Look around the room."

Hailey took a look. Stark decor, flickering white candles centered on small tables for two, beautiful waitstaff clad in black. Places like this were a dime a dozen in this neighborhood.

"What am I looking at?" she asked Dana.

"You're looking at all the cozy couples. And how the women all have long hair."

"Oh. Okay."

"We're just as hot as any of these women, Hailey. How come they're all with dates and we aren't? Should I cut my hair into a new style?"

"Definitely. You'd look even more gorgeous with layers. It would frame your face."

"So you don't like it the way I wear it now, then?"

"No! I didn't say that! You look great and you know it. . . . You know, though, I really do have to go."

Hailey looked around for their waiter, a bored-looking theatrical type. He had already told them he wanted to act on Broadway, as if they knew of a job opening and would whip out their cells and hook him up right there on the spot. He just spilled it out during the drink order.

"Maybe I'll go out to a club by myself. I can't stand the thought of going home alone again to that depressing little apartment," Dana said glumly.

"Oh, come on. It's not depressing. It's cozy."

"It's depressing. Believe me. I need to get a life, or I'm going to grow old all by myself and get a bunch of cats and eat their food and then one day the super will get a complaint that a funny smell is coming from seven-B, and you know what the smell is going to be, Hailey?"

Hailey knew what was coming, but she asked anyway. "What?"

"Me. Dead. For days. Weeks."

Hailey burst out laughing for the first time that day.

"Seriously! Stop laughing! The way things are going now, I'll wind up one of those lonely, miserable old recluses you hear about on the news, where no one even misses them. Just some rotting corpse."

Rotting corpse. Hailey's laughter died away and she looked at Dana over the flickering candle.

Even after all this time, Hailey envisioned hundreds of crime scene photos back in Atlanta, victims' faces frozen in horror in their last shocking moments on earth. She'd never forget . . . just an occupational hazard. You never get over it . . . it's always in your blood, there just beneath your skin. But at least Hailey put the bad guys away or sent them to The Row. They'd never get out.

|||||||||||||||||||||||||||||||||||||||||||||||||||||||||||||||||||||| **17** ||||||||||||||||||||

St. Simons Island,
Georgia

WHEN THE DOORBELL RANG, ALL EIGHT OF VIRGINIA GUNN'S wiener dogs ran toward the front door, barking viciously at the thought of a possible intruder.

"Shut up!" she yelled, wading through them, stooping to pet and pat as she went.

They ignored her and kept barking their heads off.

"Sidney!" she shouted. "Sidney, go! Sit! Everyone, sit!" She pointed at eight individual wiener-dog cushions that shared prime locations around the living room, on sofas and easy chairs near a huge fireplace.

The pack mentality of the tiny but hostile group egged them on, but after several minutes of Gunn shouting them down, Sidney, their leader, offered up a few more barks, then trotted toward his cushion. The rest followed.

Virginia opened the door. Renee and Dottie stood on the doorstep, accompanied by a woman with braids, wearing a long, flowered dress, and an overweight guy with a beard.

They all looked a little rattled by the audibly hostile welcome, but nobody was backing away. Virginia, who rejected all those who rejected her dogs, was relieved. She needed these people.

"They're harmless," Virginia assured them, waving a dismissive hand at the dogs. "I'm so glad you could all come."

"These are our friends Ken and Suz," Dottie said, and Virginia shook the newcomers' hands and thanked them for coming.

Then Renee, who had exchanged her hiking shorts for jeans, held out a plate of . . . something . . .

"What are these?" Virginia asked politely, peering at a dozen or so shapeless blobs on a ceramic plate.

"Mock deviled eggs," Renee said. "Dottie made them herself!"

"I hope you like them. They're my specialty." Dottie smiled proudly.

"Oh, my . . . thanks! Come on in and have a seat."

The future guerrillas trooped over the threshold. Obviously afraid to plop themselves down next to the eight angry bits of fur, they stood, imperceptibly edging toward the kitchen and away from the wieners.

"Seriously," Virginia said, setting the mock-deviled-egg thingies on the counter beside the chips and dip, "don't mind the dogs, they never bite."

Virginia tossed ingredients into the blender as Suz looked cautiously around the den.

"Have you been here long?"

"You mean on St. Simons? All my life," Virginia said, just before turning the blender on high speed, a Salem Light pressed between her lips.

Not only that, but she hadn't even *left* the Island once in over twelve years.

It just wasn't worth it.

She was sure that the moment she turned her back, the Commission would call a closed-door "emergency" meeting and suddenly a mini-mart would wind up perched on the dunes off her own back deck.

Virginia turned off the blender and wielded the foamy green slush over a waiting tray of glasses. "Allrighty . . . who wants one?"

"What are they?" Dottie—of the mock deviled eggs—asked warily.

"*My* specialty. I call them hairy margaritas." She poured five without waiting for orders, and handed them around.

"Let's sit, shall we?"

Only when Virginia rolled over the liquor cart and the dogs drifted off to sleep did the future guerrillas relax a tiny bit and move in the direction of the sofas.

"So, Ken"—she targeted him first, sensing that he, like Sidney, was the leader of the pack—"what do you do?"

"I'm in computers."

"Really? Software, programming?"

"Radio Shack."

"Ah." She nodded, sipped, and listened politely as Ken demonstrated a deep knowledge of all things tech-related.

Then she learned Dottie was a biology teacher, Renee a Wal-Mart cashier, and Suz a waitress at the Shrimp Boat. All were relative newcomers to the Island. Perfect.

The conversation flowed and a general good mood slowly seeped over the future eco-guerrillas, punctured by an occasional sharp bark emitted by a wiener obviously embroiled in a doggie night-mare.

"And what do you do, Virginia?" Ken asked.

Deflecting the question about the present, she instead addressed the past. "Well, I used to be the Chief County Commissioner."

"Really?"

She filled them in on the goofy-golf debacle, then launched into her crowning glory.

"It happened before the last vote on constructing a major bridge connecting the Island to the mainland," Virginia informed the rapt audience, as they munched chips and dips and mock deviled eggs, and sipped the all-important drinks.

"What happened?"

Virginia smiled, reeling them in. "Well, the afternoon of the bridge vote, I called Chairman McKissick's office and talked to his assistant, Sean."

Sean was a nineteen-year-old, a five-foot-nine-inch looker, a Glynn County High School grad who'd done a year at Glynn Junior College. She would soon be one in a long line of secretaries who had walked off the job after one too many booty gooses from Chairman McKissick.

Virginia still remembered when Sean answered the phone, "Chairman McKissick's office, here to serve the people of the Golden Isles. The Chairman's office is always open to his constituents. May we help you?"

"Does he make you go through that spiel every single time you answer the phone?" she had asked Sean. "I bet he made that up, didn't he?"

No answer from Sean. She didn't understand the question.

"I beg your pardon?"

"Never mind. Just put McKissick on the line. Tell him it's Virginia Gunn."

After several minutes on hold with the local easy-listening station being broadcast today from Raymond Smith's Toyota on

Glynn Boulevard, Sean came back on the line, clearly uncomfortable with lying, but maintaining all the professionalism her nineteen years could muster. "The Chairman is in a meeting. May I take a message?"

"Why do you *insist* on calling him 'the Chairman' every single time?" Virginia had asked. "Did he tell you to do that? You know what? Never mind. I know he did. That pompous ass. Just give him a message. Tell him I'm calling from over in room one-fourteen of the Jekyll Island Days Inn with a very important message for him and his wife. I'll hold."

No need to hold. Thirty minutes later, they met in person. Virginia recounted the tale for her guests. Toby parking surreptitiously outside one of the Island's only restaurants. The Oyster Box. She walked over to his car and got in.

"Okay, Virginia, what is it this time?" he demanded. "Worried about the sea turtles again? Get over it, Virginia, the Island's changing. You can't stop progress. Haven't you ever heard that? Move on with your life. Have you ever thought of actually getting a real job? And what's the deal with the Days Inn, was that supposed to mean something to me?"

Virginia said nothing, just relaxed back in the leather seats and studied McKissick's smooth pink face up close.

She couldn't believe she was noticing only then for the first time, after having known the man for twelve years, that he was the only person she had ever come across who had both a toupee *and* dandruff. Her powers of perception were diminishing.

"Then what happened?" Dottie prodded, and Virginia realized she was stalling the story with details.

"Then I pushed the tape into the tape deck"—she got to the good part—"and when that tape started to roll, McKissick nearly wet his pants right there on the seat of his Lexus! Of course, it's leased. He tried to eject it, but you know what I did?"

They shook their heads, rapt. No, they didn't know. But they wanted to.

"I pushed it right back in and turned up the volume. A truck pulled right beside us, so he couldn't very well smack me. Ha!"

Yes, both Virginia and her archenemy Toby McKissick had been well aware that a physical confrontation in the parking lot of the Oyster Box would be all over the Island by four thirty the same afternoon.

"He was over a barrel," Virginia told her guests.

"What was on the tape?" Renee persisted, and Virginia told them, explaining how she got her cleaning lady of eighteen years, Marta, to get the tape from McKissick's cleaning lady, Luisa. The audio quality was pretty good, under the circumstances, and any moron could make out Luisa and her boss, *Chairman* McKissick, on the phone planning a tryst at the Jekyll Island Days Inn twenty miles away and across the bridge.

"That first tape alone would have gone a long way to saving the ecosystem," she told her guests as she poured more tequila into the blender. "It was the second tape, though, that did the trick. It was made the same day from a recorder strategically placed under the bed in room one-fourteen, their regular."

Everyone shook their heads, completely grossed out.

"The things on that tape should never be heard by anyone," Virginia declared, "much less his wife. So McKissick had to listen to the entire tape trapped inside his Lexus while I laughed like crazy."

Virginia flipped the blender on "High."

"Then came the Commission meeting that night. I sat on the back row of the Glynn County Middle School auditorium and listened to McKissick go on and on about the old bridge."

And he did it with feeling. "It's not *just* a bridge, people. It's not *just* a road. It stands as a tribute to this Island's great history, a historic piece of art, in fact. I say '*no*.' 'No' to those who would destroy that monument that represents the spirit of the Island . . . *our* Island. Who of you will join with me and take up this cause? Who will be brave? Join hands with me, my fellow commissioners! Let us fight this destruction together. Save the old bridge!"

McKissick's forehead glistened under the auditorium's bright overhead lights, usually reserved for night basketball games.

It was clear to a blind man that McKissick was now desperate to stop the new bridge. He could have passed for a fervent evangelical preacher straight from the heart of the snake-handling, tongue-speaking bunch.

The other commissioners looked dazed and confused. Did he literally want them to stand and join hands? they wondered. Or was it figurative?

"You should have seen it," she said, laughing through her Salem Light, still pursed between her lips while she talked. The blender had stopped.

"All those middle-aged guys visibly recoiling at hand-holding in the auditorium. They were like little lost sheep, asked to improvise their votes right there on the spot. They didn't dare speak out and make it part of the official record."

So in the end, she recalled, when McKissick called for the vote and raised his own hand, displaying the very sweaty armpit of his white Brooks Brothers, the others—after searching McKissick's face for any nonverbal sign to tell them what the hell they were supposed to do—followed suit.

Virginia went around refilling every glass. "That brand-new, beautiful, and magnificent four-laner was voted down unanimously. Not one person in the room expected them to do that—not even themselves. It wasn't at all what they'd agreed to ahead of time at the Catfish Cove in Brunswick. And progress stopped cold right there in the Glynn County Middle School auditorium."

They all nodded.

The old two-lane with a single toll keeper still stood between St. Simons and Savannah on the mainland. There would be no convenient four-laner inviting in tourists by the vanload clocking sixty mph. Not on *this* island.

Not if Virginia Gunn had anything to do with it.

Atlanta, Georgia

E IGHT THIRTY SHARP, MATT LEONARD WALKED BRISKLY INTO THE darkened bar at Atlanta's Piedmont Driving Club.

He immediately spotted Sims Regard, sitting on a burgundy leather barstool. Regard, the first lieutenant for Floyd Moye Eugene, hadn't yet spotted him. Leonard paused—only for a split second— to steel himself.

Had an acquaintance been watching, they might have noted that Maltin's move was utterly out of character. As the name partner in the criminal defense law firm known simply as "the Leonard Firm"— and, coincidentally, the baby brother to the chairman of the powerful Senate Revenue Apportionments Committee—Matt Leonard was one of the most sought-after criminal defense lawyers in the South.

This deal, however, was in the big leagues.

He'd never had anything to do with Eugene—in fact he had studiously avoided him over the years.

The two of them were about to reverse a trend that had lasted for decades, and its effects would reverberate all the way down the state to the tip of the Georgia Coast.

Regard spotted him. "Matt."

"Sims."

They shook hands.

Leonard ordered a scotch, then got right down to business, speaking in a low voice though the bar was nearly empty.

"Look, I get it. It's up on appeal now and it looks pretty grim for the defense. How can Carter deliver? He's just one out of nine. Plus, this calls for an outright reversal, with prejudice, so Cruise walks and the State can't re-try him."

Regard took a pull off his drink before speaking. "Simple rotation. Carter was assigned to write the opinion months ago. That little snot of a law clerk told us right over the phone about the assignment. Otherwise, we'd have targeted one of the other judges."

Leonard nodded.

"It'll go down like this," Regard went on. "The four knee-jerk liberals on the bench dissent on principle to every death penalty that's put before them. They'll join the new majority. All we needed was the one swing vote. It's simple. The vote will now be five to four for reversal instead of five to four to affirm the conviction. The four weak sisters on the bench are always looking for a way to reverse a death case. They don't care if he walks. Both the guilty verdict and the death penalty sentence will be reversed on appeal. It's up to Carter to find a reason."

There was a long pause and neither spoke.

"You understand, right, Leonard? Carter's a piece of cake, he's already on board. What about your end?"

Leonard was slow to speak, twisting his ring, running his fingertips nervously over the three rubies in the family crest before answering. "My contact says the Committee meets to change the wording in the Georgia code tomorrow morning, seven o'clock. No press will show because the time and date were changed for the meeting, and notice won't be published in the main foyer until eight a.m., as usual . . . an hour later. Topic's not identified, it's listed under 'supplemental.' The Committee vote will be over before notice is even posted."

Leonard downed a gulp of the scotch placed in front of him and waited for the bartender to fade away before going on. "Two of five on the Committee are still back home, but three are still in Atlanta, and that gives us a quorum. They're with us on this. They're investors in the high-rise, which helps. The code change comes out of Committee and goes straight to the full Assembly by noon. It's tacked on to a big insurance bill that everybody wants . . . you know, voter pressure. The insurance bill is set to pass by eighty-eight percent at two tomorrow afternoon. That's eighty-eight percent already *locked in*. Could be even more by the time it's done."

He paused and took another sip.

"It's a blip on the screen. It'll mean nothing to anybody voting on the insurance bill." Leonard looked over each of his shoulders before finishing. "Even if they bother to read it, which they won't, even then, they won't get what it means. The wording just redefines 'tree' as any growth two feet or over, not twenty. By summer, condos will be less than a football field from the first sea oat on the beach . . . directly on the sand, get it? Asking price twelve million apiece."

Buried deep in Georgia law, Leonard found the old Georgia code reading that no structure could be erected within fifty yards of the first tree closest to beach and marsh. The word "tree" was defined as any natural, living plant growth twenty feet or over.

Naturally, the old regulation destroyed any possibility of ocean or marsh-front condos and high-rises. Nothing but grass or sea oats grew anywhere near the crystal-white sand, and certainly none topping twenty feet.

The two men wordlessly clinked their glasses.

This was good, Matt thought. It was damned good. The Cruise reversal was the only way his firm would ever get their state and federal funding back. They needed the money, desperately.

Environmentalists just assumed the beaches were protected. Every time developers tried to plant a resort, golf course, or even a simple mini-mart on St. Simons Island, the granolas went berserk. The Island remained pure while the rest of the Georgia and Florida coasts were littered with motels, snake farms, even paper mills pumping tons of smelly goo into the air and ocean.

Not so on pristine St. Simons.

But for nearly fifteen years now, Floyd Moye Eugene had slowly and surreptitiously bought up huge sweeps of Island beach. He had never used his own name—that would have been too obvious—but rather the names of a dozen fake shell corporations that had no function whatsoever created specifically for this purpose, and a few in his wife's name. Next to an environmental trust, he now reigned as the single largest private landowner on the Island.

But the land could never be developed . . . until now.

Matt Leonard downed the rest of his drink.

"Listen," he told Sims, after sipping from his glass, "Carter's got to come through on the damned reversal."

"He will."

"The firm needs it. Cruise's was the first Penalty case we've ever lost, and the hit was big. We lost all our federal funding on the Death Penalty Project . . . a couple of million . . . and we've seen a complete drain of death cases since the conviction. Plus, it made us look bad . . . made *me* look bad."

"I know, I know . . . don't worry."

Just thinking about it now, two years later, Leonard's face burned at the memory. It was the worst beating he'd ever taken in a public courtroom. Hailey Dean had gotten his client so worked up after she'd cross-examined the defense's chief alibi witness Cruise refused to take the stand.

No, instead, what did he do? Cruise wolfed down his evening sedative right there in the courtroom. The little shit had saved it in a sweat sock.

Leonard shook his head, stuck in the dark memory.

That was the first year in fifteen that a Leonard Brother didn't rule the state as president of the Georgia Bar Association. Referrals dried up, and his own client denounced him openly at sentencing. He'd shared headlines with Hailey Dean for seven weeks while the case was tried. They always painted her the hero and him the shit. Halfway through her closing argument, two jurors started crying into napkins, and the rest acted disgusted every time he tried to break her rhythm by objecting. The press loved it.

Regard snapped him out of it. "I'd love another drink, Matt, but I've got business across town."

Before he could speak, Regard slid off his barstool, walked out of the bar, and disappeared into the night.

Matt Leonard sat still, alone, second drink melting down.

All he could think was Dean. Hailey Dean.

New York City

THE PHONE WAS RINGING JUST AS HAILEY STEPPED INTO HER apartment. She dropped her bags inside the door and made a run for it.

It was probably Dana, trying to change her mind to come back downtown. She was headed for a new club when Hailey left her, whining about having to go alone.

But when Hailey picked up the phone and checked caller ID, she saw it wasn't Dana at all.

"Mother!" she said into the receiver, glad she hadn't missed the call.

"Honey, you're there!" Elizabeth Dean sounded pleased on the other end. "I was expecting to get your answering machine. I'm so glad you're not out running. It's so dangerous, you out at all hours in New York City."

Hailey wanted to remind her mother that it was dangerous down in Atlanta, too. Maybe worse . . . But she knew that would go no-where.

"That's why I joined the gym. So you won't worry! How's Daddy?"

"I'm fine. Your daddy's fine . . . tired . . . you know."

Yes, she knew. Mac Dean had been battling heart disease for years. It worried them all. And her mother had her own problems but still took care of her father non-stop.

"When are you planning on coming down to see us?"

"I don't know, I hadn't thought about it. We were just together up here at Christmas . . . it hasn't been a month! It was so nice having you here with me. I keep thinking about it . . . I miss you so much."

"It feels like a lot longer than that."

Hailey stopped short. Her mother was right. It did. "Come back and see me again. I'll buy the tickets."

The answer was prompt—and predictable. "Oh, we couldn't let you do that."

Of course, they *could*—but they wouldn't.

It wasn't just about pride. Hailey knew that her parents still held out hope that she'd "get over this," as they put it, and come back home to Georgia.

"Anyway, it's not the tickets, Hailey. You know your father hates to fly. And I can't leave him alone here, not even for a few days," she added, lest Hailey suggest it.

And she had been about to. It was on the tip of her tongue.

"You haven't been back home to visit in so long. I miss you, sugar."

"I miss you, too. I'll try, I promise. When things slow down."

The truth was, she didn't want to go back home and back to all the memories. It could trigger a depression Hailey couldn't afford.

They talked a little longer, about people Hailey used to know and places she used to visit. She missed them so terribly—sometimes her chest ached she wanted to be back home again so much. But all she had left there were her parents. They were the only link to her old life. She'd deliberately lost touch with everyone but Fincher and now he was in Iraq.

Just before they hung up, her mother said, "Oh, Hailey, by the way, they've been writing about that man . . . the last one you put on death row."

"Cruise?"

He wasn't the only one she'd sent to death row, but he was by far the most prominent—and the most cunning.

"Yes. He's trying to appeal. Like they all do. The Court won't let him out, though, will they?"

"They won't."

"I hope not. Good night, sweet girl. Sweet dreams."

The phone clicked off. Sweet dreams. She wished.

Atlanta, Georgia

C.C. PARKED THE CADDY, SLIPPED THE KEYS OUT OF THE IGNITION, and weaved through parked cars to cross the asphalt parking lot of the Pink Fuzzy. Stepping into the club's heavily air-conditioned, darkened fantasy universe, his nerves immediately calmed down and the pain of public service magically began to ebb away.

Making his way to the bar, he ordered a bourbon and found a prime seat just in time to catch a floor show featuring the most exquisite woman he had ever seen in his life.

Her dark hair fell down her back in waves, and if those curves weren't natural, there was a plastic surgeon out there that rivaled Michelangelo.

Sitting there, C.C. was mesmerized by her stunningly choreographed routine, set to music that simply chanted the same question over and over on the loudspeaker: "Who let the dogs out? *Who, who, who, who?*"

Or were they saying "woof"?

Whichever. On each "who" or "woof," she bent over and poked her fanny right out at the audience and directly at eye level. Her G-string, which she shed provocatively near the end of the song, was appropriately decorated with a spotted-Dalmatian motif on the front. Despite the limited lyrics, she performed like a buck-naked prima ballerina on opening night at Lincoln Center.

When she was finished, C.C. nearly fell off his bar stool applauding.

The girl launched into her next routine, to "You Can Keep Your Hat On." It ended with a crowd-pleasing coup de grâce, a Chinese split that brought down the house. He watched her leave the stage and disappear down the steps.

She had to rake in at least a deuce and a quarter per song, C.C. decided. Inquisitive at heart, C.C. wound his way to the back of the club to find her. Two twenty-five wasn't cheap. He wondered how much he had left in his wallet.

There, he discovered for the very first time, a super exclusive lounge area sequestered from the rest of the bar called the "Pinkie Suite."

It cost a cool thousand to get in, but once you paid up, they'd hand you a Cuban stogie, a pull of bourbon straight up with open bar from then on, and let the good times roll. No questions asked.

The best part: Select clientele could take the entertainer of their choice into private, pink-velvet-curtained booths for some special one-on-one time with your own Pink Fuzzy.

C.C. was in. No question about it.

And there she was: This time up close and personal in the Pinkie Suite.

Cigar and bourbon in hand, he made his way over. She was seated demurely on a bar stool, having a go at the salted peanuts placed out for free on the bar, her legs modestly crossed over a standard Pinkie G-string now replacing the Dalmatian.

"Your routine was a thing of beauty. I take it you're a trained . . . what? . . . ballerina?" C.C. asked, sidling onto the stool beside hers.

She looked him up, down, and over. No answer. Just a sip on her drink and another grab at the peanuts. She obviously did not know who he was.

"So how are you tonight? Has anyone told you you're gorgeous?"

"Fine. And yes."

"I liked your act. It was very creative."

"Thanks."

"Who does your choreography?"

"I made it up myself."

Impressed, he nodded. "You're quite a talent. Ever think of doing something to 'Freebird'?"

"Nope."

"Well, you should."

Her eyes narrowed at him. "I'm an artist. I need to be moved by the dancer's muse in order to create a routine."

"So? 'Freebird' doesn't move your muse?"

"It's passé."

"It's classic."

"I don't think so."

She glared. Obviously, he'd stirred up her creative dander. *Oops.*

"I'm just sayin' . . . I'm dyin' to see you do something to 'Freebird.' That's all."

She shook her head. Not a chance. Obviously, the muse frowned on "Freebird."

"The music's all wrong. Where would I work in the Chinese split? It's my trademark."

"That, I don't know." C.C. edged his stool closer. "How about you and me go continue this conversation in one of those booths?"

"I don't think so."

"Do you know who I am, honey?"

She shook her head as though she didn't care, but he could tell she was interested in finding out.

She leaned forward a little as he took out his wallet and flashed his gold-plated judge's badge at her.

"You're a cop?" She drew back a little.

"No! I'm a judge."

"Really?"

"You bet. How about you come with me to my 'private chambers'?" Again, he nodded at the curtained booths.

She shrugged. "Why not."

A half hour in the Pinkie Suite with Tina, and C.C. was in love.

Damn, they didn't have anything like this in Dooley County.

After the last floor show, C.C. trailed Tina across town through empty streets to a two-bedroom apartment she shared with Lola, one of the other dancers at the Pink Fuzzy.

"You know what I've been thinkin', C.C.?" she said as they walked up to the door. He stayed a few steps behind her, admiring the view illuminated in the arc of the headlights of a beat-up Camry parked at the curb

He was afraid to ask, but he did. "What's that?"

"I need some collagen for my lips."

Damn! She was a beautiful girl, and discreet.

But Lord, he had a feeling this was gonna cost him. He might have to actually go back to working for a living, but the thought of his old law practice situated on the little square in downtown Dooley County made his stomach hurt.

"I think you're perfect just like you are," he said, trying to dissuade talk of more plastic surgery.

"Home, sweet home," she said with a smile, and led him over the threshold.

C.C. stepped into the apartment's tiny foyer and let out a blood-curdling scream when he was met with the sight of a bloody corpse just inside the front door.

The judge continued to scream bloody murder as he took off running for the Caddy.

"C.C.! Wait!" Tina called, chasing him down the brick walk in her stilettos. "It's not real! Shut up the screaming and get back in here!"

C.C. skidded to a halt, turning back. "Not real? What the hell is it?"

"It's Lola's Christ!"

Lola's Christ? What the hell did that mean?

C.C. slowly climbed the steps again and peered inside.

C.C. was raised Baptist and was only familiar with airbrushed pictures of Christ wherein He was beautiful, clean-shaven, fair-skinned, and blue-eyed . . . usually walking on water or holding His hands out lovingly to the Universe, with the morning sky emblazoned behind Him. Not all bloody and mangy-looking.

Lola's Christ was a mangled-looking, life-size figure hanging by His hands and feet on the nastiest-looking cross C.C. had ever laid eyes on. It was incredibly realistic. The thing had to be six by four feet at the wingspan, with shiny red acrylic blood flowing down the forehead, hands, and feet. Sharpened thorns were jammed into His whitened forehead, and Christ's eyes looked mournfully to the heavens, clearly in a lot of pain.

"What is that doing here?"

"Lola collects religious memorabilia," Tina informed him as she closed and locked the door behind them. "She was going to be a nun."

"But she became a stripper instead?"

Tina nodded. "Nuns don't get paid very well."

According to Tina, Lola deeply identified with Saint Anne of Glycerine, who had been the wife of a very wealthy eighteenth-century Catholic businessman, and mother to his seven children. One afternoon at Mass, Anne had been moved by a vision of Christ to strip off all her clothes before a monastery full of monks and, on the spot, take on a vow of paupership.

"Stripped naked like that, of course the monks thought she was a saint," Tina solemnly told C.C.

"Of course."

As she explained it, Lola connected spiritually to Saint Anne. While Anne stripped during Mass in exchange for paupership, Lola stripped at the Fuzzy on the half-hour in exchange for all the tips she could cram into her garter belt. Lola attributed her success to St. Anne and claimed she kept a vision of the saint in her mind's eye every night during the floor show.

It seemed to make perfect sense to Tina.

Still rattled by the bloodied corpse in the hallway, it took C.C. a full twenty minutes stretched out on the living room sofa, two bourbons, and a dose of Tina's special talents before he could get himself back together.

"Want to see the rest of the place?" Tina invited.

"Does it lead to your bedroom?"

From what he could see, Lola was a strange one. The apartment was completely covered in shrines to dead saints and especially to

Lola's favorite, the Virgin Mary. Two large ceramic figurines of the Holy Mother guarded not only Lola's bedroom, from a table situated outside her door, but also protected the fridge. Both looked deeply saddened by the state of affairs in the bedroom and the kitchen, so, as Tina explained, Lola routinely left the two Mother Mary figurines tidbits of candy, cookies, and juice to cheer them up.

"It's the Mother Mary's fault we have roaches," she told C.C.

It was 4 a.m. when C.C.'s head hit the pillow in Tina's bedroom. The last thing he remembered was looking up at the gauzy canopy over her bed—all pink, of course. The whole room looked like the inside of the magic bottle on *I Dream of Jeannie*. Now *that* was a classic. What a show. He loved Jeannie and the inside of her bottle. Tina's choice of decor was brilliant.

Genius, in fact. Why couldn't Betty ever think up something like this . . . a bedroom just like the inside of Barbara Eden's magic bottle?

|||||||||||||||||||||||||||||||||||||||||||||||||||||||||||||||||| **21** |||||||||||||||||||||||

St. Simons Island,
Georgia

THE THIRD BATCH OF HAIRY MARGARITAS WAS KILLER STRONG. IT was time for Virginia to throw out the bait before her guests started getting sloppy—or sleepy.

"So what does Greenpeace think of the Commission's plan to replenish the beaches and dredge up all that sediment off the ocean floor?" she asked.

Nothing like plunging right in.

"It'll be the end of the sea turtles, you know. But then, Greenpeace isn't involved with that type of issue, is it? You know, *saving endangered species*." She hoped the lob would create a defensive stir.

It did.

"Well, 'Peace' normally attacks higher profile moves so that we can make an environmental difference *and* a statement worldwide. Two birds, one stone." Ken spoke up first, emphasizing the abbreviated "Peace" to modestly convey his familiarity with the Peace higher-ups.

"It's such a shame nobody's acting on the turtles' behalf. And after all the attention the spotted owl got." Virginia clucked her tongue. "But then, the owls got a mention by the vice president, so *they* live. The turtles die. God knows what's on the floor of the ocean outside those paper mills north of the Island. You *know* that's exactly where they'll get the sand to dump on the beaches."

Warming to her subject, she lit another Salem Light off the last butt. "Greenpeace started with such a wonderful concept. But then it turned into sort of a celebrity house pet, snarfing up only the tastiest treats." Pleased with her analogy, she saw that Renee, at least, was nodding in agreement.

"I guess the little guys like us get left out in the shuffle sometimes," Virginia said sadly. "Maybe it doesn't matter. I mean after all, it is just *one* link in the eco-chain."

Ken bristled, and Virginia realized that nothing else she could have said would have reached so far under his skin. To suggest that Peace was all hype amounted to pure heresy to the four Peacers hunched around the blender under the spell of the hairy margaritas. They didn't get asked out much and they didn't want to argue with their hostess, let alone piss off the wieners again.

Virginia was banking on a watershed of discontent among the guerrillas—dissatisfaction with their distant leaders, who seemed more like Hollywood celebrities than comrades united in common goals.

After a moment, Ken said brazenly, "Well, you know the bigs at Peace don't have to be in on *every* save we make."

Virginia just looked at him over the rim of her glass, saying nothing, hoping he'd go the next step.

He did. He couldn't stop himself.

"We've been misled by the *Herald and* the county commission!" he promptly decided. "Odds are they're probably in league to-gether . . . these things just don't happen by coincidence. They've conspired . . . This is a conspiracy . . . I feel it."

He was on a roll.

"If Virginia's right, we're obligated to take some sort of pre-emptive strike before it's too late for the turtles. We can't stand by and wait for this thing to make its way through all the Peace chan-nels. That could take weeks, maybe even months. The time is *now,* the place is *here,* and the people are *us.*"

He was standing now. His words unleashed a grumbling among the guerrillas.

"It's true. I've thought it for a long time but didn't want to say anything. Peace has become too big, too sensational to care for the turtles," Renee said. "They've gone Hollywood. They've turned into celebrities. When's the last time they climbed a tree?"

"First the turtles, then what's next?" Dottie wanted to know.

"We have to seize control!" Suz injected herself. "Not slogans and bumper stickers. I'm talking *action!*" She had margarita salt on her nose.

"Exactly!" Virginia trumpeted, trying not to look smug.

Atlanta, Georgia

AS VIRGINIA AND THE GUERRILLAS FEVERISHLY PENCILED PLANS on a yellow legal pad late into the night, two hundred miles to the north, Eugene waited.

In an oak-paneled office in Atlanta, Georgia, a lifetime away from the ocean lapping against the Island dunes, he waited.

Drinking scotch through the night and never leaving his desk-side phone, his cell phone burning in his hand as a backup, he waited.

The call came from a cell phone deep within the Georgia House.

A bottle sat on the floor by his desk, within arm's reach of his chair, emptied sometime around three that morning. His office was dark when the phone rang; he still hadn't pulled open the heavy drapes from the night before.

The "insurance bill" had passed.

Not a single question was raised on the floor, not a peep. No one had even noticed the change in definition of "tree."

Matt Leonard had been right all along. They didn't even know what it meant.

Democracy at work. They just voted as they were told, like sheep.

Eugene hung up and walked to his window.

Through the slit between the drapes, he peered into the dark.

The Island coast was his.

23

Atlanta, Georgia

J IM TALLEY WAS STUNNED.
Until this moment, all had been right with the world.

It was Monday morning, seven thirty a.m. The sun rose on schedule, as predicted last night by the Weather Channel's "on-camera meteorologists," as they insisted on calling themselves. What a nerve.

His coffee brewed on cue by order of his imported coffeemaker's built-in timing mechanism.

He arrived at the usual time at the State Judicial Building. His office, adjoining the Judge's, was precisely as he had left it . . . carefully jacketed in hundreds of volumes of law books, each in their appointed location, exactly where he'd left them Friday afternoon.

Jim Talley had just listened to his voice mail.

C.C. . . . reversing his opinion in a death penalty murder case?

And not just *a* murder case, a *serial* murder case. *The* serial murder case.

And not only did Judge C. want a reversal, with a new trial over some legal technicality, he wanted Cruise to walk free!

Not once in all the years C.C. had graced the bench had he ever, *ever* ruled anti–law and order, much less anti–death penalty.

Yet now, in one of the biggest cases ever tried in the largest metropolitan city south of the Mason-Dixon line, C.C. wanted to reverse his opinion? And based on a bunch of theoretical crap he rambled over a cell phone?

Jim could tell C.C. was soused when he left the message. His voice was slurred and Duane Allman was playing in the background.

Whenever the Judge had a snootful, he waxed eloquently about constitutionality, about which he knew nothing.

Jim was always astounded how a man who knew so little about the Constitution could actually bring himself to the brink of tears just talking about it. He did it every single summer at the State Bar Association meeting in Savannah, and then, just to top it off, forced everyone to suffer through a repeat performance at the law clerks' annual Christmas party.

Last year, after two or three cocktails, C.C. had "gone constitutional" with a piece of Christmas tree tinsel stuck on top of his head. The Court personnel had been to afraid to ignore him, so they all listened, which only egged him on to even greater constitutional heights.

Now Jim would have to go door-to-door within the building and hand-deliver some type of memo explaining his change of position.

Then he'd have to comb the trial transcript and record to find an actual *reason* to reverse the damn thing. It would have to be one of the issues brought up by the defense on appeal. The Court just couldn't—*sua sponte*—first raise and then sustain its own objection; the issues raised in the appellate briefs bound them.

Jim turned on his computer and waited for it to boot up. Hell, the judge might not even remember his drunken telephone monologue about how they were the gatekeepers to justice, blah, blah, and *blah*.

It wasn't the first time C.C. had left a long, drunken rambling on his voice mail . . . far from it. But it was even worse when Jim actually picked up the phone and gave C.C. a captive audience. At least the voice mail only allowed four minutes before cutting him off.

There had to be *some* legitimate reason to reverse. Something the feds couldn't argue with.

A death penalty case would normally head straight to the federal northern district courthouse for review. Jim considered federal judges truly the worst, all cut from the same cloth. Once they'd made it out of the trenches at the state court level and landed their lifetime appointments, they waited, obnoxiously looking down their noses, for every joyous opportunity to denounce their former colleagues and trash the lower courts.

The federal judges, though, absolutely loved to let killers walk, that was a known fact. But he had to come up with something legit, a solid reason to reverse. For Cruise to walk free there had to be prejudice. That would disallow the State from ever re-trying the case. Typically that only occurred when there was some sort of prosecutorial misconduct. Unlikely here. Hailey Dean was over the top, true, but misconduct? Doubtful.

Reversals were easy enough to engineer, but Dean was a good trial lawyer and very few of her cases were ever overturned. The defense lawyer, Leonard, was good, too. Jim doubted either had done anything reversible. Appeals were not mysterious. The case was tried before a judge and jury, and immediately after conviction came a notice of appeal outline, bare-bones, grounds for a new trial. When that was denied by the trial judge, the case headed up to a panel of nine judges, the Georgia Supreme Court, for review. They loved reversing death cases . . . especially four of the nine on the bench. All it took was one vote to swing the majority.

The guilty verdict and the death sentence were both up for grabs. Letting out a long breath, Jim pulled up the Cruise decision to see where it stood on the Court's rotation and how the other justices had lined up.

After skimming a few lines, he froze.

Holy shit.

C.C.'s would be the swing-fricking-vote.

His one vote change would guarantee a serial killer's death penalty reversal. And all because of one drunk drive up the interstate?

Did the Judge have any idea?

Shit.

For a moment, just a fleeting one, Jim thought back on the testimony at trial, the mauling the victims took before they felt fingers around their necks and an indescribable pain pierce their backs.

But to hell with them. They were dead.

More important, what would a reversal do to his *own* career? He couldn't name one decent law firm that would be remotely interested in hiring the left-wing liberal wing-nut that crafted the decision to let a serial killer walk free.

He had to think . . .

Resigning himself to the possibility the Judge may actually remember Saturday's phone call, Jim switched the computer over to the Lexis legal research feature to start scanning for new law in all eleven federal judicial circuits across the country covering the death penalty.

There was nothing else he could do now. The Judge wouldn't show up for at least three more hours. C.C.'s ETA, estimated time of arrival as they called it at the Court, was never before 11 a.m. and he was always in a foul mood on Monday mornings. This would be no damn picnic.

Jim dug in and, four hours later, still no sign of the Judge and no decent grounds for reversal, except a weak argument that a separate warrant should have been obtained for DNA comparison for each of the eleven murder victims. There wasn't even DNA *on* all the victims . . . so how could he conceivably reverse on DNA issues alone?

His eyes were tired and the words on the computer screen were getting blurry. Talley pushed back from his desk and put his feet up beside the keyboard for a moment, stretching out his limbs. He glanced up at the TV screen there on a shelf, sandwiched in between law books perfectly bookended with bronzed scales-of-justice figurines.

Headline News was on mute as usual and it was the bottom of the hour, time for the local cable news cut-in. The cut-in was usually just annoying, but this time the screen caught his attention. Three young men, hair cropped short, immaculately groomed and dressed in business suits, were being led out of a courtroom in handcuffs. They looked vaguely familiar.

Talley's eyes flipped down to the banner in the lower third of the screen. A guilty verdict had been handed down in federal court. Three Atlanta vice/homicide undercover cops were on the take. Talley remembered reading about the fed's investigation a few months before.

The three looked away from the screen, but the cameras were relentless and moved in for close-ups.

Wait a minute. Conally. The name rang a bell.

Suddenly it hit him like a ton of bricks. It wasn't *just* Officer Conally, it was *undercover Detective Tim Conally*, one of the lead detectives on the Clint Burrell Cruise case. Conally conducted dozens of interviews, canvassing the city's hookers, looking for leads, and if Jim recalled correctly, Conally was the cop who'd actually found the murder weapon hidden in a duffel bag in Cruise's closet.

Jim's head was spinning. He felt a little dizzy.

Headline News flashed a clip of grainy, black-and-white video, the actual FBI surveillance rigged up in some dopers' homes. The cops looked and acted like street thugs, busting into the dopers' luxury homes in gated communities, cleaning them out of tens of thousands on each rogue raid. The cops were caught on tape, robbing Atlanta's most powerful drug suppliers of vast amounts of drugs, money, jewelry, even taking their wide-screen TVs—anything and everything the dopers had that the cops wanted.

And now, every one of the detectives' cases were in jeopardy, depending on the significance of the role they played in each case. Cruise's case had to be reversed with prejudice—in other words, due to willful misconduct by the State—in order for retrial to be legally impermissible. Hailey Dean was clean as a whistle, but "the State" included the cops.

This would work. The local papers would have a field day.

It had to be divine intervention when Talley saw the screen and put two and two together that Conally was a lead detective in the Cruise investigation. Jim pulled up the trial transcript on his screen and plugged in Conally's name to search. Not only did Conally discover the murder weapon, he also transported some of the DNA evidence from a few of the crime scenes to the lab.

Perfect. That destroyed the chain of evidence, so DNA was out the window along with the murder weapon. The State screwed up.

The case was irreversibly tainted! Cruise would walk. Praise the Lord as far as Jim was concerned. He didn't have a choice now . . . he had to reverse! If the jury had known the truth about one of the lead detectives on the stand, they may have had a totally different outcome. Conally now had no credibility. You'd have thought the defense attorney would have brought this up on appeal. True, the conviction had just gone down a few months ago, but the federal indictment had been brewing for months.

Of course, the truth was, C.C. could still uphold the conviction by holding the evidence against Cruise was so overwhelming that Conally's testimony didn't matter. But Judge C.C. wanted a reversal, and here was just cause.

Maybe nobody would blame Talley after all. Whatever. He could hand Judge C.C. a reversal on a silver platter

Jim thought again, briefly, of the murder victims and their families. But hey, it wasn't his fault.

Shit. Justice sucked.

|||||||||||||||||||||||||||||||||||||||||||||||||||||||||||| **24** |||||||||||||||||||

St. Simons Island,
Georgia

THE TREES HAD WITHSTOOD THE FIERCE WINDS OF HURRICANE season and watched as twisters churned up the land around them for miles. They presided over battles played out beneath their boughs during the War Between the States. They had shaded pirates and Indians and preachers and crooks.

But they had never before been forced to wear orange markers tied around their waists.

And this, Virginia knew, was far more humiliating than anything else.

When she first heard about the markers, she told herself they were most likely placed there by the agricultural Cooperative Extension Service. With active branches in all 159 counties in the state, they routinely marked and destroyed trees that posed a danger—maybe fusiform rust disease, with its deadly orange powder, or some other contagious, coniferous malady.

But after a late-night run to the 7-Eleven, reality sunk in.

Virginia slipped in around 10:40, just before closing at 11, on her regular cigarette run. Larry was behind the counter, wearing a white T-shirt, brown polyester Sansabelt pants, and a red fishing hat that said "Kiss My Bass."

"Salem Lights. Carton. What's happening, Larry? What's with those big dirt trucks parked across from the store? I've got to tell you, not only are they unattractive and running away your business, they're against code. Heavy use trucks aren't permitted back here on the Island. These old narrow streets can't take it. They'll crack under the weight."

"V.G."—he was the only one who got away with calling her that—"it's really happening this time. You know my daddy and his daddy before him fished these marshes. We've had our home place off the point for eighty years that I know of, just us and the June bugs. Can you believe it, V.G.?"

"Believe what, Larry? Is this about the beach replenishing? Are the trucks here to start loading the sand?"

"V.G., they're dumping sand all right, but it's a whole lot bigger than the Commission's sand exchange. Plus, they claim that's just to swap sand off the floor of the water and plump up the beaches for the tourists."

"Don't get me started on that, Larry. You know damn well what it'll do to the turtles, if anybody *cares*."

Looking hurt that she'd even suggest he didn't care about the turtles, he protested, "V.G., you know how I feel. Didn't I wear a bumper sticker about the turtles on the back of the El Camino when nobody else would?"

"Yes. You did. I apologize. I know you care. What about the trucks?"

"It's a helluva lot worse than swapping sand. They're about a hair away from laying a cement base, from what I can tell. Saw the cement-mixer trucks going in yesterday. I'd have thought you'd be the first one to know about it. It's an outfit out of Atlanta. They're building right on the beach, *right on the sand*, V.G. Right *on* the sand."

Her blood ran cold. All she could manage was a strangled-sounding "*What?!*"

"Condos. Nice ones . . . real lux. Heard tell they're starting at over a *million* dollars apiece . . . over a *million*, V.G. Who'd pay *that* kind of money but Yankees or the peeps that drive down from Atlanta on weekends? Nobody from around here, I can tell you that much. And you know what'll come next, right?"

She knew. It made her sick. "Don't say it, Larry," she begged, as if his saying it would somehow make it come true.

"Yep, there goes the marshland. You know how they dry up when construction comes in. No more marshland, no more St. Simons. That's what I say."

He was right. Marshes adjacent to construction dried up like hardened Play-Doh. Everything growing in them that made the marshes one of God's lush, green creations, would die a slow, thirsty death.

Larry stared out through the plate glass and across the street at the dirt trucks, their mud flaps already splattered from work on the site.

"Who are they?" she demanded. "What's their name? Seen any locals with them?"

She tried to keep the questioning casual, but her face was hot, and she realized she had unthinkingly scratched a gnawed-looking hole into the carton of Salems.

Larry thought about her questions for a moment and she didn't rush him. She nervously opened a pack and wedged a cigarette into the corner of her naked lips. Not even Chapstick, she didn't trust it.

"Well, I seen the trucks," Larry told her. "Two white pickups in and out. Got the name 'Palmetto Dunes Luxury Living' on the side, on top of some fake coat-of-arms picture, like a family crest or a shield or something. And a heavy man with Atlanta tags has been down here a coupl'a times. First time, he came in asking about directions to the Cloister Hotel. Second time, he came in all sweaty-like, wanting a case of Diet Cokes and ice. Oh, yeah, plastic cups, too. The big red jumbo ones."

"Palmetto Dunes Luxury Living. Hmmm. Atlanta tags. Diet Coke. Let me think. What access road are they using, Larry?"

"Not sure, but he asked for directions from off what sounded like the old King's Plantation site. He was headed to the Cloister. I told him he better call ahead, because you know they're pretty picky over there on Sea Island, what with all the millionaires living there and everything. You know, V.G., they won't even *think* about letting you book a room if you don't call ahead. You know, I bet they lose a lot of business that way, don'tcha think?"

"They call it *reservations*, and whatever business the Cloister loses, it doesn't want anyway, Larry." She took a long drag.

"So, you going out there, V.G.?"

"I might just take a little drive by and take a look. Bye, you."

"Stay out of trouble, V.G. Hey, if they ask me, *I* didn't see you. You know me, V.G., I don't know *nothin' 'bout nothin'*."

"You know it, Larry." Virginia headed for the door, the carton of Salems tucked under her arm.

Thinking again, she turned back. Larry had already turned his "Kiss My Bass" hat around backward on his head again and was bent down, working on the tiny motor in the Slurpee machine.

"So what kind of car was he driving?"

Virginia would bet everything she owned that he'd know, seeing as his daddy owned the biggest junkyard and auto salvage business in the city of Brunswick.

Bent down over the Slurpee, his response was automatic, sure, and dead on the money.

"Two thousand nine Mercedes SUV, solid white. Oh, yeah, V.G., that car was top of the line, all right, top of the line. Shiny, too. Nice wax job on that baby, girl lemme tell you *what!* Even had one of those vanity tags. Looked like it was gold-plate detailed, instead of your regular chrome metal."

"White Mercedes utility, gold detail, and a vanity tag. Well, *that'll blend.*" She made a face.

The Island was more rusty-pickup style. Talk of a vehicle with gold plate–colored accessories and curb feelers would spread like wildfire.

"So, Larry . . . you didn't happen to see what was on the plate, did you? You know, the tag number?"

"Mercedes owner had to be from Atlanta, don't you think? Whole city's headed straight to hell, full of nothing but a bunch of rude Yankees relocating from jobs up north."

"Of course they're from Atlanta. Larry—*didja get the tag?*"

"Couldn't help it." His face beamed with pride. "You know how I can't help but remember numbers and stuff. It was FME."

"FME? You sure?"

"Positive. I couldn't help but think of that blinking sign up around Savannah off the interstate that says 'Food, Movies, Enjoy!' Remember the giant FME that blinked for about a mile away?"

"I sure do, Larry. I always loved that sign. It was there since I was a little girl. Thanks." She was already at the door, waving backward at Larry over her right shoulder.

"No problem, V.G." He was again submerged in the intricacies of the Slurpee motor.

A cowbell hanging on the store's door clanged when she stepped out into the muggy night. The moon shone down on the 7-Eleven's gravel parking lot as she made her way to the car. Looking up, she saw the giant arms of the Island oaks stretched out over her, waving at her in the breeze off the water.

But were they waving hello or good-bye?

She climbed into the Jeep, slammed the door shut, and looked out into the darkened parking lot before flicking on her brights, just in time to see a rabbit take off into the oaks.

Palmetto Dunes.

Damn! How the hell had *this* snuck into town?

|||||||||||||||||||||||||||||||||||||||||||||||||||||||||||||||||| **25** |||||||||||||||||||

Reidsville State
Penitentiary,
Georgia

CRUISE SAT WAITING IN A HOLDING CELL, SWEAT ROLLING DOWN the side of his face. Two hundred twenty-five pounds of law enforcement standing six-foot-four sat poised just outside the door with a high-powered long gun balanced across his chest, just hoping, Cruise knew, he would try something.

Yep, the guard was just hoping he could go home that night and tell some little tramp he had to draw his weapon at the prison that day, shoot down a mad-dog killer, save the world.

Cruise could picture her sitting there in her nightgown listening, all impressed. Then, as he told the story about gunning down Cruise, she'd be so proud. Proud of the sheriff for killing *him*! And the asshole would probably get a raise and a promotion, and for the rest of his pathetic life he'd tell everybody about how great he was, how brave he was, how he responded in a split-second and gunned down a serial killer.

Pathetic.

These idiots at Reidsville pumped iron religiously after work every afternoon, all in the hopes of being buff enough to kick ass in the unlikely event of a jail uprising.

The penitentiary was constructed in 1936 and in its entire history there had never once been an uprising. But still, they lived for the moment in crisis, or for the paltry alternative . . . taking on just *one* inmate in an ill-matched fistfight.

Well, it wouldn't be Cruise today. No way would he give these assholes the chance to shoot him dead in the hall. Why was he in holding, anyway? Who the hell wanted to see him? Who the hell had come all the way to down to Reidsville?

Matt Leonard knew better than to come near Cruise again with his BS. If it was just another visit from some lackey at Leonard's office, Cruise would bust a gasket. But he doubted it would be. Now Leonard only sent his assistants, and those visits had dwindled to practically nothing. He gave the finger through the glass window at the two that had come down a few weeks ago.

He hoped to God it wasn't another preacher, here to save his soul, either. Last time they sent a prison preacher in to rescue his immortal soul, Cruise had spit on him. A big glob right in the face.

The door opened, and Cruise looked up to see the guard come in. Behind him was another sheriff wearing a tag that said "Processing." He was soft and white and looked like he was trying to grow a mustache with no success. Huge stains were under both his armpits.

"Mr. Cruise, if you could just sign here, we'll get you processed as quickly as possible."

Cruise didn't speak. He couldn't.

Obviously, they were here to take him to the Waiting Room.

Was it time already?

How could that be?

Where was his lawyer? The chaplain? Where were all the anti–death penalty activists with their vigils and protests?

He managed to swallow over the cold lump of dread in his throat, his thoughts racing.

Shit, didn't he have another round of federal appeals to go up one more level to the Circuit Court?

Even after that, wasn't there a last-ditch appeal to the U.S. Supreme Court in Washington? Not that he expected any favors from that bunch of asses, but he knew it would at least drag things out for a few more years before he hit the Chair.

Even Leonard speculated the appeals process would take at least eight years. It had only been two. What the hell? They were that hot to fry him? Now he was headed to the freaking Waiting Room? Damn! Couldn't they at least have told him him ahead of time?

True, he hadn't bothered to read the last series of bullshit documents Leonard had sent him. He could smell the bullshit through the sealed envelope. Right this minute it was still sealed, sitting wherever it had landed when he'd shoved it up under his bunk on the Row.

The clerk cleared his throat. "What are your plans, Mr. Cruise?"

"What the hell are you talking about, 'plans'?"

"I mean, we all agree this was sudden, but where will you relocate . . . Any idea of a job out there?"

"Out there?"

"Well, I assumed you'd head to Atlanta, don't you still have relatives there?"

He stared, uncomprehending. "My mother."

The clerk nodded. "If you'll just bring your belongings down to processing, we've got three hundred dollars and a Greyhound bus ticket waiting for you."

The implication slammed into Cruise like a two-by-four, followed by a tide of pure glee.

What a monumental mistake. Didn't they realize who he was?

He knew enough to say nothing unless he had to, lest he arouse suspicion and make them realize they were releasing the wrong person.

"Your street clothes are in Property, we still have those for you. And a Bible. Think of it as a gift. From us to you, Mr. Cruise."

The clerk smiled thinly, like giving him a Bible was some great favor. Well, if this little twit expected some sort of thank-you, he got nothing. Cruise stared at him, then quickly looked down, afraid the clerk could somehow read his mind if he looked into his eyes long enough.

He limped along down the corridor, walking slowly, and not just because of his bum leg. His every breath carefully controlled, he kept his eyes down and his mouth shut. *Keep walking, keep walking. Keep it together . . . keep it together.*

This couldn't possibly be happening. It couldn't.

Any second now, they'd realize their mistake and haul him back to the Row. Probably beat the crap out of him, too.

Cruise kept a wary eye on the guard, who stayed with them every step of the way, gun locked and loaded.

When they arrived at Processing, another clerk asked, "Did you want any of your belongings that you left back on the Row?"

"No," he said simply, quietly. All he had under his bunk were some legal files and the papers he had worked on, outlining why he was innocent, especially of the last murder. And the articles about Hailey. If he made it out the front door, he sure as hell wouldn't need any of that bullshit with him.

When he finally stepped outside, he had nothing but the clothes he'd worn at trial, a folder of legal papers explaining his release, three hundred dollars, and a bus ticket voucher worth fifty-five dollars.

Cruise took a deep, expectant breath.

The air was not at all as he imagined it would be. During all those nights in a twelve-by-twelve, he imagined the sweet smell outside.

Bullshit. It still smelled bad.

He made it all the way down a long cement walk and through two series of chain-link fences with barbed wire coiled across the tops, and he still smelled the funk of Reidsville.

Would the stench be in his nostrils the rest of his life?

He said nothing climbing into the prison van, acting perfectly calm. The radio was tuned to easy listening, low and irritating in the background.

"How's it going?" the driver asked, and it took a minute for Cruise to realize he was talking to him.

Cruise remained silent but the guy just kept talking.

"You come out of a place like that, and it's gotta be awesome, dude."

Cruise managed a tight half-smile.

"Gorgeous day, isn't it? Not too hot. That's how I like 'em. 'Cause when it's too hot, I sweat. And I don't like to sweat." He glanced over at Cruise, like he was looking for an acknowledgment.

And the guy kept talking. Couldn't he see Cruise didn't want to have a *conversation*? Like they were *friends* or something?

He had to concentrate, but that damn music whining through the car speakers was driving him crazy, buzzing around his ears like a mosquito.

Cruise wanted to look out the window at the roadside, but he had to keep staring down at his hands. They were getting electric.

The music buzzed, the driver chattered, and Cruise's hands twitched with need.

Until the moment they pulled up to the bus station.

"Well, here we are," the driver announced, like he was the happiest guy in the whole friggin' world. Stupid bastard. If Cruise wasn't in a public parking lot, he'd twist the driver's head off.

"Good luck to you."

Cruise ignored him.

He stepped away from the van as if in a dream.

The van pulled away. He could see the driver glancing at him in the rearview.

Then it disappeared around the corner and was gone. Cruise waited until it was out of sight before he moved. The music, the chatter, the noise was all gone now. He was alone. Totally alone for the first time in over five years. No cellmate, no warden following his every step as he walked in and out of his cell, no camera trained on him as he slept and ate and shit every day.

Alone . . . holding his jailhouse file with the Bible inside.

Before they could hunt him down and drag him back to the penitentiary, he turned and walked toward the station.

He stepped inside and was amazed at seeing people milling about, playing video games, and eating hotdogs in the bus grill.

Stepping up to the ticket counter, he could tell the clerk knew he was straight from Reidsville. Was the haircut the giveaway?

"Can I help you?" she asked, looking almost smug.

Bitch. She was fat with too much makeup, and her perfume stank.

Cruise stared at her neck. It was freckled and fleshy with powder caked on it, same as on her face.

Nothing like Hailey's neck.

In that moment, a surge went through Cruise's body, starting in his hands and pulsing to his head, his feet, his chest, his legs.

Cruise was breathing again. A smile crossed his face and he knew.

It wasn't a dream. It was all real.

"Sir, can I help you? Do you need a ticket somewhere?"

He spoke the first words he had uttered in hours.

"New York City. One-way."

New York City

"HOW DOES THIS OUTFIT MAKE ME LOOK?" DANA ASKED HAILEY, spinning in circles in her kitchenette as they waited for the morning's second pot of coffee to brew.

"Curvy," Hailey said, and reached out to brush a speck of lint from Dana's snug blue dress.

"Curvy-good or curvy-fat?"

"Curvy-good."

"I hope so. There are supposed to be a lot of single guys at this party tonight. Are you wearing those boots, or did you bring dress-up shoes to change into?"

"I'm wearing these boots . . . home. After work. And then I'm wearing a pair of socks," Hailey told her as she took skim milk from the fridge.

"Party pooper. You said you were going."

"I said I might go."

And that was just to humor Theresa, one of the therapists who worked down the hall, who had popped over yesterday with an invitation to a housewarming party she and her roommate were throwing.

"Give me one good reason why you can't," Dana said.

"Because I don't want to?" Hailey said with a smile.

"That's not—"

"Excuse me," a male voice interrupted from the doorway.

Hailey saw Dana light up and looked over her shoulder to see a familiar man dressed in a white coat, a sterile mask dangling around his neck.

"I'm Adam Springhurst . . . I work downstairs?"

"Hi! I've seen you around the building . . . I'm Dana. This is Hailey. It's her office. I'm across the hall."

"Oh, okay . . . that's good. Nice to meet you." The dentist shook Dana's hand, then Hailey's.

There was something so familiar about him . . . as if Hailey had seen him before . . . but of course she must have. He worked downstairs. You'd have to be blind not to notice the dark hair, dark eyes, and traces of a tan that spoke of outdoors.

Dana, looking him over head to toe, held out a mug. "Coffee?"

A peek at his ring finger revealed that it was bare.

Not that it mattered to Hailey.

"You're probably wondering why I'm here."

"To borrow a cup of sugar?" Dana asked him, openly flirting, and he smiled . . . at Hailey.

"Sugar?" He recoiled in playful horror. "Do you have any idea what that stuff does to teeth?"

Hailey couldn't help but grin, and Dana laughed as if it were the funniest thing she'd ever heard.

"No, actually, we've got a leak in the ceiling right underneath this"—he indicated Hailey's sink—"and I was wondering if you'd mind if someone came up to take a look at the pipes."

"No problem. I'll be here till six tonight, so . . ."

"Great. See you later, then, Hailey."

She and Dana exchanged a startled glance.

"You're going to inspect the pipes yourself?" Dana asked dubiously.

"Oh—no. Of course not. Maybe I'll just come back up and see what the plumber finds. And to say hello again."

"Hello again?" Dana echoed when he'd walked out, closing the door behind him. "Did you hear that? What did he mean by that?"

"Who knows?" Hailey turned away, taking a mug from the cabinet.

"Hailey! Don't be so clueless. It means he's interested in you."

"How am I clueless when you're the one who asked me what he meant?"

"We both know what he meant. And in the first place, don't you think it's a little strange that a dentist himself comes all the way up here to talk about the pipes, check out your office and *you*? Not one of those old birds that works in his office?"

"I don't know . . . maybe."

"I bet there's not even a leak down there. It was probably just an excuse for him to come up and introduce himself."

"That's crazy."

"So you're not interested?"

"I hadn't even thought about it . . ."

"So you *are* interested?"

Maybe . . . but she'd never let on to Dana. The next thing she knew, Dana would skip Theresa's party to stick around here and play matchmaker.

"You know I'm not looking for anyone, Dana. I don't want that in my life right now."

"If you found the right person, I bet you'd change your mind."

Hailey thought of Will. She already found the right person. And lost him.

"Maybe," she told Dana. "But I don't think so."

Atlanta, Georgia

THE GREYHOUND TOOK OFF FROM THE REIDSVILLE BUS STATION, kicking up gravel and heading north in a cloud of dark gray exhaust.

It was headed directly to its main hub in inner-city Atlanta.

How many times had he poached the place like a fox . . . waiting for just the right woman to step off a bus from nowhere? How many times had he lurked a half block away, watching as a new crop of waitresses, hotel domestics, mall sales-clerks, secretaries, and showbiz wannabes hit town?

The bus stopped and the familiar smell of the hot, congested city's downtown slinked its way through the heavy automatic doors, stealing all the way to the back row, where Cruise sat at an angle against the bus's wall.

It hit him hard . . . the smell of the heat radiating off pavement, diesel fumes, and something else . . . something sweet and hot and familiar.

Downtown Atlanta, where it all mixed together: the heat, the exhaust, the whiff of downtown department stores full of pink-faced salesgirls meandering heavily air-conditioned aisles . . . the new steel and concrete sky-rises looking down on old flophouses right next door on the same city block, the smell of fresh boiled collard greens and cornbread served up on dinette four-tops at the cafeteria next to the station.

He was home.

Unlike the drifters pouring onto the sidewalk from all corners, this was *his* town.

He knew where to go, how to get by, where to have fun, and where to lay low when he needed to . . . when he was disgusted with the sickening presence of other people. He knew where to find everything he wanted.

But not now.

It took every fiber of his being not to walk down the narrow center aisle and down the two bus steps, leave the bus behind, and melt back into his old haunts.

But instinct told him no.

Instead, Cruise stayed rooted to his seat, staring down at the gray-and-blue pattern woven into the upholstery, knowing that if he kept looking out the window into the city's night, he'd walk out onto the sidewalk and fade into the hundreds of drifters milling around the bus terminal. He'd disappear right back into his own world, the world he had known before Reidsville Pen.

Twenty minutes later, the bus motor churned and they were off again.

He watched the last streaks of light leave the sky, replaced by total darkness.

Time seemed suspended as they headed north . . . far from the city's core, through the suburbs and cul-de-sacs of cluster homes. Past the ball fields, the shopping malls, the Starbucks, the gas stations. They fell away from the highway like empty husks, like they'd never existed.

He'd be back . . . he knew it. He'd pick up his old life again. It was all just a matter of time.

First, he had business to take care of; business he'd dreamed of for all these years, business that gave him a reason to keep breathing in the cement crate he'd been crammed into.

St. Simons Island,
Georgia

I T WAS PITCH DARK OUTSIDE, BUT THE MOON WAS SO BRIGHT VIRGINIA could see in clear detail the separate limbs of tall, thin, lanky pine saplings near the entrance to an unpaved two-mile access road that ended at the Island's southernmost beaches.

She eased her beat-up gray Jeep onto the dirt lane, then glanced into the rearview mirror.

Good. Nobody behind her. Nobody ahead of her.

She slowed to a full stop and took her time staring down the road as far as she could, until it took a rounded curve.

Just beyond her view were the most beautiful beaches on the Island, where the Atlantic first kissed the Georgia sand good morning each day.

On Saturdays, children played pirates and Civil War heroes and Indians there, hiding from parents back at home, closeted behind screen doors keeping out the onslaught of summer bugs, their curtains drawn shut against the heat.

It was to these same quiet, wind blown dunes that those very children, as high-schoolers, stole away to make love for the first time, each thinking they were the first to discover the once-in-a-lifetime spot under the Island sky.

And then even later, they would return to the familiar stretch of sea and sand as life crept up on them, the years suddenly grown too many. They came back to drink in the water and sand, and remember youth.

Then, at the end, there were last requests to see the south dunes and the ocean one more time. When Virginia's time came, she wouldn't mind if it happened right there, too; if her own last look at this earth was the Island dunes and ocean.

With a sigh, she turned off the engine, crunched down on the emergency brake, and got out of the Jeep.

She couldn't help but look up and name the constellations in her mind, an old habit. She always imagined that somewhere in the world, the people she loved both dead and alive were looking at those same stars.

Suddenly remembering why she was creeping around a dirt road at midnight, she crawled under a thick metal chain draped across the road.

She took off into the dark, keeping an eye out for wildlife off the dunes, confident that, between her and the animals, if anyone were about to be caught off-guard and take off running, it would be *them*, not her.

No sooner than three or four minutes in, she turned the curve in the road and stopped cold.

In the distance, she saw something altogether foreign. Erected in the dead center of the road was some sort of small structure, painted stark white to thwart the heat of the sun.

Some sort of guardhouse. To guard what?

She continued walking, but slowly now, taking it all in.

Beyond the new guardhouse, she could make out the outlines of cement trucks and construction materials stacked in assorted piles. They went on and on, no lack of building materials here.

A gust of breeze confirmed her worst fears.

When it blew across her face, lifting her hair from her cheek, she sniffed not only the usual salt air, but the unmistakable odor of cement mix. That, and pine timber without the protection of its hard outer bark, sliced and laid open to the elements in long, thin boards.

There was a light in the tiny booth, and she could just make out the back of a man's head.

Virginia knew she should stop, but she didn't.

Instead of passing the booth on the road and in the open, she dipped into thick trees on the side of the dirt road and continued forward, using them as cover. About twenty yards in, she edged closer to the clearing to take a look.

Larry was right.

Huge sections of land leading to the beachfront had been cleared. In the milky white moonlight, the ground looked naked without the pine-scrub covering. The gentle dips and curves of dune had been flattened like a big, square pancake and cordoned off in neat, precise rectangles with construction string, waiting to be shored up with pine timbers, then filled in with thick concrete.

Her only witness a solitary Island owl, Virginia made her way back to the Jeep, stepping surely and silently through the trees, touching them gently, lovingly, with her fingertips as she went.

The night was black and the roads were dark, even with her brights on, as she drove back, the wind whipping in through the Jeep's open windows, wet with sea salt.

The Island was no longer hers. It had grown suddenly into a strange, unfamiliar beast.

Everything seemed different now. Surreal. The curves on the back roads she had walked as a child and driven since she was fifteen jumped out at her as if she had never driven them before.

The worst she had imagined was that the beach-replenishing project was under way, started by the County Commission without her knowledge so as to avoid the predictable protests and sabotage that came with any proposed Island development.

What she had stumbled upon was much worse. This was no Magic Market, no two-pump gas station.

The development of condos on the Island's south end meant the end of the beaches . . . the end of Island life as she knew it.

It meant the end if something wild and beautiful and the beginning of something common and predictable.

High-rises mean people, throngs of them. High-rises mean paved roads, boiling hot asphalt poured over machine-flattened dunes. There would be traffic lights and crosswalks and grocery stores and water slides, possibly even . . . *a mall.*

The delicate balance between marsh, beach, dune, and salt water would be strangled dead.

Virginia couldn't let that happen.

She released the steering wheel with her right hand, reached into the glove compartment, and pulled out a cell phone and a knit cap she always wore to protect her brain from dangerous cell waves.

She veered off the soft shoulder while trying to turn on the cell, and then instinctively yanked the Jeep back onto the highway and jammed the cap on.

It was late, but she dialed the bungalow shared by her two most trusted guerrillas, Renee and Dottie.

Renee picked up on the second ring with a protective "Hello," knowing calls at this hour could only mean a death in the immediate family or eminent nervous breakdown on the part of the caller.

"Did I wake you up?" Virginia asked.

"No . . . it's okay, Dottie and I had just turned off *The Tonight Show.* Lily Tomlin was on. What's up?"

"*Code Orange!*"

"Orange? What do you mean? What happened? Did they hold the Commission meeting behind our backs? What . . . they approved the replenishing? Are you hurt? *What?*"

Virginia's throat caught. "No. It's worse than that. High-rises are going up on the south beach. The foundation's about to be poured."

"But that's impossible. Who told you?"

"Nobody told me, I saw it for myself, ten minutes ago. A guardhouse is protecting it so they must expect trouble. I've never seen a guardhouse on this Island in my life."

"Oh my God."

"Call everybody."

"Now?"

"Yes, now!"

Virginia had a feeling in her heart that if she could just do something right now, she could single-handedly turn back time and change what had happened right under their noses, on their own Island. But she had to act *now*.

"I'm sure that would wake them up."

"So wake them up. Just start the Chain."

The Chain consisted of one guerrilla calling the next in a pre-arranged manner to which they all agreed in case of an emergency.

"What do I tell them all?"

"To come to my place. Hurry, Renee. Okay?"

"Okay. We're on our way."

"Just start the Chain."

"Will do."

She tried to thank Renee, but her voice broke. She hung up, tossed the phone and the cap into the backseat, and kept on driving.

Off the sides of the road, black silhouettes of pines and oaks and palmettos blew back and forth in the wind off the ocean with such a force that they blended to look like figures dancing wildly, savagely.

She continued to speed, taking crazy turns as they came one after the next, the road jumping out from behind the oaks as if it were alive, trying to leap out and scare her.

And she was scared. For the first time in her life, Virginia Gunn was afraid.

New York City

"I'M GLAD YOU AGREED TO HAVE DINNER WITH ME, HAILEY."

"I'm glad, too," she told Adam Springhurst across the white tablecloth, and surprisingly, she meant it.

Earlier, when he'd come upstairs just as she was packing up, she'd been almost dismayed to see him. It had been a long day, and her last patient was Melissa.

Skittish as she was, Melissa clammed up altogether when her session was interrupted by the arrival of a plumber the super sent up. Hailey shut her office door so Melissa could go on talking about her fifth birthday—the last "happy" one, before her stepfather had shattered her life. But she was distracted by the sound of a wrench clanging against pipes, and finally asked if they could end the session early.

"The plumber found the leak and fixed it," Hailey told Adam when he showed up, "so you shouldn't have any more problems downstairs."

"Good. Want some dinner to celebrate?"

Her gut instinct said no, but on second thought, dinner out would really be nice. Three hours later, they were having coffee and cannoli at a little Italian restaurant a few blocks away from the office. The conversation was easy, Adam was well-educated and well-traveled, full of funny stories. He asked all about her . . . her life in Atlanta, her apartment, her hours, even the funny story about switching office suites. He seemed keenly interested in every detail.

And he came out of nowhere. No conversation in the preceding months, no hellos over the mailboxes, no bumping into each other in the neighborhood. Nothing. Just hello, need to check your plumbing, let's go to dinner.

"So if you weren't here with me," Adam said, breaking off a piece of pastry, "what would you be doing tonight?"

"I'd have gone to the gym, or for a run. Then home. Pretty simple."

He smiled. "You answered that without having to think. Sounds like you've got a routine down."

"I guess I do."

"Same here. Before the divorce, when I was living up in Westchester, I'd get off the train just in time to tuck the kids in, grab something to eat, and fall into bed. I thought *that* was a rut. Now . . . it's pretty much the same thing. Without the commuter train or the kids."

"You said you have two daughters?"

He nodded. "Cammy's thirteen, Alexis is twelve. I miss them like crazy."

Hailey sipped her coffee and wondered why he hadn't stayed near them, in the suburbs, after his divorce.

As if he'd read her mind, he said, "They're both away at boarding school in Massachusetts. My ex-wife insisted. It was her alma mater, and it's a great school, the girls love it, so . . ." He shrugged. "No reason for me to stay in Westchester without them. How about you?"

She hesitated. Hailey couldn't imagine sending children away to a boarding school. "Do you mean have I ever lived in Westchester?"

He smiled. "No, I mean, do you have children?"

Taken aback by the question, she shook her head quickly. "No."

Maybe she'd answered it too quickly, because his smile faded just a little and he said, "You're not into kids, huh?"

"No, that's not it. I mean, I love children." And she'd always thought she'd have them. It hadn't turned out that way. It was still an open wound.

What was she doing here? It was all wrong.

Suddenly, all she wanted was to go home.

Hailey looked at her watch. "It's getting late."

"I guess it is." Adam looked around for the waiter.

Five minutes later, they were outside. Adam raised his arm to flag a cab. "You said you live uptown, too, right?"

"I do, but I've got to go back over to the office and pick up some files I forgot."

"We can swing by and I'll wait," he said, as a taxi pulled up to where they stood in the street.

"Oh, that's okay. I need the walk, after all that food."

"Right. Well . . . thanks for having dinner with me, Hailey."

"Thanks for asking."

He got into the cab with a wave and a "Talk to you soon."

She started walking slowly toward the office, wondering whether he realized she hadn't wanted to share a cab uptown with him.

It wasn't that she hadn't enjoyed his company.

For the first time in years, Hailey found herself wondering whether there might not be someone out there for her after all. Someone other than Will.

She didn't like even thinking of it. She couldn't wait to get out of the restaurant and felt like running the whole way back to her apartment. That was why she'd cut the evening short. The thought of dinners and dates and movies and theater with another man was just too much like . . . cheating. Cheating on Will. She knew it didn't make sense, but the dinner with Adam was just . . . *wrong.*

But walking toward the avenue to look for a cab of her own, she decided Adam Springhurst wasn't so terrible and could be a nice friend. She'd end it there. There was nothing wrong with Adam . . . he was absolutely fine, she told herself. Young, handsome, single, educated . . . he had a great résumé. Right? He looked great on paper. But Adam wasn't the problem . . . maybe *she* was. She was sure of it. She couldn't put her finger on why she suddenly had to get away . . . from *him.*

North Georgia

THE BUS WAS IN THE COUNTRY NOW, NO SIDEWALKS, NO streetlights . . . only the gradual incline of the foothills of the Piedmont, the beginnings of the Appalachians. The bus struggled and shifted to make the gentle upward slant.

The two-lane was a curvy old thing, built decades before during Roosevelt's Work Progress Administration.

Now it was whisking Cruise farther and farther north, neatly separating objects in the night . . . people, cars, motels, sturdy telephone lines split evenly on either side of the Greyhound.

Outside the bus, the night was magnetic.

Through tinted glass he could make out shapes of things his consciousness had forgotten during his years in maximum-security lockdown. Deep down in his bones, though, in the roots of his hair, in his very skin, he remembered it all.

Cruise peered out his window at trees, trailer parks, RV camps. Tired-looking cornfields and farmhouses were flying by in the night. Split-second images of countless grassroots churches spirited past the window of Cruise's back-row seat. His eyes could barely focus on makeshift white crosses propped on the pointed centers of their roofs . . . roofs topping structures that had once passed for single-family homes, now converted to house sweaty Bible-thumpers every Sunday. It was all zooming by like a movie in fast-forward.

His right shoulder was pressed tight, hunched against the bus's rectangular thermal-glass pane. For hours on end, rarely glancing away from the old two-lane, keeping his gaze reined in as tight as his posture. He wasn't used to having unlimited freedom of motion yet. He intentionally positioned himself in the very back of the bus, last row.

He was drawn to the view out the window like a wolf to the moon.

His mouth was dry with the painful realization of all he had been denied during those years in a piss-stank Atlanta jail, followed by maximum at Reidsville Penitentiary. His neck tightened and his pulse quickened in the darkened corner there in the rear of the bus. His stomach churned. His hands clenched as he realized what that prosecutor-bitch had cost him.

The ride was getting long and they ground to a stop over and over in every bump in the road that had a stop sign. He was pissed and he couldn't believe how these morons were slowing him down, actually boarding and unboarding at stops nobody else had ever seen or heard of . . . the middle of nothing and nowhere.

Cruise glared whenever new passengers—skittish women, sullen-looking teenaged boys—hopped onto the bus. He only noticed them to the extent they disturbed him . . . slowing his flight north.

The bus lurched again, then heaved to a halt, pushing the passengers forward in their seats.

Cruise peered out to see the pickup point here, a gas station with a single outside-lamp bulb hanging from a chain to light a wooden bench situated near the pumps.

"Blue Ridge, Georgia," the driver called out in the dark of the bus.

Wouldn't the good people of Blue Ridge just *love* it if tonight, Clint Burrell Cruise stepped down off the bus and decided to make this his new home?

Think they'd show up with a welcome basket tomorrow morning and invite him to Monday's Rotary Club luncheon, packed with all the town's do-gooders and held in the conference room of the local bank?

Maybe . . . until they found out about a little Murder One conviction on his résumé.

He knew better than to even think about it anyway. The more miles between him and Reidsville, the better for everybody.

Plus, there was a little business matter for him to take care of in the Big Apple.

He'd never actually been to the city before; had only seen it in the movies.

But already, he knew where to look up some of his old friends who were there, living just north of Harlem. Or at least, they had been.

A name change, a new ID, and he'd be just fine in New York. Plus, he didn't plan to stay too long . . . just long enough.

He watched a new passenger, a spongy-looking girl, maybe nineteen, maybe twenty, lumbering up the aisle toward him.

She came all the way to the back of the bus, dragging two purple canvas bags with her, covered in sewn-on stickers and Magic Marker scrawls.

She disgusted him.

She was too fleshy, wearing low-cut hip-hugger jeans. Her sandals revealed stubby toes in need of washing and still bearing the remnants of a bluish-tinted nail polish. A silver toe ring topped it all off. Repulsive.

She turned, and he spotted a large tattoo on the small of her back . . . some Chinese-looking characters, an unreadable word permanently burned into her flesh in thick greenish-black ink.

The tattoo made him madder.

What the hell was that Chinese-looking word supposed to mean? Who the hell did she think she was, stupid pig with a Chinese word on her back? It probably said just that: "Pig."

His fingers throbbed, pounding with blood rushing through them, as if his heart were thrashing in his hands, not his chest. He balled them back into fists.

No way could he let some pudgy bitch mess it all up for him.

Why wouldn't she just sit the hell down and get out of his vision?

Her hips seemed to catch against the seats on either side as she passed up the aisle, dragging the bags on the floor behind her. Earphones hung around her neck, blaring music.

Finally, she flopped into a seat two rows ahead of him to his left.

Without moving an inch, he could see her blue-jeaned legs stretched out in front of her, the rings of leather around her two big toes to hold brown sandals in place on dusty feet.

Her right hand rested on the chair arm and her nails were bitten down to nubs, spots of polish still on the centers.

The thought of having to look over at her the entire ride to New York made Cruise's teeth bite down on nothing.

He tried to look away from the girl, but he couldn't.

He watched her chew down nervously on her nails, what was left of them. She absentmindedly gnawed and ingested germs, nail polish, and fingernail gristle without ever looking back at him.

Watching made him want to hit her in the back of her head with his fist.

Thankfully, she quit biting her nails.

But then she started thumping her dirty feet to the beat in her headphones. Even from here, he could smell her.

It poured out of her, oozing from the pores in her skin. She smelled of cheeseburger grease and Jergen's white hand lotion. They had it in the kitchen at Reidsville and both smells were now physically revolting to him

When she cocked her head to listen to the music, long, stringy brown hair fell back to reveal her neck.

The sight of it hit him like a brick. It was totally out of place on such a thundering beast. Her neck drew him.

Hot streaks pulsed down his arms to his hands.

His lips parted and his eyes took on a slant. His breathing grew labored. He stared. He felt his mouth water and his body tighten against his clothes.

Her neck.

It was beautiful. Just the sight of it brought back the old feeling, an ache, a good ache spreading across him.

He wondered if she would notice if he just walked by and happened to touch her neck . . . just once.

Would she mind? Would she scream? Would she think it was an accident?

She might complain to the driver. Then there'd be a confrontation.

Would he be thrown off the bus for simply circling her neck with his fingers? Not to harm her, but more to compliment her on the one attractive part of her body?

It would just be once, and ever so lightly . . . like a butterfly kiss.

She might be flattered. How often did this grubby cow have a man admire her?

Suddenly, she reached into a bag and dug around, peering into its bottom. She pulled out a rubber band and as he watched hungrily in the dark, she pulled the strands back into a ponytail.

How could she not sense him, just two rows back, his body on fire?

He was radioactive, the muscles in his thighs, calves, biceps, and forearms taut and stretched.

His eyes bored silently into her. Only he understood the power he possessed, that his intense gaze had a magical power that sapped a woman's strength to reject him. It was a secret power only he knew about and it radiated like a laser from his eyes, melting her, destroying her before he ever laid a hand on her, sucking her life's energy into his own.

Her neck was soft and white, almost glowing in the dark of the bus, and with her hair newly pulled back, it was now totally exposed to his view . . . all the way from the concave hollow of her throat to the delicate neck bone disappearing up into her hair.

He was imminently more powerful than her. He was just a few feet away from her, and she had no idea of his presence.

Without warning, she stood up, reaching into the overhead bin to pull down a stack of magazines out of her bag.

She glanced back at him as she turned to resettle her frame into the seat, and when she did, her eyes, briefly, met his own.

They were crystal green.

He had only seen eyes similar to that once before . . . in court. His mind reeled backward . . .

It was late afternoon, and Hailey Dean had leaped up from her chair and shouted Leonard down in a dueling match over an objection she just made.

The judge ruled against her in a packed courtroom, cutting the bitch down to size. Leonard preened obviously, in his seat at counsel table, over the legal victory, and Cruise, sitting in the midst of his defense team at counsel table, joined in, letting a smile spread across his face.

He could tell she was trying to hide her disappointment from the jury.

Hailey turned away from the judge's bench to go back to her seat, silently crossing the carpet to the State's table, a thick, sturdy, oak-slabbed monster covered in papers and exhibits. Her shoulders slumped in defeat as she glanced over at the two of them. Faced with their cocky demeanor, she'd pressed her lips together in a straight slash and visibly gritted her teeth.

After only a moment, she got up again.

Deliberately, she'd walked to the front of the defense counsel table.

Resting her fingers on its edge, her eyes locked directly with Cruise's. She'd faced him head on as she stood there in front of his table, her back to the judge and jury. And for the first time since the trial started three weeks before, she smiled at Cruise.

It was an odd smile, though, fixed, slanting up on one corner, showing no teeth.

Crystal green eyes stared into his own, and Cruise felt a hot tingling melt down his body through his spine, into his legs and feet.

It was then that he knew.

He was going down for this. She was taking him down.

He felt the rush of diarrhea and held it in only with a quick, powerful effort, his haunches tensed together.

Now, sitting on the Greyhound, he remembered. Within seconds, the electricity drained from the rest of his body, out of the muscles across his shoulders and arms, his chest and abs, and instead, all the electricity shot to his hands. They sizzled with energy . . . they'd explode if he so much as brushed them against the textured fabric of his seat.

Cruise literally *pulled* his eyes away from the seat diagonally ahead of him, willing himself to drag his face, chin first, away from the girl and her neck. He tucked himself completely behind the tall, cushioned seat reclined backward just a few inches in front of him.

Eyes burning and heart thundering, he turned back toward the night whisking by outside his window.

It physically hurt to turn away from the girl in the dark of the bus. He placed his hands, throbbing hot, against the cool of the bus window. Tall pine trees silhouetted against the lighter shade of black sky made giant figures posing in bunches, mocking him at a distance.

Eighteen hours to New York City; he'd be there by tomorrow night.

The next few weeks would fly by, just like he had planned night after night, locked down in a cell. All because of Hailey Dean.

|||||||||||||||||||||||||||||||||||||||||||||||||||||||||| **31** ||||||||||||||||||

New York City

WHEN HAILEY'S CELL PHONE RANG, WELL AFTER MIDNIGHT, SHE was wide awake in bed with a book she'd been trying to read to put herself to sleep.

She kept telling herself it was the coffee keeping her awake.

That, and the dinner. With Adam.

But there was something else, too. Some nagging uneasiness she somehow sensed had nothing to do with caffeine or Adam Spring- hurst.

Who was calling so late? Somebody who had her cell number. She reached across her bed and down to her purse on the floor, fish- ing around for the cell. This late, could it be bad news from home?

No. The caller ID displayed a local area code.

"Hello?"

"Hailey?"

"Karen!"

"I'm so sorry to call you so late, but you said to call anytime if I needed you, and . . . I do. I'm so sorry. . . ." Karen spoke the last three words on a sob.

"What's wrong?"

"He has a new phone number on his speed dial, Hailey."

"What?"

She didn't have to ask who Karen was talking about. Of course it was James . . . again.

"He assigned it to number one, Hailey. I'm number three—after his mother. Number one used to be his voice mail."

"Whose number is it now?"

"I'm not sure. I called it, and a woman answered."

"Did you talk to her?"

"Are you kidding? I hung up, plus I blocked my number. I looked up the area code, though, and it's for Tallahassee. Remember when James went to that conference in Florida a few weeks ago?"

"Yes. You think he met someone there?"

"I know he did. And I hired a private eye to find out who she is and what's going on."

Hailey gently spoke to Karen for almost fifteen minutes, work- ing through conflicted feelings for a man she thought she loved.

A man who now had a twenty-three-year-old pharmaceutical sales rep with long dark hair as number one on his speed dial.

Finally, Karen yawned and said, "I'm exhausted. I think I can sleep now."

"I hope so. For some reason, things always seem better in the morning. It's getting through the night, sometimes, that's the tough part."

"I'm so sorry I woke you in the middle of the night, Hailey."

"Don't worry. Go to sleep."

Hanging up the phone, she glanced at the book she'd dumped when the phone rang.

Instead of picking it up again, she turned off the lamp and burrowed her head under the pillows.

Like Karen, she was exhausted.

But instinctively she realized she wouldn't sleep in the hours ahead.

All was not right in her world tonight. What was it?

She didn't know how she knew, she just did.

|||||||||||||||||||||||||||||||||||||||||||||||||||||||||||| **32** ||||||||||||||||||

New York City

AS HAILEY STEPPED OUT OF THE ELEVATOR IN THE LOBBY OF HER building on a cold February morning, Ricky, her favorite doorman, flashed a familiar grin. "Hello, Ms. Dean."

"How are you today, Ricky?"

"Same as every day, just happy to be alive," he replied. "How about you?"

"I'm great, thanks," she replied, same as she did every day, and their morning ritual was complete.

She left him to his *New York Post*, folded so that most of the front-page headline was hidden.

Only the last four bold black letters were visible: R-D-E-R.

You didn't have to be a genius to figure out that the missing letters were M-U.

Murder. Never a lack of crime to report. There was always a headline. Print reporters only had to wait overnight, the TV people got it instantly.

She stepped out into bright winter sunlight. Nine a.m., and Second Avenue was already tangled in a honking snarl.

She raised her arm to hail a cab headed downtown. Ordinarily, she'd start out walking the first few blocks in the morning air, but didn't feel like it after no sleep the night before.

She had gotten home at eleven last night to find a message from Adam.

"Hi, Hailey. I'm leaving tomorrow morning on that ski trip, so I wanted to tell you Happy Valentine's Day, and . . . I'll see you when I get back."

They kept running into each other at the mailboxes in the common hallway downstairs at work.

She had turned him down for a gallery opening they were both invited to, but he didn't seem upset, and coincidentally, the two days she had actually left the office last week to go out for lunch, he'd shown up almost instantly at the same spot. It was just around the corner and had the best homemade soup in town, so maybe it wasn't that much of a coincidence. They'd shared the same table and the same newspaper. It was pleasant and she couldn't explain why, but Hailey found herself instinctively avoiding another chance meeting, staying in for lunch the rest of the week, ordering salads over the Internet that showed up twenty minutes later. Adam had appeared out of nowhere . . . and he'd probably disappear into nowhere the same way.

Why, then, had she had such a hard time sleeping last night, and woken feeling troubled again today?

Hailey felt her cell phone buzz in her pocketbook a second too late to catch the caller. Checking her messages, though, she heard her mother's voice.

"Hailey, your dad's feeling so good, we're heading down to Cumberland for a few days. We'd love you to meet us down there. We're driving but we could pick you up at the airport. I love you, sweet girl. Let me know." The phone clicked off.

Cumberland Island was just off the Georgia coast, so extreme an opposite to Manhattan Island that they might as well be on different planets. Rustic and remote, with thirty miles of undisturbed Atlantic coastline, Cumberland boasted no TVs or phones, no cell pockets, no paved roads. Maybe a dozen residents, and even fewer homes and cars. Just natural beauty.

Looking out the window of the cab, she daydreamed briefly about going back home and meeting her parents at Cumberland. A nice dream, especially this morning. A bitter wind blew off the East River.

Hailey sat back and listened to the radio, glad it was tuned to 1010 WINS.

"All news, all the time. Give us twenty-two minutes and we give you the world," the radio voice promised the backseat.

The local segment was recycling the discovery of a body. "NYPD this morning is investigating the discovery of a body at around midnight on the city's East Side. The identity of a white female, estimated to be between twenty to thirty years old, has yet to be determined. Witnesses on the scene described her as small in stature."

The news announcer's voice gave way to a taped man-on-the-street account from a male bystander with a strong New York accent.

"We were all there when the ambulance came up, but it was too late. They covered her with a sheet and took her away."

Back to the announcer. "Police investigating cause of death and matching the body's description against missing persons in an effort to identify the victim. The victim had been both stabbed and strangled, according to sources within the NYPD."

With that announcement, Hailey sat forward and frowned. Two causes of death? Strangulation and stabbing . . . that didn't make sense. . . .

Strangulation suggested a "sweetheart murder," requiring close physical contact, even a struggle between killer and victim suggestive of sex or intimacy between the two in the past, or at the time of death.

Analyzing the MO, she lowered the window for a lungful of cold air off the East River, gazing at the glass-and-concrete landscape as the cab crept another block, approaching the United Nations.

Police were most likely holding back information from the public to avoid jeopardizing the ultimate jury trial. Even worse, too many details to the media could spin off a copycat killer.

1010 WINS had jumped to the weather—cold and sunny with potential for snow flurries tonight. Hailey barely noticed, still caught up in the murder of a total stranger.

The canned news report left out crucial details and sent her mind spinning.

Where on the East Side was the girl found? In the dark waters of the East River, where Hailey jogged every evening? Thrown from a car off the FDR? Dumped in an open area—if there was such a thing in this city? Or was she stabbed and strangled right there where she was found? If so, the crime techs at the scene could make or break the case by the way they handled the forensic evidence on and around the body.

Through force of habit, Hailey methodically began to fill in details. Friends and foes alike accused her of having a clairvoyant streak, but reading minds did not account for her ability to decode a criminal mind. That talent was hard-won, via ten years in the trenches of one of the busiest courthouses in the world . . . serial murders, rapes, child molestations, and arson all routine.

"And now, traffic and transit on the eights," the radio voice declared.

The cab hummed forward, miraculously dodging pedestrians who showed neither fear nor respect for oncoming vehicles. Incredibly, few were ever mowed down. Knowledge being power, that statistic only egged them on.

Watching traffic whiz by, she knew why the news report had grabbed her attention and not let go. The stabbing/strangulation MO reminded her of her final jury trial, the Clint Burrell Cruise serial-murder case.

|||||||||||||||||||||||||||||||||||||||||||||||||||||||||||||| **33** ||||||||||||||||||

Atlanta, Georgia

C LARENCE E. CARTER WAS NOW KNOWN AS THE JUDGE WHO HAD a heart, the fair-minded champion of the people, not too proud to listen to reason nor afraid to hold the justice system to the careful scrutiny allowed only by the bright light of the Georgia Supreme Court.

In other words, he'd reversed himself midstream.

Tipped back in his desk chair on a glorious morning, C.C. gazed out the window at the glittering city, basking.

He had let a serial killer walk free with a single vote and blamed it all on the State. It was the cops' fault.

Now he was the centerfold in legal journals across the country. Suddenly, even the American Bar Association lauded him, despite his profusely and publicly ridiculing the ABA repeatedly in the past. He publicly declared it was headed up by liberals and law professors who had never been in the trenches and knew nothing about the real world, frequently describing them as bloated house pets who lounged in plush ivory towers.

Funny, he saw them in a whole new light now that they had invited him to a genuine Hawaiian luau *in* Hawaii next month, and would fly him and Tina first-class to present him with an ABA Certificate of Honor, shellacked to a high sheen and embedded in oak.

The Prosecuting Attorney's Counsel had never shelled out like this.

And then there was last week's invitation to an all-expense-paid trip for two to Italy, where the Criminal Defense Lawyers Association was planning to fete the Cruise reversal. Although he'd heard American Italian food was much better than real Italian.

Of course, not everyone applauded his vote.

His law clerk, Jim Talley, resigned. So much for *his* chances of landing a spot at Lange and Parker. For all C.C. knew, Talley was waiting tables at Cracker Barrel. But hey, if you can't take the heat . . .

Meanwhile, C.C.'s longtime supporters, the pro–death penalty groups, were furiously licking their wounds over the reversal. They hoped this single reversal must be a freakish aberration on the part of a fry-'em-like-chicken-ask-questions-later kind of judge. The reasoning behind C.C.'s swing vote remained a mystery, though the legal community was rife with speculation as to the true cause of the vote change.

Outright disgust with C.C. was evenly matched by the jubilance of the anti–death penalty camp, hailing a new era wherein future Penalty votes would now be one vote in *their* favor.

Wrong.

C.C. knew in his heart this was a one-shot deal, and it was over.

He planned all along to "leave the dance with the one who brung him." C.C. was brought to greatness by his die-hard support for the electric chair. He couldn't and wouldn't abandon Old Sparky on the cusp of his governorship. That would be bad luck.

Plus, liberals represented mostly poor, indigent clients strapped for cash. They could never fund his gubernatorial bid, much less a re-election campaign.

If he ever wanted to live in the Mansion, he had to make nice again with the "fry-babies," C.C.'s pet name for pro–death penalty groups.

He took another sip from his flask and spun away from the window.

Time to call Floyd Moye Eugene.

‖‖‖ **34** ‖‖‖‖‖‖‖‖‖‖‖‖‖‖‖

New York City

"NOW HE'S JOINED 'JDATE.' " KAREN BLEW HER NOSE INTO A Kleenex in Hailey's office. Again. "It's online dating for Jewish singles. And that's on top of Adult Friend Finders, Yahoo Singles, and Match.com."

"Is he Jewish?"

"No . . . and he's not single, either! Well, technically, maybe, but . . ."

Hailey shook her head. For a half hour now, Karen had been filling her in on James's latest. The man never ceased to amaze.

"And you should read the things he says on this JDate . . . all *bullshit*, of course."

"Like what?"

"I checked out his profile and he's got some nerve. The photo he posted of himself is half a picture somebody took of *us* one night at a party . . . and *I'm cut out of the picture*! He's just standing there with a glass of wine in one hand and his other arm reaching out off the photo. It might actually be funny if it weren't so . . . so . . ."

"Duplicitous?" Hailey supplied the word Karen was searching for.

"Exactly. Why is he doing this, Hailey?"

"He's not my client, Karen. You are."

"I know, I know. You always say that. But what's your theory?"

They'd been over and over it. Maybe someday, it would stick. Maybe Karen wasn't ready to let go, so she subconsciously remained in a perpetual state of limbo.

"My theory is that all the telephone foreplay and online flirtations make James feel like he's still out there, a 'player,' a nice-looking package of man. It's all about his insecurities. He prefers anonymity because there's no fear of failure. We've been over this. You agreed just last week."

"Remember that bootleg Viagra I told you about?" Karen avoided her avoidance.

Hailey nodded, almost afraid to hear. "What about it?"

"I told him about it, and I told him to use it. All the pills are still there, right where I left them in the bathroom cabinet. I secretly counted them so that I could make sure he wasn't using them somewhere else. He wasn't . . . at least, not according to my math."

"Well . . . that's good, isn't it?"

"It's good he isn't using them somewhere else . . . not so good that he's not using them with me. And the thing is, all this online stuff of his—it's not just about sex. Last week he e-mailed an Asian escort service and asked some hooker named Lotus if she'd like to go to dinner and a Broadway play. He wrote, 'Before the tab starts running.' *Dinner and a play*, can you believe that?"

"Taking Lotus the hooker to a Broadway play and Sardi's after for dinner? No, I can't," Hailey said matter-of-factly.

"But Hailey, do you think he'd actually go through with it? I keep telling myself no, that it's like all the other online chats and phone-sex services, that he never follows through. Or am I just fooling myself?" Teary-eyed, Karen plucked one of the last tissues from the bottom of the box and looked at Hailey, for reassurance and comforting.

"Karen, you've had the man followed by a private dick eight, is it ten times now? Phone and computer sex aside, if you're asking whether I honestly think he goes any further than just fantasizing like a million other guys in America, I'd still say no. I'm willing to bet that so far, the worst he's done is BS strippers in the clubs, and believe me, they've heard it all before. He never even takes one home. That we know of."

"So that means . . ."

"So that means I'm sticking with the international-man-of-mystery theory."

Karen burst into laughter and blew her nose. "Remember when Harry double-confirmed James never actually hooked up with that pharmaceutical sales rep?"

Hailey definitely did remember the emergency wee-hour call she'd received a few weeks ago when Karen found out James had a new phone number on speed dial. Karen matched it up with a number James stashed, hidden under "Chinese Take-out" in his Black-Berry.

Two thousand dollars later, Harry the Private Eye had discovered the woman was a married pharmaceutical sales rep James met at a hotel bar in Florida. Ever since, the two had burned up the lines with phone sex whenever Sharon hit the road out of Tallahassee to peddle allergy medicine.

That was abruptly curtailed, however, when Karen called the girl and threatened to tell Lance, her unsuspecting, redneck husband.

"Karen, I'm just curious, not judging one way or another, but how much more do you plan to spend on private dicks?" The question met with dead silence.

Hailey went on. "Is it really worth living with all the singles sites, the online chats, the hooker sites? Will you always need to know everything about what he's doing when he's not with you? Think about it . . . when you're fifty, will you still be going through his pockets and reading his e-mails? Wouldn't life be great with someone you trust? Or do you even remember anymore what that feeling is like? It's a wonderful feeling, Karen, and you deserve that in your life."

"Come on, you know I hate therapy talk. Fifty years old is still twenty years away."

"Karen . . . this *is* therapy. You're paying me one-fifty an hour, remember?"

"One-fifty's not bad, and the insurance splits it fifty-fifty with me."

"You're hedging."

"That's because I don't know all the answers. That's what you're for. I come here for answers and you beat me up with questions." Karen sighed. "Can I just have some hot tea? Maybe with milk, just to be crazy."

"I'll fix it. What kind?"

"Sleepy Time?"

"It's still morning . . ."

"To counteract all the caffeine I've had already."

Hailey, sensing Karen shifting subjects short of reaching any tough decisions, headed to the kitchen to start brewing the tea.

From her perch on the sofa, Karen called out, "And would you please not call Harry a dick? He's a certified, licensed private investigator and was highly recommended by a girl at work."

"Okay." Hailey pulled down Karen's favorite Celestial Seasonings tea from the cabinet over the counter, along with two coffee cups.

"And he's worth every penny, just like you are. Even if insurance isn't splitting his fee," Karen went on from the next room.

"I'm so flattered," Hailey called out.

Karen went into the suite's tiny bathroom and Hailey could hear her blowing her nose through the door. The commode flushed, and Karen called out through the closed door, "Hey, why do you keep all these framed law degrees hung in the bathroom? If I had all these, they'd be on display under a spotlight! What's *Law Review*?"

Hailey paused and remembered hanging them over the toilet the day she moved into this office suite and started a new life. "Oh, I don't know why I did that," she called back. "Just making fun of all the pompous lawyers I've ever known, I guess."

She tossed it off as a joke, but inside, Hailey knew why. On a Freudian level, the positioning of Hailey's law degree, awards, and achievements there in her patients' bathroom silently spoke volumes.

No more trying to right a world that was broken when Will was murdered. She had been saturated in her own crusade, a crusade that left her tired and broken at the end of the day, a crusade that forced her to relive Will's murder with every felon she tried.

Hanging her law degrees perfectly centered over the crapper seemed to be poetic justice.

How clearly she remembered packing her trial materials for the last time the night the Cruise verdict came down. She had just watched the mothers, fathers, and loved ones of eleven murder victims troop out of the courtroom for the last time.

Karen emerged from Hailey's bathroom with a red nose, but smiling.

They drank their tea and hugged good-bye, as always.

Hailey's next scheduled patient was Melissa Everett, but she still had about fifteen minutes—and that was if Melissa made it on time.

Leaving her office door unlocked, Hailey went across the hall to knock on Dana's. Her *Post* had been missing again this morning, and she had a good idea where to find it.

"Hailey!" Dana was there, with her coat on and her bag slung over her shoulder. "What's up?"

"Are you going somewhere?"

"Just getting back. I had lunch with Greg. He wanted to make up for breaking our date last night."

"That's nice." Hailey had heard all about that this morning. Of course Dana had been beside herself, worried that the new guy had already lost interest after they'd been going strong for a whole week.

Dana had really been looking forward to the date, too. She'd bragged about it for days ahead of time and obsessed over what to wear and how much she weighed.

Through it all, Hailey wondered whether to mention Adam. Dana pressed her for details after that first dinner, and for days afterward. But when Hailey had nothing more to report, Dana lost interest.

Something told Hailey not to share Adam's pursuit. She couldn't quite figure it out herself. Adam was great . . . in theory, but some lingering doubt, some nagging concern, something made Hailey leery. It was nothing she could put her finger on. But it wasn't as if she could get a word in edgewise anyway, with all Dana's excitement over Greg.

"You know, he's really incredible, Hailey. Did I tell you he told me he's going to cook dinner for me on Valentine's Day next week?"

Hailey nodded. "You did."

"Greg's just so sweet, and such a gentleman—he's got old-fashioned manners. Did I tell you he's from the South?"

She had . . . along with everything else there was to know about Greg, a recent transplant from somewhere. He was great-looking and said he'd never been married—perfect, in other words, for Dana.

"I can't wait till you meet him," Dana said. She hurriedly shed her coat and pulled out a compact. "You're going to love him."

"He sounds really nice. What does he do for a living? Does he have a job?"

"Something legal, I think. I mean, I know he has a law degree. Hey! Maybe he can get someone for you and we can double date! You're lawyers . . . you'd have so much in common."

"That's okay, I hate blind dates."

"Hailey, I'm sure you don't want to spend another Valentine's Day all alone. I'll see if Greg has a friend for you."

"Isn't he new in town? I'm sure he doesn't. And even if he does, I'm not . . ." She broke off, hearing footsteps coming up the stairs.

"I hear a client, gotta go. Thanks anyway."

She was sure it would be Melissa, but the footsteps turned out to be Dana's next appointment. Hailey made a beeline for her own office, grateful to be extricated from the whole Valentine's Day setup thing.

Only after she'd closed the door did she remember she'd forgotten to ask Dana for her *Post*. And now she finally had a chance to read it. Five minutes went by, ten, fifteen.

Hailey looked up Melissa's home number and dialed it.

"Melissa, hi dear . . . it's Hailey. We had an appointment at two o'clock . . . did you forget? Don't worry. I'm here, waiting for you. Give me a call when you get this."

She hung up. Being late had become Melissa's routine, and Hailey had come to accept it, but it didn't stop her from worrying. Hailey methodically busied herself, finishing paperwork, watering plants, and rinsing out the coffee mugs, keeping one eye on the clock.

A half hour had passed, then an hour.

Still no Melissa.

But Mazz showed up, right on time for his own appointment.

"I had a new dream about the monkey," he announced, flopping into the chair opposite Hailey.

Atlanta, Georgia

"SO WHAT DO YOU SAY, FLOYD MOYE? HOW ABOUT WE MEET TO-night at Bones for a little dead cow and some serious bour-bon and branch?" C.C. leaned back in his chair, feet propped on his desk, even more pleased with himself than usual.

"That'd be great, C.C.," Eugene agreed. "I'll see you there at eight."

"Eight o'clock it is."

C.C. reached just far enough off his chair to hang up the phone.

So it was all set. Over dinner at the most expensive steak house in Atlanta, they'd meet with the State Democratic sub-chairman to nail down plans for C.C.'s grand announcement for the governor's race.

It had to be classy and steeped in judicial decorum, something he'd learned early on from the other members of the bench. Judges could get away with pretty much anything if they just kept look-ing judicial, and even more so if they spoke *with their robe on.*

But damn, he'd have to invite Betty up from Dooley County for the El Grande Candidacy Announcement Celebration. Somehow, he'd have to ditch Betty and sneak Tina over. This would take some doing.

Think ... think ... think!

Betty's presence in Atlanta would mean he'd have to say bye-bye to any thoughts of an after-party with Tina. C.C.'s pink fuzzy would be pissed beyond belief. She loved special moments together.

How on earth could he maneuver this?

Oh, hell, he'd just have to burn that bridge when he got there.

He opened his top drawer and pulled out his flask. It was cool and comforting, smooth and familiar to the touch. It had seen him through some mighty tough times, mighty tough. He needed it now—and how.

The phone call with Eugene arranging tonight's meeting put him so on edge he could barely throw back a drink.

Shit. There was something freaky about that man, always so damn secretive, so damn uptight, meticulously demanding all sorts of details about C.C.'s calendar and whereabouts.

But hey . . . who gave a crap? C.C. was packing for the state capital, thanks to Eugene.

He took a pull before his secretary could barge back in. Now that was *nice* . . . bourbon, room temp. Why spoil it with ice?

|||||||||||||||||||||||||||||||||||||||||||||||||||||||||||||| **36** |||||||||||||||||||||

New York City

PATIENTS CAME AND WENT. THE AFTERNOON DWINDLED AND DIS-appeared before Hailey looked out the double windows into the courtyard again, and when she did, darkness was settling across the Village.

The building was silent—no more muffled noises seeping up through hardwood floors. The ring of office phones, doors below opening and closing, muffled laughter of receptionists and dental hygienists and their patients, even the occasional strains of dentist-office Muzak had all ceased for the day.

Hailey clicked off one of the floor lamps near the foyer and walked through the office, straightening things here and there, wondering uneasily why Melissa never called back.

It wasn't necessarily uncharacteristic of her to ignore a message—but she usually kept her appointments, and when she couldn't, she always called to cancel.

According to the microwave's clock, glowing green in the darkened kitchen, it was already six fifteen.

Hailey dialed over to Dana to ask if she'd like to have dinner, deciding to forgo running the East River in lieu of companionship tonight. No answer.

That was strange. Dana always stuck her head in to say goodnight.

Hailey considered trying to catch her on her cell, then opted not to.

Maybe it was a blessing in disguise; she'd logged eight hours straight without a lunch break, then another hour's work on an article she hoped to publish, about the origins of self-hatred. Her session with Hayden today had infused her with new thought and perspective, but also left her tired, more mentally than physically.

She had noticed dark circles showing under her eyes in her office bathroom earlier that afternoon when she'd splashed water on her face between patients.

Okay. So maybe she'd still skip her jog and try her best to sleep. But before she left the office, she'd try Melissa one more time. She flipped open her appointment book and dialed the number.

"Hi, it's Melissa . . . I'm not here, so please leave me a message. I promise I'll call you back."

The simple greeting was somehow haunting, almost wistful. Maybe a tiny clue of a yearning for a childhood lost.

"Hey, Melissa . . . it's Hailey again." She made sure her voice was casually upbeat. Melissa didn't need a guilt trip over the missed appointment. "I wanted to check with you about rescheduling today's session. I know you have my home and cell."

Hailey hung up, hearing footsteps heading up the hallway and into Dana's office.

She hurriedly threw the rest of her things into her bag, closed and locked her door, and crossed the hall. She'd make a peace offering of dinner at Candle Café, one of their favorites.

"Dana?"

No reply, but the door was ajar, so Hailey slipped in.

Darkness and an eerie quiet blanketed the room, though Hailey could hear distant music from a radio somewhere in the building.

"Dana?"

Maybe she wasn't here after all. *Where was she?* Hailey had just heard her come back up the steps. The door was unlocked, but Dana, like the dentists downstairs, wasn't concerned about security. She often said that if anyone wanted to steal anything from her cluttered office, they were welcome to it.

"Dana?"

Hailey glanced out Dana's windows across the street at the vacant building under reconstruction, looking shell-shocked in the night. She was so glad she had ended up with the back office—what a dismal view.

She turned away and spotted Dana's office trash can, tipped over by the door, Hailey's kidnapped *Post* spilling out of it.

Trash can spilling, no good-bye, and no returned *Post* as customary . . . Dana must have really been in a hurry tonight. She usually returned the paper every afternoon, with the same clock-like regularity as taking it.

Well, hopefully she was on a date, although Vegas odds were next to nothing Dana could have a date and not talk about it for days ahead of time.

She fished the *Post* out of the trash, the pages out of order. She went over to Dana's coffee table to spread it out neatly, reassembling it in order to read it on the way home.

Pages two and forty-three, joined at the spine, were missing.

She made another trip to the trash can and found the missing pages, oddly singled out, balled up tightly and buried in a pile of discarded bills and psych journals.

Hailey flattened the missing pages out on the table.

She froze. The grainy black-and-white photo.

It was Melissa.

Melissa Everett was on page two.

Melissa was the dead girl . . . the girl they'd found on the East Side last night.

An anguished, painful moan came from somewhere far away.

It took a moment for Hailey to recognize that it had come from the back of her own throat.

She tried to hold up the paper to look again at the photo, but her hands were shaking erratically, as if they belonged to someone else. She saw them, but couldn't make them stop. Ice water ran through her veins, instead of warm, red blood.

She stumbled toward a cushioned chair to sit down in the darkened room.

Yes . . . sit down and read the article . . . there had to be a mistake . . . Melissa couldn't be dead . . . she was scheduled for an appointment . . . Hailey could help her . . .

Before she could make it to the chair, quietly, out of nowhere, someone came up behind her.

She sensed movement, started to turn, but it was too late.

A crushing blow landed on the back of Hailey's head and neck.

Pain shot through her face as she tried to stand, but she tumbled forward from the momentum of the blow. Careening across the sidearm of the chair, she went down hard onto the sharp corner of Dana's coffee table.

Warm blood began to seep from just behind her temple. Through dark gray swirls that were closing in on her, she saw a pair of blue-jeaned legs approach her at floor level. One of them was limping.

She tried, tried with all her strength, to turn and look up to see his face, to call out for help, but her body refused to follow her brain's command.

She couldn't turn, couldn't speak, her neck and face burned by the wool of the rug, her mouth open as she tried to breathe, blood across her lips and cheek.

When the first, vicious kick landed, perfectly aimed at her kidneys, Hailey screamed out in pain, but the scream went muffled into the carpet and then, with the next excruciating kick, the dark gray swirls disappeared. Hailey Dean's world went black.

|||||||||||||||||||||||||||||||||||||||||||||||||||||||||||||| **37** |||||||||||||||||||

St. Simons Island,
Georgia

I T WAS NEARLY 3 A.M., AND THE GUERRILLAS WERE ASSEMBLED IN THE stealthiest and most mysterious black outfits they could muster, hoping to blend into the night like the cat burglars they'd seen on TV. Clustered amid the pines outside Palmetto Dunes Luxury Living, they were locked and loaded, primed and ready for the moment they'd waited for their whole lives.

There would be plenty of time ahead to plan an overall strategy for a meaningful deterrent strike at the mastermind of Palmetto Dunes Luxury Living. But for now, for tonight, the guerrillas were taking a notorious page from the Vietcong's book.

A sniper attack was the only obvious choice for a successful strike against a power much greater than the guerrillas: a construction company out of Atlanta with big money backing.

From behind the cover of dense pine saplings, twelve pairs of eyes were trained on the solitary guard inside his shack. Biding their time, they waited, poised, for just the right moment to attack.

"Anybody seen him before?" Virginia asked in a whisper.

None of the twelve were sure who he was, although they speculated in minced whispers, until it dawned on Renee.

"I know who he is! He's the guy that works security for the Brunswick Wal-Mart."

"He must've gotten a serious pay increase," Ken chimed in. Ken was an authority on many, many subjects, and apparently the compensation at Wal-Mart was one of them. "I happen to know for a fact the security guards at Wal-Mart eat free at the Wal-Mart grill."

Free lunch or no free lunch, in exchange for the speculated pay raise, he was now sitting alone in a glorified outhouse at three in the morning, watching TBS.

But there he sat, apparently mesmerized by a late-, late-, late-night TBS showing of *Conan the Barbarian*.

After fifteen minutes or so of keen surveillance, Virginia was convinced the guard was actually going to watch *Conan the Barbarian* in its entirety, so there was no use waiting for him to fall asleep. The good news was he was so engrossed in the movie he wouldn't possibly notice any movement outside.

Virginia gave the command.

The guerrillas obediently slipped through the pines.

Without speaking, they moved on, past the guardhouse—then stopped short, all of them, all at once.

There it loomed, about twenty yards ahead: a horrible, man-made clearing where once there had been a series of graceful, sweeping dunes.

They simply stood, gazing at the scarred landscape.

Then Virginia gave a firm nod.

They stepped out of the pines to begin the endless task of dragging Palmetto Dunes Luxury Living—the whole kit and caboodle, load by load—to the water's edge

Thin pine slats lay precisely over the ground to mark the outlines where cement would be poured. Now they were yanked away and placed on bedsheets they'd brought from home. Along with the slats went the strings that had been measured, cut, and staked with an engineer's unquestioned accuracy. Every vestige of orange marker was untied from surrounding trees. Bag upon heavy bag of dry concrete mixture was lugged across the sand.

Against all their deepest, heartfelt convictions against littering in *any* form, they heaped it all there on the shore. Mother Nature would have the morning tide take most of it, wave by rhythmic wave, out to sea and, ultimately, to the ocean's floor. In a matter of hours, the fishies would be gnawing delicately at the stripped-down boards, still smelling of sweet pinesap.

|||||||||||||||||||||||||||||||||||||||||||||||||||||||||||||||| **38** ||||||||||||||||||||

New York City

"HAILEY. CAN YOU HEAR ME AT ALL? HAILEY, WAKE UP."
Hailey heard it all, but from far away. She thought Fincher had been standing over her, calling her name, but then he disappeared. Hailey's eyes opened to a pale-green hospital room, the faint smell of medicine hanging in the air.

Dana was standing beside her.

"What . . . happened?" she whispered. Even her throat hurt.

"You fell and knocked yourself out, Hailey. You took a really bad blow to the head."

"What? Where? What are you doing here? Where are we?"

"You were in my office."

Right. Dana's office . . .

It was all so fuzzy, though.

"Where are we now?"

"The hospital. You've been out for hours, and I've been worried sick. How do you feel?"

Hailey opened her mouth to answer, but Dana shook her head. "No, don't try to talk. Now that you're awake, I'll call a doctor to come check on you."

"Dana, don't, I'm fine." She tried to sit up to prove her point, and a sharp pain shot through her torso.

Tears sprung to her eyes and spilled down her cheeks.

"See? You are not fine!"

She sank back against the pillows. "You said I hit my head, but it's my side that's killing me. What happened to me, exactly?"

"How would I know? I wasn't there! I can't believe you don't remember it all. Meanwhile, I'm a *wreck*, Hailey, nothing but a *wreck*! I swear I'm going to have a breakdown over this whole thing and—"

"If you don't tell me what—"

"Okay, okay, o-*kay* . . . here's what happened. I'm minding my own business, as always, on my way home after one of those *horrible* singles mixers at MOMA, I don't know why I even *bothered* to go, they're always disasters, and besides, I do have Greg, but he was busy last night, and like I always say, you shouldn't put all your eggs in one basket, am I right about that?"

"Right," Hailey said weakly, knowing Dana expected a response. It hurt to speak. It hurt to breathe.

"So I stopped back at work, thinking he might have come by and left a note on the door, because he's done that before, and I found you lying in my office, out cold. You lost a lot of blood, too, on the rug. Don't worry though, I think the dry cleaner can fix it. You split your head wide open on the coffee table. I know you have really low blood pressure. You must have passed out. Or maybe you tripped and fell—my office was kind of a mess—but how did you get those *horrible* bruises down your ribs and hips? What are you, a professional stunt girl, too? You must have done one crazy flip."

My office was kind of a mess . . .

Suddenly Hailey sat up in bed again. A sharp pain sliced through her head and an incredible ache pierced her ribs, but she barely noticed.

The *Post* article.

"Oh my God, Melissa." She felt sick to her stomach, and the warm taste of vomit came up her throat and to the back of her mouth.

"No . . . I'm not Melissa. Hailey, it's me, Dana."

"No, Dana, it's Melissa . . ."

"No, you're Hailey. *Haaay-leee.* Oh, my God. I'll go get a doctor."

"Dana, no . . ."

The door opened abruptly, stopping Dana in her tracks.

A tall, angular man in his late thirties, looking too weather-beaten and deeply tanned for a New Yorker, came in uninvited. His face was hard, with a cool glint in a pair of icy-blue eyes and a square, seemingly immovable jaw. Dana turned on him. "Excuse us, this is a *private* room."

"And *this* is an NYPD badge, miss." He casually took it out of his jacket pocket and flipped open his shield.

"Which one of you is Hailey Dean?"

St. Simons Island,
Georgia

L OOKING OUT PAST THE HORIZON, THEY SAW THE SUN BEGINNING
to show itself over the edge of the water.

"Come on, let's go." Virginia whispered it as loudly as she could, turning to the others and motioning.

They quickly made it back through the trees and past the security post. The guard, now snoozing gently, was still sitting straight up, with his back against the closed door of the guardhouse.

The guerrillas headed across the road and tried their best to blend into a stand of palmettos as they limped along.

Once past the thick stand of pointy plants, it was backwoods all the way until at last they circled back around to Larry's 7-Eleven parking lot. Without a word exchanged among them, they climbed into three cars where they'd been left. They cranked up and drove into the half-dark, half-light of the Island dawn.

They'd made it, they were home free. Months of planning, weeks of labor, and incredible expense on the part of Palmetto Dunes Luxury Living had been bravely and beautifully destroyed in a single night at the guerrillas' hands.

Vengeance was sweet.

Tonight, they had risen to greatness: shucked off their mall uniforms, their laminated company ID cards worn on chains around their necks, their plastic Radio Shack name tags.

The battle was on.

The guerrillas had struck back.

Vengeance all right, with a bullet.

New York City

L YING THERE IN HER HOSPITAL BED, HAILEY DIDN'T BOTHER TO CHECK the guy's ID when he casually took it out of his jacket and flipped open his shield.

She didn't have to. He was definitely a cop. No question about it. He had that look, immediately and easily identifiable by both fellow law enforcement and the people they spent their lives chasing.

She could spot one a mile away, even in plainclothes. They stood out in crowds of civilians like sore thumbs, if you knew what to look for.

The younger officers kept buff, muscled bodies for foot chases and arresting suspects who fought them tooth and nail. On the other end of the spectrum, cops who had been around for a while turned soft and pale. They were beaten-down, their exciting years of chasing the bad guys melted into desk jobs, brewing coffee at the precinct, and counting the days until retirement.

It wasn't just the clothes or accessories. It was the way they wore them, the way they carried themselves, the intangible attitude that screamed out, "Look at me . . . I'm a cop."

"Repeat, ladies. Which one of you is Hailey Dean?"

"I'm Hailey Dean. Who are you?"

"Lieutenant Kolker. I'd like to ask you a few questions about a young lady I think you know, Melissa Everett."

The name slammed into her and stole her breath away. Melissa. For a few minutes, she had put it out of her mind.

Too upset to speak, she paused briefly. In that moment, he went on.

"You *are* Hailey Dean of Dean Counseling, correct?" he asked, though he knew full well the room was in her name, and that, of the two women, the one in the bed wearing a cotton gown would be his best bet.

"Yes, I'm Hailey Dean," she said slowly, retracing her way through dim memories. "I had just thought of Melissa exactly when you opened the door. I . . . I think the reason I'm here is, in a way, because of Melissa."

"Really."

"I must have passed out. It's happened a few times before. Please tell me I dreamed it." Her thoughts were disconnected and her speech was dull.

He leaned forward. "Tell you that you dreamed what?"

"Was Melissa reported in the *Post* as being . . ." *No. Don't say it. Don't make it true. . . .*

"Is she missing?" Hailey finally got the question out.

"Well, Miss Dean, you're right *and* wrong. There was an article this morning in the *Post*. But Melissa's not missing. She was found last night around midnight. She's dead."

Hailey was silent, hot tears filling her eyes.

It wasn't a nightmare. It was real.

Melissa was dead.

"What happened?" she asked, and her voice broke on a sob.

"So you really don't know?"

She shook her head, turning her face away from the two of them and wiping tears on the top edge of her sheet. She managed to ask, "Was it a suicide?"

Even as she said the words, they didn't ring true.

But why else would he be here to see her?

"I was just with her last week," she said in a rush. "She seemed to be doing so much better. . . . I mean, Melissa was disturbed, but Lieutenant, she wanted to *live*. I'm sure of it."

"Miss Dean, you've got it wrong. I'm not here for your professional opinion as a psychologist. Melissa Everett was murdered. She was definitely stabbed to death, possibly strangled as well. We're waiting on the official cause of death from the morgue . . .

and she may have been molested. It's early on . . . but the way she was found . . ."

"You mean without shoes? Bare-legged?"

"Oh . . . so you remember that, Hailey? I thought it was all confused and mixed-up for you."

Why was he being so obnoxious? No wonder people don't cooperate with police.

"Well, I recall hearing that on 1010 WINS. I had no idea the body was Melissa."

"As I said, there's absolutely no question as to cause of death. Suicide was never even an option. And, Miss Dean . . . the last thing in her date book was an appointment with you."

"Yes, I was her psychologist."

Kolker just looked at Hailey.

Lying there on the single hospital bed, staring at the plainclothes officer, it all became real to Hailey.

Melissa's battle with her nightmares, her demons, her ruptured childhood was over.

She was dead. Murdered.

Hailey's chest hurt imagining the horror Melissa must have suffered at the hands of a killer.

All her prosecutions had convinced Hailey that suffocation in any form, especially strangulation, was one of the most painful ways to die. The victim was normally fully cognizant until the very end, knowing death loomed as lungs collapsed, eyes hemorrhaged, face contorted in death. But here, two painful possible causes of death? One wasn't enough?

Hailey could hardly bear it. The beautiful, tortured woman who still looked like a girl, trying so bravely to live life whole and well, not an ounce of hatred in her body, now gone as if she never existed.

Just like Will.

The news about Melissa forced her back to when she had discovered Will was murdered. Now, as then, it seemed like a big misunderstanding, mistaken information.

She remembered thinking, frantically, that Will wasn't dead, that he was fine . . . or if he wasn't fine, there had been an accident, but he *would* be fine, if she could only get to him in time.

And then, the reality.

Will *was* dead, he had been murdered, there was no accident, and there was nothing she could do to help him.

And this time, like last, there had been no accident, no mistake.

The *Post* was right. Melissa was the dead girl. Hailey's Melissa . . . her patient, her friend.

They had been through so much together, hours and hours spent alone in Hailey's suite, reliving Melissa's childhood nightmares, each trying their hardest, in their own way, to build a new life.

"I was hoping you could shed some light on her recent whereabouts, her friends, and her lifestyle," Lieutenant Kolker was telling Hailey from someplace far away. "We found your business card in her purse, with your personal cell number on it and what appears to be your home phone number and address."

Hailey's head was spinning; she could only nod, trying to make sense of what he was saying—trying to make sense of everything.

"Isn't that unusual, Miss Dean? I've never had a doctor give me his home number or address before. What exactly was the nature of your relationship with Melissa Everett?"

The questions were too much for Hailey, her head still pounding from the blow. Her eyes were unfocused and her face was hot. Sitting up in the bed, grief came over her again in waves, and with a broken sob, the tears came. "Please leave," she said abruptly.

"Excuse me?"

"Lieutenant, I need to see a doctor. Dana, thanks for coming to see about me and speaking to the hospital staff. I'll call you later, promise."

"But Hailey, how will you make it home? Let me come pick you up."

She didn't look up at either of them. "Thanks," she said flatly.

"Remember, I've got the keys to your apartment and office. I'll even stop by your place and pick up whatever you need, okay?"

"Okay. Right now I just need to get myself together. Really." She tried not to sound impatient, but her head was spinning and she wanted desperately to be alone.

The two stood looking at each other in awkward silence, not knowing quite what to do.

"Okay. I'm on my cell. Call me." Dana gathered her assorted belongings and backed out, leaving Lieutenant Kolker standing beside the bed.

After a moment's silence, he turned and left, saying, "We'll talk again, Hailey."

|||||||||||||||||||||||||||||||||||||||||||||||||||||||||||||||| **41** |||||||||||||||||||

New York City

HUDDLED INTO A BACK BOOTH IN A COFFEE SHOP OFF BROADWAY, Cruise decided he didn't like New York.

No, hate was a better way to describe his feelings. The city was dirty, and noisy—but that was no big deal. He was used to that in Atlanta.

New York, however, was cold. A brutal cold that seeped into his bones and, worst of all, chapped his hands . . . hands that were burning again.

It was Hailey Dean.

These past days he'd thought of her incessantly. Watching her go in and out of her apartment building, up and down her office steps, standing at her office window looking out onto the courtyard . . . it was all torture.

That first blow to her face felt so good. He'd wanted to for so long.

Just as he dreamed night after night back in Reidsville, it felt so good . . . the pain he'd inflicted on her. It was beyond any words he knew to describe it. There would have been more if he hadn't heard someone coming up the steps.

"What'll it be?" a heavyset waitress asked brusquely, parking herself in front of the booth where he'd situated himself to escape the cold outside for a while.

"Coffee."

"And?"

"Just coffee."

Irritated with him for taking up her booth with just coffee, she all but stormed away.

If only he had her alone for five minutes . . .

That was the other thing Cruise hated about New York. The people.

They couldn't be bothered to give you the time of day.

If it weren't for Hailey, he wouldn't be here. Again, her fault.

He waited for his coffee and thought about the first time he'd ever laid eyes on her in the Fulton County Superior Courthouse. The courtroom had been packed that morning, with lawyers and witnesses and inmates in prison orange, chained together by leg irons so they couldn't make a run for it.

He'd been chained, too, directly to the chair which was bolted to the floor of the jury box.

When everyone was assembled and the clock had struck precisely nine o'clock, the back double doors of the courtroom swung open, like a gust had blown in, and with it came Hailey Dean.

She was wearing a black long-sleeved dress that hit just above the knees. He still remembered the blonde hair falling down below her shoulders.

No one had spoken, but it was clear the attorneys and inmates alike all knew *this* bitch on wheels was calling the shots.

When the judge took the bench and the calendar clerk called his name and case number, Hailey Dean had looked directly at him, shackled in his chair.

Holding his gaze, Hailey announced in open court that the first arraignment of the morning was his. He'd tried to stand up in spite of the chains.

She said it real cold-like . . . that she planned to try the case of Clint Burrell Cruise herself and that after consultation with the elected district attorney, *the State* intended to seek the death penalty.

He never made it out of his chair; the chains were biting too hard into his ankles to stand.

Between months of court appearances came the endless shots of her, sound bites at press conferences on the local news.

He watched them religiously.

She won, of course.

Which meant he lost.

Then, after the trial, she left him abruptly.

When she was gone, it all seemed empty. He was like a dry drunk . . . stuck with nothing but old newspaper clippings to keep him company.

It sucked.

He'd had no reason to live when she left him alone, warehoused away, locked up like an animal.

But thanks to the Internet in the law library, he'd found her. Yahoo was incredible. In all the interviews after the trial, she'd been tight-lipped about her plans, but then . . . he struck gold.

The Georgia Bar's yearly directory mistakenly published a New York number under her old Atlanta address, and thanks to Yahoo's reverse lookup, her address was cake. Further proof lawyers were total screwups.

So. After leaving him there, behind forty-five feet of concrete wall, *Hailey* wanted to start all over without him, to get on with her new life in New York.

But he wasn't going to let her leave him behind.

It all came down to right now. Finally, they were back together again.

And after all these years, he wasn't ready to say good-bye just yet.

|||||||||||||||||||||||||||||||||||||||||||||||||||||||||||||| **42** |||||||||||||||||

St. Simons Island,
Georgia

V IRGINIA WOKE UP GROGGY, HER SHOULDER AND ARM MUSCLES hurting, hurting like crazy.

That was strange. Something was wrong. . . .

The night before hit her and she sat upright like a bolt of lightning . . . they did it!

Strike one against the empire.

She eased out of bed, her legs sore from the use of muscles she hadn't even thought of in twenty years. She made her way down the steps—easy-does-it, one at a time—until she made it to the ground floor.

Immediately, the wieners were awake, racing toward her en masse. The high-pitched yelps pierced her brain like a jackhammer.

"Shut up! Sidney . . . shut up, damn it!"

The pack cowered back in bewilderment, crouched with their tails between their stubby little legs.

She padded barefoot straight to the front door, opened it, and retrieved the morning paper.

The front page said it all.

"ISLAND VANDALS ATTACK!"

She closed the door and started reading. Analyzing each word, she propped herself up on the kitchen bar, lowering her reading glasses down to the tip of her nose.

She read it slowly; she didn't want to miss a single word.

|||||||||||||||||||||||||||||||||||||||||||||||||||||||||||||||| **43** ||||||||||||||||||

St. Simons Island, Georgia

A T THE VERY MINUTE VIRGINIA GUNN WAS BREAKING INTO A DEEP belly laugh over the Palmetto Dunes security guard's speculating to the paper that stealth terrorists were responsible for last night's debacle, just a few miles across town the Glynn County Commission chairman was sweating bullets, even with the office window unit on high.

Toby McKissick sat glued to the seat of his brown faux-leather office chair. Four feet of polished oak was the only thing that separated him from the other side of the desk.

There sat Floyd Moye Eugene, darkly shaded aviator glasses covering his eyes and allowing no clue as to his thinking.

But Toby knew Eugene's reputation well—and something told him Eugene knew his.

Toby's life centered around dodging his wife, seeking political favor with the bigs in Atlanta, scheming to put another dollar in his pocket, and chasing tail twenty-four/seven.

He owed so many grifters so many political favors he could hardly keep them straight in his own head. Plus, there were always the do-gooders nipping at his heels. And there was the constant fear of exposure . . . that all his "deals" and "favors" would catch up with him.

But all that was nothing compared to this.

For fifteen minutes now, Toby had been trying to explain why, exactly, the Island police had not yet pinpointed the vandals who had completely destroyed the foundational beginnings of Palmetto Dunes Luxury Living.

"Floyd, I agree two hundred percent, Palmetto Dunes is exactly what the south beaches need. I speak for the Commission in that we absolutely support you in this. It's a travesty, a *sin* that the beach has just *lain there*, undeveloped, for years."

Toby's lower parts burned like crazy. He thought he was about to pass out. His urologist warned him repeatedly about stress. In the past few months, since the hush-hush deal with Eugene started up, his kidney stones were worse than ever. He'd already passed nearly twenty of the pellet-size little monsters in all, and he could feel one coming right now.

The pain of passing his second stone of the day nearly made Toby faint. The first had been pissed straight into a Styrofoam Krispy Kreme doughnut coffee cup this morning on the way to work when he got the word about Eugene.

Eugene's stare, or at least what Toby took to be a stare from behind Eugene's darkened shades, made his groin hurt even more. Here it comes, and there's not a thing he could do about it. No way could he make it to the men's room down the hall.

"Ah . . . Floyd . . . you'll have to excuse me . . . damn!" The pain washed over him. It was all he could do to stand at the foot of his desk and whiz straight into his metal trash can. In midstream, a tiny metallic "ping" thunked loudly into the metal can, ricocheting off one side, plunking to the bottom. With a series of groans, winces, and twitches, the agony ended.

In the quiet of the office, Eugene sat unmoving, staring straight at McKissick's bare butt. Toby fell back into his chair, faint, and the chair rolled back of its own volition. His legs hung on the sides of the chair like sticks. When the chair came to a halt, the two men locked eyes.

Toby shifted his weight in his chair and struggled to keep his composure as Eugene stared hard at him.

Finally, Eugene said, "What the hell was that?" Eugene stared at McKissick, unblinking.

"Have you ever had stones, Floyd?"

"Can't say that I have, McKissick, but I can now report with one hundred percent accuracy that I truly doubt whether you and your people can handle the situation down here. Frankly, I'm not convinced you fit into the deal anymore. It may just be too big for you to handle."

"No Floyd . . . I'm on it. I'm all over it. I'll get new security and ramp it up. No more all-night shifts for one person. We'll rotate like military units do. Constantly changing guards throughout the night. This won't happen again. I swear it. And Floyd, I'll find the vandals. Probably teenagers. Trust me, it's taken care of. Go back to Atlanta, I'll call you the second we find out who tore up the layout."

Eugene sat for well over a minute in stony silence, just looking at the disheveled mess of a man sitting in front of him.

"Damn," Eugene said at last, "you're one fat, pathetic mess."

"If you just give me one more chance, Floyd, I know we can handle the whole thing. You won't be sorry. Pulling out on our people at this point is very premature and—"

"Premature? You idiot! You country-hick moron. This sets us back at least three weeks. Money's at stake here, you hayseed Billy-Bob. More money than you've ever dreamed about in your miserable little life. Now listen to me and you listen good. One more chance. And for God's sakes, keep it quiet. I'm sending the crew out first thing in the morning to restart. One more screwup on the security end, you're over. I know about every two-bit bribe you've ever taken. You don't fool a single damn soul with your Rotary luncheons and your Kiwanis membership. I know your broke-down deal in this town and I'll blow you wide open if I have to.

There'll be nothing left for the locals to do with you but indict your sorry ass. Understood?"

Eugene turned on his heel and left. Toby could hear his footsteps on the tile of the hallway, passing by Toby's secretary and heading to the front door. She brightly offered him coffee to go but Eugene brushed by her without answering. He never once removed his glasses.

The sound of the front door slamming made it all the way back to Toby's office and then the offices settled into quiet, except for the humming of the window unit. Toby sank his forehead down into his hands.

But in one brief moment of clarity, a single thought rang through Toby's head like a bell in a belfry.

Virginia Gunn.

IIIIIIIIIIIIIIIIIIIIIIIIIIIIIIIIIIIIIIIIIIIIIIIIIIIIIIIIIIIIII **44** IIIIIIIIIIIIIIIIII

New York City

HAILEY PLAYED OVER AND OVER IN HER HEAD THE LAST TIME SHE met with Melissa.

She could hardly think. Had she missed something?

Was there a clue to a problem, some sort of menace? Could she have averted disaster in some way?

Who had done this to Melissa?

Had she suffered?

Of course she had. There was no way of getting around the sheer horror of Melissa's last moments.

A double knock at her door swung her around again. Her side throbbed.

"Come in," Hailey called out in the direction of the door.

"Hi, Hailey." A man appeared, dark hair and eyes, handsome in a way, wearing a white coat. He closed the door behind him. "I'm Dr. Lopez."

"Hi, Doctor. Thank you for coming by, it's nice to meet you."

"Actually, we've already met, but you probably don't remember. I admitted you in the ER. How are you feeling?"

"Hurting." She was thinking of Melissa.

"Who's the goon with a badge outside your door?"

"Good question. I take it he's still there?"

Dr. Lopez nodded emphatically. "You took quite a beating, Hailey. Boyfriend . . . Husband? You can be totally candid with me. Everything we say is protected by my oath as a doctor."

Hailey's jaw dropped, her eyes widened, and then she laughed. "Thank you for your concern, Doctor, but I'm not keeping anything from you. I wasn't beaten. I was just . . . shocked."

He looked confused for a moment, then skeptical.

"No, *really*," she said, realizing he thought she was covering for someone. "I'm a psychologist with an office in the Village. At the end of the day, I was packing up to leave to go home or maybe to dinner. I picked up my *Post* to take with me and . . . I saw one of my patients in the paper. She had been killed. She was murdered."

"I'm sorry."

She nodded. "Even now, I'm having a hard time saying the words out loud. We'd been working together for over a year. She was so brave, braver just getting out of bed in the morning and facing life every day than I could ever hope to be." Her throat choked up again.

"I'm sorry. I know how it feels to lose a patient. It hurts. It'll take a while for it to really sink in. But what I still don't understand is how you went from reading the paper to landing in the ER, out cold with a blow to the head and serious bruising, external and internal, to your side. You've got two rib fractures, too. You know, your kidneys could have been permanently damaged."

He paused to let it sink in.

"Listen, I don't mean to give you a hard time, but your version of what happened last night just doesn't add up, medically speaking."

He stood leaning against the heat vent under the window, poised with pen and medical chart in hand, waiting to scribble some plausible explanation into her chart. She looked back at him without hesitation, shaking her head.

"Look at these." He crossed the space between them in two strides and pulled a series of snapshots out of the file.

When she took the first glance, she couldn't believe her eyes. They looked like crime scene photos. Her naked side was covered in deep black-and-blue bruises spreading across her ribs and hips like ink. She couldn't believe these were really of her.

In disbelief, she reached down and gingerly touched the same spots on her own body, and winced in pain.

She opened the side of her hospital gown and looked down at her side to see that it matched the photos, then up to meet his deep brown eyes.

"I don't understand either. My friend from work was here earlier. She said I hit my head on the coffee table. And I remember that I *was* standing there when I saw the article about police identifying Melissa's body. But . . . that's it. I don't understand the rest . . . the bruises."

"Well, when you're ready to talk about it, or to think back on it, here's my card." He set it on her bedside table. "Page me. Okay?"

She shook her head yes. "Okay."

"Get dressed, but before you go, you'll need some directions on how to function with those ribs. A nurse will come by and show you how to wrap them. You'll have a tough time walking, getting up and down, or coughing over the next few weeks. And for God's sake, don't laugh . . . it'll hurt like hell."

She couldn't imagine what she'd laugh about. "Okay. I'll be careful . . . and I'll keep them wrapped. Thanks."

"Remember, you have my card. Use it."

"Thank you."

The nurse showed up a few minutes later to explain how to wrap her ribs with Ace bandages.

Then she left, and Hailey began gathering her clothes, mentally preparing herself to deal with Detective Kolker, still skulking outside her hospital door.

She couldn't be too hard on him. He was just doing his job.

Finally dressed, she reached down for her purse, and nearly passed out again. The pain across her ribs was sharp and intense.

Hailey stood up and it hit her. It hit her like a ton of bricks. She remembered.

A pair of legs . . . in blue jeans . . . crossing the floor of Dana's office, walking toward her after she fell.

The blood had been coming down her cheek, she could feel it . . . and those legs . . . a man's legs . . .

He pulled back and kicked, putting his whole body into it, as if she were the football in a college playoff.

Again, she felt the first vicious kick to her side, then the next and the next, the tip of his boot working its way down her ribs to the soft side of her stomach.

She remembered doubling over, lying there on the carpet, her body reacting defensively to one unrelenting kick after the next, instinctively trying to cover her stomach with her arms . . . her ribs caving in onto her lungs and blood drizzling into her mouth.

But the face . . . she couldn't remember the face. She hadn't been able to move to look up.

She never saw his face.

Ribs wrapped tightly in layer upon layer of Ace bandaging, Hailey stepped gingerly around the foot of the hospital bed, sheets still rumpled. She leaned over carefully to pick up the doctor's card.

She tucked the card into her bra and made her way across the room, placing one foot after the next. Stepping through the swinging door from her hospital room out into the hallway, the first thing she encountered was Lieutenant Kolker, positioned like a vulture in the hallway.

"Still here? I'm damn impressed, Kolker."

"I have some more questions for you."

"Look, I'm happy to talk, but it's pretty hard to catch a breath with my ribs wrapped."

The smell of medicine in the hallway was heavy. She couldn't wait for a breath of cold, fresh air.

"If you'll just tell me—"

"Lieutenant. I'd like to get home to my apartment first. At least take a bath and change out of these bloody clothes."

It was all she could do to walk. But she did, all the way down the hall. He never offered to help and as she made her way toward the elevator, she could feel him watching her through narrowed eyes. She stepped on and fought the impulse to look back at him. The elevator closed, her back still turned to him.

She had a feeling she hadn't seen the last of him.

|||||||||||||||||||||||||||||||||||||||||||||||||||||||||||||||||| **45** ||||||||||||||||||

Atlanta, Georgia

CELL PHONE IN ONE HAND, C.C. GLANCED AT HIS WATCH ON THE opposite wrist and waited.

Tina had impressed upon him repeatedly in the past just how much a performer needed her beauty sleep.

It was one o'clock in the afternoon, though—she should be up by now. He didn't have lunch plans, maybe he should just hop in the Caddy and drive on over to her apartment.

Then again, he just *got here* and it was a full twenty minutes drive out to Tara Boulevard. Plus, one of the other judges might see him leaving early again.

But the thought of spending the afternoon with Tina was a temptation. God, she had a beautiful body and wasn't the least bit inhibited. And hey, locking in the announcement as Democratic candidate for governor didn't happen every day. . . . C.C. wanted to celebrate.

Making up his mind, he wheeled his office chair around, picked up the phone, and dialed Tina's number.

At first the machine picked up and C.C. heard the familiar message. It was the breathy voices of two girls, Tina and Lola speaking in unison, promising the caller they'd return the call as Isaac Hayes sang in the background.

In mid-sentence, the machine clicked off.

"Hello?" Tina's voice was all sweet and sleepy at first. He had clearly woken her up.

Was one o'clock too early? Damn!

"Hey, baby." He spoke softly and tried a form of baby talk so as not to irritate her, but the baby talk backfired.

"Damn it C., you *freakin' woke me up!* How many times do I have to tell you that?"

How she could generate that much lung power lying flat in bed under a pillow with her eyes still closed was a wonder.

"I'm starting to think you don't respect me as a performer. You continually sabotage my career this way. How am I supposed to *create* tonight on stage if I'm exhausted?"

Tina was not a morning person.

Or, technically, an afternoon person.

"Sweet potato, you'll be perfect no matter what. I just wanted to tell you I have a meeting tonight about the governor's race and I'm in the mood to celebrate. . . . Any ideas?" He couldn't suppress an anticipatory smile. Maybe she'd describe in detail just how they would celebrate the good news after she got off work.

"I only have one freakin' idea, C.C. *Sleep!* That's my big idea. Now call me back after four, okay? Is that so *freakin'* unreasonable? Just to let an artist *sleep* until a simple four o'clock? Is that *so wrong*? Am I asking too much out of you? To be conscious of *my* career demands just once?"

He paused, not sure how to answer after she posed the rhetorical question loudly into his ear.

Tina seized on C.C.'s silence and continued on.

"I mean, C.C., do you think it's all about you just because you're a big-shot judge? I mean, I'm a performer, for God's sake . . . doesn't that mean *anything*? I mean, does it count for *anything* to you? Must I be tortured every morning this way? *It's not all about you, C.C.*"

God . . . how close to the receiver was her mouth?

No way was he going to get a sex fantasy phone call at this point.

Nothing to do but retreat and forge ahead after four.

"Yes, kitten . . . after four. Sleep tight."

She clicked off without a good-bye.

Artists were so temperamental.

She'd be in a better mood tonight.

Okay, it was decided. He'd hold out through lunch and *after* tonight's meeting at Bones about the announcement, he'd head over to the Fuzzy to celebrate.

In fact, he'd just eat lunch here. To make sure the others noticed he was here this late in the day, he'd leave his chamber door wide open while he ate and then after lunch, he'd head into the law library and check out some books. Maybe he'd actually *sit* in the law library for a few minutes, for authenticity. Like he was actually *reading* the books. Maybe write in a notepad while he was reading? Or would that be overkill . . . probably yes.

He buzzed his secretary. "Amanda?"

"Yes, Judge?"

"Can you get my lunch and bring it here, to my desk?"

"Sure can, Judge. What would you like?"

"Fried chicken with mash potatoes and turnip greens on the side. A *light sprinkling* of Tabasco sauce on the turnips would be perfect."

He hoped to God she'd get the order right this time. He'd given her the exact same order fifty times before and forty-eight of those times, something was wrong . . . no Tabasco, no plastic forks, forgot the napkins . . .

Incredible, C.C. thought. Some people just had no ambition.

|||||||||||||||||||||||||||||||||||||||||||||||||||||||||||||||||||| **46** ||||||||||||||||||||

New York City

ANGING ON TO A POLE ON THE NUMBER 6 TRAIN, HAILEY NOTED that her ribs hardly hurt at all. The subway was less crowded now, it was nearly eight, and most of the after-work commuters flooded the lines at five sharp. All the seats were taken, but there was plenty of standing room.

She was lost in thought and didn't even notice all the bodies stuffed in around her. Just before she left work, she'd had a second conversation with a uniformed cop, this time over the phone. He had taken the incident report, also over the phone, when she was in the hospital. Seemed like a nice young guy, a rookie cop taking her information to create a police report. He was still new enough to the force to sound hopeful they'd find the guy. The room had been dusted for prints but so far, no match in AFIS, the nationwide fingerprint data bank. They were probably all prints of her and her patients anyway.

Over a week had passed now. Hailey was ready for her ribs, and her life, to get back to normal. She had been feeling cooped up, due to her lack of mobility, and although the doctors told her to take it easy, she had to get out tonight for some fresh air along the river.

The subway lurched to a stop at Fifty-first and Lex. Hailey made her way out of the car and up the steep steps to Lexington, took a left, and headed home. The wind was strong out of the west, but her suite at work had been overly warm today, and it felt great to be out.

Past the doorman, into her apartment for a quick change, hair into a ponytail under a hat, black plastic running watch clasped into place, gloves and an extra sweatshirt, and off she went.

It was just past nine o'clock by the time she finally turned onto the path by the river and the moment the smell of the water hit her nose, she felt great. The ribs were aching, but if she kept it light, she'd make it just fine. Hailey usually ran without music. She liked to hear the city, her own steps hitting the cement, other runners chatting as they jogged by.

She tried a light jog, but it caused an ache to spread down the side of her torso, so walking would have to do. Looking out over the water, she thought back on Dana's reaction to the assault. "Are you sure you didn't imagine it?" Dana kept asking her . . . as if Hailey could possibly mistake tripping and falling with being beaten unconscious by an intruder.

At least Dana hadn't been around tonight to drag her out for happy hour. She'd left early, saying she had a date with Greg. They were still going strong.

Dana was already wondering if he'd propose in time for her to plan a fall wedding.

"He's the One, Hailey," she had said just this morning in Hailey's kitchenette. "I can't wait until you meet him. I've been trying to co-ordinate everyone's schedule, but he's just so busy . . . and so are you."

The blocks passed and Hailey began pondering the long-ignored article she never got around to finishing. She had read something . . . oh what was it? . . . something about the inception of self-hatred in childhood. Deftly, she reached into her running bra, where she carried her cell phone religiously, and pulled it out. Dialing her office number, she spoke quickly. "Remember, word search, key words are self-hatred, inception, childhood for the article. Maybe it was in . . ."

Before she could finish the thought, an awful wail came out of nowhere. It was the sirens cranking up back at Sixty-seventh Street, Engine 39. It was a few blocks away, but it sounded like it was right beside her, and then a man's voice over a bullhorn . . .

"Sir, you are blocking the fire station. Please move your vehicle immediately. You are blocking the fire station . . ."

Engine 39 had a massive thousand-gallon pumper, and it needed all the room it could get to pull out. Hailey imagined if the guy didn't move, the firemen would jump off the truck and move his car for him. She'd call back later and leave the rest of her message to herself.

She had slowed down when the sirens started and, losing the momentum, she realized that even walking, her ribs were really starting to ache.

She turned and started the long walk back and the cold set in. She had left without money or ATM card, so walking was the only option.

It was getting late. Suddenly, she realized how stupid this was. It was after ten o'clock, and here she was out alone, armed only with her apartment key and her cell phone. She tried to pick up the pace.

It seemed like such a great idea when she was crammed into a stuffy subway, but now the path had become empty. She was getting closer to home . . . but still, a dozen blocks to go. Deciding it was safer on city streets, she turned right and started up a flight of steep steps, leaving the East River path and going back up to the avenues. Walking south on First, instinct made her turn back and glance behind her.

Only one guy was trailing about two blocks behind her, and Hailey was sure it was the same guy right behind her when she slowed down at the sirens a while back. She couldn't see his features; his face was covered by a hat riding low . . . like every other New Yorker on a night like this.

He could be anybody. Having counseled countless victims in the past, she knew a common aftereffect of a violent attack was fear of going out and being afraid of your own shadow.

A block later, when she looked back again, the guy was still there. Even though it hurt, she tried to pick up the pace. The wind was biting across her face where the skin was unprotected. She could always hop into a diner, but she hadn't brought money . . . that wouldn't matter. And even if she did, then what? She had to come out sometime; she couldn't stay in a diner all night. And if she called police on her cell, what would she say? "Help, I see a man walking on the street?"

She looked back. She caught him suddenly turn, as if he were looking intently into the darkened overhang of an antiques-store window. She paused in her tracks, something about him when he abruptly turned away . . . a body movement, a mannerism, was so familiar to her . . .

Whoever he was, she wasn't about to go introduce herself. Now she was limping, favoring her injured side. Fifteen more minutes, and then she made it to her cross-street. Hailey turned back just in time to see him turn in toward D'Agostino's automatic doors. Okay . . . he was right behind her for twelve blocks, but he wasn't following her. So this must be his neighborhood, too. He was stopping at the local grocery.

No one's following me! she scolded herself . . . she had to get control . . . mind over matter. The attack in her office had been random.

But then why no robbery? It was an obvious question . . . a break-in and assault, for what? No robbery, no sex assault . . .

Okay, she had to stop. The guy was likely scared off by someone coming up the steps or one of the dentists slamming a door on the way out.

She slid onto the elevator and headed up. Glancing down, she saw that she'd been out close to two hours. It was ten forty-five.

A tingle went down her body.

Ten forty-five. He couldn't possibly have gone into D'Ag's, they locked the doors at ten sharp. He didn't want her to see his face.

She moved as quickly as she could down the hall, twisting the deadbolt, letting herself in and quickly sliding it, along with the chain lock, into place behind her before leaning back against the door, her heart beating wildly.

New York City

A STRONG, BRACING WIND MADE IT DIFFICULT FOR HAYDEN TO breathe as she walked home from her cubicle in the graphics department. The thin slice of her face exposed to the freezing air was numb.

Why, tonight of all nights, with the lowest temperatures on record for this time of year, had her Metro card run dry? She could have sworn there were at least three rides left on it, but when she tried to run it through the turnstile, it was empty.

A cab would be perfect, tucked away in the backseat with the heat on high. She also could have sworn she had a few dollars and a credit card in her wallet, but somehow, that was empty, too. That meant no bus and no subway for her, and certainly no cab.

Tiny snowflakes danced around her, and she momentarily took in their beauty before going back to worrying about her job, a job that made no allowance for beauty in art. How creative could she be when she worked for a corporation with no heart?

Reminding herself that "art" and "corporation" don't mix, she decided she had to go freelance, but first she'd have to line up enough work to tide her over until she was established.

The light changed. Hayden resumed walking

Her backpack was heavy with art materials and her poetry notebooks. Maybe she should try to get some of them published. Was there even a chance?

Hailey said there was.

But having her work published seemed too wonderful for someone like her, like winning the lottery or falling in love. Those kind of miracles were for other people.

Would you listen to yourself? That's just the kind of talk Hailey hates.

Hayden kept walking.

According to Hailey, Hayden *could* make something wonderful happen, if she just believed in it hard enough.

But did Hailey really mean it when she said the poetry was beautiful? Or was she just trying to boost her confidence?

Hayden hadn't had the guts to show her work to anybody else, but during her last therapy session Hailey reminded Hayden again that she knew somebody in publishing who could look them over.

But what if they were rejected? Hayden didn't know if it would be worth risking that kind of blow . . . the work was a look straight into Hayden's psyche.

She'd love to put down her backpack, it was so heavy, but her poetry and sketches were her treasures. Her shoulders were actually hurting, the ache reaching down her back. Waiting at the next cross-street, she shifted the backpack from one shoulder to the other.

Fifteen more blocks to go.

Somehow, the snow was getting inside her boots. She couldn't feel her toes anymore.

Was there anything in her fridge or would she have to order in? Definitely Thai, if that were the case.

Then she could finish one of the pieces she had started last week. This time she was changing themes and she knew Hailey was going to love it. Her new piece was all about hope, and—

In one shattering moment, her backpack was wrenched so hard Hayden didn't know what had happened. She reeled backward and sideways at the same time, then was jerked upward by her own backpack with incredible strength, and whirled sideways into an alley Hayden had walked past a hundred times and never looked down.

Desperately trying to gain traction, her feet skidded in the slush. She struck out wildly into the cold air with balled fists, but never made contact with her attacker.

Opening her mouth to scream, she felt something nylon, like pantyhose, crammed down her mouth, deep into her throat. She could hardly breathe.

In one last bizarre, frozen moment, she hung suspended in the air from the straps of her backpack, arms and legs flailing like a drunken ballerina in a frenzied dance. Then a brutal kick to her back sent her sprawling face-first into the alley, her head hitting the concrete with a thud. She tasted her own blood.

Her backpack ripped open and her precious notes, months of labor contained on page after page of penciled scrawl, went flying to the four corners, the wind lifting them up sharply, threatening to hurl them down the alley.

She wanted to tell him to take her wallet . . . just don't touch her notes . . . get the notes back . . . she had to get the notes back . . .

The nylon hose jammed deep down her throat made it impossible to speak, hard to breathe . . .

She could still gather them and save them if . . . she was sure of it . . . if she could just get loose. Her eyes followed them as they gusted up into the air, seeming to pause there, captured on an icy upward surge. But before she could offer her wallet in exchange for her papers, now wet and dirty and scattered down the alley, she felt her jeans yanked from behind, hands on the flesh of her hips and back, and then on her neck.

The blood from her head was in her eyes, her knit hat was pulled down over one side of her face so she could hardly see ahead of her. Deep-seated survival instincts kicked in and she waged war the only way she could . . . scratching, clawing, until her nails broke backward at the quick and bled . . . clawing at the set of hands now digging into her flesh . . . trying to pry them from around her neck . . . trying to scream, to inhale. The hose in her throat wouldn't allow her to inhale and scream out . . . just some air . . . God please, some air . . .

Suddenly, she saw her mother and little brother standing together at the end of the alleyway. Mom had her arm draped loosely around her little brother's shoulders . . . they were looking at her.

But why were they here? And how?

They had both been in the family sedan when it plunged off a slick roadway, skidded through a metal guardrail and dove headlights first into the cold, dark waters off Long Island.

That was two years ago, but tonight the two of them looked warm and toasty, even though they were wearing the same summer clothes they had on when they drowned, her mom's favorite sleeveless summer dress with green and gold flowers on it, Chad in jeans. The freezing cold gusts up and down the back alley didn't seem to bother her mom and brother at all.

Why did they just stand there, watching what was happening to her? Why wouldn't they help her?

All at once, a sharp, burning pain pierced upwards through her back.

The hands around her neck didn't budge, remaining hard, like a vise crushing the fragile front hollow of her neck so that it touched all the way back to her spine.

Her eyes hurt, a bulging, throbbing pain that gained momentum every time her heart pumped more blood into their delicate vessels as they hemorrhaged one by one . . . hurt worse than anything she had ever felt in her life. They felt like they were exploding out of her eye sockets . . . out of her head.

It wasn't cold anymore.

The snowflakes floating through the air seemed like fuzzy angels dancing around her head. Her mom was smiling at her.

Atlanta, Georgia

I T WAS SILENT IN THE PRIVATE SIDE ROOM TO THE ROBERT E. LEE Ballroom at Atlanta's Marriot Marquis.

C.C. sat back limply on an overstuffed leather sofa. The world seemed warm and amber-colored through the haze of whiskey. Eyes closed, tie askew around his neck, his jacket was carelessly tossed beside him, legs stretched out in front of him, feet up on a matching leather ottoman.

The announcement of his candidacy for the Democratic bid for the governor's spot went off without a hitch. Well-wishers, flacks, hangers-on, and party honchos had all crowded the ballroom, and oh how the liquor flowed.

The Democratic hordes ate all the free food, drank all the free booze, and left, along with reporters from the *Telegraph* and the rest of the local news media. Which was worse? Demo party flacks or journos? Who ate the most free food? That was a toughie, C.C. decided. Lay out a plate of sandwiches and you could put money on journos and party hacks to appear out of nowhere.

Hell . . . who cared? It was all business-expensed anyway.

Once C.C. was in the Mansion, he'd be able to throw any soiree he wanted, and the already-bloated state budget would pick up the tab. The state budget was so fat, none of it mattered anyway.

Eugene himself had made a brief appearance, wearing those damn aviator sunglasses again, even in the darkened ballroom. He spoke only a few words of congratulations as Sister Sledge's "We Are Family" pulsated so loudly C.C. could hardly make out what Eugene was saying.

Whatever it was, it was something warm and supportive, C.C. was sure.

Before melting back into the crowded room, Eugene clapped C.C. on the back and spoke directly into his ear, saying something about C.C. deserving not only the governor's bid, but one hell of a celebration.

C.C. planned to do just that as soon as he could lose his wife, Betty, up from Dooley County since the afternoon before on one of her rare trips up to the big Sin City.

He had to hand it to her, though. Betty had stood by him dutifully throughout the onstage regalia. She actually looked damn fine, decked out in a navy blue long-sleeved suit, hair back in a 'do courtesy of her beautician at Cut and Curl back home in Dooley.

The memory of another woman intruded as he thought wistfully of Tina. He had noticed that woman at the party tonight, in her mid-thirties and wearing a low-cut red dress. What a rack that one had.

Suddenly, the red dress stirred up surprising thoughts of romance that broke through C.C.'s hazy buzz.

Should he wrestle his way out of the easy chair and go try with Betty? For old times' sake? Just to see what would happen?

It had been nearly four years since he'd last attempted such a thing. The rebuff was still fresh in his mind. Betty could be a cold, cold woman when she wanted to. It was after a bitter breakup after a brief affair C.C. had with a former court reporter, Janice. When he couldn't "commit," Janice had dumped him. He was sure Betty never knew about Janice, but the fact that his own wife rejected him when he needed her the most still hurt C.C. deeply.

Thank God Tina came into his life.

He started humming "their" song, "Freebird."

He hadn't seen her in nearly two weeks, and missing the club was making him cranky and antsy. To hell with it—after a stop at Phipps Plaza for some power shopping tomorrow, Betty would be long gone. Praise the Lord.

His first order of business once he got to the Mansion would be to re-examine the damn Hope Scholarship.

Currently, all Georgia Lottery proceeds, repeat *all proceeds*, went to education. That was just wrong. The state was sitting on a pile of money and it was all going to education. Whose idiot idea was that anyway?

Reform. That would be his platform! Genius!

Oh how he wished he could write that down so this thought wouldn't just evaporate in a few hours the way so many of his break-throughs did . . . but he had no idea where he could get a pencil.

Kicked back there in the leather chair, C.C.'s mind wandered, and surveying the world around him, he happened to spot his own shoes.

They were absolutely stunning. Italian leather, shined to a sheen. Who did that? he wondered. Made his shoes so shiny? Someone. Whoever did the laundry.

What a night. C.C. dozed.

IIIIIIIIIIIIIIIIIIIIIIIIIIIIIIIIIIIIIIIIIIIIIIIIIIIIIIIIIIIIIIIIIII **49** IIIIIIIIIIIIIIIIIIIII

St. Simons Island,
Georgia

MONDAY. MORNING. EARLY.
Something stirred in the morning quiet.

Virginia Gunn awakened and rolled over, twisting herself in the sheets, resisting the urge to open her eyes.

Something woke her up . . . hadn't it?

Everything was silent in the house, upstairs and down . . . so what was it she just heard? Was it anything? In the still of her bedroom, the only sound was the waves outside, lapping up against the thin strip of beach beyond her house.

She rolled over again, yawning.

As she tried to fall back to sleep, her thoughts naturally drifted to the pressing problem at hand.

Time was of the essence . . . there were millions riding on the Palmetto high-rises, and she knew it. She did some digging around at the County Clerk's Office and discovered the possible money-man was Floyd Eugene, a cutthroat . . . a political majordomo out of Atlanta. Property in surrounding blocks had changed hands during the past two years, and Virginia smelled a rat.

Her raids on his property were costing him money. How much longer until payback came around? She'd have to—

A loud thump suddenly ripped the silence.

Immediately, the old wooden beach house was filled with an intense storm of barking from a pack of hysterical wiener dogs . . . *her* wiener dogs.

Obviously, the newspaper boy had driven up and stepped through the gate of the high wooden fence surrounding her yard to sling the morning paper, rolled and rubber-banded, at the front door. The boy's bull's-eye hit in the center of the front door sparked the usual fear of deadly attack among the wieners and, in an effort to protect everything they lived for, i.e., Virginia, the house, the doggie treats in the kitchen, they commenced to throw themselves violently at the door in the entrance hall.

"Shut up, damn it . . . *shut UP!*" she screamed into the empty space in her bedroom, not bothering to roll over off her stomach, much less trudge out to the top of the stairs and yell down at them.

She could see them in her mind's eye right now, a snarling, furry mass at the foot of the front door, barking their lungs out at the tiny slit of light between the base of the door and the hardwood floor . . . prepared to maul to death their would-be attacker.

The sharp reprimand she screamed out didn't make a dent. It just bounced off the bedroom walls and disappeared into the carpet, while the barking continued at the same fevered pitch.

The newsboy would have been toast if Virginia hadn't locked the doggie chute at the bottom of the front door last night.

Opening one eye only, she looked over to see the digital clock display. It was only 7:15 a.m. What the hell. They'd never let her sleep now, and the furious barking had woken up the birds, all housed in elaborate cages in the dining room.

Claudine the parrot was squawking full blast and attacking the little row of bells Virginia had attached directly beside her water bowl . . . a distraction. . . . something for the bird to play with. Quietly. Delicately. In a manner befitting a beautiful bird . . . a beautiful tropical bird that Virginia had paid good money for in order to spring her from a pet store in Baxley, Georgia. What the hell was the bird doing? Tearing the bells out of the cage with her bare claws?

Then came the last straw.

The phone began to ring.

She still refused to move. It was too early. She lay on her stomach, face to the side underneath a pillow, counting. She silently counted fourteen rings.

In Virginia's mind, fourteen rings at this hour amounted to stalking. Any idiot would know that after four to five rings, either the callee wasn't at home or obviously *didn't want to be bothered. Hello!* Didn't anybody have any damn manners on this Island?

At last, the phone went quiet, the barking subsided, the bells on the bird cages were stilled . . . peace.

Virginia burrowed down under the covers and tried to re-enter the deep REM state she was in earlier.

The phone started again.

Eighteen rings this time. It was either a stalker or an emergency. The odds were against sleeping any later, so she finally gave in, rolled over, and eased out of bed toward the phone.

"Hello. It's early. It better be good."

"V.G., can you come down?"

Larry was on the other end, and he sounded choked up.

"What's wrong, Larry?"

"Today's the anniversary of the D."

She needed some coffee. "What the hell is a D?"

"Dale!"

He broke off abruptly. She could tell he was crying.

Dale . . . Dale . . .

It took a moment to make the connection.

The walls of Larry's garage were covered in huge, colored posters of his idol, the late, great, Dale Earnhardt. More than once, his father had driven him for hours, crisscrossing the Southeast just to see the D race round and round a NASCAR track.

"V.G., they're memorializing him on TV. I've been watching the instant replays of the crash all morning on the thirteen-inch here in the store. I can't take it."

"Listen, I'll be right there."

Virginia hung up and stepped into a light pink sweat suit she had taken out of the dryer the night before and thrown on the easy chair in the corner of her room. After clamping her old Atlanta Braves baseball cap down snug on her head, she pulled her long, dark ponytail through the adjustable hole in the back. She picked up her favorite windbreaker, one she had bought on the side of the street during the '96 Olympics. It was covered in the interlocking Olympic rings with eagles swooping across the back. It had seemed glorious and patriotic at the time.

She pulled the door to her bedroom gently shut, hoping not to alert the dogs she was going out and avoid a mob scene.

Quickly and quietly, she went down the stairs and out the back door. She tiptoed to the Jeep, knowing that the moment the engine turned over, the pack, led by Sidney, would resume their hysterical barking, throwing themselves at the door and running in circles around the den.

Virginia backed out of the gravel driveway. She shifted and turned it wide to swing out into the street.

The morning was still cool and wet . . . the sun hadn't scorched everything in sight just yet. The breeze off the ocean smelled fresh and salty. No other cars were out yet.

New York City

T HE AIR WAS STILL FRESH AND THE SIDEWALKS WERE COVERED IN a blanket of glistening snow, still undisturbed, when Hailey went into work. Her walk the night before in the cold air had left her feeling so much better. Her mind was clear, and while still sad over Melissa, at the same time she felt happy to be alive and rededicated to helping her other patients. But the eerie similarities between Melissa's death and a string of cases she prosecuted in Atlanta wouldn't leave her mind for long. Of course, murders didn't happen just in Atlanta, and she really didn't know all the details about Melissa's death yet.

Hailey stepped into the foyer, kicked snow off her boots, went upstairs three flights, and put on hot water. Not a soul was stirring in the little brownstone this early. She puttered around the suite and flicked on the computer to work on the outline for her article. Hayden wasn't due for another forty-five minutes. She was often late, but never early.

Hailey was seated at her computer when a light rap on her office door broke the silence.

"Hello? Who's there?" Hailey called out, rising from her seat, heading to the door. That was odd . . . she hadn't heard a sound . . . no one had gotten buzzed up.

No reply.

Hailey opened the door to Kolker.

"Mind if I come in?"

"Hi. What's up? Come on in. Any news on Melissa?"

"I think you know," Lieutenant Kolker said cryptically.

"Excuse me? What happened?" she returned, as his handheld police band radio squawked.

Kolker held up the index finger on his right hand to her as he listened to a handheld police band radio he held in his left, signaling her to hold on. She did. He then finished the transmission by barking a series of numbers into the lower end of the radio.

"I'm really feeling much better now and I'm happy to talk to you. I do have a patient coming in just a few moments, would later today be okay? I can definitely meet you when I break at lunchtime." Hailey walked around to her desk, sat down, and started flipping through her appointment book, a thick full-size black spiral notebook.

"Ms. Dean, I wish it were still that simple. Things have changed since we last met. For you, anyway," he said flatly.

He leaned over toward her with his palms spread on her desk. "Ms. Dean, Hayden Krasinski was also one of your patients, correct? Just like Melissa Everett was?" His voice was cold. His eyes never left her own.

"Lieutenant, you know as well as I do that any communications between Hayden Krasinski and myself are protected under the doctor-patient privilege. I will say, though, that I know Hayden very well."

He nodded. "That's what I thought."

"I spoke with Hayden last week and plan to see her this morning, as a matter of fact. Why do you ask? Wait . . . Kolker, please don't tell me you think Hayden has anything to do with Melissa's death."

When he didn't respond, she went on, "I assure you—no, I'll go so far as to *personally* vouch for Hayden. She's incapable of violence. She's a very caring and sensitive person."

He let her go on with neither comment nor reaction.

"Listen, I give you my word on that, as both a psychologist and an officer of the court. You *do* know that I am an officer of the court, Lieutenant? You seem to know everything else about my clients and me."

"Believe me . . . I do."

What was with his attitude?

"Then you know I've probably handled just as many felonies as a prosecutor as *you've* handled as a detective. And I swear to it . . .

Hayden's not involved in Melissa's death, and if you're trying to find her so that you can—"

"Ms. Dean, we don't think Hayden was involved."

She looked back at him across her desk, closing the appointment book and standing. "Then why all the questions about Hayden?"

"I don't think Hayden was involved. This is about you. We don't want to locate Hayden Krasinski. We know where she is. She's at the morgue, Ms. Dean. Hayden Krasinski is dead. She was stabbed and likely strangled in the last twenty-four hours, and not too far from your office, either."

Stunned, Hailey grasped the edge of the desk to keep her balance. The pain showed in her eyes and her immediate, gut reaction was one of disbelief. Her mind couldn't accept the news, and the color drained from her face.

"Don't bother to look so shocked," Lieutenant Kolker said dryly. "That stunned, hurt look might have fooled me once, Hailey Dean, that's right. It worked the first time you used it at the hospital, but it ain't workin' this time. You nearly had me snowed in there. Man, was I a fool. I guess you've used your looks before. It's not working this time, Counselor."

"What?" Her thoughts were spinning. She couldn't take in the news about Hayden. "Lieutenant, I'm not—"

"Don't bother to tell me what you're not," he cut in rudely, "because I'm going to tell you what you *are*. You're under arrest."

"For what?!" Anger took her over. Her patients were being singled out for death, and her words came out sharp as steel.

"Do you want me to repeat it?"

She said nothing back, the desire for revenge against the killer so strong now, her whole body was coiled and ready to spring.

"Melissa Everett *and* Hayden Krasinski are both dead. Two innocent women murdered just weeks apart, and you know what, Ms. Dean? You're the only connection to the both of them."

"But that doesn't mean—"

"Same MO. Single females in their twenties, both slight of stature, both emotionally troubled and easy to take advantage of, both strangled *and* stabbed—very unusual—both in the evenings on a city street, no robbery . . . sound familiar? Both murdered just blocks from your office. Both had your business card on them. Both had your home number and cell in their address books. Both trusted *you*, Hailey Dean. They'd do whatever you told them, wouldn't they? They never saw it coming, did they, Hailey . . . just walking along and the stab in the back. Too much of a coincidence for my taste."

This wasn't real. It couldn't be happening. The man was an imbecile. How could she be connected to violence, much less murder . . . and of her own patients?

"Oh, and nice touch, leaving that little message on Melissa Everett's answer machine . . . as *if* you had no idea where she was when you knew she was lying stiff and cold in an alleyway. But nice touch. You're a real pro, Dean. A jury's gonna love that!"

"Kolker, you know this is impossible. Why are you doing this? I can't believe it. . . . Hayden's been killed? What happened to her?"

"Don't ask me. It's up to headquarters if you get any more information up front. I'm sure your defense lawyer will file discovery and tell you anything you need to know about your *patients*. For now, that information's off-limits to you. All you need to know is that they're *dead*." He eyed her as if she were a dangerous snake loose in the office. "Look, cut the crap. I know you lawyer types . . . anything we tell you, you'll just use it against us in court. Isn't that the game you lawyers play?"

Hailey hardly knew where to begin. "What in the hell are you talking about? What are you saying? I cared about Hayden *and* Melissa. They were both friends to me."

He continued as if she hadn't spoken a word.

"You handled serial murders, didn't you? Never lost a case, did you, Dean? Always a winner, right? Well, you're not a winner now. You lost this time. We're on to you."

Kolker was having a field day. He kept talking, hoping for a reaction, a statement, an outburst, maybe even an admission. Anything he could use against her in court. She knew this. Far in the back of her mind, the wheels started turning. Years and years of courtroom strategy were piercing through the shock.

"I'm actually a little disappointed in you. Should have tweaked the MO. Changed it up just a little bit. Hell, a smart ex-prosecutor like you can afford to be creative once in a while . . . right? Not make it so easy for us dumb cops to figure out."

"What are you talking about?"

Kolker went on, unfazed. "But what I don't get is . . . is it some sick sex thing for you? Because I just don't seem to pick up on that particular vibe from *you*. Or did you just crack?"

"You moron!" She shrieked it. "You're arresting me while a killer's out there stalking my patients? You're wasting time!"

"Hailey, Hailey, Hailey, temper, temper." Kolker waggled an index finger at her like she'd been a bad schoolgirl.

That was it.

Hailey pulled back and gave Kolker what he asked for. Before he knew it was coming, her right elbow wound back and released with a force neither of them could have predicted, landing a right punch to his left chin. It landed with a loud *thwack*, slicing up to his nose, too, and blood immediately began gushing down the front of his shirt.

It happened so fast and was so unexpected, Kolker was caught completely off-guard.

Grabbing a bandanna out of his back pocket, he wiped his mouth and nose, furious and embarrassed at the same time over the fact she'd been able to land a hit square to his face. Now he'd be the punch line back at the station for this and he knew it. Maybe he'd just leave it out of his report.

"Oh, the jury's gonna love this. A temper out of control. Fits right in with my scenario. Want to tell me all about it? I'll listen. I'll even make sure they go easy on you downtown. What happened? Get a little too involved in your cases back home, Hailey? Push yourself a little too far? You couldn't take it anymore . . ."

She had committed a horrible tactical mistake—she showed anger. She actually punched a cop. She had to rein it in for her own sake. With immense self-control and a throbbing right hand, she now remained perfectly silent, taking in everything she could, gleaning every fact possible before he got wise and clammed up.

"That's my theory . . . you cracked and left the law, didn't you, Hailey Dean? I've read about you. We checked up on you, we did our homework on this one, don't worry about *that*. You quit prosecuting after that last big-deal serial murder case you won. And now . . . your patients start dropping like flies, dead . . . *just like them* . . . *just like the hookers in Atlanta.*"

She lifted her head and looked him square in the face. Surely he couldn't mean it.

"I mean, come on, these killings are copycat to the max . . . right down to the four-pronged stab wound. Can't you come up with another plan?"

Four-pronged stab wound?

She knew there'd been a strangulation-stabbing . . . but this was the first she knew of a four-pronged wound. Her blood ran cold.

"What I don't copy is what you *get* out of it all. No robbery . . . no previous hatred or animosity with the victims. Do you just want to be in the spotlight again? Somehow swoop in with vital evidence and make yourself the big star all over again? Is that it, Hailey? You know . . . to look so good, you're one twisted chick."

She finally answered.

"Shut up, you stupid son of a bitch. You know this is impossible. What's the real deal, Kolker? You guys need to make yourselves look good with an arrest instead of admitting the truth . . . that you don't have any remote idea who's committing the murders?"

In the back of her mind she knew it was deadly to "chat" with police when you're clearly a criminal target. Whatever you said was guaranteed to be misconstrued, but she went on anyway.

"For your information, I didn't 'crack.' I just got sick of it . . . the bloody crime scenes, the murders, and the double-dealing in the courtroom. The cruelty . . . *that's* what I quit. Don't you ever think of it yourself, Kolker? What is it . . . do you *like* dead bodies?"

He looked pained. She kept going.

"Don't you ever get tired of defense attorneys who beat the system, Kolker? And the morons who sit on the bench and call themselves judges? The witnesses who lie with a straight face? Ever wake up at night dreaming about the last victim . . . the last trial . . . the last investigation? Ever get worn down from just fighting the fight . . . finishing one case and forty more land on your desk? Or is it you just don't have the *guts* to do anything else?"

At last, he rallied. "Save it, *Counselor.* Don't fight me on this. I'll end up taking you in anyway, so you might as well make it easy on yourself and not cause a scene. Remember this, Hailey Dean . . . I don't *need* to figure it out. I don't *need* a motive. All I need is a perp, and the perp is you. I've got you on motive and opportunity, plus, *we've got forensics to back it up.* I don't have to untangle the snakes in that little blonde head of yours. I'll leave that up to your court-appointed *psych.* Hell, you'll need one to explain this to a jury. Nice going, Counselor."

Forensics? How could that be? Forensics . . . blood, fluid, DNA? Linking her to the murders? Impossible!

Hailey clamped her mouth shut while he cuffed her, knowing at this point that anything she said could and would be held against her in court. Why her? What did they have? But she wasn't getting any more out of Kolker, not right now, anyway.

How many times had she repeated those same Miranda warnings to how many suspects?

You have the right to remain silent, anything you say can and will be held against you in a court of law, you have the right to an attorney . . .

She knew the words by heart and they rang like a nursery rhyme through her head.

The cuffs were cold metal and tight on her wrists. Her side was hurting so badly it felt like it was on fire. Throwing the punch had cost her, but it was worth it. Kolker's nose was still dripping blood.

He grabbed her purse from the rug beside her desk and shoved it under his arm.

"Let's go, you're under arrest for double murder, the stabbing deaths of Melissa Everett and Hayden Krasinski," he said, leading her out her own door, his grip tight on her arm above the elbow, as though she would take off at any minute and try to outrun him

She prayed no one would be there to see her go. Dana's office door was closed, thank God.

But the door to the dentists' office on the first floor was propped open as the UPS guy wheeled in boxes of supplies. She could see them all . . . the waiting room full of patients, secretaries behind the counter, one of the dentists. They'd all know soon enough.

They stared at her as she passed, hands in front of her, wrists obviously shackled together. No one spoke. It was if they were characters in a silent movie, or those life-size cardboard cutouts of people . . . people who didn't move or speak, just stared.

She tried her best to cover the cuffs with her coat so onlookers wouldn't see. But she knew they could see.

They could see.

IIIIIIIIIIIIIIIIIIIIIIIIIIIIIIIIIIIIIIIIIIIIIIIIIIIIIIIIIIIIIIII **51** IIIIIIIIIIIIIIIIIIII

St. Simons Island,
Georgia

V IRGINIA PULLED UP IN FRONT OF THE 7-ELEVEN. SHE COULD SEE Larry behind the counter, slumped between displays of chewing gums, Sweet-and-Sours, even ginseng root.

The cowbell hanging from the door clanged when she walked in, and Larry sat up. His eyes were bloodshot and his face was pale except for his nose, which was red.

He didn't speak at first, just slid off the bar stool, walked to the Bunn-o-matic, and reached for the glass coffeepot. He poured coffee into a Styrofoam cup and topped it off with heavy cream before nuking the contents for exactly twenty-five seconds in the mini-microwave next to the Slurpee machine. In somber silence, he handed the Styrofoam cup to Virginia.

"Just like I like it. Thanks."

"V.G., I'm not some nut, some obsessed freak." He reclaimed the bar stool. "It's just that he was a hero. You know, he came from nothin' and nowhere, and he was king, V.G., king of the NASCAR."

"I know, Larry."

They sat in silence, Larry flipping through a NASCAR magazine, Virginia beside him sipping her coffee and looking out through the glass storefront at the parking lot.

A white pickup pulled up, and she watched a man in a blue uniform get out of the driver's side and slam his door.

An officious-looking "crest," reminiscent of Great Britain's royal House of Windsor coat of arms, was proudly emblazoned on the driver's side door. It was tacky, pompous, and fake.

It was the Palmetto Dunes Luxury Living logo.

The man in the uniform certainly was at work early this morning. So . . . they hadn't given up after the attack . . . but why should they?

Why should a guerrilla foray onto the property scare away millions of dollars of backing and even more to rake in once the condos sold? Of course the developers weren't giving up.

While the guerrillas had staged only one attack, word was they had at least slowed down the dune developers. After the assault, there had been no further attempt to re-pour the foundation. At least not yet.

The cowbell on the handle clanked as the man pushed open the glass door.

He looked vaguely familiar to Virginia, but she looked down instinctively when the cowbell sounded. Virginia noticed his navy uniform was already blotched dark with sweat.

"Hey, Larry."

"Hey, Clyde. How's it goin'?"

"Well, I went out there and got 'em ready to start up the construction again. Got the security cameras in place. Guess you heard about it already. Bet there won't be any more kids tearing the place apart this time. And it's a good thing, too. The boss out of Atlanta rolled some heads. Got the security guard so nervous, he's poppin' Tums like you wouldn't believe. Near 'bout lost his job after that last time."

He stopped dead center in front of Virginia and turned back to Larry. "Got the Coke with lime, Larry?"

"Nope. That company never could leave well enough alone. Seems they'd have learned something after the 'New Coke.' Remember that big mess?"

"Yep." He kept talking with no instigation. "Yes, sir . . . these cameras'll stop 'em. Got 'em all the way from some outfit in Atlanta. Damn, Toby McKissick and the whole County Commission's in on it. They got their hands in everybody's pocket, you know. Nothing new about that."

He reached into a glassed-in refrigerated area, pulled out a Diet Coke, walked back to the counter, and put down a dollar. " 'Course the work crew said it wasn't kids . . . that it was a curse. You know, voodoo. Everybody's always said the south beach was haunted. My aunt Rosa said it to me twenty-five years ago."

"I always heard that, too. My grandmother told me," Larry told him.

So had Virginia. The ghost stories surrounding the Island's south beach, which dated back to before the Civil War, as far as anybody could tell, were about a burning slave boat that had landed on St. Simons's southernmost shore. No such ship had ever been documented, but the lore continued.

Clyde pulled a cloth handkerchief out of his back pocket and ran it across his face. "*Damn* it's hot out there. What time is it, for Pete's sake?"

They all three turned to look at the clock plugged into the wall behind the register. Over the Coca-Cola logo, it read eight fifteen.

"Not even eight thirty in the morning! Whew!" Clyde exclaimed. "Got to be eighty-five degrees already. Thank God I finished up before it *really* heats up."

"Musta been tough out there," Larry said, alluding to the camera installation. "It's like a jungle in some parts. Hot as hell."

"Oh, yeah, and they wanted the damn cameras hidden out of the way so they can catch the kids. Don't know why . . . prob'ly just a bunch of high-school kids having fun. It ain't like it's a federal case, ya know? Just kids. But you know folks out of Atlanta . . . ever' thing's got to be just so. They start up construction again tomorrow morning and had to have the cameras in place first, come hell or high water . . . whatever, I got paid." He waved the dollar at Larry. "You gonna ring me out or what?"

"Hey, keep the dollar. The Coke's on me. So where'd you finally end up puttin' 'em?" Larry asked it without the slightest change of inflection in his voice.

"Put what?"

Damn this guy was slow. "The security cameras . . . this morning . . . remember?"

Virginia didn't dare move a muscle, keeping her nose in Larry's NASCAR magazine, specifically, a close-up of Dale Earnhardt getting Rookie of the Year back in 1979.

Clyde snorted. "Oh yeah . . . *them*. Put 'em up high on those two big pines just inside the guardhouse, one on either side, 'bout twenty feet in, just off the road. They're kind of hidden behind the pine needles. You'd never notice 'em in a million years," he added. The more he talked, the prouder he got of his job that morning.

"That was smart," Larry kept it going. "Just two of 'em?"

"Yep. Two'll do it. Look right down on the driveway into the site. I had to go in all the way to Brunswick and get a ladder special order to make it to the top. Damn Eddie over at the Georgia Power Company wouldn't let me use one of their trucks. But don't blame Eddie, it wasn't his fault. It was the lawyers that said no."

Larry nodded. "Yep . . . it's always the lawyers."

Not a word from Virginia.

"Thanks for the Coke, Larry."

"Any time, Clyde."

Out of the corner of her eye, Virginia watched Clyde go out through the glass doors and head to the pickup. But just as she opened her mouth to commend Larry on his detective work, Clyde stopped in mid-stride.

Now what?

They watched through the glass storefront as he threw his throat back and took a deep gulp of the ice-cold Coke.

"Good Lord," Virginia muttered, shaking her head.

Neither Larry nor Virginia moved a hair sitting there on the bar stools behind the counter, watching as Clyde finally got into the truck, cranked up, and headed out of the parking lot.

Only when he'd eased out onto the highway and screeched off did Larry turn to Virginia.

"Man, V.G., you make me *nervous*! I gotta calm *down*. This whole morning's giving me an aneurysm. I guess you wanna drive over there right now to check out the cameras."

"I can go by myself. It's okay."

"Hell, no, you are not going by yourself. Anyway, I want to get a look at those cameras stuck up on a pine tree. Go wait in the El Camino while I close up. We'll take my car. She's unlocked. Better let the windows down. Might be hot."

Virginia smiled. Larry always did the driving.

Virginia went ahead, sat in the El Camino's passenger's seat, and watched Larry lock up.

He climbed into the driver's seat, flicked on the El Camino's AC, and they headed out of the lot toward the Palmetto Dunes development site.

It was nearly 10 a.m. when they reached the area. The sun was just starting to heat up, burning the cool out of the air and off the road. Minute by minute, the damp, frosty feel in the air was giving way to another hot Island morning. In another half hour, heat waves would begin to snake up off the dark gray asphalt on the Georgia back roads.

Virginia and Larry traveled along several miles of bumpy access road. Keeping it casual, they eased past the entrance of Palmetto Dunes Luxury Living at about fifteen mph. He kept it in the road while Virginia surveyed the area.

"See anybody around?"

"No, but keep going straight a little bit. Just in case."

He nodded and continued on toward the south beaches for about a mile, then U-turned and doubled back to the construction site.

"Wanna go in?"

"No other way to find out where the cameras are. Plus, you have tinted windows. They can't see us, but we can see them."

Larry turned in, inching down the private drive toward the plum spot picked for the high-rises.

"It's the sweet spot, that's for sure." He was right. There at the cusp, where grassy, firm ground turned to pink-white sand under your feet, was the exact spot Palmetto Dunes planned to erect two grayish-red high-rises, twenty-four stories each.

The two of them leaned forward in the El Camino, looking up to the tops of a cluster of tall pines.

And there they were, two black security cameras perched high above Palmetto's entrance, glinting down toward the guardhouse like computerized metal birds of prey, waiting to catch their victims on videotape

"Clyde was right," she told Larry as they both still squinted upward. "No one would ever spot those cameras unless they knew just where to look."

"Okay, so, now that we've seen 'em . . ." He pointed toward the guardhouse. "Let's get out of here before Deputy Dog burps his coffee and turns around."

The rest of the site looked exactly as it had before. From what they could see from inside Larry's El Camino, not much more had changed since Virginia had led the second foray against Palmetto to destroy the construction ground work.

The guardhouse stood just as it had for weeks. Virginia could even make out the back of a head, resting against the glass . . . the same head as before. It was the former security guard from the Brunswick Wal-Mart. He hadn't been fired after all.

The window AC roared away right beside his head and, true to form, the guard sat oblivious to two spies thirty feet behind him. He was absorbed in his TV, same as before, but this time he was engrossed in *The View*.

Larry gently eased the El Camino into reverse and they backed out undetected.

When they were back on the main road, he glanced over at Virginia. "Well, what'd ya think?"

"We'll just let them lay out the foundation again and then, the night before they're ready to pour the concrete, we'll tear it all up again."

"Don't tell *me*. I don't know *nothin' about nothing*! I'm just working reconnaissance here."

"Right . . . you're just a spy. So how can we get in without using the trail by the guardhouse?"

"Don't know . . . lemme percolate."

They headed back toward the 7-Eleven.

Virginia's mind was spinning over the game of cat-and-mouse she was playing with some of the most high-powered financiers in the South. Could they possibly be outwitted a third time?

When she got back, she'd round up the guerrillas from their various daytime callings . . . the Radio Shack, the local high school, the Wal-Mart, and the Shrimp Boat Restaurant. Construction was under way again, and they had to be ready for action forty-eight hours from now.

Once the concrete was poured and set, destruction of the foundation would be almost impossible without the use of explosives. Time was of the essence. Millions of dollars were riding on the Palmetto Dunes high-rises. She learned a lot from the County Records Office. She wondered how long Eugene had been buying up the land. . . .

Larry broke the silence with three words.

"Amphibious sneak attack."

Virginia pulled her sunglasses down to the tip of her nose, just barely keeping them on, and looked at him over the rims. The look posed the obvious question.

"Clyde's damn cameras cut you off from the main entrance." He turned down the radio. "The only other path in is off the highway . . . too dangerous. Might get spotted. They're on to us now. . . . They'll be waiting up front for somebody to sneak in. So we got to go from another angle."

"Another angle?" Virginia didn't get it.

"V.G., didn't you ever see *Caddyshack*? My God, it's a classic."

"Of course I saw *Caddyshack*, I haven't been living in a cave, for Pete's sake. But what does *Caddyshack* have to do with Palmetto Dunes?"

"V.G., you saw it, true. But I've seen it twelve times . . . minimum. If I only learned one thing from the movie . . . just one thing . . . it's this. If you want to beat a varmint . . . you got to *think* like a varmint. These varmints are using the beach. So'll we. We come in after dark by dinghy, shore at the south beach, and walk in. They'll never suspect a rear attack."

Brilliant.

" '*We*'? So you're in the foxhole with me?"

"I got to stand for something, V.G. I've let the Seven-Eleven take over my life. Running a convenience store takes on a life of its own . . . it's sucking me dry, V.G. The deliveries, the gas pumps, the customers, the damn Slurpee machine. They've become my raison d'être."

She didn't want to interrupt, so she just nodded her head and kept looking straight ahead, watching the yellow line in the middle of the road as it flew under the front grille of the car, disappearing then popping up again behind them.

"It takes a toll, V.G. The grind of business. It's robbed me of my purpose in life. The D reminded me of that. So, yeah. I'm in, V.G. I'm in the foxhole with you."

New York City

H AILEY HADN'T SMELLED THE INSIDE OF A JAIL IN A LONG TIME.
But the moment she was pushed through iron doors into
the crowded holding cell and took a deep breath, it all came back.
Nothing so much as the sense of smell speaks to the human memory, instantly dredging up the good, the bad, the painful and long-
buried.

Days-old human perspiration mixed with heavy perfumes the
hookers had worn since the night before. Somebody, somewhere,
had puked. And the stench of urine on a heroin junkie managed to
pierce through it all, hanging heavy in the still air.

Hailey could feel the eyes of the other women on her from the
opposite end of the cell where they were all gathered. A card
game was going in one corner, and little knots of women congre-
gated to mull over their charges and the hard luck that landed
them here.

Ignoring them, she made her way over to one of the only vacant
seats, a wooden bench bolted to the floor.

As she lowered herself onto it, she found herself sitting right
next to the source of the sickening smell . . . a heroin junkie sleeping on the bench in urine-soaked clothes. Her deathly white com-
plexion highlighted angry red needle marks along her inner elbow
and wrists. Hailey could see the familiar puncture marks on the
woman's left hand, between the knuckles and fingers. She looked
like a wizened, shrunken version of what she must have been before
she took heroin as a lover.

The others had edged away from the smell toward the other end
of the room. Hailey took a look around. It was a large square room
with no windows and plain walls devoid of hardware that could be
forced off and used as a weapon.

"My babies . . . what about my babies?" a woman in her twenties sobbed into a handkerchief. Listening to the others trying to comfort her, Hailey calculated the woman's misdemeanor prostitution bust would mean a probation revocation and a six-month good-bye to her two infant children on the outside.

"I can't stay in here that long," the woman cried.

She wasn't the only one crying. Each one faced charges ranging from prostitution to distribution of meth, to a knifing on Third Avenue outside a deli, driving under the influence, and grand larceny. For the most part, they were either drugged-up, drunk, or strung-out on the roller-coaster ride of a first-time arrest and the shock of literally being thrown in the can.

And the "can" stunk.

"What you in for?" one of them would occasionally sidle up to ask Hailey.

"Bad check." She lied, of course.

She wasn't about to tell them the truth, much less reveal her identity as a lawyer, a criminal prosecutor in another life. Now was not a good time to be besieged for free legal advice.

She had to think.

All she knew was that she'd been linked to two murders by the fact that Melissa and Hayden were both her clients, her name and home and cell numbers were found on their bodies, both had sessions scheduled with her the night of their murders. The police weren't that stupid. They had to have more to arrest her. But what?

And they'd both been strangled and stabbed—apparently like the string of dead women she'd represented in Atlanta.

Hailey looked down at her own hands, clutched together in her lap.

She spread them and imagined them circled around the throats of dark, fragile Melissa and Hayden—young, creative, so alive.

Her throat tightened and her face flushed hot.

Her first murder prosecution as a rookie ADA had been an asphyxiation . . . manual strangulation coupled with the killer forcing a plastic laundry bag over the head of his victim until she died.

Hailey still remembered walking onto the crime scene. The clear plastic laundry bag was still over the woman's head, parts of it lodged deeply up into her nostrils as she had sucked it in, struggling for the last bit of air left in the bag.

Hailey never knew the woman in life, but the memory of her face contorted in death with a common laundry bag inhaled into her nose had never really left the back of Hailey's mind.

It came back to her now, but she couldn't stop substituting the faces of Melissa and Hayden.

Kolker really believes I did it, that I murdered my own patients, that I stabbed them in the back, that I posed the strangulations, that I have the heart to watch them lying there, the life draining out of them. . . .

She knew she had a right to a single phone call . . . but who was there to call? Her family was away at Cumberland. Fincher was half-way around the world in Iraq. The realization that she was alone in the world was painful.

A standard, battery-operated, institutional metal-rimmed clock hung high on a wall in the holding pen.

Slumped beside the sleeping junkie, Hailey literally watched the minutes pass, her eyes following each forward jerk of the long red second hand, her ears hearing the loud tick that came with every movement.

It was becoming unbearably hot in the cell as more women crowded in, one by one.

Although the holding cell was packed, Hailey was alone and weary. Her face was drawn, her lips were dry, and her hair was plastered to her head, damp with perspiration. The sweat between her breasts soaked through her blouse and a dark pattern appeared and spread, seeming to blossom, slowly across her chest. As she slumped against the wall, her head fell loosely down toward her right shoulder. Numbness took over. She slept.

The stench in the holding pen seeped through her nostrils and into her dreams.

In the dream, she was back in an Atlanta jail with Fincher, looking through the first set of mug-shot books. They had spent over two weeks, working into the night, to comb through thousands of photos and, ultimately, cull a newly created photo album to present to strippers and prostitutes across the city for possible leads.

The police department's profiler had suggested that the serial killer stalking the city was a white man in his late twenties to early thirties, muscular, middle-to-high income bracket, and extremely meticulous, but with artistic tendencies, possibly an only child.

"Fincher, it's so damn hot in here and the smell is giving me a headache." She rubbed her temples and pushed her chair back from the table. "I'm worried."

"About what?" He didn't look up at her but sat staring at the pages of perp photos on the table in front of him. "I mean, other than a stalker who's strangling one girl after the next and City Hall doesn't give a damn . . . at least, as long as it's not some socialite or a rich little cheerleader gone missing."

"You're preaching to the choir. What's bothering me is that we're losing time. The more we chase down some profile APD cooked up, the more likely he'll strike again before we can get a line on him."

Moments passed before he broke the silence.

"I know what you want, little girl. Forget it. They're not giving you anybody else on this case. No way will they take personnel off the burglary ring in Buckhead. The rich people are worried about their stereos. So it's just you and me . . . as usual. Unless the mayor's office gets worried over this one, no more funding, no more bodies to help patrol the strip, nobody canvassing the area, nothing. Nada. Nobody. Don't even ask. They'll just say no, and you'll get your feelings hurt. Okay?"

She pushed another album toward him across the table. "Thanks. That helped. Just keep looking."

They resumed scanning one shot after the next.

Another hour passed before static crackled on the police-band radio Fincher wore at his hip.

"Hold on," he said into it, and turned to her. "Hailey, I'm stepping out to get better reception."

"Okay, but don't leave me in here for long. That door locks on the outside, remember? *And no cigarette break, damn it.* If *I* have to keep working, so do you. This ain't no tea party, old man."

"Keep *that* talk up and I will take a smoke. How did you say I'm supposed to lock you in here?"

Laughing, she threw a file folder at him as he closed the door.

She sat sorting photos in piles like a deck of cards and was still smiling when he came back in five minutes later.

Without looking up, she said, "I smell *smoke! Cigarette smoke!*"

When he didn't answer with some retort, she glanced up.

One look at his face and her smile vanished.

He stood frozen at the door, looking at her square in the face.

"What? What happened?"

"Hailey, they found another body."

She said nothing, just looked back down at the piles and piles of photos.

"It was off Stewart Avenue again. No robbery, same MO, possibly posed manual strangulation, stab wound lower back. Victim partially clothed, mouth and nose full of dirt."

She swallowed hard, and nodded.

"They're processing the scene now," Fincher told her. "Body may be too decomposed to get a DNA match at this point. Looks like it went down sometime after midnight on Friday. No ID on the girl yet. In her twenties, though, they think. Should we head on over and make sure they don't ruin the crime scene?"

Hailey couldn't speak, the image of another horrific torture-murder scene creeping into her brain like green mold edging over bread in the fridge. Then there would ultimately be the discovery of the victim's identity, the late-night visit to her family's home to tell the next of kin.

What would they find this time? Kids waiting for Mom to come home? A family? Or would there be just another middle-aged or elderly woman rushing to answer their knock, peering through the screen door, wondering where her daughter had been the last few nights?

And the look on the women's faces when Fincher flashed his badge . . .

They always knew at that point.

They knew their daughter was dead as soon as they saw the badge.

"Come on, Jezebel. Let's go."

Hailey stood and, still without a word, began packing up photos.

Fincher watched her from the door. His radio began crackling again. More news from the crime scene, no doubt. He didn't answer, standing rooted at the doorway. Then he propped the door open with the chair he had been sitting in, and got down on his knees. Together, they packed their bags.

They left the jail in silence.

The sun was setting and the tall, slender lights lining Atlanta's streets suddenly clicked on in front of them, lighting up the roadway as far as they could see.

He was out there, laughing, probably. Maybe he was going to work, maybe just coming home. Maybe he was at a movie with his wife or watching TV with his kids.

Or maybe he was cruising the strip at that very moment, stalking the next girl who would die with her neck mangled and twisted . . . the skin on her back ripped by vicious puncture wounds.

Then suddenly, Hailey was standing by the side of the highway, watching the taillights of the county cruiser disappear into the Atlanta night. Fincher faded into the traffic as the dream scene flickered in and out, and then faded out of her mind.

The real-life smell in the holding pen still assaulted her nostrils.

But then it all morphed into one heavy, cloying scent. A familiar scent.

Carnations.

Carnations not found in nature, but the kind that were over-treated in florist shops for maximum aroma value.

Everywhere she looked in the dream, carnations surrounded her, nauseating her with their sickly sweet smell.

Through the doorway was an open room and in that room were even more carnations: pale pink, yellow, white, blankets of them, arrangements of all shapes and sizes, sitting in vases on every possible stick of furniture.

Trapped, desperate for fresh air, Hailey looked for a doorway.

She found one and peered into the room and stepped in. Her eyes widened and her heart stopped.

The room whirled around her.

There was Will, lying dead and made up in heavy funeral home makeup to cover the bullet wounds to the side of his face.

His face. Asleep? No, dead. Will was dead.

The smell of carnations closed in on her, choking out the fresh air and suffocating her with a deadly overdose of funeral perfume. She gasped it in, sucking in the flowery smell as hard as she could for any trace of oxygen, but there was none—

"Dean!" Her name rang out.

No answer. Hailey's head was still slumped on her shoulder, her eyes closed.

"Dean! Answer up! Hailey Dean!" A female bailiff barked her name at the entrance of holding. She was holding a clipboard in her left hand, staring down at the pages of a computer printout to make sure a Ms. Hailey Dean had not already left the cell.

"Hailey Dean . . . where are you?"

It took a moment for Hailey's head to clear . . . to realize this wasn't just more of a bad dream. The dream was over. She truly was in the bowels of a Manhattan holding cell.

Hailey rose from the bench, weak-kneed. A stabbing pain shot through her ribs as she spoke. "I'm Hailey Dean."

"Let's go. This ain't no garden party, Missy. They want you upstairs an' I got to take you."

Hailey stepped carefully over several women sleeping it off on the filthy linoleum-tiled floor.

Making her way out through the others, it hit her that the smell no longer nauseated her.

She'd take a packed holding cell any day over the sick, sweet scent of death and funeral home carnations.

New York City

THE FEMALE WARDEN WAS TIGHT BEHIND HAILEY, LIGHTLY TOUCH-ing her shoulder as they walked single file down a worn, pale-beige institutional corridor.

"Left," the warden called out, and Hailey turned into an interrogation room. She naturally and immediately took in the lay of the land. In lieu of a window, a long, wide, seamless mirror covered one of the walls.

Hailey was seated in a metal folding chair. She looked around. These four walls had seen it all, and it showed, in layer upon layer of semi-gloss paint jobs. Hours of interrogations, confessions, threats, denials, hushed whispers between lawyer and client, witnesses, victims . . . it all played out between these four walls.

Now it was Hailey's turn . . . forced to match wits with some of the best homicide detectives in the business, skills honed by years of working the streets and solving the unsolvable.

But so are yours, she reminded herself.

She wasn't shackled, so she got up and walked over to the two-way mirror. It covered the entire length of the interrogation room's wall, from the chair rail up to the low-hung ceiling of industrial perforated squares. The detectives were undoubtedly leisurely kicked back in worn chairs on the other side. She decided to spoil their fun and chose a straight-back office chair, setting her back squarely against the mirror, keeping her face hidden from their view.

She looked straight ahead at the opposite wall, taking in the blank expanse covered in peeling beige paint. They'd be so disappointed they couldn't watch her face as she sweated it out . . . no nail-biting, wringing of hands, fidgeting, let alone crying for them to enjoy. Nothing. Just the back of her head.

But forget the goons on the other side. How the hell was she going to get out of this mess?

Think . . . think . . . think . . .

Her mind kept churning over bits and pieces. It all had to be connected.

Crumpled up on the floor of Dana's office with the carpet rough on her cheek while she took a manic beating from . . . whom? And why? Just before she had passed out, she was sure she'd heard a voice.

It was low and soft, almost a hiss . . . drifting out of the grayness closing in around her, familiar.

But as hard as she struggled, she couldn't remember what it had said or place who it was. It remained just a voice—angry, evil, spit out close to her ear there on the carpet.

Reliving the night of the attack was getting her nowhere fast. She could worry about her aching ribs and the break-in later. She hadn't even been able to process it all, much less to mourn the loss of two patients.

But right now, she had to somehow convince hard-boiled New York City homicide detectives that she was not the perp in the double murders of two longtime patients. She was armed only with a few facts she gleaned from the *Post*, combined with a little information Kolker unwittingly gave up.

Footsteps in the hall . . . She tensed, waiting.

But then the hall beyond the door fell quiet; no more footsteps to be heard.

So she sat, not twitching even a muscle, forcing herself to gaze neither at the mirror nor the door.

Commanding her mind to shift gears, she focused on the circumstances surrounding the deaths of Melissa and Hayden.

If she could just think just one step ahead of the homicide detectives. . . . Over and over she spun the story in her head, to think her way out of this beige-painted hellhole and get home.

First, what did Kolker spill? In his attempt to come off like the big guy, he had likely spouted off information known only to police. Same old story . . . a self-important official leaking like a sieve.

Even if he couldn't actually be a captain, he could at least feel like one for a moment. His bragging may have given her all the information she needed.

She predicted an interminable wait before Kolker showed up to meet her, and she was right.

But those were the rules of the game, and in order to win, she had to play by the rules. A frustrating wait in the interrogation room, after hours in lockup, sitting on a hard wooden bench and pacing a concrete floor, was meant to wear her down and soften her up.

She knew it . . . and they knew it.

Finally, after a good twenty minutes more had passed, Hailey made the next move. She stood up from the metal chair and strode purposefully up to the two-way mirror.

|||||||||||||||||||||||||||||||||||||||||||||||||||||||||||| **54** |||||||||||||||||||||||

Atlanta, Georgia

C.C. COULD HARDLY FOCUS HIS EYES THIS EARLY IN THE MORNING. He looked down at his wrist.

Eleven thirty?

Eleven thirty!

Where the hell was he, anyway? What was his room number? His head felt fuzzy and even he, C.C., recognized that the taste in his own mouth was from beyond the grave. Of course, he had no idea how bad it actually smelled, and assumed it was nothing a cup of coffee wouldn't fix.

He staggered off the couch and looked around.

This was definitely not his room. . . . His room didn't have a leather couch. Wait . . . maybe it did. Nope, it didn't, of that he was sure. He flopped back down on the sofa to get his bearings.

Where *was* his room?

He felt the outline of his plastic magnetic room key in his pocket. Pulling it out, he realized it did not have the room number stamped on its surface. Damn. When did they stop putting your room number on the key? Ridiculous. Another issue for his agenda.

Spotting a phone on a table beside the couch, he reached over, picked it up, and dialed zero.

"Welcome to the Atlanta downtown Marriott Marquis, the home of the world's elite travelers. This is Ellie, and how may I direct your call?"

That was a mouthful. It was almost too much for C.C. to comprehend first thing in the morning.

"Yes . . . ah . . . ahh . . . what room am I in?"

"Excuse me, sir?"

"I said what room am I in?" C.C. raised his voice on the last three words to help the receptionist better understand his question.

Marquis phone operator Ellie Jostad duly noted the nasty tone on the other end of the phone. Who in hell was this moron? What room is he in? How can you be sitting in the middle of a damn ballroom and not know it? Why was she, Ellie Jostad, destined to answer morons on the phone all day? Her mother was right . . . she should have finished classes at DeKalb Junior College and maybe she wouldn't have to listen to idiots like this for a living. Man, she needed a cigarette.

Instead of throwing down her headphone and lighting up a Merit, she answered. "Sir, you are calling from the Robert E. Lee Grand Ballroom study, if I understand you correctly, sir."

C.C. tried to lower his voice and attempt to reason with someone clearly suffering from a mental disorder.

"No, let me repeat so you can understand me. What room am I in?"

I should hang up on this rashy jackass, it's just not worth minimum wage. I can hardly put gas in the car and now this . . . If Ellie's supervisor wasn't four feet away at the coffeemaker, she'd blast this guy. . . . "Sir, how can I help you? You don't know where you are? Do I have that right?"

"I mean what room am I registered to? What is my room number?"

"Sir, I am not allowed to release that information over the phone."

"Ma'am, you are talking to the next governor of the great state of Georgia."

"Excuse me?"

Dumb bitch. C.C. had to go to the bathroom badly, and he had an intense aversion to all public bathrooms. He would actually only sit on certain commodes . . . in his homes, and then, only in his master bathroom, his office, the Supreme Court men's room . . . his country club was questionable. . . .

"This is Supreme Court Justice Carter," he said succinctly. "You're saying you can't tell a Supreme Court judge his room number?"

"Sir, it is against the Marquis's security policy to—"

C.C. hung up on her, slamming the phone down as hard as he could at a seated angle. He dragged himself out of his chair and stepped into a wide, sunlit hallway outside the Robert E. Lee Ballroom. His eyes were immediately assaulted with light, and his head pounded.

After walking in what seemed to be a circle, he came upon the elevator. Head still pounding, he leaned up against the wall beside the buttons to wait, his eyes closed against the light filtering through the hall.

This was ridiculous.

Once he was in the Mansion, there would be no meetings before noon.

After a lengthy and unpleasant argument at the front desk, C.C. managed to convince a thin young man in his thirties with a pencil nose, that he was in fact Georgia Supreme Court Justice Carter.

It required producing his driver's license and undergoing a thorough comparison of his person to the photo on the plastic rectangle.

Reluctantly, the clerk handed him a new magnetic strip card and reminded C.C. that the room number was not displayed on the strip for his own safety.

C.C. wouldn't let it go. "It's just damn inconvenient."

"Sir, as I said before, your room number is not displayed on the card for your own safety."

Sanctimonious little shit.

C.C. fumed as he turned away from the marble-top desk and headed back across the expansive lobby to the elevator bank.

He would refuse to set foot in this shit-box again when he made it to the Mansion. And he'd see to it that no other Democratic Party soirees would ever be held here on principle.

C.C. made his way down the carpeted corridor and unlocked the door to his and Betty's room, number 1112.

He started talking before he was even fully in the room, calling out to Betty as he opened the door.

"Betty? You'll never believe what happened to me!"

Maybe if he talked fast enough and filled up the room with chatter he could avoid the fallout. He had long ago realized his best strategy when coming home after misbehaving was to simply pretend it hadn't happened.

"Hey, Betty. What a night! Did you have a good time? That was some dress you had on, honey."

Damn! Before the words were totally out of his mouth he realized his mistake. What if she asked about it? What the hell did she have on? Why did he have to open his big mouth? Wait . . . he could just say how great her figure was. That was easy. He could fake it.

But the question just hung there in the still air of the hotel room. The AC was off and the curtains were pulled open, letting the sunlight pour into the room.

"Betty? Sugar Pie?"

Uh-oh—not a sound. She must be sulking in the restroom.

The TV was on with the volume muted, having reverted back to the hotel channel offering in-room movies and games. It even offered porn, C.C. knew, and a pretty damn good selection, too. Especially the ones with nurses.

Of course, it would be a cold day in hell before Betty would even think the word "porn," much less order some. C.C. tiptoed past the two neatly made double beds and rapped on the bathroom door.

"Honey, about last night . . . I just had to meet up with some of the party people until it was so late . . . I hated to wake you up late after your drive, so I just let you sleep."

No answer still. He rapped the door again and finally opened it. He knew she would be there, sitting at the vanity, either in tears or staring at him disapprovingly.

He sucked it up and went in.

Other than the faintest smell of hairspray, Betty was gone.

Nothing . . . not a suit in the closet, no eyeglasses by the bed, no damp towel on the rack, no tissue in the trash. Nothing.

On the vanity was a note, though. "Leaving early to avoid delays southbound between Atlanta and Forsyth. B."

Man, she had nerve. If that didn't beat all.

After all he had done for her. Truth is, he'd made her. She was a skinny nobody before him and now she was Mrs. Clarence E. Carter. And her leaving the hotel like this without even a word?

C.C. left the room and headed for the valet. No reason to tarry.

Easing himself behind the wheel of the Caddy, he put the AC on max and the stereo on high. Luther Vandross's voice melted through the speakers and sunk into the car's soft leather interior.

Reaching under the driver's seat, C.C. dislodged the super-secret silver flask he kept wedged beside the seat controls. Looking into the rearview, he waved good-naturedly at the poor schmuck just behind him driving an old burgundy Toyota Camry.

Poor guy was close enough that C.C. could see his face pressed up against the front windshield, squinting because the glass wasn't even tinted. The sun was brutal at this time of the day. You just didn't know what driving was until you'd had a Caddy.

Atlanta, Georgia

G RAVEL FLEW AS C.C. TURNED IN TO THE PINK FUZZY. HE GLANCED at the clock embedded in lacquered wood on the Caddy's dash. Tina should be here by now, having a salad for lunch as usual.

She rarely dined at home, and who could blame her, with that roommate?

That Lola, she was a strange one. Not only did she strip full-time at the club with Tina, she was a devout Catholic who collected reams of religious memorabilia. She was born deep in the bayou in Slidell, Louisiana, a Cajun who dabbled in the art of "white magic," as she euphemistically called it. Lola practiced Santeria, voodoo, and was not at all afraid to throw a little hank on somebody now and then, if such a hex were absolutely necessary. Lola was forever cooking up some foul stank on the stove in order to heal the sick, bring home a loved one, or seek Christian vengeance on an enemy. Lola's "enemies" were normally other girls at the club who cheated her out of lap dances and tips, obnoxious customers, and, quite often, the phone company, who routinely disconnected her phone for nonpayment.

On good days, Tina and Lola's apartment smelled heavily of flower-scented potpourri, Glade Plug-Ins, and hairspray. On others, it reeked of boiling chicken entrails stirred up with who knows what. Lola occasionally threw the gooey stuff on the enemy's car, smeared it on their front door at an opportune moment, or, in special cases, actually fed a tiny voodoo replica of the enemy *to* the stank as it boiled on the kitchen stove.

C.C. made it his business not to ask what exactly stunk, but for safety's sake, he stayed on Lola's good side and never, ever ate out of the refrigerator.

Tina avoided it as well, and had as many meals as possible at the Pink Fuzzy.

C.C. was aware that some people didn't enjoy eating at strip clubs, citing sanitary concerns such as pubic hair in the food. C.C. personally pooh-poohed such reviews. Food and theater critics are always asses anyway. Too snooty to review food in a strip club . . . fine, they were the ones missing out. Food. The little bit he'd eaten at the announcement party last night had been just enough to pad his stomach for his assault on the bar.

The lot was only about a third of the way full at this hour, and C.C. parked in his usual spot under a telephone pole with a security light attached. That always helped to locate the car once the parking lot had grown dark and jam-packed with vehicles. Damn SUVs and pickups would end up towering over the Caddy.

Now *there* would be some innovative legislation that everyone could appreciate, parking spots delegated for SUVs, pickups, and the like, allowing the rest of the world to see their cars when they came out of clubs at night. Hey, it could apply to grocery stores too, not just strip clubs.

This governor thing was going to be good.

C.C. had been on a roll with the press lately, especially since the Cruise reversal. They actually liked him now that Cruise had walked free. He just hoped the little freak didn't kill somebody else, but of course he would. With any luck, though, he wouldn't get caught and it wouldn't come back on C.C. Maybe he'd commit the next murder in another jurisdiction.

By that time, the election would most likely be over anyway.

C.C. opened the driver's door and rolled out his left leg first, his black leather shoe crunching down into deep gravel. He took another pull on the flask before his right foot joined the left and he made his way across the parking lot to the heavy wooden double doors of the club.

Not one to ask for special treatment, he reached backwards for his wallet to get his ID as he stepped inside.

"Hey Judge. How's it hanging?" asked a burly bouncer, squeezed into a shiny, dark-gray suit and sitting on a stool behind the ticket counter–type lectern. His biceps were straining against the cloth like he had two Virginia hams stuffed into them.

"Good, Sam, good."

Sam smiled out from above a collar that was bound tightly with a maroon tie. C.C. noticed his diamond tie tack. Always classy here, he thought approvingly.

"Saw you on the news last night, Judge. Looking good."

That gave C.C. pause. The news? "What was that? I was tied up for both the six and eleven."

"Don't be shy, Judge! Congratulations! The announcement last night! About throwing your hat in the ring for governor! It was everywhere, especially at eleven."

"Oh, yeah! The announcement. It was something, all right. You know I just want to serve the people, Sam, just want to serve the people."

"We turned all the screens in the whole place on you all at the same time . . . even the JumboTron was on you, instead of the dancers. It was something, it really was."

"Thanks for the support, Sam." C.C. smiled widely, tipping Sam a ten for future favors. "Where's Tina? She here yet?"

"Nope. But she should be. Her show starts in an hour. When she gets here, I'll tell her to come see you at the bar first thing. Go on over there to the bar, Judge. Burger's on me, just the way you like it, bacon and cheese, double-meat . . . right?"

C.C. smiled again, then sidled up to the bar and took a seat, accepting his due as the front-runner gubernatorial candidate.

"Jack straight up . . . and just show it the water, boss. Just barely show it the water. Just a sprinkle."

The drink appeared before him and he fixed his eyes on the JumboTron, where a new girl was dancing in pink patent-leather boots that went up over her knees.

Sitting there in his leather swivel bar stool waiting for his free burger, C.C. realized he could easily pull a Reagan. Go from governor to a national platform. It was his for the taking. Washington needed him. His foreign policy was brilliant. He hated Iraq and North Korea and wanted to nuke them both till they both glowed yellow. God wanted him to be in Washington.

Who *was* that girl in the pink boots? C.C. tried his best to place her as the music blared.

The din of the football game blared from several widescreen plasmas, serving as background for various women onstage in the "entertainment" area. C.C. watched one after the next, each more beautiful than the last. He had lost count of how many bourbons had come and gone.

The new girl in the pink boots was now making her second appearance since C.C. had settled in at the bar well over an hour ago. Her platinum hair was pulled high on the back of her head in a ponytail that swung halfway down her back, and she writhed to a Gwen Stefani tune.

The pole was a wonderful thing and this girl knew how to use it. C.C. marveled at how a waist that tiny could physically support boobs so huge. The girl was great, true, but she couldn't compare to Tina.

Who was late . . . again.

C.C. checked his watch, growing impatient.

Two new girls in an Asian motif were on the stage. One had something like a fly-swatter in her hand. Okay. C.C. settled back for the show.

"Lenny, hit me one more time . . . just to take the edge off. And, the cheeseburger?"

Onstage, the girls began a series of elaborate contortions, one doing a backbend, G-string and pasties toward the audience, while the other miraculously managed to hang upside down by her ankles on the pole, dangerously waving one leg out toward the audience.

Mesmerized, C.C. didn't break his gaze, but as a second thought, called out, "And Lenny, make it well!"

Rare meat disgusted C.C. Always had. He always liked to taste a little grill in his steak, lighter fluid and all. He only wished he had stock in A-1.

He almost didn't notice when Tina finally showed up, breezing through the front door past Sam and straight to the bar to hug him lightly from behind, reaching her arms across his chest. Startled, he looked down. The long, hot-pink enamel nails studded with rhinestones were a dead giveaway.

"What do you want to drink, babe?"

Disentangling herself, she carelessly dropped a huge metallic silver Prada bag to the floor beside their stools and settled in beside C.C.

"Pink Cosmo for me, Lenny. I only have ten. I'm due onstage." Tina called out her order, then swiveled around to look C.C. in the eye.

"I saw you on the eleven o'clock news. You were standing in front of the mikes."

C.C. waited for the same old complaint she hadn't been allowed to come to the party.

"You looked good, babe. I've never seen you in a tux before."

"And you look great!" he said, trying to sidestep the party last night as Lenny set two drinks with napkins in front of them. "What's your song? Got a new routine for me?"

She looked back, coyly eyeing him over the rim of the frothy drink.

Using her long pink nails, she dug into the froth, fished out the lime, and started tearing the fruit off the rind with her teeth.

"Maybe I do have a new routine just for you . . . you'll have to see. Right now I'm feeling all left out and hurt about last night. I saw Betty standing behind you. I bet you still haven't told her, have you?" Her tone took on a childlike whine.

He turned toward the widescreen. The game went to commercial and came back to two men in painful-looking sports coats who began discussing the game, laughing as if they'd told the funniest joke ever. C.C. couldn't make out what they were saying.

Tina pulled his sleeve. When he didn't answer, she continued, "You know, I'm starting to think that after I pulled you through all this, I'll never even be invited to the Governor's Mansion, much less live there with you like you promised."

"Baby, you know now's not the time to announce our engagement. Just be patient. You'll see."

Tina glanced at her watch, drained her drink, and slid down off the chair until her spikes touched the floor. Gathering the Prada and the full-length amber fur coat she carried everywhere, she whispered into C.C.'s ear.

"I got you a little surprise tonight."

"What's that?"

Her last "surprise" had been when she tattooed his initials inside the top of her thigh. It had led to a nasty infection and cost him thousands in doctors' bills.

"You'll see!" With a tongue-kiss in his ear, she was off. A thick cloud of perfume hung in the air behind her.

The music blared, the players ran up and down the field onscreen, the girls danced, and Tina made her way to her dressing room. C.C. pulled a nice Dominican from his shirt pocket and lit up.

The two with the fly-swatter were still onstage. By the looks of it, C.C. figured they must be professional gymnasts.

The cheeseburger came with a huge side of fries. After smothering them with ketchup, he dug in. He waved at the next man down the bar and gestured for the salt. Before the guy could respond, a feminine hand came between them. It was wearing a full-length, hot-pink evening glove, with plenty of bling on the slender fingers outside the glove. Reaching between the bar patrons, it was holding a salt shaker.

"Hi, Judge. I'm a friend of Tina's. How are you tonight? Feeling good? You're *looking* good!"

C.C. looked into the eyes of one of the most beautiful, tall, statuesque women he had ever laid eyes on. She was the color of mocha, with brunette hair falling nearly to her waist in waves.

"Well, hello! It's nice to meet you. Have we met before?"

"I don't think so."

After all the bourbons, C.C. couldn't quite make out her accent, but it was husky and exotic.

What a beauty! C.C. was thrilled. Could she possibly be . . . ?

"Are you my surprise? From Tina?" he asked tentatively, hopefully.

Would Tina be so magnanimous?

Of course she would! She was being squired by the next governor!

This was his victory lap!

She smiled at him. Her lip gloss smelled like cinnamon. It was so thick he could smell it, even over the cheeseburger.

"Surprise? Yes, that's what I am . . . your surprise . . . your special, private surprise." Her words came out like honey being poured from a jar.

He knew it. Tina was an angel.

"But for the rest of the surprise, Judge, the cherry on the icing, we need privacy. It'll only take a minute. But my special surprise for you has to be in private. Tina said so."

Private? Just the two of them?

Just at that moment, right on cue, Tina emerged onto the stage dressed in an Egyptian-style headdress and sandals with straps crisscrossing up her legs. Her eyes were rimmed with elaborate blue and black kohl eye shadow, and she wore a shiny black Cleopatra wig. She lithely stepped up onto the backs of two muscle-bound guys on all fours on the stage floor. Just before she swung into gyrations, balanced on their backs, she tossed a kiss onto one index finger toward the JumboTron, her secret "hello" to C.C.

He took it as a sign that he was meant to fully enjoy his "surprise," with no guilt attached. Tina truly was his dream girl.

The surprise whispered into his ear, "Go to the VIP men's room, far end stall. I'll meet you in five minutes."

Without a word, C.C. drained the remainder of the golden liquid in his glass, turned, and headed toward the men's room in the VIP at the rear of the club.

Making his way through the club, C.C. adjusted his eyes to the darkened VIP Pinkie Suites.

"Hey Jack. How are you tonight?" C.C. asked the attendant outside the bathroom.

"You're looking good, Judge. Looking good."

C.C. breezed through the swinging door and, amazingly, found himself alone in the john. By instinct, he squatted over and checked. No feet below.

Perfect!

This was incredible, just the beginning of his new life and all the wonderful opportunities that would come with it. As instructed, he marched directly into the last stall.

Wait . . . maybe he should freshen up.

Peeking outside the stall's metal door, he noticed he was still alone and ventured out over to the multiple sinks lined beneath a huge horizontal mirror. A long counter ran below the mirror, covered with men's hairsprays, condoms, lotions, and aftershaves.

He quickly squirted himself but good with something called Drakkar Noir. It sounded foreign and exciting. He added squirts under each arm and one quick, discreet but drenching spray down the front of his pants aimed directly at his crotch.

You never know.

C.C. scurried back to his stall and sat down, waiting. It felt like Christmas morning!

Not more than a few minutes passed when he heard the swinging doors to the bathrooms swish open and heels clicking across the tile floor.

C.C. tensed, sitting there on the toilet.

There was a light tapping at the door, and he could tell from her feet under the stall door that it was her. He opened the stall door and let her in. From where he was sitting on the ceramic bowl, Mocha looked six feet tall.

"Don't get up, Judge, just sit back and relax. Baby got a surprise for you."

Baby kneeled down on the tile in front of C.C., unzipped his pants, and buried her face in his lap, his right hand resting gently on the top of her head, his left palm braced against the metal wall of the stall.

She tossed her hair back and started giggling.

C.C. giggled too, his eyes nearly closed, his head rolled back, leaning against the back of the toilet.

Then he saw it—C.C. was never sure whether he caught the first few bright flashes.

Then another and another . . .

At first he thought he was seeing strobe lights in his head, but when he squinted his eyes open, he was staring right into an expensive-looking black metal camera attached to a long lens.

It was hanging to his left, over the side of his stall.

What? A camera in the crapper?

He jerked forward and caught something in his right hand. With much confusion, he looked at the long brunette wig he held in his hand as Mocha squirmed up to attention and began rearranging her clothes.

"No-no . . . Baby's leaving. Y'all too kinky for Baby in here. Nobody told Baby 'bout no camera." She blurted it out in a deep-pitch baritone.

Still clutching the long weave, C.C. was frozen on the cold commode seat, unable to absorb what was happening.

Looking up straight into Mocha's nostrils, he noticed for the first time a large and distinct Adam's apple. Not good.

Urine threatened to expel. C.C. absolutely could not wet his pants. He had to act.

With the two of them struggling to rearrange themselves in one stall over a toilet, C.C. could barely get up and zip up. The stall door flew open, Mocha flounced out, and the man attached to the Nikon jumped down off his perch on the neighboring commode seat, lid down. He had apparently been crouched there, straddling the toilet's water with one foot on either side of the bowl, since before C.C. first came in.

"What the hell is going on, you son of a . . ."

Jumping down off the bowl like a monkey, he lurched directly in front of C.C. and continued to snap away . . . catching C.C. arranging and zipping.

Just as C.C. made a grab for him, he took off like an Olympic sprinter, not even bothering to push the swinging doors open, charging them shoulder-first like a linebacker.

The music from the VIP room blared into the bathroom as C.C. started after the guy, only to stumble and fall face down onto the cold tile floor. He got up and ran for the door. What the hell was going on?

He charged from the brightly lit fluorescent-tiled bathroom through the doors and back into the darkened club room; he couldn't see but knew enough to head for the door.

Too late. The guy was gone.

|||||||||||||||||||||||||||||||||||||||||||||||||||||||||||||| **56** |||||||||||||||||||

New York City

"WHAT THE HELL IS SHE DOING?" OFFICER KEVIN DUNNE ASKED, as Hailey leaned into the two-way mirror and wiggled two fingers like bunny ears saying hello. "Does she know we're here?"

"What do you think?" Lieutenant Kolker responded, lowering all four chair legs to the ground and watching her intently. "I told you, she's a lawyer."

Not just a lawyer, Dunne knew.

Kolker had instructed the detectives to pull up every LexisNexis article they could find on Hailey Dean.

It made them all a little edgy to learn that she was considered to be a brilliant criminal trial lawyer, perceived by many civil libertarians as a zealot, a renegade crime fighter who used all means necessary to win a case.

"Maybe she really is crazy," Dunne's partner, McKee, muttered, reaching for a Marlboro, contraband in the new "smoke-free zone" era.

They'd tossed that theory around when they'd read about how, out of the blue, she had packed it all in after ten years of clawing her way to the top. It was rumored she'd bid farewell to a million-dollar civil practice waiting for her.

Nobody was sure what triggered her departure. Rumors ranged from a disastrous love affair with a defense attorney in Atlanta to disgust with the jury system to a nervous breakdown following her last major trial.

Kolker was opting for the breakdown. It fit much better with his theory that Dean was motivated to kill her patients due to a mental imbalance linked to that last prosecution. The MOs were far too similar not to be connected. They thought about a third-person copycat, but between the obvious connection, the forensics taken in the field, and the other evidence Kolker developed—it added up to her. And it made a much more sexy story. There'd be nowhere else but up for Kolker after this . . . outsmarting a lawyer-turned-killer.

"Sure looks like she's lost it," Dunne agreed, incredibly uncomfortable beneath her studied gaze that laid bare their hiding place.

"Damn, it looks like she's staring right at us." McKee pulled uncomfortably at his necktie.

Of course, she couldn't see them . . . could she?

No.

That was ridiculous.

But the way she was staring . . .

It just wasn't right. They were supposed to make her nervous . . . not the other way around.

"Kolker, go ahead . . . get in there."

"Not just yet. I'm gonna make her sweat."

"Yeah, well, she don't look like she's sweating," McKee commented as Hailey smiled into the two-way.

"Shut the hell up," Kolker barked, and shifted his weight in his chair.

They continued to watch, studying her, trying to get a read on her emotions.

Was she nervous? Was she tired? Would she break into tears?

At last, Kolker cracked.

"All right," he said, standing, "it's time to play bad cop. I'm going in."

|||||||||||||||||||||||||||||||||||||||||||||||||||||||||||||||| **57** ||||||||||||||||||

St. Simons Island,
Georgia

TOBY MCKISSICK STARED AT THE PHONE ON HIS DESK AS IF IT WERE LIABLE to bite him on the wrist if he reached for it, and squirmed in his seat, now noticeably slick with sweat, especially along the lower back and contoured seat.

He wanted to shoot himself. No, not himself, somebody else. He definitely wanted to shoot somebody else.

The intercom system made a second obnoxious buzzing sound, and he slumped down even further in his prized Naugahyde office chair on wheels. He pulled it as close to his desk as his stomach would allow.

He knew it was Sean, his secretary, buzzing him to tell him Floyd Moye Eugene was holding on the phone, long-distance from Atlanta.

He could pretend he wasn't there like he normally did with unwanted and intrusive calls. It probably wouldn't work this time.

Sean wasn't too smart, but her legs were long as a colt's and she had a perpetual, miraculous coppery brown tan.

Even though Sean was beautiful, her blind hero worship of him was actually irritating sometimes.

Quite a contrast to his wife. When she wasn't at home playing bridge with her foursome, Lois made constant trips back and forth to the St. Simons United Methodist Church. The bulletin had to be written on Monday, typed on Tuesday, mailed on Wednesday. Then there were the Hand Bells Choir, the Kids' Choir, and the Adult Choir. Lois was involved in all three, plus knee-deep in church politics. Toby still loved her in his own way, like a child loves an old teddy bear whose fur was rubbed off and eyes torn out, in other words, no longer attractive.

"Who is it, Sean?" Toby asked.

"It's Mr. Eugene, long-distance from Atlanta."

Toby felt like every ounce of energy had drained from his body.

He knew it was hopeless, but he asked anyway. "Does he already know I'm here in the office?"

"Well, I told him you were in a budget meeting . . . like I normally do. Was that wrong? Should I tell him you're 'in conference on a matter of grave importance to the constituents,' like I did last time?"

"No. I'll take the call."

"Yes, Mr. Chairman."

The dreaded buzz came again and the call passed through to Toby's desk.

He put on his game face, kicking back in his chair and putting his feet up on his desk, trying to get in the mood. "Hi, buddy . . .

how's business? Hot as hell here, Floyd, you ought to come on down and go out fishing with me on my boat. How is it up north in Atlanta?"

There was flat silence on the other end.

Toby involuntarily sucked in his breath and held it there. He didn't have to wait long.

"You stupid piece of shit." Floyd was speaking low. "Don't even start the glad-mouthing. Save it for the locals you brainwashed into voting for you every two years. I'm not buying. Your boat . . . *my ass.* It'll be a cold day in hell before I'd let you steer anything with me in it. I rue the day I picked a complete imbecile for an operation this big. You wanna tell me how you managed to totally screw this thing up?"

This morning's "Huevos Ranchos" egg special he'd ordered at the Huddle House was making loud churning sounds in Toby's stomach. "Floyd, I understand why you're upset and . . ."

" 'Upset' isn't the word for it, moron." Eugene never raised his voice, but his unique hissing quality was worse than a rattlesnake's. "I've got eight million in equity tied up in Palmetto so far. And that's *pre-construction.* Do you understand what I'm telling you?"

Toby couldn't answer—a whiny stutter came out instead of words.

"Because of you, McKissick, there've been delays. Timing is everything."

"But, Floyd, I can't control a group of kids tearing the place up. We tried to . . ."

"And because of your delays, I'm out an extra two hundred thousand. The place is guaranteed to open its doors for occupancy in two months. Two months. Another delay and we could lose committed buyers. You know how much that'll cost me, you moron?"

"We hired extra weekend security . . . the best." Sweat rolled down the side of Toby's temple.

"Bull*shit!* You got one sad sack from the Brunswick mall and the other from Wal-Mart. I already checked them out, idiot. Just for once . . . just *once* in your miserable pea-brain life, *try not to bullshit.*

I can smell it on your breath, two hundred miles away over the damned phone line."

The Sansabelt waistline in Toby's madras-print pants was soaked from the sweat coming down his back, and his mind was a blank.

"We're starting up again in twenty-four hours. If anything goes wrong, McKissick, you've got more than a couple of thousand riding on it. You're about to put some skin in the game. Now buzz your secretary so I can hear you send her to lunch. And keep it on speaker."

"Why? She can't hear what you're saying. She has no idea what's going on anyway."

"Just do it, McKissick. Now."

Toby left the line open and buzzed Sean. "Honey?" He struggled to keep his voice level. "Why don't you go on to lunch early and take your time . . . do a little shopping?"

She buzzed back immediately. "What? Shopping for what? And I'm not hungry. I just ate a Slim-Fast bar and they're great. . . . Want one?"

"No, lemon-pie. You go ahead. I need to have a private conference."

"Okay . . . but it's not gonna be private. Two gentlemen are out here in the front office waiting to see you, from Atlanta they say. They said you're expecting them."

She buzzed off before Toby could say anything, and frankly, he didn't know what to tell her even if he'd had the chance.

He heard the front door to the office slam shut behind her as she headed out to her Geo, sitting in the office parking spot.

For a moment, there was only the even, grinding sound of the air conditioner, cranked up on high even this early in the day.

Then two men appeared, standing silently at his office door.

They didn't speak, just strode uninvited straight through his door, into his office, and toward him. The taller one silently massaged the knuckles of his right hand and took in his office like it was a two-bit flophouse. Toby knew instinctively that all the Kiwanis awards, civic trophies, and local celebrity snapshots covering his office walls—each one carefully evocative of his own importance—didn't impress these two in the least.

The shorter man trained his eyes on Toby like a Doberman, watching him as if he were some sort of a doggie meat-treat. He spoke in a low, guttural tone toward the speaker on Toby's desk. "We're here, boss."

"Good. Keep the speakerphone on for me, boys. I like to know when a job's finished."

They were on him immediately.

The first punch was sharp and to the stomach. The Doberman's fist disappeared deep into Toby's gut, the pain doubling him over and smashing him facefirst to the floor. His head hit the metal trash can and it toppled over, papers flying across the floor, now at his own eye level.

His favorite Mexican egg dish came up in a blur of brownish salsa and egg. It spurted across the carpet and dribbled down the sides of his mouth.

They pulled him up and, despite the intense pain, Toby struggled with one hand to keep his toupee atop his head.

As the intruders looked down as if Toby were a giant garden snail they were about to salt, he managed to adjust the hairpiece to a perfect center.

"I knew it was a piece," the shorter one paused to snicker.

"Shitty piece, dumb-ass. We spotted it a mile away. Not only are you a dumb-ass, you got no style. I hate a guy with no style. Don't you hate a guy with no style?"

"No style whatsoever. It's disgusting." Even thugs have standards. This one looked down at Toby like he was something foul smeared on the bottom of one of his snakeskin boots.

He reached down, ripped the piece off Toby's head, and threw it like a Frisbee across the room, where it landed on a shelf covered with local softball trophies.

Toby had never, not even once, been seen publicly without his toupee, and it was quite the topic among the locals. Moreover, he never even went to bed in the dark of the bedroom he shared with his wife without his hairpiece carefully adjusted on his head, much less allowed the shiny red skin covering his skull to ever be seen by strangers. Of his many vanities, it was the greatest.

With vomit dribbling down his chin, his hairpiece stripped away, and his gut aching, he was terrified of what was about to come.

He'd known from the start that Eugene was dangerous, but how did things go so wrong? And the money . . . it had seemed like a dream come true, a deal he couldn't turn down. . . .

The second punch made the room go dark.

Toby fell back to the floor, faceup and prone against the wall behind his desk.

The smell of the eggs managed to reach through the hazy pain to his nostrils. He retched again onto the floor under his desk and all over the side of his prized briefcase—alligator, pre-governmental ban.

"Okay . . . talk. The boss wants to know who did it."

Toby could barely hear, much less talk.

A punting kick from a sharp-toed cowboy boot landed at the small of his back.

"I don't know. . . . It was kids," he blubbered it out.

"Bullshit! The boss wants a name. Talk, you fat turd, or you'll be picking up your teeth off this carpet."

Tears streamed down Toby's cheeks.

He recalled the hours of veneer and porcelain work the cosmetic dentist had placed in his mouth, creating a megawatt smile that shone out of his tanned face.

The big one lifted him up off the floor by his collar. A punch landed on his nose. Warm blood oozed down his face onto his golf shirt, and bloody bubbles formed between his lips when he managed to speak.

"Virginia Gunn. She probably did it."

"Crybaby snitch. I knew you'd talk." The big one looked down at him. "Didja get that Tony? Virginia Gunn . . . whoever the hell that is."

"Got it. Virginia Gunn. We'll find her."

Sharp kicks in quick succession landed to his lower back and stomach, worse than either of the previous blows.

As the savage kicks continued, one after the next, Toby instinctively curled into a fetal position to protect his vital organs.

After a few moments, he felt nothing more.

The vomit dried brown on his face. He was out cold when Eugene clicked off the speakerphone and the Dobermans disappeared into thin air, out in the sweltering mirage of the strip-center parking lot, as if they'd never existed.

||||||||||||||||||||||||||||||||||||||||||||||||||||||| **58** ||||||||||||||||||

New York City

HAILEY LOOKED UP AND SMILED BRIGHTLY WHEN KOLKER ENTERED the room, face red and notebook pressed tightly under his left armpit.

"Hi, Lieutenant."

He eyed her suspiciously when he caught her smiling over at him, leaning back casually against the two-way. He was all prepared to be the "bad cop." A good mood was too weird and it threw him off.

"Hailey." He nodded curtly, pulled out a chair, sat down, and crossed his legs ankle to knee. "Sit down."

Hailey walked over to the conference table, pulled her chair in a little too close to Kolker, straight into his personal space, and sat, knowing he'd feel it was too awkward to pull his chair away from her.

"Feel like talking?"

"Sure." She didn't move a muscle, keeping her hands loosely clasped together in her lap.

"Mind if I use a recorder?" He took it casually out of his jacket pocket and laid it on the table in the tight space she'd left between them.

Hailey knew it was a well-practiced move, keeping it all very nonchalant.

"Go ahead," she said. "But shouldn't I be read my rights again?"

"Excuse me?"

"A substantial amount of time has passed since you last read them and I'm now in official custody, aren't I? Might not hold up in court, you know." She was practically quoting straight from police manuals used in cadet training all over the country, reminding him that she knew the rules and had played the game as many or more times than he had.

He rankled. "Of course, Counselor." Sarcasm dripped off each word.

She held the smile.

He flicked on the recorder, took out the standard Miranda card all cops carried, and started reading it out loud. "You have the right to remain silent. Anything you say will be held against you . . ."

Halfway through the reading, she made eye contact with him and held it hard.

As if challenged to a duel, Kolker quit reading, slipped the card back into his wallet, and continued reciting Miranda by heart.

They squared off and the questioning began.

"So Hailey, how long had you treated Melissa and Hayden . . . and was it purely professional?" He asked it suddenly, with a smile.

Interesting. Was he switching to the good cop routine? Did he think she was crazy? That maybe she'd forgotten all the crap he'd put her through at the hospital?

She hadn't.

He went on. "And when I was in your office, I noticed some papers on your desk. They were in plain view, I couldn't help but see them. They're about murder victims, stabbing victims to be exact . . . written by someone who gets a thrill out of it."

"Well, Kolker, sorry I waited for you to get all set up with the recorder here and get all the way through Miranda, but maybe I shouldn't talk without a lawyer." She knew she could bring it all to a screeching halt by demanding a lawyer *now*. But the truth was, the lawyer might not show until the morning, and the overnight delay would give the cops enough time to trump up probable cause to rifle through her home and office—that is if they hadn't already. Plus, it always looks bad to lawyer up when you claim you're innocent. Like you have something to hide . . . which most suspects did.

He looked confused.

Encouraged by the reaction, she went on, "Frankly, I'm concerned about the way this investigation is being handled. You questioned me at the hospital before you read me my rights, and they had me on meds, meaning everything we discussed in my hospital room and office would be fruit of the poisonous tree. Much less a search. It'll be suppressed in court, of course. And it's not just your word against mine. Remember my colleague, Dana? She was present the whole time and will swear under oath that no rights were read before you questioned me."

A scarlet pattern began to creep up his neck, spidering out of his shirt to blotch his face.

She pressed on. "Kolker, you are familiar with the fruit of the poisonous tree, aren't you? You know, any evidence that flows from illegal beginnings is no good. I mean, they do run you guys through a little Crim Pro class here before they dump you out on the street . . . don't they?"

Kolker might be screwed legally and know it, but that didn't stop him from continuing the interview while he still had her on his turf, still banged up, and still minus a defense lawyer.

"Good try, Dean, but the evidence isn't based *only* on what you said to me. The facts surrounding the deaths of Melissa Everett and

Hayden Krasinski point directly to you. You're the common link, Hailey, between two dead bodies. Not only that . . . there's the forensics I mentioned. Yep, you're locked in pretty tight on this one. And remember those eleven decomposed hookers, back home, Hailey? The last case you ever tried? Remember you were the big hero back then? Same exact MO.

"Four-pronged stab wounds, Hailey. Both Melissa and Hayden. You stabbed first, then posed the strangulation once they were down. Yeah, I checked it out, Dean. Lots of people down there say the case drove you kind of crazy . . . said I should have seen you in court. I hear you tried the case like you were possessed."

Hailey remained carefully expressionless, but Kolker knew he hit a raw nerve.

The memories of the eleven dead women in Atlanta rose up in her mind's eye, and she thought of her own clients, Hayden and Melissa, dying the same death. She could feel the sweat on the back of her neck making her hair wet underneath, but the rest of the loose blonde hair covered it.

She had to make it out of this stifling hole. If she didn't, she wouldn't be able to work the case on the outside to build a defense and figure out who was responsible. Surely something Melissa or Hayden had said over all those months would give her a clue that the two murders were somehow linked.

"Female victims, right?" Kolker said. "All in their twenties, staged manual strangulation, four-pronged stab wound from a gourmet poultry knife, wallet and driver's license intact, partially clothed, always with dirt and mud smeared on their faces, and of course, the fancy baker's twine on every victim. It's sick. What, you want to swoop in and be a hero again? Wanna talk about it, Hailey?"

His eyes bored straight into her as he struck a match on the bottom of his shoe and lit a cigarette.

"You could do it, all right. You could pull it off. We know you work out. We know you work out every night, running, weights, the whole thing. You're strong. With the element of surprise on your side . . . not to mention the element of trust you had with your patients ... listening to all their problems day in, day out. Picking out just the right ones ... the weakest ones. Probably had 'em doped up on Prozac, lithium, sedatives, all arranged by you. ... Oh, yeah, you could do it ... no doubt about it. Did you sock them in the head with something first, Hailey, just to stun them before you gave it to them with the poultry knife? And those journal entries of yours about stabbings ... *twisted*!"

Hailey reached down deep. She was a lawyer. ... He wasn't. So hit where he was soft ... legalities of the arrest.

"Poultry-lifter, Kolker, not poultry knife. And, nice job ... but you know I'm right about the interview being suppressed as poisonous fruit. You screwed up, Kolker. Now it'll all be thrown out of court, and you know it. But forget about that for today. You've got *plenty* of time ahead to worry about your case getting thrown out. There's something else even *more* rudimentary."

Sitting there, she discovered for the first time that Kolker had a tic ... in his right eye. It was twitching now, and she knew she had done it. In the space of five short minutes alone in the conference room together ... he was *pissed*.

Kolker snapped off the recorder.

She kept on. "It doesn't take a lawyer to figure this out, but it seems to me the first thing you should do in a *murder* investigation, much less a *double-murder* investigation, is establish times of death. Of course, that's after determining cause of death, I assume *at least that's* been done."

She paused, desperately wanting a glass of water. The verbal sparring was wearing her down and her mouth was dry.

"But hold on a minute, Lieutenant ... didn't somebody mention there was a crack on the head? Or have you even had the morgue check for head abrasion under the hair? So is it strangulation, stabbing, or blow to the head? Better get that straight before you start comparing MOs from other unrelated cases, no matter how much you want to nail me for this."

Kolker's face twisted. She had obviously hit upon something with the possibility of blows to the head as the actual causes of death. Plus, in the Atlanta murders, strangulation *and* stabbing were causes of death, each lethal enough to cause the death in and of itself. Here, from what she was hearing, one of the wounds was postmortem.

The strangulations here could actually have been staged postmortem, in some sick game. The killer could have posed the bodies as if they'd died by strangulation, or even have strangled them after they were dead, just for the thrill of it.

And then there were the unmistakable puncture wounds to the back. . . .

Her head was spinning. If a blow to the head was the true cause of death, it would only be worse for Hailey, since a crack to the head with a blunt object would take much less upper-body strength than manual strangulation. The same for stabbing.

What was the true cause of death? She'd bet he wasn't even sure yet. . . .

It didn't matter now. All that mattered was throwing a wrench in Kolker's preconceived theory. That was the only prize for Hailey right now . . . keeping him off balance. And the times of death . . . there was a weakness here. She sensed it.

"But back to the time of death," she said, trying her best to wheedle information out of him so she'd have something to go on in her own defense. "I mean, that *is* step one, wouldn't you say? Time of death?"

"For your information, we have officially set the time of death for Hayden Krasinski at eight thirty p.m. Melissa Everett died at nine fifteen p.m. the preceding Wednesday. Nice touch playing dumb, Dean, as if you didn't already know. So while we're on that topic—"

She cut in coolly. "I'll continue the interview as long as you keep the recorder going. The trial judge might not like it when she finds out you turned it off."

The twitch in his right eye went crazy, and Kolker punched the recorder's red "On" button again.

They both knew it was highly inappropriate to tape only portions of a police interview. If the case made it to a courtroom, such a practice would lead to successful motions to suppress the entire discussion, thrown out on claims police had edited or tampered with the defendant's statement.

Score two for Hailey.

Sweat appeared on Kolker's upper lip, and his collar showed dark, damp areas where it met the skin of his neck.

"Where were you at nine fifteen last Wednesday night, Ms. Dean?" he asked crisply. "Or do you need a lawyer to dream up an alibi for you?"

Wednesday . . . nine fifteen . . . Where *was* she?

Where *was* she on that night, for God's sake?

Her mind stretched to the limit, but she couldn't remember.

Then it hit. She leaned forward from the waist, as if she was making sure the recorder picked it up, heavy on the drama for the benefit of the peanut gallery watching from behind the two-way mirror.

"Get this, Kolker. I don't need a defense lawyer to protect me from you because I don't need protection. I don't need a defense lawyer at trial because there will be no trial. And I certainly don't need a defense lawyer to dream up an alibi . . . because I know exactly where I was. Check it out. I was at the New York Sports Club on Third Avenue at Fortieth Street. I showed my club ID, the computer read it and logged it. There should be a computer record to verify it."

"Nice try, but I checked you out. . . . I know your drill. You're just like clockwork . . . always the same thing, every night of your lonely little life. When it's nice, you run the East River, when it's not, you run the treadmill and lift weights at the gym. Out running alone doesn't amount to an alibi. And for all I know you could have left that night right after you signed in, just to create an alibi. Would have been a decent story, too. But sorry, no good, Counselor."

Damn . . . he had done his homework. Who the hell had told him her workout schedule?

Then the truth hit. Who else could it be but Dana?

Hailey could just see her, drinking in every drop of attention Kolker or any half-decent-looking man was willing to feed her. Dana could talk forever and apparently had.

But it wasn't over *yet*.

"Well, *normally*, that would be correct. If you did your homework instead of listening to office gossip, you'd already know Wednesday night was a little different. Change up in the routine." She paused for effect, just long enough to get him nervous.

Leaning back into the tape recorder, she went on. "Wednesday night, when I signed in at the Sports Club the weather was bad. Too cold for me, anyway. Check it out, Kolker . . . call the Weather Channel. And as for the treadmill, that particular night management was redoing the treadmill room to install individual televisions on each machine. I couldn't use the treadmill, so I signed into an aerobics class—probably two dozen witnesses, maybe more. I got stuck in the very front row and I didn't know the steps, plus my ribs ached, so I'm sure they'll all remember me."

Kolker looked as if he had taken a punch to the gut. If she was telling the truth, and her steady gaze straight into his eyes suggested she was, his "airtight" case against her was falling apart in front of his eyes.

"It was a funk-aerobics class . . . and it went from eight thirty until ten o'clock that night. Then I took a shower. And, Kolker, I walked out of the building that night with the instructor. I was there when she locked the glass doors in the front of the club. Check the security camera in the gym lobby. You'll see me, but you'd better hurry. In case you didn't know, banks, convenience stores, ATM machines . . . those cameras tape over every seven to eleven days *at best*."

Before he could respond, she continued on. "After that, I went across the street to the mini-mart at Thirty-eighth and Third. A few of them are open twenty-four hours, you know that much, right? I bought groceries."

Almost immediately, his eyes lit up.

Before he could even blurt it out, she held up her hand. "Don't get excited. . . . I didn't pay cash. Used a debit card. Comes right off my checking account. Immediately. If you have wireless in here I could pull it up for you right now. You know how to use a computer, right? You know . . . e-mail . . . online banking . . . surfing the Internet. . . . It's easy now, Kolker, it even shows the time— somewhere around ten thirty. How does that fit into your theory? Pretty well, if you totally want to throw out the time line your Medical Examiner established for the time of death. Or, hey, your theory could still conceivably work . . . if the body had been found in the dairy section at the mini-mart."

She saw him glance over at the mirror. They had to be laughing into their fists at him back there by now, and before he thought it through, he shot back.

"The time is fluid, Dean. And I've still got you on Hayden's murder. You may talk your way out of one—and I'm not saying you did—but not the other. You're dead in the water, Dean."

The veins on either side of his temple were bulging, and his face was red.

You'd better watch it, she told herself, realizing this might not be the right time to be a smart-ass.

After all, he did have the keys to the jail, literally. "What about Thursday night? Where were you?" Kolker asked without a pause.

She pulled back. "I'm clear on Thursday, too. I ran the East River."

"Alone?"

"Yes." The tables turned abruptly. She knew she was in trouble.

"Running alone along the East River? No witness? No running buddy?" Kolker smiled, rummaged in his pocket for a quarter and pushed it across the worn tabletop with the pink eraser tip of a yellow pencil. "I know it hurts, Hailey . . . but don't feel too bad. Here's a present. It's from me to you . . . to call your lawyer. Nice try, Hailey." He stood up and gazed triumphantly toward the mirror, nodding his head slightly to his cronies on the other side, as if he were taking a bow.

She knew he was right. Running by herself . . . all alone along the East River jogging path . . . wouldn't work. No witnesses . . . but wait . . . what could she do . . . Was there any way she could alibi herself? They'd still hold her, even on the single Murder One count, even if the other was weak. Without thinking it through, she spoke.

"Well, you have a point. But, Kolker, I ran with my cell phone tucked into the pocket of my sweatshirt. I was thinking as I ran. I had an idea about an article I'm working on, and before I lost the thought, I called my office. I left a message to remind myself."

"So what does that prove? You could have easily made the call anytime from anywhere . . . maybe leaving the body warm on the ground at the scene of the murder, for all I know."

He was right. Again. She had to think faster.

"So the call, if it does exist, only proves one thing—you're even more cold-blooded than I thought. Cold-blooded enough to stab some mixed-up, innocent kid and then before you even turn the block, you set up your own alibi."

He was gaining ground. "And everybody knows that even a high-schooler knows how to change time and date stamps on incoming and outgoing calls. This'll make a hell of a closing argument for the prosecutor, won't it, Hailey Dean?"

He sat back in his chair, now relaxed, grinning into the two-way. Kolker's moment of triumph. He was loving it.

But it didn't last long. Watching him carefully, Hailey pulled the trump card. "No."

The moment faded for Kolker and he turned slightly in his chair to look at her.

Her voice was cold now. "In the middle of the message, fire trucks from Sixty-seventh Street pulled out onto Third. It's Engine 39, I'm sure. It had to have been. I could hear the ladder man over a bullhorn shouting so that they could get the big pumper truck out. I heard him telling drivers to back up so they could get out. Cars were blocking the driveway. The pumper couldn't pull out onto the street. If the machine picked it up and I'm sure it did . . . it locks me in on the time. I'm clear across town, practically in the Seventies, the murder is at the other end of the island, in the Village, you said."

He didn't respond, but looked briefly toward the mirror as if for guidance.

"Check the message, Kolker. I know I saved it because I didn't have time to work on the article yesterday before . . ."

Before you barged into my office and you brought me here . . .

She held her tongue, saying only, "I can play it back for you right now on remote if you want. You'll hear the ladder captain in the background and the sirens. They'll have a record of a fire-truck detail being sent out that night . . . that time. And you do know how to triangulate, right? To ping? You know, to pinpoint the exact location, sometimes down to the square block, where a cell call's made?"

Kolker was looking down at the table between them, deep in thought.

She didn't let up, she went for the kill. "Go ahead . . . ping me. And oh yes, my doorman, Ricky, saw me when I came back in."

Hailey put her right index finger on the face of the quarter and slowly pushed it back across the tabletop toward Kolker.

"Keep it, Kolker." Hailey stood up, preparing to leave. She'd won her way out of the jail and she knew it.

She glanced over her shoulder at the two-way mirror and nodded her head.

"Not so fast, Counselor. Your hair's usually pulled back, right? Maybe you should have kept it back the nights of the murders, Hailey."

She stared at him full-on. "Get to the point, Kolker."

"I told you we have forensics. Can't argue with the crime lab. You were on the crime scenes all right, both of them. DNA puts you there."

"There is no way my DNA was at the crime scenes."

"Save it. We got top-notch crime techs working Melissa's body within the hour. Hayden's, too. The best in the state, maybe even the country. They combed the scene, Hailey. It didn't take them ten minutes to find long blonde hair—not one piece, Hailey, several.

We've already had it tested, mitochondrial DNA, Hailey, maybe even some nuclear DNA, too . . . and *they're yours.*"

Her hair? At the scene?

"And Hailey, they weren't just *at* the crime scene. They weren't just *on* the body. Melissa was clutching them in her right hand. She was fighting to live . . . fighting with you. I think you had them doped up on some of your shrink meds . . . and they never saw it coming . . . and from someone they trusted. It's sick. On Hayden it was caught in a bracelet she was wearing.

"And one last thing, as if we needed it. What about this? Any idea who *this* belongs to?" Kolker stood up, stretching his long legs. Reaching into his pocket, he pulled out something shiny, something silver.

Hailey turned and froze. Hanging from his right hand, on its black silk cord was a small, silver necklace, a tiny Tiffany's ink pen.

"Recognize this, Hailey?" Kolker asked, gloating.

She did. Of course she did.

She didn't have to look any closer to know what was engraved: *For Hailey, Seeking Justice, Katrine Dumont-Eastwood.*

"We found *your* jewelry, *your* necklace from Tiffany's. It was on the Krasinski murder scene. And it wasn't in her pocket or sweatshirt. She didn't just pick it up accidentally. It was under her body. And to top it off . . . the cord's broken. Lose it during the struggle, Hailey?"

She had once treasured it dearly but now it dangled in Kolker's fingers like a noose.

Atlanta, Georgia

FRANK LAGRANGE HADDEN (THE THIRD) HAD BEEN WORRIED ABOUT being able to walk, let alone run, after being folded into the crapper stall for so long.

Thanks to the burst of adrenaline shooting through his body when he sprang up and snapped the first shot, he somehow found himself sprinting through the hot breeze of the parking lot with amazing agility for someone so horribly out of shape. Tall and thin, he never exercised, spending most of his time online, parked in front of his big screen, or closeted away in his darkroom.

But once he was off the toilet, he unfolded long, thin legs and ran like hell.

His Nikes dug into the gravel and he pumped his arms furiously, weaving through hundreds of parked cars to get to his own burgundy Toyota.

Laying the camera on the passenger's seat, Hadden cranked up, jerked the Camry into reverse, put it in drive, and took off spewing gravel. He burned rubber pulling onto the asphalt, locked the car doors, and belted himself in all while gunning the gas, surreptitiously glancing into his rearview mirror just in time to see C.C. lurch out of the club, a burly bouncer on either side of the Judge.

Damn fool.

Looking back, he could see the Judge and his two goons running through the strip club parking lot, looking for him in the wrong direction.

By now, he knew, Baby was long gone and wondering who had given "her" the two thousand dollars cash. He/she should have known that was way too much for just a Monica. But there was no way a hooker would turn down a cold two thousand dollars, and Frank knew it.

He also knew, after following this jackass for weeks, a judge no less, that there was no way he'd turn Baby down.

What a way to make a living.

His legs had fallen asleep while he'd been crouched on the toilet seat for nearly an hour, and now they felt like fiery daggers were tearing through them.

Hadden snaked through the back streets of Hispanic neighborhoods surrounding the Pink Fuzzy until he made it back to I-85.

Once there, he floored it, going north of the city, keeping one eye on the rearview mirror, just in case.

In minutes, the traffic and streetlights began to fall away. He picked up his cell and dialed the number he had been given.

No one ever answered, but he always got his payments on schedule, like clockwork.

The line was picked up by a machine, identified only by an outgoing beep.

"It's me, Frank. I got the photos. The ones you wanted and plenty of extras. As soon as I get the last payment, they're all yours. Negatives included, as promised."

Another beep came, signaling the end of the allotted recording period.

He hung up the phone and tossed it onto the seat beside him.

Frank finally began to breathe easy. He dropped his speed to fifty-five mph as he continued heading north to his home on a cul-de-sac in one of thousands of nearly identical suburbs surrounding the city of Atlanta.

His neighbors had no idea what he did for a living.

But everybody who was anybody in certain circles knew that he was the best in the Southeast. He got it all—on tape, audio, and video—for people all over the country. Private dicks, the mags, sleazy divorce lawyers, jealous lovers—they all knew where to come.

If they had the money.

But even with business being good, he could always use more fat wallets like this one.

This was a major gig, and that moron Judge Carter made it easy. Frank had tailed him for seven weeks, and the idiot never even looked in the rearview mirror. Not even once. Oh, wait, there was the one time Carter had actually waved at him.

For the first few days Frank started out with rented cars and elaborate disguises, which of course he billed to the customer, along with the entire stakeout. The bill was never questioned. The disguises didn't last long, though. No need.

By the end, Frank was parking his Toyota right behind Carter's car over at his girlfriend's apartment. No fear of detection whatsoever.

Frank had hated people like Carter his whole life, ever since kindergarten. The ones who had it all, got it all without even trying. The Haves. Carter was so drunk off his own sense of self-entitlement, so used to the world being his oyster, he never looked up from his own front zipper.

Speaking of which, he was probably out in front of the Pink Fuzzy right now still trying to get his zipper up.

If he could find it.

New York City

AILEY FROZE . . . HER MIND WRESTLING HAND-TO-HAND WITH her vision. She was speechless . . . staring at the impossi-ble . . . the illogical. It couldn't be true. . . . It didn't make sense.

Her silver Tiffany pen, engraved on the side, given to her by Ka-trine years ago after a murder trial.

She and Fincher had torn apart the courtroom looking for it . . . spending hours down on all fours between the pews of the court-room, where Hailey had wandered during her closing arguments. They'd searched through all the evidence, the trial files and notes, even retracing Hailey's footsteps back and forth to her office there in the courthouse. Finally, they gave up. Hailey remembered walk-ing to the county parking garage that night feeling a loss, repeat-edly touching her neck where the black silk cord normally hung down.

She never saw it again until now . . . years later in the interroga-tion room at the NYPD.

"Surprised, Hailey?" Kolker rolled the glinting silver back and forth gently between his thumb and fingers.

She had her back to the wall. The only strategy she had was to play him. Let him do all the talking. He was incredibly pleased with himself, barely able to contain his elation over the pen. Could he hold it in? Was Hailey wrong?

It took about thirty seconds.

"You thought you pulled it off, didn't you. But you left *this* little calling card. You were there with Hayden when she died, Hailey, and this proves it. And I want you to know . . . I picked it up my-self."

He actually turned toward the mirror, his back to her as he went on.

"It didn't take me long to realize it belonged to none other than the treating psych for both dead women. That's no coincidence, Counselor. By trial time, believe me, we'll come up with a way to explain your alibis. Just be glad New York got rid of the death penalty."

So her pen had turned up after all this time . . . under Hayden's body. In a single thoughtless boast, Kolker had given away a major prosecution strategy. Now she knew the strategic significance of the pen, where they'd found it, how they planned to use it against her, and, significantly, exactly who had picked it up. She knew about the hair, the article, the timing of the murders . . . it was no small amount of evidence . . . and this was just the beginning of the investigation.

Mustering every ounce of technique left in her body, she managed to keep a stoic mask in place. But now she understood the State's case, what tied her to Hayden's murder and, connecting the dots, to Melissa's as well. Now she had the ammunition she needed to fight back.

But she had no choice. It would mean lying to the police. She wanted desperately to tell the truth but . . . they'd never believe the truth about the pen disappearing. It was a major gamble because if she were caught lying, she'd look guilty as hell. But tonight, there was no other way out. She reminded herself that Kolker couldn't possibly know the history behind the pen. She swallowed hard and it hurt her throat.

"Hey . . . I've been looking for that. It's my favorite. But Kolker, even coming from you, I'm shocked. This can only mean you searched my office without a warrant. I haven't seen my pen since Hayden's last visit. She was twisting the cord, wrapping and rewrapping the silk portion between her fingers while she talked. She played with it nearly the entire session. So it was there, in the office, but then . . . you came by . . . Kolker . . . did you take the pen from my office?"

The words were poison to any major investigation, accusing the cops of planting evidence, and they hung, foul-smelling in the close quarters of the interrogation room.

He was speechless. In one minute, the momentum shifted.

Realizing she had a tiny advantage, Hailey pressed on.

"Kolker, is that the only way you can crack a case, planting the pen as evidence? Even coming from you, I'm shocked."

Sensing that he was faltering, she leveled her eyes to his and put the accusatory shoe on the other foot. "Did you go in without a warrant? Did you find it, read the engraving, and place it there under her as she lay dead? You're the one who's sick, Kolker, not me. It's so much more sensational to try and pin this on me, isn't it? A regular street thug wouldn't do, would it? Just how far will you go to make a name for yourself?"

"I didn't—"

Suddenly, Kolker was keenly aware that his colleagues and superiors behind the mirrored wall were watching him.

All right, Hailey, that's enough. Keep it simple, she warned herself.

How many times had liars done themselves in by creating an elaborate story that could be attacked from countless angles?

Learn from their mistakes . . . say no more . . . see where he goes with it.

She could see the wheels turning as it slowly started to dawn on him that the discovery of the pen wasn't exactly the airtight piece of evidence that would clinch the case for him. In fact, there were any number of explanations why Hayden may have had the pen. She could have borrowed it, swiped it, used it, and then, unthinking, dropped it into her artist's notebook.

"You mean that's it? This pen is why you're holding me? And the fact I was trying to help Melissa and Hayden?

"The *kinky* journal entries, as you so eloquently put it, Kolker, is research I've been doing for over a year on the psychopathy of serial killers. All of them, Gacy, Bundy, Zodiac, Boston Strangler, BTK . . . the notes weren't about my patients at all, and I've sent the theory to over a dozen psych journals to see if they'd be interested in publishing. There are records. Try that on at trial. Oh, and they'd never get in at trial anyway because they *weren't* in plain view on my desk, they were in a file drawer beside my desk. You searched without a warrant. . . . I knew it."

She looked him square in the face, unrelenting. "Oh . . . and the hair . . . your big *forensic evidence*. It means nothing. I hug nearly every patient when they leave each session, Kolker. I'll have a string of patients testify to that at trial, so dig in, Kolker. They're transfers from me to them. Or maybe they caught a hand in my barrette or touched my shoulder."

He had lapsed into silence. Hailey didn't let up.

"But she was clutching it . . . her hand was in a fist!" Kolker was limping now.

"Says you. By the time my lawyers and experts finish with your so-called crime tech, the jury will think you planted the hair just like you did the pen. That is, if they don't see the obvious, that it's a simple transfer. It's not enough. And Kolker, the word 'mitochondrial' doesn't scare me. It simply means DNA without skin, without the nucleus, the root attached to the hair. Big deal. Even if you have nuclear DNA with the root . . . so what? If a few hairs were torn from my scalp when one of them pulled away from a hug or when I pulled a sweatshirt off my head and it transferred to them . . . I never even felt it. Struggle? There was no struggle. It proves nothing . . . *nothing*, Kolker."

She could see the wheels turning, that the magnificent dream he'd nurtured for days on end was fading. He hadn't cracked a serial-murder case after all, not yet, anyway. He was not headed for a promotion and could forget being heralded in the press.

"You kept mementoes of the murders. I found Hayden's poems in your office like the ones that were in her backpack the night she was murdered, and a photo of Melissa. Just like Gacy kept underwear and driver's licenses off his victims. Killers keep them like normal people keep ticket stubs and photo albums. Explain *that!*"

Without a pause, she spoke evenly. "So you *did* search without a warrant. I thought so before, now I know for sure. Hayden gave me a stack of her poetry to show to a publisher who lives in my building. And Melissa showed me that photo because it pictured her with her sister. She left it at my office on the coffee table and I put it in her folder to give back.

"Kolker . . . this isn't a murder investigation," she said, "it's a frame-up so you can claim you cracked the case. Just a grab for headlines. The whole thing makes me sick. Two innocent women, murdered brutally in your own backyard, Kolker, and I'm the best you can do? Wait until the papers hear that you arrested a woman even though the victims may have been molested."

She got him again, on pure speculation. Instead of protecting the case, he protected himself and blurted a retort.

"But there wasn't any sperm! We don't know if the molestations were premortem or post-, whether the attacker was a man or woman."

"You're not even sure there was a molestation . . . are you? A partially clad victim doesn't equal rape, Kolker."

As he started wildly searching through his papers, she dropped the bombshell.

"I refuse to be questioned any further. I want to call a lawyer . . . now. When I thought you were actually investigating the murders, I wanted to help, but now . . ." She closed in for the kill. "And I want Rube Garland."

She had never even met Garland, but she saw his name in a news article when she Googled Kolker's name after he showed up in her hospital room.

The story detailed Garland's client who walked free on a murder rap because of a legal loophole. It was Jack Kolker . . . then just a beat cop . . . who had neglected to sign his name on a bag of evidence.

That bag contained hair samples taken from the victim's bedroom, the murder scene. The DNA just so happened to match up with Garland's client's. The paper's front page had a shot of Kolker storming out of the courtroom, an angry snarl on his face.

The photo was accompanied with an interview with the defense attorney, Rube Garland, in which Garland gloated over NYPD's failure to protect the chain of custody, leaving a hole in the case and making it ripe for a defense claim of planted evidence. Hailey insinuated now, as then, Kolker screwed up DNA hair evidence.

Before Kolker could utter another word, the door to the interrogation room burst open.

Two cops, both wearing suits, walked into the room. One was short, gray, and pensive . . . the other tall, dark, and looking incredibly angry.

"Kolker, you're needed upstairs." The little gray one spoke.

Without another word, Kolker gathered his papers and left the room, throwing one last glance over his shoulder at Hailey as he left.

It was a look of unmistakable hatred, pure loathing. She had totally humiliated him in front of his whole team, the brass, too.

But it didn't matter now. Hailey sensed it. She was headed home.

It was over . . . at least for now.

The two detectives handcuffed her to the table, which was bolted to the floor.

"Wait here," the short, gray cop said, and the two of them left her there alone, unattended.

Fully aware that others might still be seated in the observation room, she said nothing and remained expressionless.

After another long wait alone, they returned.

As the taller one jangled keys and reached for her handcuffs, she saw that the short cop was holding a large plastic garbage bag containing her empty purse, wallet, cell phone, and pager. All the wallet and purse contents were loose in the bag, having been searched thoroughly.

Hailey's ribs ached as she stood.

"Ms. Dean, you may be required to return to headquarters for questioning." The little gray one again, short but not curt, giving no explanation as to her detainment or her release.

She expected neither.

Nobody needed to tell her why she suddenly was being released. Kolker's interrogation had bombed miserably. The department had obviously pinned their hopes on his theory, and with the discovery of Hailey's pen at the second murder scene, the interrogation of

Hailey Dean should have been the icing on the cake . . . case closed.

In their plans, the evening would have ended with drinks all around at the Irish pub around the corner, and tomorrow morning, a front-page story in the *Post* listing all their names, describing them as the elite force that stopped a cunning serial murderer who turned out to be none other than a beautiful criminal lawyer-turned-psychologist. Of course, no front-page story would be complete without photos of themselves.

But it hadn't turned out that way.

"I'm happy to do whatever will help with the case." They began the circuitous route out through the bowels of the building, the detectives leading the way. Once on the ground floor, the short gray one pointed toward the imposing front entry.

"A right, then a left. It'll take you straight to the front exit. Good-night."

She continued walking down the corridor, fighting the impulse to turn back. Just as she made the first turn to the right, she glanced quickly sideways to see them still standing there in the middle of the hallway, staring at her, clearly unhappy at the sudden turn of events during the interrogation. She turned the corner and they were out of view.

Hailey made the rest of the walk alone.

Pushing the heavy doors forward, she stepped outside. The night was dark and fresh. Lights were beginning to twinkle in thousands of buildings across the city. It was biting cold; the wind whipped around her legs and blew blonde hair away from her face.

She was out, true. But for how long? She braced her body against the cold. And it wasn't just the freezing wind howling up the street that made her shiver.

Somewhere out there in the city, blended in with nearly eight million other people, there was someone willing to wrap his hands around the necks of two young women and strangle the life from their bodies . . . to pierce their backs with a four-pronged murder weapon jutting from the spine all the way through their lungs . . . all in a twisted effort to frame Hailey for double murder.

Her silver pen was the key. The realization sunk in slow and heavy as she stood there on the top step of the jail. Two women were already dead at the hands of someone targeting not them, but Hailey. Would there be more? She had lied, true . . . but if she told Kolker the truth about the pen, she'd still be in the interrogation room instead of on the street.

Police were no help to her now; they wouldn't accept defeat. An invisible weight settled on Hailey's shoulders as the lights continued to blink through the misty darkness settling over the city. One thought burned into her consciousness.

Who planted the pen?

||||||||||||||||||||||||||||||||||||||||||||||||||||||||||||||||| **61** |||||||||||||||||||||

St. Simons Island,
Georgia

VIRGINIA UNLOCKED THE WOODEN DOOR THAT WAS PART OF THE tall, weathered fence surrounding her house, and stepped into the yard. It was all grass, sea oats, and scrub pines growing wild and unmanicured, still wet from morning dew and sea mist.

As she approached the front door, she could hear tiny yelps and barks as the dogs hurled themselves at the door to welcome her back, their little doggie toenails digging at the bottom. When she pried through the tiniest possible opening so as not to let them escape, they leaped on her, all tongues and fur.

First, treats, and then, the guerrillas. With Sidney curled in her lap, she took out her old address book, BlackBerry be damned, and started dialing.

"Good afternoon, Radio Shack."

"Yes, may I please speak to Ken?"

She was on hold for the duration of a Britney Spears song until, finally, she got her first lieutenant, Ken, on the other end. They spoke in agreed-upon code.

"The beach is hot. We need to cool off."

The undercover talk thrilled Ken no end.

"When?" he whispered into the phone, and Virginia could just see him, turned away from the others and being all Barney Fife.

"Nighttime, and we go by boat. Call me tonight but start the chain."

"Chain commenced. Over and out."

The phone clicked off and the gig was on.

The other dogs were all sacked out on the den furniture, sleepy after their treats. Virginia pulled herself out of the chair, depositing Sidney on his paws, and started upstairs to make the bed and take a shower.

After that, she'd head back to Larry's. She had to locate some sort of a boat they could take around the bend of the Island. Shouldn't be hard, no water patrol that time of night. It would have to be large enough to carry the shovels and hedge-clippers they'd need to tear apart the layout.

In the back of her head, somewhere remote and tucked away, she knew it was all temporary. The money man would find a way to lay the foundation regardless of their attacks on the work site.

And then what? Chain herself to the site's chain-link fence? Mount another petition of Islanders that opposed development?

That was beginning to wear thin as more and more Islanders got paychecks *from* developers.

It would be a long war, and this was simply one battle.

At the top of the stairs, Virginia turned right into her bedroom. She opened the curtains and looked out at the waves rolling in one after the next after the next.

It was beautiful and hypnotizing and worth fighting for.

"That's what it's all about," she whispered to nobody. She would find a way.

A thump at the front door snapped her out of her daze.

The damn paperboy. She'd told him a million times, *don't hit the door*. It would throw the dogs into a fit. But luckily, they continued to snooze off the treats.

She bent to pick up a pillow off the floor, then stood up straight, eyes wide, locked on the window.

The paper had already come.

Something wasn't right. All at once, Virginia could feel it.

She stood absolutely still, listening.

For a moment, all she could hear was the distant sound of the ocean and her own breathing.

Then, the faint but unmistakable sound of a footstep creaking on the stairs.

She was no longer alone in the house.

Panic washed over her and she looked around for a place to hide. Knowing she was trapped, she made a futile move toward the closet.

Just before she reached it, she glimpsed, through the corner of her eye, movement in the doorway.

It was too late.

She turned around.

Two of the most massive men she'd ever seen looked back at her with flat gazes.

"Who the hell are you and what the hell do you want? Get out of my house before I call the police!" She eyed the phone on the other side of the bed, and without waiting for an answer, she lunged for it.

Diving across the bed, they tackled her. She hit the floor, her face sliding along the rug, burning. One of them kicked her hard in the backside when she tried to stand up.

"Take it . . . my purse. It's over there." When she spoke her tongue tasted blood.

The shorter one backhanded her and she flew against the wall.

"Somebody likes the beach, doesn't she?" The pointed toe of a snakeskin cowboy boot crashed into her ribs.

The tall one yanked the neck of Virginia's shirt and ripped it down around her hips. Her arms crossed her chest and she stayed flat on her stomach. One of them turned her over, but she couldn't see which. A pain went crashing through her skull when a fist made contact with her jaw.

Far away, she could hear the wild barking of her dogs . . . and then it faded into silence. The last thing Virginia saw was the carpet under her face on the floor.

|||||||||||||||||||||||||||||||||||||||||||||||||||||||||||||| **62** ||||||||||||||||||||

New York City

HE'D ALWAYS HAD EXCELLENT NIGHT VISION, EVEN AS A CHILD. The super-heightened sense, his uncanny ability to see in practically pitch-dark conditions, had served him well in the past. On the streets of Atlanta, he'd been able to spot the silhouette of a lone woman on a darkened sidewalk blocks away, even in shadowy pockets where the streetlights had been shot out for target practice.

And then later, in the penitentiary, he would sit nightly, unmoving, in the dark of his cell, looking straight forward through the bars of his cell door, seeing yet not seeing.

He always had the advantage at night, and tonight was no different. His eyes had been trained on the front entrance of the New York City Women's Detention Center for nearly seven hours. As the daylight faded, he had to focus even more keenly as people came and went about their business. His back to a wall across the street, he continued staring, watching every single person who emerged.

Darkening winds whipped up the street to fly above him and around the building that rose like a mountain in the middle of a New York City block. He melted against the stone of the building.

Then suddenly, the hours spent hunched there against the building came to an abrupt end.

It was her.

The moment was perfect . . . just like he dreamed . . . the precise moment he saw her emerge from the giant front doors. A huge overhead lantern-fixture hung down in the middle of the old building's entrance, glowing golden in the night and spilling light down over the steps. It bathed her body with light against the dark and when it did, the sight of her hit him hard in the gut. He sucked in wind so cold it hurt his chest and made his teeth ache.

The blonde hair, the pale face, the slight frame . . . the figure precisely matched the one etched into his memory.

He watched her step out of the building and into the night air. He refused to even blink, drinking in the sight of her as she stood for a fleeting moment on the gray-streaked solid granite landing of the NYPD. She was poised there, topping thirty or so sharp granite steps leading down to the street level, like a tiny, delicate marzipan ballerina decorating a giant cake.

She almost seemed to lean back and rest against the heavy doors. Her coat fell back, away from her body. He could barely breathe.

What was she thinking?

She could have absolutely no idea he was this close to her.

But then, none of them had.

How does it feel now, Hailey? The hunter is the hunted. The destroyer is being destroyed. Does it hurt, Hailey?

His eyes were sharp and he spotted the bandage on her left hand as she reached up to grasp her shoulder bag.

She was lucky to be walking at all. She better not complain. A few cracked ribs were nothing compared to what the others got.

When she pulled her scarf off to rearrange her blonde hair, he was nearly sliced in two by the sight of her face, pale after hours in lockup, blonde hair blowing against her cheeks.

The others in Atlanta had meant nothing to him. He couldn't possibly have cared less when they died. He was only interested in that beautiful moment, the intense eclipse of pain he gave them at the very moment of death.

Maybe it was something the two of them, Hailey and he, could discuss back at her place.

As she came down the long flight of granite steps to the street, he stepped out of the shadow and onto the sidewalk.

She never even looked back, not nearly as sharp as she was during her days as a prosecutor.

This was going to be easy.

He tried to imagine the look on her face if she were to turn around by chance and see him so close, just behind her.

Would she be scared? Would she fight? Would she confront him, here in the streets, alone? Or would she turn and run as best she could with her ribs bandaged?

The thought of her trying to run from him made his whole body tense.

God, his hands had started to tingle in his coat pockets. The electric heat pulsed past his fingertips up through his palms. Even his wrists ached.

He was so close to her now, he could call out her name and she'd turn around.

He wondered if her hair smelled the same as it had in the courtroom five years ago. He'd been fantasizing about the inside of her apartment. He had gazed up at it from the street for hours at night, watching until her bedroom light went out. He could tell she left a light on somewhere, maybe the kitchen, over the stove.

Once he was inside, maybe he'd even find a scrapbook in her apartment. Maybe there'd be news clippings with him in it.

He knew in his heart she thought about him just like he thought about her.

The big difference was that he hadn't made her suffer for five years in the bottom of a stinking hellhole.

He followed along behind her. It would be tough for her to get a cab tonight, especially in this neighborhood. It was cold as hell and late. She had a nice long walk ahead of her. He noticed she favored her right side as she continued walking, and he saw from behind that she was wearing old cowboy boots.

Nice. They were walking through the city together. How romantic. Just like a movie.

His fingers were starting to feel like they'd explode straight out of their skin inside his pockets, and his groin throbbed in sync with the blood pulsing through his temples.

He could feel it all. He was here, now . . . with her. He'd dreamed about this moment for the past five years, waking and sleeping.

Everything would be okay.

St. Simons Island,
Georgia

T HE BELL WAS RINGING OVER AND OVER, BUT IT SEEMED FAR
away. . . . Then something else . . . a pounding sound.
Virginia opened her eyes.

It took her a while to get her bearings. Why was she on the floor,
wedged between the wall and a love seat? She was lying directly
beneath a tall bedroom window and looking under the love seat
toward her bedroom door. She could make out the bottoms and
legs of the furniture, and could see straight under and through to
the other side of her bed, and on to the hall beyond the bed and
bedroom door.

She closed her eyes again, her head in a vise of pain.

The house was still, completely still. As her vision corrected, she
realized she was staring straight into a set of deep, brown eyes that
stared right back at her, trained and unblinking.

Sidney.

The wiener lay flat on his stomach, all four sausage legs splayed
out to his sides, gazing mournfully at her. Immediately recognizing she was awake, he army-crawled on his tummy across the
carpet to where she lay trapped between object and wall. He
crawled all the way, till they lay nose to nose. Lying on the carpet, inhaling his doggie exhale, she tried to speak his name. The
pain in her throat was so intense she caught her breath mid-
syllable.

She tried to roll over and up, but she couldn't. Summoning up all
the strength left in her body, she managed to rise up halfway and sit
with her back against the wall, her head spinning with the effort.

What the hell happened?

Sidney's joy that she was alive could not be contained and he began rapid-licking her calf. The wiener looked for the world like he had been crying. She tried to reach out to pet his head, but the fierce pain in her side wouldn't let her extend her arm.

When she looked down at her right hand, she saw that blood had dried down two of her fingers where there should have been nails. The nails had been broken off backward.

What day was it? Why was she on the floor? Confused, she glanced around and spotted her phone and digital clock radio, both torn out of the wall and broken in pieces on the floor.

It all came back in a rush. . . . the two men with no necks. The threats about the beach. Her shirt being torn from her. . . .

She looked down with momentary panic and was relieved to see that the shirt was still around her waist and her jeans were still on, buttoned and zipped.

At least she only took a beating from the no-necks. It could have been worse. So much worse.

But how did they know? How had they found out about her?

And what about the others . . . her little band of misfits . . . her guerrillas? Had they been beaten as well? Were they even alive? Had they fought back? Could they? Could the two intruders possibly know how to get their names, much less locate them?

Virginia stiffened; there was movement downstairs.

The sound of the sliding glass door onto the deck opening . . . She could hear the metal slide down the floor groove and then catch. A pause, then the door was slid shut again. She heard the glass door's lock click back into place.

They were back.

They must know she was still in the bedroom. They must think she was still alive. She looked wildly around the room for an escape . . . other than down the stairs and directly into the path of her attackers.

The only other way out was the bedroom window. Better to jump from the second story and risk a broken arm or leg than the alternative.

She caught Sidney's eye.

Please, please don't start barking. . . . just this once . . .

Sidney seemed to get it . . . that he had to remain silent . . .

She couldn't stand, so with her heart pounding frantically, Virginia started to crawl toward the window.

They must know she was still in the bedroom. How much time did she have? Not enough.

She rounded the bed, her body screaming in agony. She inched herself past the bed . . . then just a few feet more to the window . . .

She was there! She'd made it!

Now, to lift herself up, unlock, raise the pane, stand, and get out . . .

It was impossible.

No, it isn't. You have to save yourself. It's the only way.

Struggling, she pulled up on the sill and reached for the lock, stretching . . . stretching . . .

All she had to do was open the window. She could try and scream. Maybe the neighbors would hear . . . Someone . . . Anyone . . .

The pain, so acute it took her breath away . . . No scream escaped her lips. It was futile anyway, her house was set apart from the others; her neighbors would be sealed into their air-conditioned houses, insulated from the day's heat. Her voice would be drowned out by the surf.

She silently reached to unlock the window. Straining for the lock, she stopped, tried again. She managed to reach it, turn it.

Wincing in pain, she began to raise it, just enough to get her torso out, then fall to the ground twenty feet below.

She gazed out the window, and when she looked down, the ground was swirling, her vision blurred from the beating.

Concentrate. You have to keep going . . .

The window was up.

Now . . . if she could get her leg up and out, the rest of her could follow. . . .

It was too late.

Two hands grabbed her shoulders, pulling her back, away from the window.

The pain was so intense. She couldn't fight anymore. Where was Sidney? What did they do to Sidney? The room disappeared in black.

|||||||||||||||||||||||||||||||||||||||||||||||||||||||||||| **64** ||||||||||||||||

New York City

HAILEY HUNCHED FORWARD INTO THE COLD WITH HER ARMS crossed over her chest, moving quickly up the street toward her own apartment.

Her own apartment.

It seemed like months had passed since she'd been home.

Ricky was there, manning the front door, holding it open for her, and she stepped into the familiar warmth of the lobby.

Habit carried her through the lobby, nodding good-night to the snoozy second doorman manning the desk, past the mailroom hidden behind the elevators.

Now, finally, she slipped into the elevator alone, humming its way up. She leaned back against the wooden panel and focused on the one thing that had consumed her for the past three hours.

Her silver pen.

Now, years after she had lost the memento of one of her most famous murder trials, it turned up again. Not in an old trunk or trial file, not crammed to the back of her underwear drawer where she often put letters and cards she wanted to keep, but in the hands of the NYPD, lifted as evidence off the dead body of one of her own patients.

When the elevator's muted bell rang to a stop at her floor, Hailey stepped off and headed down the carpeted hallway to the end of the hall to her corner apartment. It seemed amazing to her to take out her key, open the door, and find everything as it had been when she'd left. The light still burning over the stove, the window still cracked slightly in her bedroom to let in cool, fresh air, her clogs still sitting at the edge of her bed, as if nothing had changed.

But it had. It had changed horribly.

Home. Home at last.

She could hear her own footsteps in the quiet of the apartment, stepping back to the bathroom attached to her bedroom to fill the tub with hot water.

Leaning over to plug the stopper, her thoughts raced. She was clearly the cops' chief suspect. They'd be out for blood now that she'd trumped their theory from behind bars. They'd want to nail her on this no matter what. They'd never admit they were wrong, especially after she'd humiliated Kolker. Plus, if she *wasn't* the killer, they'd be screwed at trial. How could they testify under oath to a jury they were *positive* they had the killer, when a few short months before, they'd been were positive *she* was the killer? They couldn't. They were locked into her, and they'd make the evidence fit.

She knew it. She felt trapped.

Hailey turned abruptly, leaving the bath water running. She went into her closet and kicked off her boots and socks, leaving them there on the closet floor. Barefoot, she went silently across the hardwood floor into the kitchen.

The pen. That's what they had against her, that, the hair match, and a few pieces of circumstantial evidence. They'd be working the case against her now harder than ever. They wanted her at all costs.

She was going down. They'd find a way to do it . . . unless she could figure it out before she was re-arrested.

She robotically went through her cabinet until she found the tea she wanted. Filling the kettle at the sink, she wondered . . .

The pen had never been in her apartment or her office here in the city; she was certain of that. That ruled out Hayden lifting it by accident. It hadn't happened that way, but for the very first time, Hailey had lied to police. To save her own skin.

Standing there in her kitchen waiting for water to boil, her lips curved up wryly on one side. The shoe was finally on the other foot.

How many dozens—no, hundreds—of times had she shredded criminal defendants and their lawyers in open court when they had been caught in a lie to cops after a crime? And when defendants were foolish enough to take the stand, she carefully dissected their every word, twisting them, slicing them, slowly roasting them until sometimes they broke down and cried. Sometimes they had confessed . . . and sometimes they lunged at her across the witness stand. Unsuccessfully.

The stillness of her apartment was disconcerting compared to the sounds of the city, so alive outside, far below, even at this time of night. The water was heating and she walked from room to room, innately seeking some sort of comfort from the things around her. She glided back across the hardwood floor onto the cold slate kitchen floor.

The only sound was the hot water running on high in the bathtub. She stopped at the den window beside her mother's piano and leaned against the built-in heater, staring out at the Empire State Building. She was hundreds of miles away from the old life full of murder, rape, gun violence, child molestation, and drug lords. She thought she'd left it all back in Atlanta to come here, to start over lost in crowds where nobody knew her name, where every time she ate out, she wasn't surrounded by a potential jury pool.

But tonight, she was right back where she started.

Images of Hayden and Melissa appeared in her mind's eye, then suddenly blurred with the dead and decomposing bodies of the murder victims she represented for so many years. They all blended together.

Shaking it off, she turned away from the window and walked back through her bedroom to the bath. Reaching across the tub to twist off the hot-water tap, she was relieved, once again, to see that all was as she had left it.

Back in the master bedroom, she went to the rosewood wall unit at the far side of the room, directly across from the bed. She'd had it specially made and installed, and it covered the entire wall.

The shelves on one side were full of volumes and volumes of research, both legal and psychological, notes, presentations, and oral arguments. The other side, when opened, revealed a built-in desktop computer topped by shelves that held a fax, printer, dictionary, thesaurus—all tools of her trades.

Hailey adroitly reached beneath the computer's slide-out keyboard, pulled a lever, and a panel along the back swung open.

It had been nearly a year since she'd opened the cabinet's concealed door to survey its secret contents. Tonight, it was pure instinct.

A small overhead light in the back of the unit automatically illuminated the gun and knife collection she had amassed over a decade of prosecuting everyone from bank robbers to drug lords to street gangs.

Yes, she'd been the only assistant district attorney who, on principle, never carried a weapon.

But these weapons—which were entered into evidence in Hailey's more memorable prosecutions—were always carefully stored in a locker in her office. At some point, when the appeals process was exhausted, they'd all be auctioned off or just melted down somewhere.

Unbeknownst to Hailey as her flight jetted her from Atlanta to LaGuardia on the day of her move, somewhere below her on the interstate snaked a moving van full of an arsenal she never intended to bring with her. When the movers had packed her belongings from the office, they had simply shipped the huge lockbox along with everything else.

It had taken a while to discover what happened. She was in no hurry to unpack the boxes she thought contained old trial files . . . in no hurry to relive the violence, the hatred, the crimes that had worn her down . . . that caused her to leave her roots for a so-called regular life.

But the day she finally unpacked the box and realized what was inside had actually not been upsetting at all. She hadn't been upset . . . no . . . she was almost . . . nostalgic. Nostalgic for her old office, the friends she'd had there, and the dedication that propelled her for so long.

She handled, checked, and polished every weapon. They totaled forty-three guns, ranging from a Colombian Uzi to a hooker's twenty-two to a sawed-off shotgun with its blunt end covered in black masking tape. The knives included plenty of switchblades, but also a machete polished to a high sheen, a kangaroo knife, a Smith and Wesson boot knife, and a Puerto Rican pig sticker.

Now she stared at them all, taking stock.

At last, she reached out, and with a firm hand, chose the .38. It fit better than the others in her hand, and she'd used it more often at target practice.

Hailey shook open the chamber and peered inside.

It was loaded.

Setting it on top of the computer, she took down from a peg a specially designed shoulder holster made of black, flexible Lycra and Velcro. Leather bulked up and was easy to spot outside clothing. Not this.

Hanging the holster on the side of her bed, she closed the cabinet and secured the computer overlay. She slipped on the holster and weapon to keep her hands free. She walked, surefooted, gun at her side, into the kitchen and turned down the flame under the copper kettle.

As she lifted it up and over, away from the flame, something caught her eye.

There was light where there shouldn't be: lamplight pouring from inside her home office, pooling outside the door.

Hailey never, ever left any light on in the apartment while she was gone—nothing other than the stove hood, whose glow streamed into the entrance hall as she walked in each night.

No other light, ever.

Her thoughts whirled back over the last twenty-four hours. She remembered packing up a stack of files. She remembered noting that the plants were green and growing in spite of the cold, straining toward the winter sun at the window.

She remembered checking the lock on her patient file cabinet, pulling the office door almost closed, walking out through her kitchen, and leaving for the day.

Same as every morning.

But now the door leading into her home office was fully open . . . and were all the lights in the room on?

Someone had been here while she was gone. They could still be here. Or out there, somewhere, watching her.

As Hailey stood there at the stove, hand on the kettle, trying to grasp what had happened, she became acutely aware that every window in her apartment was in plain view. All the shades were up their highest to let in as much daylight as possible when she was there each morning.

But now, in the dark outside, the Manhattan skyline was a million pinpoints of light, each one representing a person's apartment or office, suspended in the night air.

If she could see them, they could see her.

Hailey gently placed the kettle on a cool burner and reached for the .38 with her trigger hand. Pulling it, she held it down against her right side, the stovetop island protecting her maneuver from prying eyes in the night. Gripping the .38, she backed up against the sink and counter and began making her way toward her office. The handgun was now clutched firmly with both her hands, right index on the trigger, pointing down.

Keeping her back to the kitchen counters, she walked sideways across the expanse of slate. Beyond the folding doors, she could see the floor lamps on, as well as the desk lamp. The wooden cabinets discreetly concealing hundreds of patient files, as well as all her old trial files, stood there. Their drawers were ajar.

The room was empty. She couldn't just see it, she could feel it; she knew no one was concealed in the shadows, watching her. Still, she checked. Just to be sure.

Whoever had come into her apartment was gone, leaving only the trace of lights on and cabinet door ajar.

Keeping the gun firmly in her hand and her back to the walls of the room, Hailey pulled the cabinet doors open wide. What were they looking for?

And why not ransack the apartment in the search?

She glanced at the window that faced the apartment buildings next door, with terraces growing trees some twenty floors above the earth. She could see people in lamplit windows, going about their business cooking, reading, watching TV.

Keeping the gun firmly in her right hand, Hailey reached up with her left to close the shades.

She turned back to the cabinet, where her trial files were arranged alphabetically in rows of precise horizontal lines across the first three upper shelves. On the top shelf, a few of the files appeared slightly pulled forward from the rest.

Heart pounding now, she put the gun down and began sorting through the folders, fingering back the tabs on which she had handwritten defendants' names and charges: *Clay Rape Trial, Clemmons Drug Trafficking, Collins Arson, Cook Domestic Homicide, Dixon Weapons Violations . . .*

Her mind was spinning, calculating rapidly.

Something was missing. What was it?

Hailey closed her eyes and visualized the rows of files.

Then her right hand went instinctively to her throat, where the silver pen had once hung from its silken cord.

Her eyes flew open, and she felt a flash go through her body.

She knew, even before she looked . . . it was her last death penalty trial folder. It was gone.

The Clint Burrell Cruise file was gone.

The realization came in a sickening gush. In her mind's eye, she again saw her attacker walk by her as she lay there on the rug, blood oozing down her temple, across her cheek, and into her mouth.

The man who beat her unconscious in her office, who crushed her ribs with the toe of his boot, kicking her over and over until a dark gray film rolled in around her . . .

A limp.

It was years ago, on local Atlanta Channel Eleven News. She'd noticed it first when the press closed in on the all-important perp-walk from the back of a squad car into the precinct station the night of the arrest. When she went to the jail to draw additional blood for a second DNA match, it was there. And later, she'd seen it in court when he walked in and out, surrounded by armed sheriffs.

He walked with a limp. Clint Burrell Cruise. The killer.

She felt it in her bones. He was here. Here in the city.

Atlanta, Georgia

". . . SOON AS I GET THE LAST PAYMENT, THEY'RE ALL YOURS. NEGATIVES included as promised."

Eugene deleted the message and hung up the phone after listening to Hadden's message.

Hadden . . . another pawn. It all fit together like he had planned. He had known it would work out from the get-go, ever since C.C. wanted to take a cart at Augusta. From there on in, it was like shooting fish in a barrel.

Next the glossies would be mailed and the dominoes would begin to topple one by one. The race for governor would be back to normal.

The Cruise death penalty had been reversed and the federal grant money was headed back into the pockets of his partners at the defense firm. They had already gotten the beach vote through . . . the reps on the floor at the Georgia House and Senate had been herded like sheep. Not one of them had bothered to ask the significance of the definition of "tree," as in the "first tree on the beach."

Maneuvering the change in how "tree" was defined by the Georgia Code would pocket Eugene millions of pure profit by the time the last condo sold.

It all went down smooth as silk.

Now all he had to do was wait.

Within a matter of days, if not hours, the glossies would be in the mail and on their way.

He looked out over the city from his office chair, smoothing down the crease in his cashmere pants with his hands, staring into the dark, a thousand lights blanketing the city.

There was still the matter, though, of Virginia Gunn.

SOMEONE WAS OUT THERE; SOMEONE WHO WANTED TO HURT HER. She had to be wrong. It couldn't be Cruise. He was in prison. On death row.

Her mother's voice echoed back . . . something she'd said when they were talking on the phone one night.

"They're saying he's still trying to appeal, but the Georgia courts would never let that happen."

They wouldn't . . . would they?

Surely she would know, though, if Cruise had won his appeal by some miracle and been released. Surely she would have been warned. . . .

By whom, though?

She picked up the telephone and dialed her parents.

"You've reached Mac and Elizabeth Dean. We're not home right now, but leave us a message and we'll get back with you."

No, Hailey realized with a sinking heart, they wouldn't. They were on Cumberland.

And Fincher was on the other side of the world in Iraq.

Heart pounding Hailey fired up her computer and went to the Georgia Corrections Web site.

Clint Burrell Cruise.

She had long railed against a system that didn't warn victims of violent crime when perps were paroled. She'd even testified before the Georgia Senate to demand a change in the law as part of the Victims' Bill of Rights. Since a large percentage of the Georgia Legislature was made up of defense attorneys, it failed. Victims of rape, robbery, assault, even murder victims' families were never warned . . . much less former prosecutors who had left the job and moved hundreds of miles away. And any press about it would have been local.

How often did headlines in the morning papers deal with parole releases from another state? Never. Nothing within the law required that she be notified. And victims and their families had no rights under the Constitution. She'd learned that when Will was murdered.

Within seconds, her worst fears had been confirmed.

He was out.

|||||||||||||||||||||||||||||||||||||||||||||||||||||||||||||||| **67** ||||||||||||||||||

St. Simons Island,
Georgia

WHEN VIRGINIA'S HEAD FINALLY CLEARED, SHE WAS LYING ON her back on her own bed. She opened her eyes slowly, prepared to see the two no-necks towering over her. Instead, she looked directly into the eyes of Larry.

It was clear he'd been crying.

"My God, V.G., what happened to you? Who did this?"

She was alive. Lying in her own bed. With Sidney, wagging his furry little stub of a tail. And Larry was here.

She was alive.

Her throat aching from an earlier blow near her trachea that sliced under her chin, she struggled to speak.

"V.G., say something. Anything. Just let me know you're okay."

"Get the vodka. And Diet Coke. On ice. Hurry."

Larry stood up and turned. Just as he turned through the bedroom door into the hall, she added, "And the cigarettes."

She was alive all right.

Hours later, Virginia sat propped on one of the kitchen bar stools, the hushed group of eco-guerrillas gathered around.

No chips and dip, no cheese and crackers today. No whirring blender churning mushy frozen drinks. No stereo playing Nina Simone on low in the background. No theorizing or pontificating.

Virginia finished telling the story exactly as she remembered it, in detail, right down to the Diet Coke and vodka—which she sipped as she spoke. This was no time for her usual Amaretto. This was an emergency.

The guerrillas couldn't drag their eyes away from her face and she knew it wasn't a pretty sight. She'd accidentally glimpsed herself in the bathroom mirror.

Her eye was black and some of the blood from her mouth was still dried where it had trickled near her right ear, even after she rinsed her face at the sink. Along the bottom of her jaw, the skin was just beginning to bruise. Her gums were bloody and her arm was in a makeshift sling made of a cut-out section of fitted bed-sheet, the elastic pucker still showing on one side. Her nails were torn down to the quick on one hand. Her wrists were both ringed with red welts that were beginning to turn deep blue in little dots across the red.

But she didn't dare go to the hospital, as Larry wanted her to do.

"That would mean cops," she told him. "And we don't want *that*."

Larry didn't want to leave her there for even a second, but she sent him to the liquor store for more booze. She didn't want to scare the group with talk of hospitals and police. Plus, it was going to be a long night.

The rest sat unmoving when he left through the sliding glass door and Virginia was met with stone silence now as the guerrillas either stared down at their Birkenstocks or gave her the "blink," staring fixedly away while blinking rapidly. The silence spoke volumes.

They were scared shitless . . . and they should be.

"So do you really think this was because of what we did?" Dottie asked, unable to drag her eyes off the bloody quicks of Virginia's fingernails.

The tiny group was having a hard time accepting the truth . . . Virginia's beating was because of Palmetto Dunes. Hell, it was just digging up wooden markers and plucking off orange plastic ties . . . just ripping out a little string . . . string that had been tied meticulously from marker to marker across hundreds of square feet of dunes, dunes flattened by giant industrial machine rollers. In fact, up until now, they hadn't truly been convinced anyone had really noticed the late-night vandalism they'd taken such joy in.

Virginia took stock of her ragtag warriors, all too meek to retort to nasty customers or refuse unreasonable shift demands. Teachers intimidated by pushy parents and school principals. Clerks who gave money returns to "customers" they knew had shoplifted. No receipt? No problem!

They let soccer moms swipe parking spots they'd trolled for thirty minutes at Wal-Mart. They stood speechless when mall rats cut in front of them at Cinnabon. They endured protracted conversations with telemarketers at dinnertime. Sometimes, it was just easier to consolidate their debts or sign up for a new phone plan than argue into the phone or, God forbid, hang up.

They were the tormented souls who were never chosen for the basketball team or cheerleading squad, football being totally out of the question. The last ones standing awkwardly between two schoolyard teams, the ones who walked away pretending they'd really rather stand on the sidelines. The ones who always got zonked first playing dodgeball.

And now they were facing the prospect of physical pain in exchange for continued vandalism of somebody else's beachfront property.

This was not what they'd signed up for . . . but they all shrunk under Virginia's gaze or, in the alternative, looked the other way.

While Virginia hadn't expected them to lead the battle like Eisenhower, she hadn't expected this either—total silence and fear when faced with adversity. Virginia had given it her best, egging them on with a rousing pep talk. During the silence, she glanced over at the sofas gathered around the fireplace, the light pouring into the den. Even the wieners lie there lifeless, draped wheezing on the sofas and floor, like they, too, were too drained to fight the good fight any longer.

Virginia cleared her throat, making the only sound other than nervous breathing coming from Kenny, who sounded extremely stopped-up. Head cold.

She lit a cigarette and took a long, deep drag, exhaling through narrowed eyes to avoid her own smoke. "Okay, guys, you think about it and we'll talk tomorrow?"

"Fine . . . good . . . that's a plan . . . okay . . . see you tomorrow . . ." They all murmured at once, blending soft voices nervously together into one low, quiet buzz while adroitly grabbing their things and shuffling past the wieners to the door.

Virginia sat still on the bar stool until she heard the last of the cars crank up, twist in the gravel driveway, and motor off.

The house was quiet and turning dark. She hadn't turned on any lights yet. The dogs lay there forlornly, not even rousing to bark their heads off for dinner.

For the first time ever, she hated their quiet.

Walking out the back door onto the deck, Virginia stopped in her tracks, looking into the sky over the water. Dark, wet evening air was blowing off the Georgia coast. It was breathtaking.

Her ribs ached and her fingers felt like they were broken. She could still wiggle them and they were currently curled around a drink, so they must be intact.

The sea oats swayed on the dunes, and instinctively, she flipped off the patio's outdoor lights so as not to disturb any sea turtles mating or burying eggs out in the sandy curves. The gestation, birth, and nurturing of the Coastal Sea Turtle was time-consuming and laborious, but what sea turtle wouldn't be lured by a night like tonight?

Staring out at the dunes, she pondered her next move against Palmetto.

A fire? No, too destructive to the Island. A bomb? She didn't know how to make one, although if that freak McVeigh could make one out of horse manure, she could do the same. There was plenty of dog poop around her house . . . the wieners had awful manners.

Okay, she was not making a bomb out of wiener doo-doo. She snorted into her glass at the mere thought of it.

But another day of construction had passed. The attack on Virginia had postponed the amphibious sneak attack. The high-rise was inching toward the moment when they could no longer sabotage it as easily as they had so far. As soon as the cement foundation was poured, they would be at a loss.

There had to be a way. . . . She had done it before. She, Virginia Gunn, had single-handedly stopped a gigantic new four-lane bridge from crossing the water from mainland to Island. It took all her skills and cunning.

You did it, though, she reminded herself as she sipped her drink.

But what about Palmetto Dunes? The County Commission had clearly been bought off. She could always file a lawsuit on behalf of the citizens, and as guardian protecting the sea turtles.

But she knew that in the end she would lose in court and likely be outed as the midnight marauder at Palmetto Dunes. Then, one way or the other, the others would be dragged in and likely lose their jobs and what little money they made at the mall, the IHOP, the Radio Shack, and the local public schools. Jobs and money . . . maybe more.

Virginia poured another drink and downed it. Why bother with the glass? It just slowed things down. She swigged straight from the bottle, hoping for inspiration. Sidney led the other wieners out onto the deck and they hopped up into her lap and nestled in.

She needed a fresh idea. She'd wait until this time tomorrow night—no, a little later, when it was pitch black. A late-night drive out to the south beaches. She'd go back to the construction site alone to check it out. Maybe there was another angle she'd missed, something, somehow, some way they could put the skids on the high-rise again.

Something short of a wiener-bomb.

The water lapped up; she could hear but not see it. The spray blew across her face, not bracing, but in a gentle way instead. The Seven Sisters, the Cassiopeia constellation, smiled down at her. Over the dark curve of the ocean, on the other side of the stars, she saw a glow against the dark of the sky. Then she saw it in full. There was a new moon rising.

|||||||||||||||||||||||||||||||||||||||||||||||||||||||||| **68** |||||||||||||||||||

New York City

THERE WAS NO TIME TO FEEL AND NO TIME TO WASTE. FUELED BY grim reality, Hailey went methodically to each window in the apartment and pulled down the shades. In the kitchen, she put the kettle back on the flame.

Wherever he was, he was either watching her now or watching the exit nearly thirty floors below. She double-checked all the locks on windows and doors.

Did it matter? Somehow, he'd managed to get in here once. He could do it again.

A shrill whistle pierced the silence.

Hailey instinctively placed her right hand on the grip of the gun . . .

It was just the kettle.

She left the window and crossed the stone floor to turn off the gas flame. Pulling open the kitchen drawer for a spoon, once again, the old chill went from jaw to spine and stomach down to calves and toes.

It was there . . . entangled in the knives and forks and spoons.

Something that shouldn't, couldn't have been there. It hadn't been there before. It wasn't there when she'd pulled out the last spoon before she left for work so many hours before.

Kitchen twine. An oblong wind of it was peeking out from under the rows of silverware, some of it curled up into the utensils, all neatly in their kitchen drawer dividers like she'd arranged them.

Hailey whirled and in a frenzy began yanking open drawers and tearing through cabinets, their contents falling harshly to the floor. She ransacked her closet, looked under the bed, tore the mattress off the frame, thrust her hands down pillowcases, unzipped the pillows themselves, and felt the foam rubber for lumps. The laundry closet, the washer and dryer, the umbrella stand . . .

It was here . . . somewhere. It had to be . . . but where?

Somewhere in her apartment was a ticking time bomb. How many were there?

Back to the kitchen, she knelt on the floor to reach a low drawer dedicated to cloth napkins, pot holders, and place mats. Reaching far to the back, she began feeling her way through them as if she were blind, feeling for something . . . and found it at last.

It was wrapped inside a set of old kitchen towels she'd brought up from Atlanta.

It was still crusted in blood.

Hailey unfolded a single, four-pronged poultry-lifter. The last time she had seen one like it was in an Atlanta courtroom, when she'd held it in her left hand, arm outstretched, walking the length of the jury rail.

Instinct made Hailey raise the lifter up under the vented hood over the stove to inspect it. It was the same. . . . She knew before looking.

A Norpro, identical to the one used in Atlanta. A solid, stainless-steel Norpro . . . an evil-looking poultry-lifter with steely sharp prongs.

Glancing again at the shades pulled down snug over the windows, she walked back to the silverware drawer and pulled out the twine.

Again, she knew, before she'd even turned it upside down to read the label, that it would be the exact same type as used in the Atlanta murders.

Sisson Imports, made in France. Three hundred inches of it, glossy and white.

When did he plant it?

In her other hand, the four-pronged lifter felt like it weighed a hundred pounds.

Whose blood was crusted on the tines? Melissa's? Hayden's? Someone else's? Another one of her patients whose body was yet to be discovered?

The pressure in her head was unbearable; she could literally feel the blood draining from her lips.

How long would it be until the police came to search her apartment?

They would find her here with the weapon and the twine.

No explanation would suffice. She had to destroy it. What else could she do? Go to Kolker and tell him, *"Gee, I just found the murder weapon in my kitchen drawer and I can't imagine how it got there . . ."*

What to do? . . . what to do?

What would they *expect* her to do?

Wrap it in a plastic bag and throw it out in the garbage? Then throw it down the trash chute, where it would be discovered in the main receptacle? Identifiable in the same bag with all the junk mail with her name and address on it mixed with kitchen debris and other trash? Traceable right down to batch, lot, and specific D'Agostino's grocery store where she'd bought the trash bag? They'd probably even dig up some grainy surveillance video of her actually *at* D'Ag's buying trash bags.

Or should she hurl it into the dark waters of the East River while out on a run?

Too predictable.

How many times had she sent divers down to retrieve a weapon? Piece of cake. She had even gone on dives herself to then explain the process to jurors in openings and closings.

It rarely took more than three hours underwater to find the knife or gun in the waterway closest to a suspect's home or office. Or at least part of a gun. Occasionally, the perp might be wily enough to remove the barrel from his automatic, rendering it useless for cross ballistics identification purposes.

But this was no gun. It was a seamless, shiny, solid piece of steel, no way to dismantle it.

It was a four-pronged lethal weapon disguised as a kitchen implement, and it had sliced through the lungs of two of her patients . . . that she knew of.

The East River was out.

The blood was the thing. Simple bleach wouldn't work. Ajax . . . no. Clorox . . . no. Laundry detergent . . . no. She needed something with enzymes. . . .

Reaching far back to the rear of the cabinet, she found it: Black Swan Muriatic Acid. The stone worker had left it behind it when he laid slate in the kitchen and the cement bathroom base beneath the tiles. Muriatic, or hydrochloric, acid would be most likely to destroy DNA. For now, she lined the kitchen sink and surrounding counters with layers of plastic wrap, turned on the hot water in the kitchen faucet, and slowly washed her patients' blood off the steel tines of the lifter.

Then she poured the cleaner from its plastic container across the sink and into it, completely immersing the lifter in pure muriatic acid. It might not be perfect, but it was the best shot she had. She did it gently, so as to cause no spatter on the sides of the sink. One swipe with Luminol would catch each drop, but this was the best she could do, tonight anyway.

After rinsing the sink and drying the lifter with paper towels, she carried the ball of twine to the bathroom sink. With her, she took the matchbook she kept in the kitchen drawer beside the gas stove and turned on the overhead shower vent. It took three matches to set the twine on fire.

She added in the paper towels, the hand towels that had wrapped the weapon and the plastic wrap from the kitchen. She watched as it was totally consumed, until there was nothing left but ashes.

On the fourth flush of the toilet, it was all gone.

Back in the kitchen, she again rinsed the entire sink with the muriatic cleanser, took out the drain stopper, unscrewed the bottom of it, and allowed the pieces to fall apart. Heading to the trash chute, she threw the pieces down, hearing them fall against the metal sides of the shaft until the sounds disappeared.

Now, the weapon. She walked through the apartment . . . searching. Then, in the den, her eyes focused on a mosaic lighting fixture, amber mosaics beautifully pieced together in a bowl-form, facing upward against the ceiling. Dragging over a bar stool, she stood up on it and gently placed the weapon inside the fixture. There.

She climbed down and surveyed the room.

The murder weapon, State's Exhibit Number One against her, was completely concealed.

For now.

She sank into a chair, sitting there in the dark of her apartment.

Clint Burrell Cruise.

Here in the city.

Was he here to kill her? Or just frame her and send her to the electric chair, just like she had sent him?

She methodically searched her apartment again and found nothing more planted. But one thing was missing . . . her favorite hairbrush was gone from the drawer beneath her bathroom mirror. She always kept it there. That explained a lot. The "forensics" Kolker had been so thrilled about . . . she didn't need to see the lab report to know that the hairs found on Melissa and Hayden were hers . . . straight from her own hairbrush.

She looked at the clock. It was 2 a.m.

In four hours, the morning rush would be in full swing at the Century Diner a few blocks away.

She'd be ready.

IIIIIIIIIIIIIIIIIIIIIIIIIIIIIIIIIIIIIIIIIIIIIIIIIIIIIIIIIIIIIIIIIIIIIIIIII 69 IIIIIIIIIIIIIIIIIII

New York City

HE STILL WASN'T CRAZY ABOUT NEW YORK, BUT CRUISE COULDN'T complain about the food.

Roast Long Island duckling.

Filet mignon.

Stuffed lobster.

He was visiting the best restaurants in the world . . . restaurants whose chefs were once friends of his back in culinary school.

Imagine if they knew he was here, dining on their creations, all picked out of metal dumpsters behind each restaurant.

Most of it was barely touched, having been served to thin, wealthy women who frequented Manhattan's five-star restaurants strictly for the scene. Forget the food . . . they couldn't care less about the artistry behind each dish.

Most people would likely recoil at the thought of devouring the remains of food that had first been on somebody else's plate. But they'd never eaten at Reidsville State Pen.

He was definitely eating better than he was sleeping . . . seeking out park benches, subway tunnels, and, when the cold was the worst, the city's homeless shelters.

He imagined Hailey in her apartment in the sky, asleep beneath blankets on her bed.

What did she wear when she slept? A nightgown? A T-shirt? Did she have silk sheets or high-count cotton? What did she keep in her refrigerator? What was in her closet . . . her drawers?

All he had to do was get past the doorman and up to her apartment door. He'd been watching the service entrance and underground parking entrance. Visitors, movers, and work crews were in and out all day. He could easily slip in there . . . but what floor? Oh, yes, the bar directory had given him that on a silver platter.

For now, though, he'd have to settle for watching from a distance.

Tonight he was lurking on the steps of a brownstone down the block, keeping an eye on the entrance to her building, hoping she would emerge. Nobody seemed to be home. He wondered how he could get in.

He hadn't seen her yet . . . but he was sure there were no other entrances than these two, and he had a bird's eye view of both.

The wind off the East River was bitter. Soon he'd call it a night and find a place to bed down. Probably at one of the shelters, he thought, and sighed, his breath puffing out frosty in the night air. . . . Unless he could jimmy a door or window here at the brownstone.

Then a shadow loomed behind him in the glow of the street lamp.

"Cruise."

What the hell?

Who here knew his name?

Cruise turned around.

Stunned, he managed to ask, "What the hell are you doing here?"

He spotted the glint of a butcher knife's blade. Cruise twisted away and it struck his arm, just inches from a vein.

Ignoring the gushing blood, he fought off the attack.

Working out daily for years in prison had made him even stronger. After throwing a brutal left jab to the throat, Cruise took off as best he could. He found a filthy rag in a garbage can and used it to stave the flow of blood from the gaping wound on his forearm. If he hadn't turned at the last second, he'd be lying in the city's morgue right now wearing a John Doe toe-tag.

|||||||||||||||||||||||||||||||||||||||||||||||||||||||||||||| **70** |||||||||||||||||||

New York City

A T 6:30 A.M., HAILEY'S HEAD SNAPPED UP FROM WHERE IT RESTED on her chest for the last two hours.

It was time for breakfast.

The walk was just a few blocks, the shorter the better, and getting there was crucial. There was absolutely no reason for them to stop her, question her, detain her. But cops didn't always need a reason. Who would a jury believe? Two cops or her, carrying a murder weapon concealed inside her sweatshirt?

In her bedroom, she pulled on sweats and running shoes, and snapped on her plastic running watch. Over her clothes, she pulled on an extra, baggy sweatshirt. With no time to waste, she headed into the den.

Climbing up on the kitchen stool, she removed the sharp-pronged lifter from the mosaic ceiling fixture where it spent the night.

The sweatshirt was several sizes too large and hung loosely on her, leaving plenty of room. Wrapping it gingerly in a bath towel, she gently turned the deadly tines away from her stomach as she slipped the weapon into the pouch in front of her sweatshirt. Taking one last look around the apartment, she left, locking the door behind her.

It was 6:38 a.m.

The elevator descended from the floor just above her. When the doors slid open, there stood a man in running attire like herself, but with a golden retriever attached to a leash. He stood in the far corner. Not recognizing him, she almost backed off the elevator, but realizing that would seem unusual and, more important, memorable, if asked by police, she stepped on as normal. She kept her eyes down, focused on the dog.

The security cam in the upper corner bored into her.

She shifted to the corner and glanced over. He was staring straight into her face.

"Out for a run?" he asked.

Red flag. He was engaging in unsolicited conversation. Her antennae shot up immediately. A normal New Yorker would never do that.

She nodded politely.

"Me too," he responded, trying to engage her in conversation.

The guy was standing there stiffly, just like a cop would. And his shoes. He said he was going running, but his shoes were tennis shoes, not running shoes. His jacket was extremely lightweight, not for outdoor winter running. Were those slacks under his running pants? She couldn't tell. . . . This was bad.

The bell dinged. Lobby. She was out like a shot, as fast as she could walk without breaking into a full-blown sprint right there across the lobby floor.

It was empty but for the doorman, who called out after her, "Have a good run, Hailey!" Ricky blurted it out after her just as she darted past him and his morning newspaper.

Great . . . if the elevator guy hadn't been sure before, now he definitely knew it was her.

She might have one thing on him though . . . she could run.

She didn't bother to answer, just blew out the door. The cool air off the East River hit her and she ran north for all she was worth.

Cutting the corner against a red light, she glanced back over her left shoulder. She heard wild yelping and saw the elevator guy, fifty feet behind her now, trying to jog, but his retriever had tangled immediately in a knot of other leashes—a dog walker coming his way with an even dozen dogs, all shapes and sizes.

One block north, she looked back: no sign of him.

It was 6:43 a.m.

She cut left, heading west up the incline. She heard barking in the distance behind her . . . at just the right spot, she darted left into a parking garage and circled back south toward her own apartment, cutting through alleys and garages until she made it back just two doors from her own building's entrance. She headed north, and in the distance, she could see him . . . the elevator guy. He looked to be getting farther and farther away with every step.

She had four city blocks on him and turned left, heading west crosstown. Two more blocks and two more avenues, and she was right where she wanted to be.

Ducking into the Century Diner, she immediately saw that there was a wait. She made her way politely through the crowd made up of the early business crew, all of them headed to offices around the city. In an hour, they'd be replaced by the more laid-back bunch: designers, sales, elderly retirees still on work schedules. Then would come the leisure brunch crowd, followed by moms with their babies in strollers.

Not a single suited male looked up from the business sections. They barely noticed her graze past.

She walked straight to the single bathroom positioned just across a narrow hallway from the diner's kitchen. The kitchen was a madhouse, already in the throes of a hot, sweaty, frenzied morning rush.

The tiny bathroom was empty. She locked the door at the knob and with a latch, and looked at her little plastic Casio.

It was 6:53 a.m.

The bathroom was hot, overly heated by its next-door neighbor, the kitchen. Putting the lid down on the commode, she stepped on top and reached up to remove one of the perforated ceiling blocks above her. Staring up, she realized there was no way to hoist herself up. She placed the square back into position and looked around the tiny bathroom. There had to be a way. This was her only plan . . . if she could just get up there. . . .

Only one other choice. She stepped up off the commode and over onto the sink, a full foot higher up. Standing on its two outer edges, she reached up again, lifting away a second block.

Pay dirt.

Using all her upper body strength, she pulled herself up on the two-by-four over the door beside the sink. Her foot kicked loudly against the door when she used it instinctively for leverage and she froze, waiting for a reaction from the other side.

Not a sound.

She hoisted herself through the opening and gently placed the square back where it belonged. She was in the pitch dark now and began to crawl through the dark, clammy ceiling space. It was musty and filthy, obviously undisturbed for years, if not decades.

Peering down through tiny holes in the ceiling squares as she crawled, she could see there was no one in the tiny hall waiting for the bathroom . . . yet. But she'd have to hurry.

She kept moving forward. She only had about fifteen more feet to go. She could see through the tiny specked holes in the ceiling squares that now she was over the kitchen. But the kitchen wasn't good enough.

She needed the sinks . . . deep, steel industrial sinks, by this time, inches deep in gray soapy water and dirty dishes.

Pressing her eye to a hole in the ceiling tile, she spotted it on the far wall.

On her stomach, she army-crawled across the filth, making her way over and looking down through another tiny hole, just in time to see a short, thin busboy dump a stack of gooey egg dishes into the sink. She was right. The sink was half-full of dishes covered in water, iced with liquid soap bubbles.

Her right hand was outstretched above her. The Casio glowed in the dark.

It was 7:03 a.m.

Hailey lay there on her stomach, barely breathing. She slid the square over just a few inches, and then reached down with her right hand and gently, gently, pulled the lifter, sharp tongs facing away, out from under her shirt. Unwrapping the towel, she held the lifter by its base, the towel still wrapped around the handle.

Careful . . . fingerprints.

She watched as the busboy stood there running more hot water into the soapy goo. When it reached almost to the top, he wrenched the hot water off and turned away. In that split second, Hailey moved the ceiling square six inches further to the right and dropped the lifter directly into the sink, eight feet below.

It hit the top plate underwater and slid left to the bottom of the sink.

Instantly moving the square back into place and almost afraid to look, she forced herself to peer through another pinpoint speck hole. To her amazement, nothing had changed. The kitchen continued on and the busboy returned almost immediately with another load of plates for the sink

Still on her stomach, Hailey turned back on the night-glow feature of her watch.

It was 7:10 a.m.

Backtracking, she crawled as fast as she could toward the bathroom, just in time to hear the first of a stiletto of sharp knocks on the bathroom door.

Moving the bathroom ceiling square, she lowered herself to the sink, returned the square, hit the floor, and opened the door.

Would the elevator man be there with a pair of handcuffs?

She looked straight into the prunish face of a Wall Streeter, who brushed by her without a word, as if somehow she had insulted him by just being there.

She did the same, worming her way through the crowd at the door, and finally lifting her face only as she stepped onto the sidewalk and back into the morning air.

Turning left, then left again, she made her way back to the East River, sprinting east until she was back to her regular path. She ran crosstown to her building, then two steps at a time up to the front door and quickly tucked into the high-rise lobby.

Ricky was there still, smiling. "That was a quickie for you, Hailey! No pain, no gain!"

"I can't pull anything past you, Ricky . . . but don't worry, I'll make up for it tomorrow." She breezed past him and into a waiting elevator.

Her head buzzed as the elevator climbed the thirty floors, minus floor thirteen, for good luck.

It was 7:18 a.m.

Stepping off the elevator, all was quiet.

With the murder weapon safely soaking in the soapy water of the sink at Century Diner, Hailey had one job left on her to-do list.

Catch the killer before he caught her.

Atlanta, Georgia

"D AMN! DAMN! DAMN!"
Why the hell couldn't anyone do anything on their own?
Why did he, Floyd Moye Eugene, have to do everything himself?

Eugene was steaming under the collar; his face was red and his temperature had to be soaring. Sitting there behind his mahogany desk, which was completely free of clutter, not a single stray piece of paper or even a tiny silver gem clip out of place, he fumed.

Just off the phone with the Palmetto Dunes "leadership" down on the Island, Eugene decided, as he slammed the phone down mid-conversation, to make good on the threat to fly down to the Island and straighten things out himself.

If you want anything done right, you have to do it yourself.

That moron of a commissioner at St. Simons couldn't foul this thing up any better if he tried.

Two months of constant delay had cost Eugene over two hundred thousand dollars so far. The bill was rising. Time was wasting. Failure to open the doors in time for tourist season would drain millions from short-term "flip" investors hoping for a quick recoup to then sell out before moving on to another so-called paradise high-rise development.

Eugene and his backers out of Vegas already had their eye on a "protected" strip of land in Hawaii—nothing but fisherman's huts dotting the beach for miles.

Perfect.

But that was a no-go until Eugene could make good on St. Simons.

This should have been a freaking shoo-in, right here in his own freaking backyard.

With all the strings he'd had to pull with that moron Judge Carter; the reversal in order to get the federal funding back . . . in order to get the statute changed; the bust at the strip club . . .

Eugene breathed in hard and exhaled.

He had to calm down. Reaching for his right top drawer, he unlocked it and pulled out a manila folder, just to reassure himself.

Ah—the black-and-white photos of C.C. in the bathroom stall with the tranny.

They were beautiful. Thank God Hadden knew how to take a shot, even though he was a drunk. And excellent quality. You could make out every single hair combed over C.C.'s head.

C.C.

The idiot had to be shitting himself, waiting for the bomb to drop.

Then it would be bye-bye "Mansion," as C.C. insisted on calling the governorship.

Wonder if he'd ever put two and two together and figure out that it was no coincidence that just after the reversal and the re-funding of federal money to the law firm, he got busted with a tranny.

Probably not.

C.C. would probably blame it on some right-wing Republican conspiracy. Self-important moron. As if the Republicans would go to so much trouble to destroy a pimple on their ass like C.C.

Still seated behind his desk, Eugene patted the photos gently, as if they were a little pet, then locked them back away in the drawer.

Eugene realized he actually looked forward to the inevitable phone call from C.C., 'fessing up and begging Eugene to save his jiggly ass. He reached under his jacket into his short pocket, pulled out his dark aviator sunglasses, and touched a button on his phone.

"Yes, sir?"

"Call Peachtree DeKalb and get a pilot ready. I want to leave in thirty for St. Simons. I want the Gulfstream. I refuse to be cramped in a Citation. And for God's sake, no stewardess yammering. I only want to hear from the pilots, and then precious little. And get the car and driver. And have a white Escalade waiting on the Island."

Eugene clicked her off before she could utter the usual, "Yes, sir. Thank you, sir."

Minutes later, the traffic blurred as Eugene's limo sped up I-85 toward PDK, Peachtree-DeKalb Airport, one of Atlanta's most exclusive private airports. With pilots on the ready for those who could afford it, PDK had a steady stream of veteran Delta pilots standing by to fly your plane, carry your luggage, fix you a drink, and shine your shoes if you wanted. Pilots were in the surplus in Atlanta, thanks to carrier layoffs and gas prices at the biggest Delta hub in the country.

The limo pulled up in front of EPPS Aviation with Eugene seated in the back, behind tinted windows.

Like the Wright brothers, the Epps started off as bicycle repairmen. Now they catered to an elite clientele that was willing to drop $8,000 for a one-way forty-five-minute jet charter flight.

The limo door was opened for Eugene, and he crossed a few feet of hot asphalt through wide glass automatic doors and onto a red carpeted walkway, leading to a white birch front desk.

To one side past closed frosted doors was the pilots' lounge, and to the other, an elaborate setting for waiting passengers, complete with food, liquor, coffee, and widescreen televisions flush against polished birch walls. Magazines and newspapers from practically every major city in the world lined one side of the lounge.

Eugene breezed past it, heading straight through the lounge area to a second set of glass doors opening out onto private runways.

Standing there holding the door for him were two former Delta pilots, one gray with a deep tan, the other younger, paler, and taller.

"Mr. Eugene, happy to have you back. . . ."

"Skip it. Let's go." Eugene cut him off mid-sentence.

The two pilots exchanged a glance and fell silently into step behind Eugene. They'd flown for him before.

Eugene was one of only a handful of customers who made them question their decisions to leave being true captains in exchange for opening doors, saying "Yes, sir," eating shit, and cashing a big, fat paycheck every other Friday.

At the plane's metal steps, Eugene looked up and barked, "This isn't the Gulfstream V. What the hell is it?"

"It's a Citation X, Mr. Eugene. This is all that was available at short notice."

He climbed the steps without a word and sank down into a creamy leather seat.

A flight attendant who had also flown with Eugene before knew better than to speak. She waited silently until he signaled by holding up the aisle-side index finger.

"Bourbon on the rocks."

"Yes, sir. Right away."

She disappeared for just a few moments, reappearing on his left with the drink and a napkin. He took it silently and she melted away into the air-conditioned seats just outside the cockpit.

The engine whined and they were off, suddenly looking down at a crazy slant onto the city. Eugene sipped his drink and eyed the familiar landscape. The Capitol shone bright gold, the Georgia Dome, the Fulton County Courthouse, the Georgia Supreme Court building, CNN Center, all closely woven together in Atlanta's downtown.

Eugene's bourbon was down only an inch or so when the city fell away and they were flying over deep, deep green fields that stretched as far as the eye could see.

This was the "other Georgia," the dream that Sherman had coveted, the land that had sparked hundreds of tales and a body of folklore . . . the Deep South. Thousands of square miles of peanuts and soybeans and peach orchards and pine trees, swamp and live oaks and the remnants of vast plantations, with great white lines, Interstates I-75 and I-16, slicing the state generally down the middle.

Here lay the voters: voters who didn't like six-foot-tall transvestites getting it on in a bathroom stall with a gubernatorial candidate.

Eugene drained his first drink and was soon on his second.

Before thirty-five minutes had passed, out the window he saw water, a million sparkles playing on the dark ocean from the sun. Marshes and sand melted into each other at water's edge. The white beaches of St. Simons shined like a string of translucent pearls beneath him.

How gorgeous that beach would be with Eugene's Palmetto Dunes high-rise luxury living, right there on the water's edge.

For the first time that day, he nearly smiled.

‖‖‖ **72** ‖‖‖‖‖‖‖‖‖‖‖‖‖‖

Atlanta, Georgia

"YOU SON OF A BITCH."

C.C. winced at the shrill volume and held the telephone receiver away from his ear. "Baby, what's wrong?" he asked, and dared to hope Tina was pissed at him for something lame . . . like not showing up last night at the Fuzzy or forgetting to call earlier.

C.C. was suddenly opting to keep a low profile. Very low. He hadn't left his apartment since the incident in the men's room.

With any luck, she'd never find out about that.

"How could you?" she shrieked in his ear, and his heart sank. She knew.

He'd been fooling himself if he thought he could keep it from her—or anybody, for that matter.

"And with a tranny? You sick son of a bitch!"

"How did you find out?"

"Are you freaking kidding me? CNN? Headline News? How about Fox? They're talking about you, C.C. It's freaking *breaking news*. They even cut into my soap this afternoon, you stupid son of a bitch! You're the crawl, C.C., the crawl at the bottom of the screen!"

He opened the nearest drawer, found his flask, and threw back a shot of bourbon as Tina screamed all kinds of accusations into his ear.

"Baby, you don't understand what happened," he said when she'd stopped to take a breath. "I thought you were the one who set it up. I thought it was your special surprise for me ... and I ..."

"What the hell? Why would I—"

"You said you had a surprise for me. I thought she—he—was it!"

"Are you out of your mind, C.C.? That's sick. You're sick."

"Tina, just listen. I'm sorry. I didn't mean it. You know I love you. I did it for you. You can't—"

He never did get a chance to tell her what she couldn't do, because there was a click in his ear, followed by a dial tone.

He reached for the remote, braced himself, and turned it on.

St. Simons Island,
Georgia

"WHY THE HELL IS IT SO HOT IN HERE?" EUGENE DEMANDED of the flushed female clerk behind the desk at the Hertz rental car office as she hunted for papers that should have been ready.

They weren't.

"I'm sorry, sir, the air-conditioning blew out yesterday."

"Yesterday? It happened yesterday? And what's the explanation for it being out today?"

"Needed parts," she said apologetically, and slid the clipboard across the counter at him.

He continued to glare at her across the counter.

"From Atlanta." She felt he wanted more of an explanation.

Signing the papers, he decided on the spot that the stupidest people in the world weren't in Atlanta after all. They were here on St. Simons Island. Bunch of hayseeds. No wonder he had to fly all the way down to straighten things out at Palmetto Dunes.

After an interminable wait, Eugene strode across the sun-baked parking lot to the white Caddy Escalade he demanded his secretary locate for him.

The sweat rolled down the back of his neck as he climbed up and in, switched the ignition, and cranked the AC on high. A local country station was pre-set and blared out of the radio. He jabbed at the controls to turn the thing off. Quiet. He wanted total quiet and another Jack on the rocks . . . wondering if he'd find anything but moonshine in these parts. Idiots.

He pulled out of the gravel driveway from the private landing strip and onto a paved surface road, the dashboard-mounted GPS instructing him to "Turn right."

Floyd Moye turned and headed straight to the only five-star hotel in the region, the Cloister. Perched on the upper waters of St. Simons Island, it was surrounded on the other three sides by a world-class golf course in the Scottish tradition. Every evening, a single, lonely figure in full kilt regalia would wail the bagpipes out near the water for the residents.

Screw that.

All Eugene wanted was a cold drink and the AC on high in his room. He hoped to God they had him in the lodge where a private butler was assigned to each room. The butlers weren't great, but at least they were something. And what a bar that place stacked. His mouth was dry as he put down the pedal.

After a twenty-minute drive, he was there. The Lodge at the Cloister welcomed Eugene like a long-lost son, ushered him straight up to the Presidential Suite looking past a croquet lawn and on to the trickle-back of the Atlantic. The marshes swelled up across the salty water and shimmered in the last streaks of sun pouring down onto the Georgia Gold Coast.

None of it fazed him. He called over his shoulder to the room's private butler, "Jack on the rocks."

"On its way now, Mr. Eugene." Bent down slightly in a perpetual half-bow, the butler backed out of the room, shutting the door noiselessly behind him.

Eugene turned away from the balcony and came back into the AC, picked up the bedside remote, and clicked on the room's TV. There was an immediate close-up of C.C., dressed in the long, black robe he wore on the bench. A large font across the bottom of the screen screamed out BREAKING NEWS in red letters, all caps.

Floyd Moye turned up the volume.

". . . is just the latest high-profile politician to become embroiled in a sex scandal," the reporter was saying. "Having recently achieved notoriety after a stunning vote to reverse the conviction of serial killer Clint Burrell Cruise, the judge was formerly considered to be a strict law-and-order advocate. Shortly after that decision, he launched his campaign for governor . . . a campaign now scuttled by a spectacular fall from grace. CNN has managed to locate the young man *allegedly* photographed in the men's room of a local club, the Pink Fuzzy, with Justice Carter. He promises to reveal *in detail* about his life and his night with the judge in his upcoming book . . ."

Eugene turned off the television and stepped back out onto the balcony. The sun was just dipping down into the horizon, sending millions of shimmering bursts of light dancing onto the dark water.

He silently did the math: How much would people pay for a view like this over on the formerly protected sands at St. Simons?

Millions.

Millions were in the balance.

Everything was in place now for the condos to rise up directly on the sand.

Floyd Moye felt the chilled air from inside pouring out through the open doors onto his balcony and he turned around. The drink he had requested was sitting on a napkin there on the coffee table, no sign of the butler who had come and gone. Eugene walked over and drained it, setting the glass back down as he turned again toward the water.

To hell with it. Enough was enough.

Time was money, and every day of delay cost him thousands in potential profit. If Eugene couldn't pull off Palmetto Dunes, he'd lose the deal in Hawaii . . . at the very least. His "friends" in Vegas backing the deals were not the understanding sort.

He had trusted others to handle the problem. They failed miserably.

He'd drive out to the construction site on the Island right after dinner, find out exactly what the problem was, and solve it. Himself.

Tonight.

Dooley County,
Georgia

Of ALL THE PLACES C.C. HAD IMAGINED HIMSELF LIVING, OR even visiting, Dooley County was not among them.

An upscale Atlanta penthouse, yes. Tina's place minus the voo-doo roommate, yes. The Governor's Mansion, definitely. The White House, a distinct possibility.

But never did he imagine the rambling former farmhouse that had been in Betty's family for over a century would be his perma-nent abode. Her family barely tolerated him, practically holding their noses at him just to get through a single dinner. He could feel it emanating from the walls of the front room when he walked in. And the feeling was mutual.

"Betty? I'm home!" C.C. called out after he opened the screen door, flipped on the wall switch, and dumped his bags in the floor. He'd just have to make the best of it . . . for now.

True, he'd lost his reputation, Tina, the bench, the governor-ship . . . but he still had Betty.

And more important, he had Betty's money.

After the dust settled, he could regroup and get his campaign back up and running again. Show 'em C.C. was still in the race.

"Sugar Pie?" he called, leaving his bags lying there in the hall and making his way through the house. Betty usually unpacked them for him.

Speaking of pie . . .

She usually welcomed him home with a homemade peach pie, hot from the oven.

Sniffing the air, he smelled only a hint of Lysol and all the musty antiques Betty's family was so hung up on. He briefly re-membered when he'd placed a glass of ice tea on her grandmother's antique buffet without a coaster. It was as if a possum got in the house and climbed on the dinner table, the way they'd all rushed around.

Walking room to room, he noted she'd changed things around a bit. Bought some new furniture, gotten rid of some of the old—including his favorite recliner, he noted, as he glanced into the living room. He loved that thing!

She'd probably just sent it out to be re-upholstered. It had seen better days. Or better yet . . . she'd ordered him a brand new one! To surprise him now that he'd be spending more time here with her.

And he would—in the immediate future, anyway.

"Betty?" he called, making his way to the kitchen in the back of the house and opening the screen door out into the backyard.

The house was silent.

And not just the house. It had been so long since C.C. had been back home to Dooley County for any extended period of time, he had actually forgotten how quiet it was. Even with the kitchen door wide open, he couldn't hear a sound.

Finally a dog barked in the distance . . . and that was it.

What the hell would C.C. do with himself, stuck here with Betty for who-knows-how-long, and nothing to do?

Turning back and heading into the kitchen, he went directly for the high cupboard where he kept his stash of bourbon . . . he stopped in his tracks.

There, squarely in the center of the table, sat a big, yellow manila envelope, his name scrawled on the front in black Sharpie, Betty's handwriting.

Something told C.C., even before he opened the flap, this was not a love note.

He was right.

In fact, it was quite the opposite.

Divorce papers . . . along with all the newspaper clippings about the trouble he'd gotten himself into at the Pink Fuzzy.

There was a note from Betty, too.

Don't bother looking for me. I'm on a Carnival Cruise to the Bahamas with John David. P.S. don't bother going to the bank. And remember, the house belongs to my aunt Fruttie.

So.

That's how it was.

His wife had run off with the farm overseer, leaving him high and dry.

C.C. found a bottle of bourbon and took it out onto the back steps.

There he sat in the hot, still darkness, slapping at mosquitoes and blowing upward through his bottom lip to keep the gnats off his nose and eyes. He couldn't stay here—glancing at the papers in the folder, he saw that even the lawyers said so.

He wondered what Tina was doing tonight. She'd gotten over the tranny, but she'd told C.C. how "the trust was gone" between them.

God, he missed that girl. For the rest of his life, he'd go to sleep remembering the routine to "Freebird" she'd finally worked up. It was a doozy.

C.C. sat in the silence awhile longer, looking out the screen door into the backyard. Hell, he could make a comeback. He still had a law license.

He could always practice law.

St. Simons Island,
Georgia

HE MOON RODE HIGH AGAINST A BLACK VELVET SKY. VIRGINIA parked her Jeep and got out just at the point before sandy grass turns to pure beach. She reached back in to cut the lights so as not to scare the sea turtles.

It was that time of year, the magical few months when, only under the cover of darkness, the loggerhead sea turtles swim ashore, find their way across the sand, dig their secret nests, and lay tiny eggs. Endangered, according to the feds, they searched the world and chose the Golden Coast to raise their young. A safe haven . . . until now.

Inside the Jeep, the wieners, the whole yapping bunch of them, made it vociferously clear they wanted out.

"*Sshh!* I promised a ride, not a walk."

They didn't care what she'd promised and continued yelping frantically like all their little lives depended on getting out the one window.

The turtles would not appreciate the wieners' sincere attention, so Virginia pressed the button to automatically lower the window on the driver's side, just enough to give them some air, but not escape.

"Don't even think about it, or it's no treats forever," she told Sidney, turning to find his watchful gaze on her, both ears standing straight up in the dark of the Jeep's cab.

Just to be on the safe side, she raised the window another quarter inch.

"I'll be right back."

The salty air whipped Virginia's hair when she stepped away. She had eased up, hoping her engine wouldn't disturb the turtles.

They were here first, after all, inhabiting the beach long before the Indians roamed the coast, before the Spanish came searching for gold, before slaves were finally set free, before German subs trolled this very shore, spying on the Rockefellers and Gettys who summered here.

Now Palmetto Dunes was set to do what even the German subs didn't . . . destroy their habitat.

Walking out halfway to the water, she sank down on the damp sand, sitting Indian-style, her body still aching from the beating.

What next?

How long could her band of misfits, amateurs all, thwart the multimillion-dollar plans of powerful developers and local politicians in league with God-knows-who.

Speaking of God, it had been a long time since Virginia had had any contact with Him/Her.

Now was as good a time as any to break the ice.

"God, it's me, Virginia. I don't blame You if You don't accept this call. I know You only hear from me when I need something." She hesitated. No other way to say it, so she tried the direct approach. "But guess what? I need something. I need help to stop this."

She nodded her head backward toward the construction site in the distance. She knew He'd know what she meant by "this."

"This is Your creation I'm trying to save. This beautiful beach, and all Your creatures that call it home. I've kind of run out of ideas. Show me what to do. Help me, please. Amen."

She fell silent—and so, it seemed, did the world around her. The water lapped ever so gently; even the breeze seemed to ebb.

Gazing out at the dark sky, she wondered if God had heard her prayer, and whether He had a plan, because she certainly did not.

Suddenly, coming out of the dark behind her, a car motor, the gas gunning. Virginia jerked around, twisting from the waist up to look backward.

She spotted headlights just a few yards away, barreling toward her on the beach.

Scrambling frantically out of the way, she had no time to move . . . it was too fast and too close . . . a huge Escalade with the brights on, plowing across the sand, straight at her.

"No, no!! God, no!"

Face down, she braced herself, throwing her arms over her head in what she knew would be a futile effort to protect herself from the SUV's crushing tires. For just a second, she heard nothing but her own panicked breathing and music blaring from the car's stereo, and . . .

A miracle. The tires on the white metal behemoth ground to a halt, wedging down into deep, wet sand just feet from where she lay, arms still over her head.

She had been so sure it was gunning for her, but maybe she was wrong. Maybe—

The driver's side door flung open, and a man stumbled out. The Escalade's stereo continued pumping out Glen Campbell's "Wichita Lineman."

She got to her feet quickly, peering at him. She couldn't make out his features against the headlights cutting through the dark, but his voice was slurred and angry. Did he actually try to run her down?

"Who the hell are you?" he shouted out.

"I'm Virginia Gunn, who the hell are you?"

Eugene sagged against the car. Virginia Gunn . . . Virginia Gunn . . . he knew that name

It came to him through a haze of alcohol. Here was the thorn in his side . . . the thorn that had already cost him hundreds of thousands and possibly millions if investors started to pull out. Obviously the two "friends" he hired to take care of Gunn didn't finish the job. Here she was . . . alone . . . on the beach . . . an isolated beach.

His prayers were answered.

He quickly closed the few feet between them, pulled back, and threw a right punch straight to her face, landing just below her left eye. She went down hard, sprawled on the beach again.

The blow was blinding and the next thing Virginia knew, she was facedown on the beach with a mouthful of sand.

He aimed a hard kick straight to her right thigh . . . and she cried out in pain. But she scrambled with amazing tenacity, clawing at the sand to get up and run, her feet digging into the sand, slowing her down.

She took off running toward the dense undergrowth surrounding the construction site.

Enraged, Eugene gave chase and, just as she made it to the edge of the site, caught her by the shoulder of her jean jacket. Wrenching her backward, he felt the two of them tumble to the earth together.

When they landed hard on the sand, she was on her back and his hands were around her neck, clamped hard, determined to rid himself of her, for good.

Virginia could see the stars shining behind Eugene's face, just inches from her own, and she clawed at his hands as they locked around her neck. She was too tired, she couldn't fight him off.

The stars were going out; the world was turning dark.

She knew she was dying, there on the beach she had tried to save. Somehow, it seemed fitting . . . for a moment.

Then, instinctively, she doubled her legs in front of her chest and, using her knees and feet, heaved Eugene's weight off her body.

Suddenly, she could breathe again; the stars reappeared twinkling above her. Sucking in air through burning lungs, she careened toward the trees with Eugene at her heels.

He caught up with her just as she reached the edge of the forest, grabbing her at the waist and spinning her around. A pair of brutally strong hands encircled her throat once more, closing off her windpipe.

It was at that precise moment she became aware of a rustling in the undergrowth, and then, erratic barking.

The wieners. The wieners had managed to squeeze their little bodies through the cracks she'd left them in the windows to breathe, escaping the cab of the Jeep and were there, beside her, beneath her, all around her.

The barking took on a fever pitch and they began yapping, gnashing the air, nearly screaming, and all the while biting every inch of Eugene's suited body they could get their teeth into.

"What the hell?" He released Virginia's neck and batted his arms at the fierce little dogs, blindly stumbling back to fend them off.

Sidney leapt through the air and managed to take a bite of the upper thigh, latching there and hanging on wildly, his eyes glaring straight up into Eugene's face. Kicking and hitting at them all, Eugene stumbled back and lost his balance, landing with a dull thud.

Everything went quiet.

The wieners encircled the spot where he lay, all of them wheezing for air.

Virginia stood up, peering through the dark. What happened?

In the moonlight, she could see Eugene sprawled out on the grass at the sandy base of the tree, eyes wide open staring straight up into the night sky.

She edged closer.

Was he playing possum, trying to lure her into a trap?

Or was he really . . . dead?

Cautiously, she circled him a few times and then went closer. His foot was still entangled in the vine that tripped him. Surely he hadn't hit his head hard enough on the roots to kill him . . . had he?

Cautiously, Virginia inched over to his side.

Blood was oozing from the back of his head into the white sand.

She crouched beside him, trying to revive him.

Placing her hand under the back of his head, just under his skull at the top of his neck, she found it . . . the top of a rock protruding up from the sand . . . the rock that tore into Eugene's skull.

But it wasn't just a rock; something was carved deep into the bloodied stone.

Pushing him aside, she dug away the sand with her bare hands.

It was a marker.
A slave marker dated 1843.

LUCY MINERVA AND OVID STOKES
FROM PALM POINT PLANTATION.
PROPERTY OF PIERCE BUTLER NO MORE.
IN DEATH WE ARE FREE.
1 8 4 3

Virginia looked up at the night sky and smiled. They weren't just building high-rise condos on the beach . . . they were building high-rise condos on a sacred slave burial ground.

Her fight was over.

God had taken her call after all.

||||||||||||||||||||||||||||||||||||||||||||||||||||||||||||| **76** ||||||||||||||||||||

New York City

CANCELING THE DAY'S APPOINTMENTS TO STAY HOME HAD seemed like a good idea this morning.

But now that Hailey had spent hours alone in her apartment, pacing, paranoid despite the lowered shades, locks, and a .38 at her side . . .

Maybe she'd feel safer somewhere else.

Here, she couldn't help but feel like a sitting duck. He'd gotten past the doorman and locks once before. He could do it again.

She paced relentlessly from room to room, making tea, straightening things that didn't need to be straightened, ignoring the phone every time it rang.

It had been ringing a lot.

Dana had called several times, leaving messages.

"Hailey, are you sick? Why aren't you here today? Call me. I need you." She sounded like she was crying. "Greg dumped me."

Of course. Hailey knew he sounded too good to be true.

"Hailey, it's me again. Please call me back. I'm so upset."

Man trouble.

"Hailey, come on . . . I'm sorry to keep bugging you, but where are you? Pick up if you're there."

She felt vaguely guilty, but she couldn't talk to Dana. She couldn't talk to anyone.

Including Adam Springhurst, who had also called. She'd thought about it. Adam had it all: the degree, the successful dentistry practice, looks, charm . . . but something was sideways. Maybe it was just her. Even after all the years, she wasn't ready for the dating scene, the dinner conversation, retelling all your funny stories to a different person every Saturday night. It probably had nothing to do with Adam at all.

Bottom line . . . she couldn't trust anyone right now, including Adam and Dana. Not until this was resolved, one way or another.

It didn't make sense of course . . . but Dana was the only person in the city who could have gotten into, or let someone into, her apartment to plant the murder weapon, even if unintentionally.

She had a copy of Hailey's keys. And then there was the night Hailey had been attacked, in Dana's office . . . right after she'd found out about Melissa. Hailey was almost positive she'd heard Dana just moments before the first blow.

Hailey sternly stopped herself. Looking out her window down the twenty-one floors to the avenue, she felt ashamed for suspecting her friend. Hailey wished she could be a different person . . . a sweet, trusting person. The person she was before Will's murder, before she spent so many years surrounded by violent crime. She wanted desperately to be that way again.

But the world had changed her.

As the day wore into night, Hailey sat alone in the darkened apartment, clutching yet another cup of tea gone cold. She couldn't sleep, couldn't eat, couldn't call anyone because she didn't dare trust anyone.

There had to be an answer, something she was missing. Who knew so much about her? And who knew so much about her last serial murder prosecutions in Atlanta all those years ago? Where did her Tiffany pen come from and who planted it? Would they stop at merely framing her for her patients' deaths? Did they want her to be shamed? To lose her bar license and psychologist license in one fell swoop? Who wanted her behind bars? Who wanted to destroy her reputation and credibility? Or was she the next victim to die with four metal prongs slicing through her lungs?

Cruise.

It all made sense.

But the pen . . . how did he conceal it for all these years in prison? Wouldn't it have been discovered? Taken away? Returned to her . . . or at the very least confiscated from him?

Hailey had torn through her apartment inch by inch today, exploring the heating and cooling units and behind the fridge, checking the washer/dryer, inside commode tanks, and inside the other light fixtures; checking for slits in mattresses and sofa cushions; searching inside fuse boxes, the dishwasher . . . even inside the air purifiers.

Other than finding her files askew, she'd found nothing else.

She should be relieved.

But she wasn't.

Someone was playing a game with her . . . a deadly game.

She couldn't just sit in the dark, wondering, waiting.

Her life depended on it.

It was nearly midnight when she strapped on the .38 under a raincoat and headed down to Second Avenue to hail a cab.

The streets of Manhattan were nearly empty. Hailey held her arm up in the air. Almost immediately, a cab materialized.

It took less than twenty minutes to get to her office downtown.

Opening the street door in the night chill, she pulled it closed and locked it behind her before heading up the stairs to her office.

Stepping inside into her office foyer, she found it silent and undisturbed, just as she left it.

She locked the door behind her and crossed the room to a neat row of filing cabinets. Thumbing through the files, she reached back toward the end of the row, pulling out a cream-colored manila folder titled "Hayden Krasinski."

Hailey settled into the wingback chair by the office window, flicked on the floor lamp just beside her, and started reading. The gun and holster dug into her shoulder, so she took it off just while she was reading and hung it right beside her over the wing of the chair.

Two hours passed and she still had no idea exactly what she was looking for; only that she hadn't found it, despite going over and over everything in Hayden's file. Now for Melissa's.

Her head ached and her eyes were burning, but she didn't dare give up. There might be a clue to the murders here. There had to be, because she didn't know where else to look.

Rubbing her fingers into her forehead, she stood up and walked across her office floor to the kitchen to brew tea. Just as she was adding milk, hoping the tiny shot of caffeine would keep her going, she heard a single clicking sound.

In the instant, before she spotted the human figure, she heard his voice.

"Hello, Counselor. That's a standard door lock. Easy to pick. I'm surprised you wouldn't do better."

He was dressed in solid black and stood blocking the door of Hailey's office, facing her, his head and face completely obscured in a green ski mask leaving nothing visible but eyes and lips. Just before hurling the tea cup at him from across the room and turning to run, it registered in the back of her mind . . . perpetrator approximately six feet tall, 185 pounds, dark clothing. Race, hair color, other identifying features and characteristics, unknown.

The shot was a perfect aim, but he ducked his head out of the way a few inches and the cup smashed head-level into the wall beside the door. Darting backward, she lunged for the door out of her little kitchen and into the shared back hallway. Before she could get out, he closed the space between them, grabbing her from behind at the waist, yanking her hand off the knob so violently it felt as if several fingers were instantly broken.

He pulled her backward, hard. She hit the floor and tasted blood. He came down on top of her. As she struggled forward to get away from him, her hand grazed the cord to the coffeemaker on the counter above.

She pulled hard.

The coffeemaker, filled with scalding water for tea, smashed down, drenching the ski mask.

He screamed in pain, clutching his face. In that second, she scrambled up off the floor and ran.

She made it through the door and out into the hallway. She knew the door to the street was locked with a key—she had locked it herself. The key was back in her office. . . . There was nowhere to go but up. One of the older dentists notoriously left his back office door unlocked. She could only pray that was the case tonight. Her boots still lay at the foot of her reading chair; she ran up the hardwood stairs as noiselessly as possible.

What if it's locked? The thought ripped through her brain in the last second before she grasped the knob with her uninjured left hand.

She almost cried out in relief when she turned the handle: it was unlocked. Slipping in, she maneuvered through a darkened file room, sliding through the tall metal stacks of patient folders reaching floor to ceiling, then through a side door to the waiting area, closing the door behind her as silently as possible. Her goal . . . the third-floor fire escape.

Negotiating the darkened room, Hailey passed by the coffee table stacked with magazines, a large ceramic umbrella holder, a magazine rack. Then, in search of the fire escape window, she stepped into the dentist's clinical exam room.

To her horror, there were no fire escape steps outside the exam room's window. She had chosen the wrong room.

With nowhere left to go, Hailey huddled down behind a massive piece of diagnostic machinery looming over a cushioned, reclining hydraulic dentist's chair.

She waited. She hardly breathed for fear of making noise.

It seemed like forever, the silence hanging in the room as she crouched there on the floor . . . the quiet ringing in her ears . . . when finally she heard it . . . a far-off click as the front door lock was jimmied and snapped open.

She stifled a scream and tried to scrunch down even further onto the floor.

She couldn't hear a thing.

Seconds passed; minutes. She could hear movement now in the waiting room she had just left. . . . It was the metal magazine rack, she was sure, that crashed to the tile floor.

Then quiet. She strained to hear in the darkness. Nothing more, and then . . .

The air moved in the room and she knew. He was here.

She could feel him, lurking there in the room with her.

Silent tears flowed hotly down her cheeks.

Why? Why had it come to this? Who was he?

Nothing stirred in the room, yet she didn't dare believe he had moved on. She could sense him, could feel him in the air. She could see nothing in the black of the room, crouched down near the floor.

All at once, he pounced from behind, heaving her up by her neck.

She screamed out in pain and fought wildly, lashing out in every direction, kicking at his knee, his crotch, anywhere she could make contact.

He gripped her neck from behind. She wrenched free and scrambled away.

He came after her with a curse. Again, his hands closed around her neck. Again she broke free and tried to claw her way to the doorway.

She didn't make it. He picked her up and literally threw her across the room. She landed against an antique sideboard. Pain shattered her body, yet somehow she managed to stand. He was on her, strong fingers digging into her neck as he bent her forward at the waist, over the sideboard.

Suddenly, a cloud passed away from the moon outside. In the dim light filtering through the office window, Hailey looked into an ornate mirror above the sideboard and saw his shoulders and head, still shrouded in the ski mask, looming behind her.

She struggled against him. He wrenched her arm and she heard the crack of bone. Searing pain, poker hot, shot through her arm and shoulder. "What's the matter, Counselor? Still don't recognize me?"

With her one good arm, she managed to get hold of the mask, pulling at it. But it hit her—just before she saw his face in the dim moonlight—she knew his voice.

After all the years of courtroom practice, this was one with whom she never shared a cup of coffee, a Christmas card, a sandwich at lunch, or even a joke over the phone or in pre-trial plea negotiations. Instinctively, she had always kept her distance.

Now she understood why.

"You don't have to do this. . . . Stop now before you make it worse on yourself," she gasped out. "You know they'll get you . . . maybe not now, not tonight, not tomorrow—but they will."

He held her in a vise grip as he talked, his lips against the side of her head.

"Not if they never find your body, Hailey. That's the mistake I made with LaSondra. It wasn't supposed to go down like that. I got a little sloppy with a cheap hooker just once . . . just once."

Matt Leonard's hands circled around her throat and squeezed. Facing the mirror, she saw her own mouth open for air, saw her eyes begin to bulge. As she watched in silent horror as her own life drained away, she saw it.

The ring with three rubies.

And just before the ring twisted inward to the palm during the struggle, she understood. In that moment, she understood the trident mark on the neck of LaSondra Williams. . . . She understood why a man like Leonard would volunteer to take the case of Clint Burrell Cruise pro bono. Her mind flashed back to the courtroom and Cruise gnawing his nails down to the quick. He was a nail biter . . . he couldn't leave fingernail marks on LaSondra's neck. She understood it all. Leonard murdered Victim Eleven. He'd strangled LaSondra Williams and set up Cruise to take the fall for her murder.

"Don't you see, Hailey? I have to . . . I have to do it." Leonard breathed it into her hair. "Cruise is out. When I went looking for him, I heard he came to find you. Only you could put it together, only you, Hailey. Only you."

His fingers dug into her skin, the rubies tearing at her throat.

"I knew the deal with Cruise's MO—can't keep a secret in APD Homicide. So I set it up to look like Cruise's work and took the case pro bono. Brilliant. I knew he'd take the fall. Until the feds nailed your detective for stealing from dopers, and caught on tape, too! Good cop, Hailey. Too bad he was the one that found the murder weapon. But the reversal wasn't all bad, Hailey. My firm needed the money we started losing after the Cruise conviction. But then Cruise headed up here. I knew once he found you, between you two, you'd put the pieces together. Once you got my Internal Affairs file from APD. There's no other way, Hailey. Go out with a little dignity. Let me remember you that way . . ."

In one last spurt of strength, Hailey pushed backward, and they both went sprawling on the floor.

Hailey began crawling again, trying to get to the door.

Leonard grabbed her again by the back of the hips and jerked her back. She flailed, reaching—reaching for anything.

Her fingers wrapped around something and squeezed, and in the moment, she didn't even know what she had.

She heard a whirring sound just as she sunk the object into Leonard's neck, hot blood spurting onto her face and shoulder.

The dentist's drill.

Two things she hated most in the world . . . a sleazy defense attorney and a whining dentist's drill . . . united at last. It was her final thought before she slumped forward.

New York City

"HAILEY! HAILEY, WHAT HAPPENED?"
From far away, she heard Dana's familiar voice mingled with the buzz of others blending together through the haze.

Forcing her eyes open, she saw daylight. She was looking up, surrounded by faces. She recognized a few—one of the dental hygienists, and the receptionist, and Adam, and . . .

Dana . . . mascara streaked down her cheeks.

"Hailey . . . I don't understand. What were you doing here with Greg? Did you kill him, Hailey? He's dead. My God . . . he's just lying there, dead."

Confused, Hailey followed her gaze and saw a sheet-covered figure on the floor not far from where she lay.

It came back to her in a flash.

Leonard . . . Leonard attacked her, and she . . .

"Did you kill Greg, Hailey?" Dana asked again.

Greg?

What was she talking about?

"Easy, there, Ms. Dean," said a paramedic who was kneeling beside her. "Don't move just yet. You're pretty banged up."

"I can't believe Greg is dead," Dana sobbed.

That wasn't Greg.

It was Leonard. Leonard had—

Suddenly, the truth hit.

It had been him all along, Hailey realized.

Posing as Dana's new boyfriend, infiltrating her life so that he could get close to Hailey. He must have slipped her keys away from Dana and made a copy, setting him free to come and go from her apartment when she wasn't there.

From across the street and half a block up, Cruise stood jammed inside a doorway . . . watching. He'd been here ever since circling back and tracking Hailey from her apartment to her office. He'd been waiting for the two of them to come out. But now, an ambulance and police had arrived. He naturally shrunk further into the shadow of the door frame. It didn't make sense. Why was Leonard here? Why the attack the night before? What did he have to do with Hailey? He didn't know now, but he'd find out. And he'd be back.

Cruise turned on his heel as yet another squad car pulled up, and no one noticed a man with a limp and a hat riding low on his face, slowly blending into the crowded street and fading away.

"Step back, please. I need to speak to Ms. Dean. Excuse me. Excuse me. NYPD."

Hailey recognized Kolker's voice even before the crowd parted and she saw him there, badge in hand.

"Looks like you took quite a tumble, Hailey Dean," he said— but not unkindly. He knelt beside her. "Want to tell me what happened?"

"Later," she murmured.

"I just need you to know—"

"She said later." It was Adam who stepped in.

Adam, too, who squeezed her hand and said, "Hailey, you're damned lucky to be alive, you know that? If the office cleaning lady hadn't come in and found you when she did . . ."

In time, she knew, it would all make sense.

For now, he was right. She was just lucky to be alive. But purposefully releasing Adam's hand, she motioned Kolker over and down, close to her face so he could hear. The crowd parted, and he knelt down beside her. Her throat hurt so terribly as she tried to speak, but couldn't. She looked straight into Kolker's eyes.

"I just want you to know, Hailey . . . I'm sorry."

||||||||||||||||||||||||||||||||||||||||||||||||||||||||| **78** |||||||||||||||||||

Atlanta, Georgia

THE SUN WAS SHINING DOWN WARM ON LEOLA'S FRONT PORCH. Ivy and plants surrounded it, dozens of hanging baskets placed across the top of the porch created a canopy overhead. A single tear made its way down her wrinkled face as she sat alone, rocking. In her lap was today's *Atlanta Telegraph*. A gentle breeze breathed across the porch, barely rustling the paper's headline.

The detective's taillights disappeared around the corner as they drove off. He'd been there a long time, trying to explain how attorney Leonard had taken Cruise's case to cover up a murder of his own, the murder of LaSondra. Leonard's history with prostitutes was apparently well known among the APD brass; his police file was full of brutality incidents with hookers as well as others. But nobody knew it continued after he was pushed off the force. After he became respectable, a lawyer.

Leola sat perfectly still there on the porch for a while, feeling the sunlight hot on wooden planks beneath her feet. She sat down in a rocker and opened up the front page of the *Telegraph*.

Finally, her little girl could sleep. Years ago, Leola had given up on the hopes and dreams she had for her girl, but at least now LaSondra could sleep in peace. Leola glanced down at the headlines.

CHARGES DROPPED AGAINST CRUISE
IN WILLIAMS MURDER

Well, all right, it wasn't so much the headline that mattered. It wasn't even the topic of the article or the fact that her daughter hadn't been murdered by Cruise, but by his defense attorney—who couldn't hurt anyone else, ever again, because he was dead.

Miss Hailey Dean herself did the deed.

Thanks to her, the papers weren't calling Leola's baby girl all those awful names anymore.

Leola Williams reread her favorite phrase in the article.

"LaSondra Williams, an aspiring dancer from Atlanta . . . "

Oh how she could dance. When she was little, Leola would put on a record and the minute the music started, LaSondra would twirl around and around, arms outstretched, calling out to Leola, "Mama! Mama! Look! Look at me, Mama! I'm a dancer, Mama. Can I be a dancer when I grow up?"

"Yes, baby, you're my sweet ballerina girl," she would say.

A good girl. Her LaSondra.

Leola set the newspaper aside, not noticing the other front-page headlines below the fold.

LOCAL BUSINESSMAN DIES IN FREAK ACCIDENT;
BUILDING PROJECT CURTAILED AFTER SITE
NAMED HISTORICAL SLAVE BURIAL GROUND

Humming to herself, Leola closed her eyes and said a silent prayer in her head.

God bless Miss Hailey Dean, and make her well, wherever she was.

New York City

THE SHEETS WERE COOL WHEN SHE LAY DOWN.

She was so tired, her body ached.

Not one light was on inside the apartment, but the window was cracked open with the shade pulled nearly all the way down. Gray-white light from First Avenue filtered in under the shade, and she could hear the tires of cabs whiz by, slicing through the rain on the asphalt.

She no longer knew what time it was, but it was late in the night . . . so late that other sounds were gone. No voices or activity, no horns, even—just the wheels turning in the rain.

She was hungry, but so bone tired she didn't have the energy to make it to the kitchen and look in the fridge.

She just lay there, drifting, floating.

Leonard's face appeared in her mind, contorted with rage just before she'd killed him. She blamed herself for not fitting the pieces together sooner. Of course Leonard had learned all the details of the serial murders from his cronies who graduated to APD Homicide long after Leonard was forced out. They still hung out at Manuel's Tavern, the local cops' bar, practically every week. Details like the baker's twine and the poultry-lifter were never leaked to the press or the general public, so naturally investigators believed the same killer murdered LaSondra. Now, APD was launching investigations on other unsolved prostitute homicides with Leonard in mind.

And now Leonard's Internal Affairs file had been made public, including that when he was investigating a string of burglaries, he held on to burglars' lock-picking tools. Her office and apartment were easy pickings, and he'd gotten most of his information from his new and unwitting girlfriend, Dana, and maybe even Hailey's keys as well. He'd been wooing Dana for weeks, milking her for information and spying on the two women from the abandoned building across from Dana's office. He first thought it was Hailey's.

After his attempted frame-up and attack on Hailey, it had all gone public. When his sixth wife learned of the multiple incidents of brutality on hookers and suspects he'd arrested, she appeared devastated, for about five minutes. His house and law practice were already up for sale, and Leonard was buried in a non-denominational cemetery near the interstate.

Even now, Hailey could feel his hands tighten around her throat. She forced her thoughts back further. To something pleasant. She was somewhere, maybe as a child? At home in front of the old black-and-white? Maybe it was in law school at the end of hours and hours of grueling study? Or was it after a long day in court?

She couldn't name the time or place, but the TV had just finished the American anthem. . . . She knew what it was now: It was WMAZ, the old Channel Thirteen of her youth.

It was fuzzy and static. At the end of the U.S. anthem every night, the broadcast signed off with Ray Charles singing, rocking side-to-side at his piano to the beat in his head. He sang it soft and sweet . . . *Georgia.*

Her heart felt like it would burst with longing . . . but for what?

The lyrics came rushing through her head . . . loving arms reaching out . . . moonlight pouring through tall pine trees. The rain outside began coming down in torrents . . . but now, in the half-dream, it was pouring down onto the hard red dirt of home.

"*. . . Georgia on my mind . . .*"

The pine smell filling her up, before she had ever seen an autopsy photo or smelled a bloody crime scene or looked through a microscope to compare markings on bullets dug out of a body. Before she ever stood sweating through her bra in front of a jury or read an indictment out loud in front of a waiting panel to commence a trial . . . before she saw it all, felt it all, became old with the knowledge.

Back when it was all bright and shiny, too bright to even touch or look at.

She would fly out of LaGuardia in the morning. First thing, before the shops opened or the *Post* hit her door.

She'd leave early, early when the street was hers alone and fifty cabs would race straight toward her arm held up in the dark of morning. She'd book the flight from the back of the cab.

LGA to ATL.

One-way, for now.

First, my deepest thanks to my friend and editor, Gretchen Young, who has had great faith in me and *The Eleventh Victim*. You have made so many wonderful things possible for me. Thank you.

To Wendy Corsi Staub, you are a wonder! Thank you!!

To Jim Walton and Ken Jautz, thank you for the support, the opportunities, the trials we've covered, and of course, the friendship. I owe you both so much, it can't fit onto a page.

To our wonderful staff on *Nancy Grace*, and especially Liz, thank you. You are the backbone.

Without Dean Sicoli, "the muse," there would be no *HLN Nancy Grace*. First e-mail in the morning, last e-mail at night . . . my friend and my EP, thank you.

And last and dearest, thank you, David. What would it be without you? Nothing. You and the twins are the joys of my life. And to my Father God and Christ, thank you for these and all your many blessings.